Three hybrid werewolves

Eve Martin

Contents

Chapter 1

"**F**uck you Sin!" She screams, Ah, it's like music to my fucking ears. I love it when a woman screams. Do it some more baby. She stomps away from angry.

"Awe come on Storm don't go away mad!" I fake plead with her. Just go away! I think to myself. She stops in her tracks picking up a book from dresser drawer beside her, she throws the book at me. The book whizzes by my head barely missing me. What the actual fuck?

After a long night of vigorous and hot as hell sex, I finally dropped the bomb on my current girlfriend Storm this morning. And as you can see she is not taking it very well at all.

For weeks I've been planning to break up with her jealous conniving ass and every time I start to do it I become a wimp and back out. I have no idea why. Storm has this certain insatiable control over me.

One being that she can fuck like a damn goddess and the second, well, she gives great head too. Man that mouth can do wonders. My dick twitches just thinking about it.

But my brothers have been on my ass consistently lately for me to drop her ass. She's well known around the pack as the packs she-slut. Spreading those luscious thighs to whomever she can just so she can climb the hierarchy ladder.

With all three of us being the Alphas of our pack, Storm set her greedy eyes on us three without any shame or compunction at all. I'm just the stupid one that fell for it.

I knew all along what she was after. I'm not an idiot. I just thought that I could have a little fun before I had to rain all over on her greedy parade and look where that's got me.

In my bedroom with a foul mouth vixen who has murder flowing intently through her damn devious eyes.

I'll never fucking learn.

"Why Sin? Why now? Weren't we having a good time?" She purrs at me seductively. Boy did her mood change swiftly. Doing her sexy strut as she walks up to me giving me those sexy fuck me eyes.

Fuck me!

I never claimed to be strong man. With her long fingers tracing slowly down my hard pecks my dick, that I have so lovingly named Fido, salutes to her automatically. I cant help but to release a damn groan with my eyes nearly rolling to the back of my damn head.

"I can change your mind sexy." Storm drops to her knees effortlessly her long fingers wrap around the elastic band of my boxers pulling them down my legs in one quick go.

My traitorous dick springs to action.

She wraps those supple lips around my stiff cock, swallowing it all the way down to the base. "Fuck Storm!" Yes, there's no doubt I'm a weak fucking man!

Her warm little mouth keeps bobbing up and down my cock like a fucking pro. I fist my hand in her curls pushing her face closer to me. "Fine you want to suck my cock, then suck it!" I groan, pushing her head back and forth roughly. I don't fucking let up!

I fuck her mouth like a ravaged beast making her gag around my dick so wonderfully. Her hands press against my legs trying to pull herself away from me but I won't fucking have it.

She wants me, well she will damn well sure fucking get me.

"Suck it Storm!" I demand of her aggressively, making her go to and fro rapidly. "This is what you wanted isn't it?" Oh fuck, my balls clench up. My spine begins to tingle. I pick up my pace forcing her mouth to take all of my cock. She keeps squirming, fighting against me, trying to catch her breath.

Fisting up my hand I grab another handful of her curls moving her head with both of them, steadily pushing her against me. "Fuck!" Here it comes, literally. I shoot my load all into her mouth but I don't let go of her hair. I just hold on tighter.

I make her swallow down every last drop of my fucking tangy cum.

When I finally release her, her ass falls on the floor spitting and gagging. I shake my head at her giving her a dark chuckle. Pulling up my boxers I look down at her completely repulsed.

"You got what you wanted. Now get the fuck out!" I demand angrily pointing my finger to my bedroom door.

Storm stumbles to her feet a tad bit ungraciously wiping her mouth with the back of her hand she glowers over at me.

"Your a prick." She tries to insult me, I just give her another chuckle.

"No I'm not but you sure got one." She drops her sneer suddenly glaring at me.

"Please Sin don't do this. I know you love me. We can work this out. Just give me a chance." Storm whines. She has to be bipolar. Fuck why can't she just get the damn hint?

This girl has truly got to be completely desperate. I just raped fucked her mouth viscously and she still acts like she wants me.

I hate it when my brothers are right but Storm apparently just wants what she can't get from me. She wants to be the Luna of the Blood Claw Pack the fiercest pack in the Southern Hemisphere.

After our parents died in a fucking plane crash three years ago we had to take over the pack. Along with me and my two brothers, Sun and Slay, and my baby sister Lila, we have managed to turn our pack around from being at the bottom three packs in the well known south to the number one position by perseverance, hard work, fighting, maiming, and killing.

We had to do what he had to and I don't regret a single fucking moment of it. But now I'm having to fight off women left and right because they all seem to fucking think that I'm the easy going one out of the three of us. Just because I'm the one who is always joking around and smiling.

My twin brother Sunny is basically the easy going one. His disposition in life is to just go with the flow. Mine on the other hand is visceral. Most don't see that side of me. I hide it very well.

"Storm just go. I'm tired of fighting. We can talk about this later." I urgently suggest because I know my bother Sunny will be dropping by my bedroom unannounced as he always does every damn morning.

"Okay. I'll go. I'll see you tonight baby" she smiles up at me hopefully but all I can do is cringe.

"Fine." I huff as she makes her way out of my bedroom giving me a final wave of her freshly manicured hand.

Fuck! Why me?

I may be visceral but I have an Achilles heel when it comes to women.

My mom always taught me to be respectful and to treat a woman right and if I didn't do it that woman would gladly tan my hide.

"Why didn't you just break up with her?" My brother Sun ask as he's strolling into my room staring at me with disappointment etched all over his face.

"I tried. I fucking tried Sunny but that damn girl does not take no for answer." Grabbing my jeans I slip them on me quickly.

"Just do it." Sunny quips. Really!

"Do I look like a damn Nike commercial?" I grumble at him. He shrugs his shoulder dismissively.

"All I'm trying to say is if you don't put your foot down now she will expect you to make her our Luna and that my brother is never going to happen." Sunny insist. Well no shit!

All three of us agreed after we took over the pack as Alphas that we would definitely not make just any woman our Luna without the others approval. Unless of course it's our mates then that is no brainer.

Sunny is holding out for his mate to come along. He's a lovesick dreamer. Slay doesn't care one way or the other. He's only a year older than us so he thinks he has plenty of time before he meets his mate.

Me? I don't want a fucking mate. I could actually care less if I ever have one. I love the idea of being able to fuck who I want and when I want without someone breathing down my damn neck all the time.

"She will never be our Luna." I tell him while grabbing my t-shirt, I slip it on over my head then put my boots on.

"That's good but you need to call it off Sin. The sooner the better." He says it with so much urgency. I don't get it.

Both him and Slay seem to think that they can control my fucking love life.

"Why are you in such a hurry for me to break it off anyway?" I ask him curiously, tilting my head to the side I wait for his reply.

"You forgot didn't you? I knew you would. Damn Sin it's not like we haven't been planning this shit for weeks!" I watch as Sun starts to get flustered. I have no idea about what the hell he is referring to.

"Enlighten me." I say.

"The She-Wolf Parade? It's fucking tomorrow night how can you forget something as important as that?" He huffs.

Fuck!

The damn She-Wolf Parade. I did totally forget. Probably because I think it's rather stupid and pointless. It's all in the dumb name.

A bunch of fucking She-Wolfs parade about drinking, dancing, and eating in front of a bunch of unmated male wolves in hopes of finding their mates.

"So we really have to?" I grouse. I hate these damn things.

"Yes we do Sin. We have put off hosting it for two years now we can't put it off any longer. Lila is going to cut off our heads if we don't participate in it. She's been looking forward to this all year." He tells me.

I can't believe this! I guess I have no choice but to go then. Lila would definitely cut off my damn balls if I even think about backing out.

She's been hoping to find her mate lately. Both her and Sunny are nothing but lovesick dreamers. Not that I don't want her to find her mate nor him. It's just that I hate the idea of a mate period.

"Fine I'll go but I'm not wearing a damn monkey suit!" I hate them.

"You know Lila is going to have a fit if you don't." He grumbles.

"If I wanted to dress up as a penguin I'd do it for Halloween not for some stupid hormonal parade." Sun laughs while shaking his head.

"Fine but if she comes after you don't come running to me to hide behind." He jokes.

"Like I need to hide behind you." I quip.

Lila is very sweet natured but he does have a point. She can be a major bad ass when she wants to be.

"We better go down Slay is impatiently waiting for us." What the hell does Slay want now?

"Why?" I ask.

"I don't know he just said he wants to talk to both of us." Well damn.

"Then let's go before he pops a blood vessel." I laugh at my own stupid joke.

"Eat!" Slay commands both of us as soon as we both entered the dining room.

A buffet of wonderful food is covering the dining room table. The smell of freshly cooked sausages and bacon make my mouth water.

Sitting down next to Slay I load up my plates with all of the meaty goodness. I'm a damn glutton when it comes to food. The meatier the better in my book.

"What did you want to talk to us about?" Sun ask as he is piling up his plate also. He takes a seat on the opposite side of Slay. We usually have a our meals privately. Most packs don't but we like the comfort of it and of course if we need to discuss certain things we like it better when we don't have a live audience.

"Where's Lila?" I ask Slay. She usually joins us breakfast it's strange for her not to be here.

"She's running around like a chicken with its head cut off trying to get all of the last minute details done for the Parade." Slay informs me. Chomping down on a crispy piece of bacon I just nod my head at him.

"I wanted to talk to you both about helping with the parade. Lila has her hands full. Sunny if you wouldn't mind can you help by checking with the cooks to make sure they have everything done and enough food prepared in time for the Parade tomorrow night?" Slay ask Sun.

"Sure." He agrees with his mouth wide open while chewing his sausage.

"Damn close your mouth Sun, you disgusting pig!" I complain. Fucking disgusting.

"The pig is in my mouth." He comments with a smile with his mouth still full. Ewe.

"Sin if you don't mind would you please check with the unmated males and see how many are going to actually attend? So far we have over two hundred guest coming and I need a final headcount?" Easy enough.

"Sure." As long as I don't have to dress in a monkey suit I don't mind helping out at all.

"Oh and I want you both there tomorrow night no excuses and if you happen to find your mate please alert me as soon as you do." Slay states.

"Why?" Sunny ask.

"Because I'm the official counter tonight. I hate it but no one else volunteered to do it." Slay groans.

I don't blame him. The official counter has to go around writing down everyone's names and who they are mates to. It's a fucking headache to do.

"Have fun with that but I doubt I'll meet my mate and if I do I'll just reject her." I reply nonchalantly.

"The hell you will!" Slay voiced his opinion very loudly. His damn voice vibrates all throughout the dining room.

"What's crawled up your ass Slay? Why do you care if I reject my mate or not?" I ask him completely dumbfounded over his attitude.

"Because dear brother what you say and do reflects on all of us. If you so carelessly reject your mate that the Moon Goddess has so generously paired you up with then how do you think that would look to all of our loyal pack members? They would hate you for it." Slay does have a point but that still doesn't dissuade me from not wanting a damn mate. I don't want to be tied down. That's the bottom line.

"Fine. I wouldn't reject her but I don't want anything to do with her either." I lay it all down on the line glaring over at my older brother with a hint of disdain.

"I don't think you have to worry about that brother. The Moon Goddess blesses us wolves with a mate who actually deserve a mate. You truly don't deserve one. Not if you seem to always think that you are far too good to even have a mate." I glower over at my brother Sun. How can he think so poorly of me?

"Just because I don't want a damn mate doesn't mean I don't deserve one. Any She-Wolf would be happy to have me as their mate." I established it clearly to him with a heavy huff.

"Yea any She-Wolf would runaway from you if she found out you were her mate. She would probably be more than terrified of that idea thinking that she may catch some sort of disease." Slay mocks laughing darkly at my expense.

Laugh it up assholes.

"Wolves can't catch those type of things jackass. Besides it doesn't matter, if we haven't found our mates by now we probably never will. We may just have to pick a chosen mate for our Lunas." I laugh at their expressions.

Slay looks disgusted and poor Sun looks down right pitiful at the very idea.

"That will never happen it's either our destined mates or nothing. I will not allow any fake Lunas to help lead our pack!" Slay foolishly admits. I shake my head at the moron.

"And why not? It's all the same Slay. One pussy is just as good as the others. I don't see why you and Sunny are so damn adamant about it having to be a true mate to be our Luna. As long as one can handle the responsibilities that are bestowed upon her I think any woman would do." I tell them both shrugging my shoulders finishing up my plate of food. Leaning back in my chair I observe how both of them are taking my news.

"Then you are a complete moron Sin. Not just any woman could do this job and no matter how you view it and I will not repeat myself again about this, only our true mates will ever be Lunas of our pack. Get me?" Slay gruffly tells me. I sit there silently soaking it all in.

"If that's the way you want it then so be it. Let's just hope that your mates will be able to the job for all of us because I will definitely not be getting one." I tell them both with a bit of authority laced in my voice. I don't care how he views it. This is my decision and that's final. He can not get me to change my mind about this.

It's just the way it is.

"He didn't break up with Storm either." Sun fucking tattle-tales on me like a little kid.

The asshole.

Slay is stunned for a fraction of a second then he turns his heated gaze to me. "Why not?" He ask.

"I tried. I really did but Storm is so fucking hardheaded she wouldn't even listen to me." I try to get him to understand.

"How can she listen to you when you got your cock stuffed all the way down her mouth?" Sun replies with rambunctious laughter.

"Really Sin? You know as well as I do about her reputation and you also know what the hell she is after. Why do you keep her around if all she is going to do is use you?" Slay ask me somewhat confused.

What can I say that her pussy is like fucking gold? That she can suck me off better than a Hoover can? Or that she will take it up the ass without lodging any complaints? I can't tell them that! So I resigned myself to state the obvious.

"She's good in bed." See simple.

"Yea well I can ask any of our guys around here if she is and I'm sure they will know the answer to that one." Slay can not stand Storm. The way she is always flaunting herself and bragging about it always seems to upset him. I just can't figure out why? Who cares if she is slut? I for one like that she's into touch with her sexuality.

Most women aren't and to me it's a bit refreshing and a little bit of a turn on.

"Are you upset because you never had a piece of her? If you want her you know that I wouldn't mind sharing." I snidely ask him. He undoubtedly just gives me another glare.

"I don't want someone who has been used by the entire pack. That's not my fucking style Sin." No it's not.

Slay hardly dates anybody. For the longest time I thought he might be gay. But one night I saw him with a pretty little She-Wolf sneaking off into his bedroom.

I mean he still could be into men. Hell I don't know. He's not one to talk about his private affairs even if you press him too. He just clams up. The tough guy act doesn't fool me though. I know he's lonely. You can see it in his eyes every time he looks at someone that has a mate.

I wish I could change it for him but it's not up to me it's all up to the Moon Goddess. I honestly wouldn't mind if he did find his mate at this stupid Parade tomorrow night. It just might make him a little bit more easier to be around. Then maybe he would get off my ass and worry about his mates ass instead.

No I don't mind if either of my siblings find their mates, in fact I hope they do. I just want them to be happy and I would be happy if the Moon Goddess decided to bless them all.

As long as the Moon Goddess leaves my ass the hell alone!

Chapter 2

Waking up in my fathers dungeon is not what I would refer to as having a good time. With my head swimming and a strange foul taste in my mouth, I search the room groggily.

The asshole really did it. I can't believe it. How could I be so damn foolish?

I trusted him. I mean come on he is my father, though sometimes he could be a cruel bastard especially to his own damn children but I've never expected this.

I wish my mother was still here. We were such a happy family unit while she was still alive. After her death my father, the well known Alpha Baker Rose of the White Moon Pack, changed dramatically. He went from being a well respected and caring Alpha to someone that I don't even recognize anymore.

His loving nature slipped away from him two years ago when some vile and malicious Rogues attacked our pack for some unknown reason. They tortured and killed my mother along with a few other pack members, after that my father was never the same.

With my head feeling a little fuzzy I try to recall exactly what had happened between us last night.

The last thing that I can remember is arguing with my father again but unfortunately I can't even remember what our argument was about. Why can't I remember? Ugh!

And why would he throw me in his dungeon? Damn! I need to get the hell out of here! Whatever our argument was about it had to be bad because I can't think of any reason that would result in me having it be thrown in his damn dungeon.

"Dad!" I scream out loud with both of my hands fisted up pounding heavily on the damn dungeon door. "Dad! Let me out!" I scream louder.

But after what seems like hours of me screaming and pounding on the door with no reply back my throat is now dry as a desert and I my hands freaking ache. Damn! The cold dungeon room smells of old tainted blood and soured urine. The revolting aroma is making me nauseous along with a headache blooming inside of my head that just won't seem to go away, it's all making me feel truly miserable.

What could I have done or said that was so bad to warrant this type of punishment? I have always tried to be the best daughter that I could possibly be so why am I being discarded this way? It doesn't make any damn sense to me.

Dropping down on the little moldy mattress that's tucked in the corner of this gruesome dungeon prison I start to cry. My tears keep escaping my eyes they keep rolling down my face precariously. Why? Why me? These same questions keep echoing in my mind.

Finally hearing loud footfalls entering the dungeon halls I spring up from the old mattress racing toward the dungeon door. Peeking out of a little rectangle opening on the door I see my fathers face suddenly appear at it before me.

Startled I jump back a step eyeing the door nervously. The lock on the door starts to rattle when the door finally opens the creaking sound of the door makes me shiver it's an ominous sound that makes me feel like I'm waiting for my own perilous doom. As my father enters the room he places the door keys in his front pant pocket. Closing the heavy wooden door behind him. When he suddenly turns to me I blanch back when I noticethe fierceness displayed all over his face.

"Dad." I nervously drawl out his name.

He saunters in the room with a heavy stride, the stomping of his boots reverberate throughout the cold daunting room hauntingly.

My father decidedly chooses to lean up against the grey stoned wall, facing me he offers me a viscous glowering glare simply folding his arms across his his barreled chest.

"Well princess it seems like we have a problem." He finally speaks, I hint a very discouraging roughness to his tone. I can't understand why he would be so upset with me.

"What problem dad? What did I do?" I rush out my questions frantically wanting so badly to know the answers.

He darkly chuckles at me, shaking his head. I scowl watching him clearly confused about his abrupt behavior toward me.

"You denied me and that just won't do." He replies sucking on air between his teeth still deathly glowering over at me.

"Denied what? I don't understand." The way he is behaving toward me right now is not unusual per say it's just at this very moment there's a touch of madness added to his usual fierceness that absolutely confuses and terrifies me.

"When I lost your mother I also lost my Luna. My pack lost one of their leaders. The best one anyway. I loved her deeply the loss was so damn traumatic not just for me but for everyone. For two years I have mourned her, yearned for her, and weeped for her. Now I think it's time for a change." Chills run down my spine from the hard calculating look he's throwing at me.

"What do you mean?" I ask with my voice quivering slightly. What does this have to do with me?

"I think our pack needs a new Luna one that was just like your mother. One like you." He harshly comments pointing his long finger directly at me.

Does he plan on letting me take over his reign? But I'm the youngest with my brother being a year older than I am it was always a foregone conclusion that he would be the upcoming Alpha of our pack, not me.

"But what about Fier he is suppose to be the next Alpha, not me. Why would you do this to him? He has been training for this his entire life to take over the pack from you when you retired. You can't do this to him dad. He would be so upset." Fier has always stood by me, through thick or thin, I could always rely on him. He has always looked forward to the day when he becomes the Alpha of our pack.

For my father to take this dream away from him is nothing but cruel. I won't let him do it to him. I can't.

"You're misunderstanding me princess. I'm not going to retire. I am still going to remain as Alpha of my pack." I stare at him beyond confused, furrowing my brows, I start to fidget bouncing on the back of my heels.

"I don't understand." I mumble lowly.

He tsk at me shaking his head then pulls himself from the stoned wall walking over to me slowly, he halts when he is finally standing directly in front of me. His reaches his hand up to my face tenderly tracing my cheek with his thumb pad.

Sliding my eyes up to look up at him, I flinch when I read the sudden announcement of lustful desire quickly flooding his eyes.

No he can't mean this? It's beyond absurd. He's my fucking father.

"I want you to become our Luna. My Luna. I want you to become my lover." He says gruffly with desire laced in his tone. Oh please Goddess let this be a damn joke. He can't mean it!

"You're fucking disgusting!" I bellow out at him stepping away from his revolting touch. The nauseating feeling I had early comes back to me hitting me at full tilt.

The man is mad! Crazy! Who would actually think about their own daughter in this sick depraved way?

"No I'm not! I will make you my Luna Thorn! Our pack needs you. I need you!" He barks out to me with anger as I step further away from him shaking my head vehemently.

"Fier will never allow this. He will stop you! He will kill you!" I venomously spew at him.

Fier will stop him. He will save me from this madman! He has to.

"Fier will not be a problem. Neither will our pack. Our pack is behind me one hundred percent. I had him taken care of. There is no one that can stop me Thorn. This will happen. We will have the ceremony tomorrow night when the moon crests. You can try to fight it all you want sweet one but no one can help you. You will be mine." He snarls, walking closer to me with his arms held up high in the air to grab me. I frantically look around the cell room searching for anything that can remotely help me.

My eyes hit upon a a broken piece of plywood leaning up against the stone wall beside an old brown bucket.

As my fathers paces pick up coming forward I duck low under his outstretched arm, rushing across the room I swipe up the plywood with both of my hands.

Before my father can even register my swift movements I take the chunky plywood in my hands rear back and swing it just as hard as I can toward his head. Swinging upwards the plywood crashes across the back of his head hard. He stumbles from the impact but still is able to brace himself.

Continuously swinging the plywood I eventually managed to knock my father completely out. His body begins to fall to the cell floor clumsily, with my arms stinging and my breathing erratic I hastily drop the piece of plywood onto the cell room floor staring at my unconscious father on the floor unbelievably.

Quickly coming to my senses I rush over to my fathers prone body digging through his pant pockets I was finally able to clasp my hand around the cold metal key to my freedom.

Jerking the key from his pocket I rush over to door, opening it with a bit of ease. I walk though it slamming it behind me as I exit I lock the dungeon door with a loud resounding clink of the lock clicking into place. I relax blowing out a heavy breath.

I throw the key down the dungeons hallway then briskly turning on my heels I begin to run out of the dungeon to my freedom with no apparent plan of where the hell I was going I just rush off. All I know is at this very moment I needed to run and get away fast and find somewhere far away from here to hide.

I needed to find my brother Fier.

Rushing through the isolated town of Retron I kept low hiding behind old buildings with no planned destination in my mind.

I had nowhere to go basically. The only relatives that I have is my deranged father and of course my brother Fier but I have no idea where he is or what's happened to him.

I couldn't even ask for any type of help from anyone that is in our pack. According to my father they all knew and supported his crazy idea for him to make me his. So disappointingly I have no one.

I don't know what I'm going to do? It all feels so damn hopeless. How did my life turn out this way?

Hearing a train whistle blowing loudly in the distance I search around the town looking for the train tracks. I spot them past the alleyway. If I could possibly jump into one of the cargo boxcars maybe just maybe I might have a chance to escape away from here unharmed and unnoticed.

Rushing to the tracks on the far side of town I bustle through some oncoming people that are straggling about behind some old abandoned buildings on the east side of town. Almost stumbling over some trash bins that were left out in the alleyway haphazardly, I quickly right myself jumping around them hurrying as fast as can to the upcoming train.

Out of breath and growing abundantly tired I finally make it to the side of the railroad tracks. Now all I have to do is figure out how I'm going to jump onto a fast moving train that's going close to fifty miles per hour along the train tracks.

Watching nervously as the train is approaching I happily notice that the train is starting to slow down. The loud train whistle blows one long whistle signaling that it's about to stop. Yes! Yes! Yes!

The delight I feel encompasses me fully knowing that I won't have to break my own damn foolish neck trying to jump on a fast moving train.

One short whistle from the train signals its impending stop. I creep around the side of railway depot building to hide inconspicuously.

As the train finally comes to a jolting stop I silently make my way down the side of the train searching for an open cargo boxcar.

Finally near the end of the long train I find a cargo boxcar that was left slightly open. Climbing into the boxcar as my hands grip the metal clasping on the sliding door I almost fall over. Gripping the clasp tighter I pull myself up inside of the boxcar breathing heavily from over excursion.

Falling on my back in the boxcar on the cold steel flooring I stare up at the top of the boxcars ceiling thankful that I was actually able to make it.

This would be so much easier if I could actually shift into my wolf form but unfortunately that won't happen for another two days when I finally turn eighteen and I can't wait.

Hearing footfalls outside of the boxcar I scramble to my feet rapidly. Traipsing across the boxcar hurriedly I edge my way behind two wooden crates hiding myself away.

Voices travel up to my ears from outside of the boxcar. Two gravely voices speak randomly for a few minutes until the boxcar door suddenly closes with a rattling vibration rattling throughout the car.

Blowing out a very long held breath I settle back against another wooden crate panting out heavily in complete darkness.

After awhile the train finally starts moving again, it jolts me forward off of the crate I was leaning on. I smash into another crate catching myself with both of my hands pressed against it. I steady myself as the train continues to glide on down the tracks.

Restless, I climb up onto one of the wooden crates. Nestling down upon it I curl myself up into a ball. Closing my eyes I start to drift off to sleep with the steady rhythmic movements from the speeding train.

I can't believe I actually done it. I escaped my deranged father without anyone seeing me.

Now all I have to did is somehow find my brother which sounds a hell of a lot easier than I might think.

My last thought before I drift off into slumber was that of why is this shit happening to me?

I get jolted awake when the train suddenly comes to a screeching stop almost falling off of the crate I was restlessly sleeping on.

Standing abruptly, I train my ears listening closely for any sounds near the car I'm in. Not being able to hear anything but the trains slow screeching, I edge my way around the wooden crates before me until I get to the car door. Fumbling around with my fingers on the darkness trying to find someway to open the boxcar door I get a shock when the door suddenly comes sliding open.

Standing at the door looking down I get startled when I see a big burly man glaring up at me.

"Who are you? What the hell are doing?" He ask me confused but apparently frustrated. Hurriedly I jump from the cart landing on some gravel as I fall helplessly on the ground. Scraping my leg I ignore the pain as I jump up quickly and scramble to my feet.

Without any hesitation I take off running from the train and the burly man as quick as my feet will allow me. When I reach the caboose of the train I run behind it swiftly only to arrive at the edge of a forest.

I hesitate looking at the foreboding forest scared to enter it that is until I hear men screaming out loudly from behind me.

Without having any other damn choice I rush forward into the foreboding forest.

I have been aimlessly walking through the forest for what seems like hours now.

My feet are aching, I think I have fucking blisters on top of blisters from walking so damn much. I'm tired, exhausted, and fucking hungry as hell.

I have no clue about where the hell I'm at and the sun is starting to set making the forest seem even more foreboding than it was before.

I need to find some substantial food and I definitely need to rest but I force myself onward with what little strength I have left heading off to Goddess only knows where.

This is ridiculous.

After a few more hours of walking I suddenly hear faint music coming from the west end of the forest, I trudge my way over to the sound. The crumpling dead leaves on the forest floor and broken branches never dissuade me from my task. I finally come to a clearing through the woods where a bright light is cascading threw the trees up head.

Standing behind a large oak tree I peek around it trying to be as discreet as I possibly can. When I peek around the tree I see a large party of some sort going on before me.

Tons of people are scattered about either dancing, eating, or talking with each other. The loud cumbersome music is casting out through an enormous backyard. There's a buffet table sitting off to the side against a large old Victorian white two story house.

The aroma wafting from the enticing food arouse my taste-buds to almost salivating from the delicious smells.

My stomach grumbles loudly notifying me of my hungry state.

So with resolve in my step I invade the party walking around the people that are happily chatting amongst them-selves I edge my way to the table very slowly.

Reaching my destination I almost jump from glee. Eyeing the table of its robust contents I grab a small saucer from up off the table and start filling it up with different food varieties.

With my saucer full I creep over to the side of the big house, standing at the corner I dig into the food ecstatically. The delicious flavors of the succulent lamb in my mouth explode on my tastebuds. I moan out in derisive pleasure enjoying the immaculate taste until someone roughly grabs me by my bicep turning me around to face them abruptly.

The succulent food that was on my saucer and my saucer goes crashing down to the ground I could almost cry seeing all of that food go to such a tragic waste.

Angrily I look up at the rude offender who dared to spill my food so damn effortlessly.

When my eyes suddenly clash with the rude offenders eyes I nearly choke on the lamb.

Before me stands a God. A very handsome and alluring God.

His sexy chiseled body is hosting a ton of beautifully amazing tattoos that would make a woman scream. His dark hazel eyes draw me in like a long lost lover and his aroma is overwhelming divine. A mix of heady musk and spring rain is quickly overloading all of my senses.

I swallow the lamb down with a loud gulp as I wipe my mouth with the back of my hand I honestly think I'm actually drooling. Damn! He is one sexy as mother fucker but unfortunately his sexy ass is glaring daggers at me.

Mate!

My wolf, Maya screams inside of my head.

Oh hell no! I don't want or need a damn mate!!!

"Who the hell are you?" Fuuuuck! I think I just creamed in my pants. His gravely voice holds a deep baritone that can make a girl swoon.

"I-I'm....hungry! And you just spilled my damn food all over the ground!" I huff peering back down at my poor demolished food I pout.

"I'm serious. Who the hell are you? I don't remember you being on the list." What list? I have no idea what the hell he's talking about. Oh yea, I crashed his party. Well shit!

"You must have missed it. It's no problem though I'll just be on my way." I anxiously tell him taking a large step around him I begin to walk away.

"Not so fast." Fuck! Just my luck! He wraps his big hand around my wrist halting me.

"Please I was just hungry I didn't mean to cause any problems if you would just let me go I'll leave and won't bother you any more." I try to plead with him but by the look on his face my pleading doesn't faze him a damn bit.

"You're coming with me." What? No! He tugs my arm pulling me forward.

"Please I'll just leave. I was just hungry. Please don't do this." I continue to plead but it falls on deaf ears as he pulls me along through throngs of happy people at the party.

All of which are now staring at me very curiously.

The sexy as hell guy pulls me threw the doors of the big two story house with ease. He yanks me into an open faced living room and kitchen area where another sexy as hell guy is standing by an island talking freely with another sexy as hell man.

What is the water around here?

"Look what I found." The big guy holding my wrist tightly says, pulling me toward him until he has me standing right in front of him facing the two other sexy men.

With both of his hands on my shoulders he lowers his hands then starts rubbing his hands softly up and down my arms. I can feel sparks ignite up within me making me moan out load from the intense sensation of it.

The two other sexy men turn to me Instantly when the sexy man that's holding me speaks again.

"A trespasser." He says gleefully. I roll my damn eyes at him.

The other two sexy guys walk over to me and this time I do drool. Fuck! Such fine specimen. Both of their bodies are rocking hard. I fucking moan again.

They stop right in front of me, when I raise my eyes to meet theirs all hell breaks loose in the giant room.

"Fucking hell! Mate!" One of them says.

Fuck me!

Chapter 3

Fuck me!

How did this delicious piece of morsel in front of me just walk into my house and knock me completely on my fucking ass?

Her hypnotic dark blue eyes locked unto mine and I knew instantly that she was my mate.

I lick my bottom lip roaming my eyes down that tantalizing body I go from her luxurious mane of sandy brown hair to her plump provocative lips all the way down to her vavascisous breast. Stopping at her enticing breast I almost bite my damn tongue when my eyes drop lower to her firm tanned legs. My fucking dream girl is standing right here in front of me.

Damn! She is the entire fucking package all rolled up in one. All I need is for her turn around and show me her full round plump ass and I'll be heaven. Please let her have a a big enough ass that I can wrap my hands up in Goddess.

Then her intoxicating aroma hits me like a damn Mack truck. Fuck!

Cinnamon with a mixture of a vanilla slam into me hard evoking my damn senses. My dick jerks in my pants suddenly when she starts breathing heavily making those damn scrumptious breast rise up and down so damn sweetly. Fuck me! I look down to my dick and roll my eyes at how damn hard I actually am. Down boy! I take a deep breath to try and mentally calm myself.

"What's your name beautiful?" I ask her not quite recognizing my own damn lust filled voice.

"Thorn." She whispers her name up to me, her little soft voice has a slight tremble to it. She's notably scared I noticed, I can see the fear rotating in her dark blue eyes.

"Thorn. We won't hurt you there's no reason to be scared beautiful." I smoothly assure her. Cocking my head to the side I lower it so that she is able to see my eyes more clearly.

"Look at me." I softly command her placing my fingers on her chin I raise her pretty little head up toward me so she can see the honesty in my eyes. As soon as my skin graces hers the tingles shoot straight threw me alighting a fire within me easily. Damn!

"We won't hurt you, I promise, but I need to know what you're doing here." Ignoring my brothers I focus mainly on her.

If she's here searching for her mate at the She-Wolf Parade then I will gladly tell her that her search is finally over because here I fucking stand ready, willing, and completely able and all just for her.

"I was just hungry. Please I only had one bite of the lamb, I will pay you back as soon as I am able to just....please don't hurt me." She pleads with me so damn sweetly, damn! I would love to see her begging me to release her when I have her all tied up and on my bed.

Fuuuuck!

I need to get my mind out of the damn gutter. Taking a long breath I drop my hand from her pretty face observing her.

She was hungry? She didn't come for the party? From the look of her attire it seems like she's been traipsing through our woods for some time.

Her disheveled state leaves me furrowing my brows at her. Dirt and grime are covering her t-shirt and jeans randomly. She even has a couple of black smudges on her beautiful face.

She acts like she is running from something or someone. Interesting?

"Release her Sin." I tell him with a touch of veiled protectiveness in my tone.

"Slay we don't know her. She could be anybody. She could be working for somebody. For all we know she could even be a spy for that asshole Alpha Wallis." Sin tells me cautiously. He may have a point but I don't believe that she is actually a spy for Wallis.

Wallis has been a pain in our side for years now. Every since we all became Alphas he has done everything in his power to try and overthrow us.

Regardless Thorn doesn't look the type to be associated with a creep like Wallis.

"I said release her." I provide him with no further explanation. I stand there folding my arms across my chest and glare at him.

"Fine. But I know who she is and like I told you before I don't want one nor do I need one. Got it?" How the hell does he know who she is? Scowling at him I watch him as he gingerly takes his hands away from her arms albeit very slowly.

Thorn looks over her shoulder at him completely perplexed by his demanding statement and attitude.

"How do you know who she is?" I inquire, perplexed myself by his statement.

"Because I can feel it. I can see sit when I look into her eyes. I can even fucking smell her!" Sun says it aggressively. I scowl again peering over at him but then I notice Thorn raising up her arm.

She sniffs at her underarm a couple times then looks back at Sin with a questioning look.

"I don't smell that bad do I?" She innocently ask him I can't help but to laugh at that pure innocent look that's on her face. Covering my mouth with my hand I try to hide my smile from Sin.

He looks down at her like she's lost her ever loving mind. Now he is the one that is looking perplexed. I can't help but to laugh again.

Sun starts barking out with laughter right beside me with his hands on his stomach he is doubled over in laughter. I shake my head at him, Sun can be a bit childish.

"It's not funny!" Sin grouses. I immediately sober up my laughter when I see the tense look on Sins face.

Poor guy doesn't know what to think. I think he has just met his match with Thorn. This should interesting.

Thinking of Thorn I recalled what my brother said to me earlier.

"What do mean you can feel and see it?" I ask him with an abundance of curiosity flowing through me. It can't mean what I think it does can it?

"Fuck Slay! Do I really have to say it? She's my mate! I felt it when I touched her. I saw it when I looked into her eyes and I can smell her alluring scent!" Sin grumbles.

No fucking way!

"She can't be. She's my mate Sin! How can she be yours too?" I ask dropping my hands down to my sides I glance down at Thorn suspiciously.

"Wait a damn minute. She can't be either of yours because she is definitely mine!" Sunny states with gruffness in his tone. I side eye him obviously confused at his declaration.

"How did this happen? Is the Moon Goddess punishing us?" Sin hastily replies combing his fingers through his hair.

"Would anyone like to hear my opinion about it?" Thorn speaks up finally alerting us all.

"What?" Sunny ask her as he takes a small forward toward her. I take notice of how edgy he's acting toward her. It's like he's trying to control himself from touching her. Maybe it's his Wolf Stinger keeping him on edge?

"Well for one all of y'all are acting like I'm not even here and it's rude and for two I don't even want a mate. I have too much going on in my life right now anyway. Don't worry I won't reject any of you but I can't stay here so could you please just let me go and I'll be on my merry old way." She says with a giant smile on her face that doesn't come close to reaching her eyes.

"No way. I don't know what's going on in your life right now but there's no way we are letting you go when we you just found you." Sunny states vehemently refusing her demands.

I just can't seem to get over the we part in his sentence.

How I'm the hell are we three suppose to share one mate between us all. I've heard of it happening before of course.

Our very own Queen has multiple mates but I never once thought that my brothers and I would fall into that category. I always thought we would eventually have a mate each not just one for us to share.

I wouldn't even know how to do that shit anyway.

"I don't care either way. You guys can leave me the hell out of this one. Have fun with her because she's all yours." Sin rudely says as he turns on his heels and storms away from us.

I watch him as he stomps away highly disappointed by his actions. The guy clearly has some issues he needs to work out.

Glancing back down to Thorn I observe her face watching it closely as she eyes Sins back or is she admiring his ass as he stomps away? I grin at her obvious desire toward him apparently she is drawn to him in a way at least sexually anyway. Now I'm feeling a bit jealous over my own damn brother. I want her to look at me that way.

With fire and desire floating in those dark blue spheres just as they are now.

Clearing my throat to get her attention she jumps slightly startled coming out of her horny daze. I release a huffy breath at her display.

"You said you were hungry and it looks like you also need a change of clothes. Why don't you eat something right now and I'll try to scramble up you up some clothes so you can get a shower and change and if you like there's a guest room waiting for you upstairs for you to sleep in." She starts to protest but I hurriedly cut her off before she can.

"Look you look completely exhausted and like you said you're hungry. Why don't you just stay here for now and we can help you with whatever or whoever you're running from." I suggest keeping my voice at an even tranquil tone so as not to frighten her away.

"Who said I was running from anything?" She insist but for some reason I can just tell. She's like a frightened little skittish doe and that bothers me more than I can say.

"I just assumed. I don't know what's going on but as you heard from all of us apparently you are all of our mates and that alone is reason enough for me to over my services to you regardless if you want them or not you have them and you have me at your disposal." I try to best to assure that I'm not her enemy. I want to earn her trust. Hell I want to make all of her problems go away.

But I have to take this slow because unfortunately she doesn't have time for a mate right now and that is going to drive me completely nuts until I can change her attitude toward me and my brothers. I just have to make her see that I'm or we are on her side.

"Same here. We're not bad guys Thorn. We won't hurt you if you need our protection we will gladly offer it to you. Just give a chance." Sunny grants her a wide smile with a flash of hope twinkling in his eyes. The guy has already got bad for her.

"Okay. Thank you I would greatly appreciate it but I don't want to be any trouble that guy Sin doesn't act like he wants me around or even likes me. I don't want to cause any problems and I don't want to be a burden." She says it with a hint of modesty and vulnerability in her voice.

"Sins my baby brother and this guy here is his twin Sunny Vallor. I'm Slay Vallor their older brother and this is the Blood Claw Pack we are all the Alphas of the pack and you my beautiful mate will soon be our Luna." I staunchly inform her with a grain of authority laced in my voice.

She may not want a mate as of yet but I will change her pretty little mind about that soon enough.

"I didn't agree to that. You apparently assume a lot. I do appreciate your offer to allow me to stay but I can't stay long. I'm sorry there is a lot going on with me right now and I can't drag either of you into it." Thorn briskly says waving her arms decisively in the air. I grunt out in disproval.

She's not getting away from us that damn easy.

"We can work all of that out later right now you need to eat." I remark lifting my arm out to her I offer her my hand with my palm held up. She tentatively places her little hand into mine the sparks hit me full force when we make contact. Her eyes widen glancing up at me I offer her a genuine smile.

I gently pull her along to our private dining room in the back of our house with Sunny trailing along closely behind us.

Letting go of her hand I pull out a chair for her sit on as she passes me to sit down on the chair I finally get a good look at her ass and fuck me has the Moon Goddess blessed her.

I groan out heavily viewing that perfect ass of hers. Nice round plump lumps that would I would love to sink my dick deep into. I love a fine ass and she definitely has one.

Sunny catches me glaring at her fuckable ass he slyly smirks at me wiggling his damn eyebrows up and down silently laughing at me.

I don't care, it's mine, she's mine, and I will look at it all I fucking want and boy do I want to. Hearing her chair scrape across dining room floor brings me out of my lustful state quickly. Shit!

I suck in a breath trying to calm my desires for her but unfortunately her head turns in my direction as soon as she hears me take in a deep breath.

Her dark orbs lock directly onto my swollen cock that's pressed tightly against my snug jeans when I see the expression on her beautiful face I groan out again. Fuck!

She licked her bottom lip with that mesmerizing tongue on those juicy plump lips slowly, making me want to throw her ass on the dining room table and ravish her completely.

This sexy ass woman is definitely going to be death of me and I don't think I would have one damn complaint about it even if she did. Fuck!

I left Thorn alone to take a shower with a new change of clothes from my generous sister Lila in her guest room to go find my obnoxious ass brother Sin.

I politely asked Sun if he would stay in our home while I went out looking for my arrogant brother he gladly welcomed the idea to do so. Who can blame him? Thorn is like a fantasy come true I just can't understand why Sin doesn't think also.

Thankfully the stupid She-Wolf Parade is finally over. We still have a few stragglers that have stayed behind using our guest rooms in the pack house that traveled a long way just to attend the massive event.

With the rest of them gone I make my way into the backyard searching around for Sin but I can't seem to find him anywhere. I already checked his bedroom and he wasn't there unfortunately.

Where could his stupid ass be?

I pick up his scent near a row of houses that have some of our pack members living in them. Following the scent I stop dead in my tracks when I realize whose house he's in.

Fuck! The bastard will never learn.

Stomping up on the porch I bang my fist loudly on Storms front door. Making the door rattle on its damn hinges.

"Open up Sin! I know you're in there!" I shout still banging harshly on the damn door.

It finally creaks open revealing a disheveled Sin standing there only in his fucking boxers. I grab ahold of his ear with my fingers pulling him out of the house roughly.

I let go of his ear when I finally have him on the front porch with me.

"What the hell is fucking problem Sin? You met your mate just hours ago and I find you shacked up in Storms fucking bed. Are you delusional?" I am fuming mad. I knew Sin protested about having a mate but I never though he would be so callous as to sleep with a woman right after he found one.

"Damn Slay I told you I didn't want a fucking mate! What is your damn deal?" He grumbles rubbing his ear.

"My damn deal is that there is a beautiful young vibrant girl in our home that is your mate and instead of wanting to be with her you are here fucking the pack slut! I told you that when we found our mates that I didn't want you with her and you still went ahead and did the exact opposite of what I told you. What is it with you and this fucking woman Sin? Is her fucking pussy that damn good?" I grind out him with my temper flaring. I just don't get it and he's pissing me the hell off!

"He doesn't want her. He wants me. Why else would he be here after he found her? You may be one of my Alphas Slay but you have no right saying those nasty things about me and coming to my own and making a scene!" Storm tells me as soon as she appears at her door glaring up at me.

"Just reject her Sin and accept me in her place. I would make a far better Luna for you than any other woman." Storm suggests seductively. Strolling over to stand by Sin with her hands placed upon his chest.

"I can't." Sin miserably states.

Of all of the...

"Why the hell not?" Storm steps back from him placing her hands on her hips. The damn woman is standing there with only a small revealing nightie on. She has no damn shame.

"Because I promised my brothers Storm. I can't accept you as my Luna. Neither of them will allow it." Sin tells her with remorse but he can't seem to look her in the eyes.

"I'll be damned. Slay you can't do this to us. He has a right to choose his own Luna and neither you nor Sun should dissuade him from choosing who he wants." Storm glowers over at me. I try suppress my smile but I fail miserably.

"You are not Luna material Storm and you will never be. Thorn will be our Luna and no other. If you ever raise your voice to me again I won't hesitate a second to throw your ass out of my damn pack. I'll make you go rogue without a second thought or worry about it. Try me Storm and I will see to it that you never have another pack you can run too I promise you that!" Now it's my turn to glower at her but I do it with an enormous smile on my face.

I can't stand this bitch standing in front of me and whatever Sin sees in her ass is beyond me.

"You can't do that. Sin tell him. Tell him what you want baby! Tell him you want me and not some dirty old hag." She pleads with him but he ignores her pleas.

Hearing her call Thorn a dirty old hag sets me right off.

"Look you despicable slut bag if I ever hear you call your Luna another foul name I will gladly rip out your damn tongue and throw your skanky ass in my dungeons do you fucking hear me?" I growl out lowly pointing my finger direct-ly in her backstabbing face.

"Come on Slay that's going a bit too far isn't it? You just met Thorn you don't know anything about her. How you can you be so protective of her already?" Sin scoffs. I just shake my head at his stupidity.

"Sin she is our mate picked by the Moon Goddess herself just for us, how can you be so disrespectful about it? I won't have you hurting her Sin. Not by your words or by your despicable actions. Get yourself together and lose the trash!" I gruffly demand of him stepping off of Storms porch.

"If she has you and Sun why would she need Sin? Just let him do what he wants Slay. He's your brother you should allow him to have a choice." Storm says halting me in my tracks. Turning back to her I look at Sin he's just staring at me with pleading eyes.

I hate to do this to him but Storm is just not good enough for him. I have to make him see that one way or the other. Even if I have to fight him over it.

"I am allowing him to have a damn choice Storm. He either chooses to accept Thorn as his mate or he has nobody. Not even you." I say as my last parting shot.

Turning around from them I walk away smiling deviously.

The first round goes to Slay!

Chapter 4

Sneaking up the stairs as quietly as I can. I press my ear against the guest room door that Thorn is in before I knock.

I don't want to catch her in the shower and frighten her. Hearing her rustling about in the bedroom I gently tap on the door, dropping my arm to my side I patiently wait for her to open it.

When the door finally opens I almost trip over my own damn tongue.

Thorn is a damn fucking Goddess. She stands in front of me holding on to the doorknob with one hand while the other is holding up a blue towel that's wrapped around her breast. The top of her voluptuous breast are enticingly pried up over the towel. I watch as the steady fall of her breathing causing her breast to rise and fall. Fuck! Now my damn dick is throbbing.

"Did you need something Sun?" He sweet little voice calls out to me. Shaking my head to rid myself of my disobedient thoughts I peer up at her face trying to fight my carnal urges.

"Uhm, I just wondered if you wanted to talk." I say hoarsely. Clearing my throat as I wait for her reply.

"Sure just let me get dressed. Your brother Slay brought me a pair of jeans and a shirt but I have nothing to sleep in." I swallow down a loud gulp.

"Would you like me to get you one of my shirts to wear to sleep in?" I ask her with slight trepidation. The thought of her sleeping in my shirt does strange things to my imagination.

"If you don't mind? I hate to bother you though." She says shyly.

"It's not a problem. I'll be right back." I rush to say, quickly running to my bedroom I grab one of my shirts off of the hanger not caring about which one I chose, I rush back into her bedroom with my hand out offering her one of my t-shirts.

She takes it from my hand then heads off to the bathroom. Walking further into her room I take a seat on the side of the bed waiting for her.

When she finally reappears my eyes suddenly glue heated-ly on to her. The shirt that I chose for her to wear is my old Journey t-shirt. It reaches all the way down to right above her kneecaps and she looks sexy as fucking hell in it. I shyly look away.

"What did you want to talk about?" She ask me as she makes her way to me. She sits down on the bed beside me with one leg folded over laying flat on the bed the other one is hanging off of the bed. I take a chance and glimpse down with her legs slightly parted I try to peek under the shirt she's wearing but I feel like a perverted peeping tom. I divert my eyes away quickly clearing my throat again.

"I just wanted to get to know you a little better." I finally answer her. I hate that I'm so damn shy sometimes. It makes me feel inadequate in some ways.

After a person gets to know me I open up to them eventually. It's the getting to know a person part that makes me so damn shy and nervous.

"Sure. Ask me anything." She replies smiling at me.

Man she's so beautiful.

"Uhm, how old are you?" I ask her the first question that just pops into my head.

"I'm seventeen almost eighteen in two days that is." Wow she doesn't look that young. I thought she was around nineteen.

"How old are you?" She ask me timidly.

"Twenty two. My birthday is in July." I tell her wanting to push the conversation along.

"Do you have any siblings?" I ask but her eyes suddenly look away from me.

"Yes just one. A brother. He's a year older than me. I miss him." Her statement seems so sheltered. I look at her curiously but don't broach anymore on the subject.

"You've met my brothers. I also have a sister her name is Lila. That's where the clothes came from that Slay brought you earlier." I inform her kindly.

"How old is Slay? I know Sin is your twin right? So which one of you two is older?" She ask wanting to know more about us. Which makes me happy. Maybe if she gets to know us better she won't want to runaway from us.

"Slay is a year older than me. Sin is only nine minutes older than me but he thinks that makes him the boss of me." I honestly tell her.

"Why is Sin so mad all of the time? I mean, I just met him but he seems so angry." I can understand why she's asking me this. Sin is a very complicated person.

"He's just cocky. He seems to think he is a prize to all women. He doesn't mean anything by it though. I just think it's his way of coping." I lowly tell her.

"Coping with what?" Stick foot in mouth. That's apparently something I'm very good at. Damn!

"Coping with our parents death." I tell her but don't elaborate any further.

"I'm sorry. I know how you feel I lost my mom two years ago." Damn! Well I guess unfortunately we have that in common.

"I'm sorry. H-how did you lose her?" I press wanting to know everything I can about her.

"A rogue attack on our pack. They killed six of our members that day one being my mom." Damn! I hate that for her. Rogues are viscously arrogant wolves that could care less about anybody.

"We lost our parents in a plane crash three years ago. They were traveling to a distant pack in the north to visit and help another Alpha. He was having trouble with rogues. So my parents flew out to help him only they didn't make it." I confess this all to her with a profound sense of sadness. I miss my parents every fucking day.

"I am so sorry Sun I know how hard that is." I so appreciate her thoughtfulness. How did I get so damn lucky to have such a sweet mate?

"Thank you. Okay on to happier questions. What do you like to do?" She looks over at me with her whimsical dark blue eyes concentrating.

"I love to read, paint, listen to music, and dance. How about you?" She beams up at me.

"I like to ride my Harley, shoot pool, and hunt. I also like to listen to music." I tell her grabbing the hem of my shirt she's wearing to show her.

"Oh right. I love Journey. I also like some hair metal bands from the eighties and I'm completely in love with Harry Styles." I don't know who this Harry Styles is but I already don't like him. I scowl at her with jealousy coursing through my veins. "He's a singer that use to be in a band called One Direction." She states when she sees my tempered look.

I've never had this emotion before. I've never been jealous over anybody or anything. It's a very unpleasant emotion. I hear my wolf, Stinger, howling in my head.

"Are you okay?" She ask me tentatively, with worry on her face.

"I'm fine. Why?" I ask.

"Because your eyes are turning a bit red." Fuck!

"Calm down Stinger you're scaring her!" I growl at my wolf.

"I don't care I so don't like her talking about loving others." Stinger angrily replies.

"He's just a professional singer. It's no one you have to worry about. Calm the hell down!" I growl again.

"Fine." He huffs.

I roll my eyes mentally at him. My wolf can be stubborn.

"I'm part Red Wolf my wolf got upset when you said you loved Harry Styles." I quip.

She giggles at me. The soft little giggles coming from her makes my heart swell.

"That's so cute. What is his name?" She ask me with a spike of curiosity.

"Stinger. He's basically a softie but he does have a temper sometimes." I half laugh with her.

"Mine is named Maya. She randomly talks to me because I haven't shifted yet." That surprises me. I shifted when I was fourteen.

"Why haven't you shifted?" I ask.

"Well I'm half Fae the Fae side of me is resisting my White Wolf half for some reason but when I turn eighteen in two days then I will be able to." Uhm. I've never heard of that before but I've never met a Fae either.

"I've never met a Fae before. What can you do?" I speak my own thoughts to her.

"Not much. Not yet. Not till I shift fully but when I do I'll be able to preform magic in both of my forms." I don't understand.

"Both of your forms?" I ask.

"Yes. I'm a winged fire Fae. When I shift I'll be able to use my wings also." That's actually incredible.

"You said you were half Red Wolf? What's your other half?" She ask edging closer to me on the bed.

"I'm half Pyromancer. I can manipulate fire." It took awhile for me to learn how to control it but thank fuck that I eventually did.

"Wow we have that in common. Fire I mean. I can't wait to finally be able to use mine. My mother was a Fire Fae also. She could do incredible things. Once she conjured up fire and made it into the shape of a giant flaming heart. It was so beautiful." I can see the love she has for her mother captured on her beautiful face. She must of been one impressive woman. I wish I could have met her.

"She sounds awesome." I tell her and I mean it if she was anything like Thorn I could only imagine how beautiful and sweet she was.

"She was. I miss her." She says sadly and I definitely can tell that she really does. It's such a shame though. I know exactly how she feels and it sucks.

"You told me about your music preferences what about movies? What kind do you like?" I ask her changing the subject quickly. Diverting her from her sadness.

"You may not believe it but I like horror movies. My favorite is Get out and I like some thrillers also. What about you and please don't tell me it's all action packed type movies that would be so typical." I flash her grin. Watching how animated she gets over her favorite things is mesmerizing.

"Believe it or not I like fantasy movies. Maybe some action adventure movies sometimes but I'm all about the magical stuff. My favorite is The Lord of the Rings Trilogy I think it's awesome." Her eyes twinkle up at me when she smiles.

"I like that to." She says at least we have a few things in common then.

But I want to desperately know what or who she is running from. I put on my serious face, bracing myself I just point blank ask her.

"Who are you running from Thorn," she freezes, I search her face as it quickly goes from happy to solemn instantly, "I just want to help you. I know you don't know me Thorn but I am your mate I will do anything to protect you. You can trust me." I calmly inform her. Placing my hand on her knee to comfort and have contact from her.

The tingles shoot straight through me as soon as I touch her delicate skin causing me to unintentionally groan out desirably from the sensation. I close my eyes to enjoy the enticing feeling.

She reflectively pulls her leg away from my hand springing up from the bed, the lose of contact to her makes me nearly want to weep.

I open my eyes to see her frantically pacing back and forth. She's stressing over something vital.

"Please Thorn I just want to help." I plead with her. She stops her pacing peering over at me with discerning eyes.

"You don't know me. Why would you want to help a complete stranger? You don't even know what you're asking of me. I don't mean to sound like I'm ungrateful but I don't know if I can trust you." She replies with sincerity. I slide off the bed walking up to her, I stop right beside her soaking in her wonderful scent of cinnamon and vanilla.

"Believe me when I tell you that you can trust me Thorn. You may not understand it just yet but a mate bond is the strongest bond in the world one that the Moon Goddess has generously blessed us with and I won't take that for granted. I will do everything in my power to always love and protect you." I insist, placing all of my cards out on the table for her.

I understand that since she has shifted yet she may not feel the blessed bond we have with each other just yet. But I'm hoping and praying that within two days on her birthday that our bond will click into place automatically for her.

"Love? Now I know your just pulling my leg. How can you love someone you just met? That's just preposterous." Now I know just from her actions that she definitely doesn't feel the bond exactly like we do.

"When you shift into your wolf Maya you will understand the bond more. Until then Thorn I just want to help you. Who is after you?" I press her once again this time I feel as if I'm practically begging her though. She lets out a trembling sigh then bowing her head in defeat.

"My father. My father is after me." She barely whispers it to me. The desperation in her tone is completely disheartening.

"Why? Why is your own father after you?" I'm dumbfounded by the idea of hearing it's her father that has running scared.

"Fine I'll tell you but please don't tell anyone else. I don't want anyone to know or to get caught up in between this battle." I nod my head taking her hand into mine I walk her back over to the bed.

We both sit down on the edge as she tells me why she's running scared. I listen closely to every detail. How her father locked in his dungeon after an argument they had the previous night. How she can't seem to remember how she got there.

She tells me about her brother Fier, it strikes a cord within me when she mentions her brothers name it's sounds awfully familiar.

Hearing a creaking on the floorboards I pry my eyes up seeing my brother Slay standing in the doorway. I don't let on that he's there because deep down I know that he needs to hear this as much as I do.

When she finally gets to the reason as to why her father is so desperately after her I become furious and obviously sick at the very idea of him wanting to make his daughter his own lover.

It's repulsive! What kind of sick father is he?

"What's his name?" Slay finally speaks up from the doorway. Thorn gets startled from his sudden appearance. She practically falls off of the bed when she hears him, I reach out quickly to catch her. Grabbing her by her biceps I pull her back onto the bed those damn sparks light up again as soon as we make contact.

I can't control it this time I let out an audible moan startling Thorn once again. She places her tiny hand up to her chest breathing erratically.

"What's his name Thorn?" Slay ask her more aggressively as he strolls into the room he stops at the edge of the bed glaring down at her.

"Alpha Baker Rose of the White Moon Pack." As soon as the words tumble from her mouth my spine stiffens.

Glancing up at Slay the haunting look that plasters on his face from hearing her father name is frightening.

"Baker Rose is your father?" I ask basically floored by her admittance.

"Yes why do you know him?" She ask scowling.

You could say that we do. We know his ass very well and we fucking hate him! Well resent him mostly.

"Yes we know him. So if your dad is Baker Rose that means you are his famous daughter Thorn Lee Rose right?" Slay ask her haughtily.

"Yes. H-How...do y-you...know about me?" She stammers out with a hint of confusion written all over her beautiful face.

I sigh, this isn't going to be easy.

"We've heard about you. You are a well known rumor around these parts. The infamous White Wolf and Fire Fae. I should've realized it when you told me earlier. There is a damn prophecy about you that's been passed down through the years. Damn I should have known it was you. I'm a moron!" I grouse combing my fingers through my hair. Why didn't I see it?

"I don't understand what prophecy are you talking about and how do you know my dad?" How can she not know about herself? Didn't her parents ever inform her of it?

"The prophecy states that once the White Wolf Fire Fae reaches her full potential and finds her mates that she will rule once again over the Invivus Realm. A Realm that as of now has no ruler over it. It's been that way for many years because of the lost Princess. It is rumored that she was kidnapped one night while she was attending a social event in King Zeniths Realm. There has been an interim ruler since she went missing a man named Samuel Drake, he is the Princesses long lost cousin so he claims and he is an evil and vile man. The Fae have been waiting patiently for their Princess to arrive and take back her Realm hoping that she will dispel them from Samuel and his vile ways and that appears to be you." Slay relates the prophecy to her.

I watch her closely as she absorbs the information he just told her.

Her face goes pale instantly and her breathing begins to pick up more rapidly. I'm afraid she's about to faint from the shocking news. I edge closer to her just incase she does but she surprises me when she springs up from the bed nudging Slay out of her way she starts to pace the room again.

"So you're telling me I'm this long lost Princess? That my mother was actually going to be the Queen of this Realm? Then that would mean that my father...that my father either kidnapped my mother and held her against her will or.....but what about my brother? Wouldn't he be the rightful King? I mean, that would make more sense, wouldn't it?" She rambles mainly to herself.

"Not quite. Is your brother a Fae also?" Slay ask her, he watches her curiously as she continues her frantic pacing.

"No. He's just a White Wolf like me but he has no Fae in him. But if that's the case then...." She trails off deeply scowling and confused.

"That would mean that Fier is your half brother." I finish her thought for her.

"They lied to me. They all lied to me! Why? Why would they do that?" She ask us bewildered but at least she's stopped her pacing now.

"I don't know beautiful but we need it find out why. We also need to find a way to let everyone in the Invivus Realm know that you are alive and well." Slay insist. Thorn just shakes her head vehemently.

"No. We can't. Not until I shift. If I have to face down this Samuel I need to be at my full potential. Until then no one can breathe a word about this. Hell what am I saying they wouldn't believe you even if you did tell someone. Damn, I don't believe it! Fuck! I've been lied to my entire life now my father wants me for his....that's why he wants me? He wants to rule over this Realm? That has to be it!" She rambles again answering her own questions aloud.

I can't stand to see her in such a frantic state. This is all too much for her to bear at once. It would be for anybody.

Sliding off of the bed once again I walk over to her. Standing behind her I wrap her up in my arms tightly basically cocooning her. The sparks hit me again this time I try to control my audible groan. She doesn't need that right now.

Placing my chin on top of her head I squeeze her lithe body tighter to me.

"It will be okay Thorn we will work this all out for now we need to only concentrate on your shifting. Everything else can wait." I assure her. She nods her head numbly at me, making my head bounce up and down as she does it. I stifle a laugh at it.

"Like I said before beautiful I am at your disposal. We are at your disposal. We will help you through all of this. What are mates for after all?" Slay says slightly chuckling at her.

"I can't ask you to that. You hardly know me." Thorn states miserably.

"You're not asking us Thorn we are volunteering. Besides it's in the prophecy that you will have your mates by your side. We can't go against a prophecy can we?"Slay states trying to lighten the mood.

He may have said it just to lighten her up but what he states is actually true. It is rumored that her mates stand beside her to battle her enemies with her. I just hope it doesn't have to come to that though but if it does I will definitely be there for her.

"We will be beside you the entire time Thorn. Not just because it was foretold but because we actually want to be." I tell her hugging her tighter.

And we so do!

Chapter 5

Maybe Storm has a point.

A little while after Slay left I came back to Storms bedroom. Where it didn't take long before Storm fell asleep. I stayed up contemplating every thing that's happened in the last few hours.

It nearly crushed me seeing him so damn disappointed in me and my choices. I've always respected my brother. He had the unfortunate job dropped into his lap when he had to take over raising us after our parents sudden demise.

I respect him more than anybody on this fucked up planet but Storm may be on to something also.

After our unfortunate meeting tonight on Storms porch when she said that I should be able to make my own choices it got me to thinking.

She's right. I'm a grown ass man and I should be able to make own damn decisions. That's where the problem lies though.

I may be old enough to make my own decisions but I always seem to fuck things up for me and the people I love whenever I make them.

I act before I think.

But is it so wrong of me not wanting this Thorn girl as my mate?

What if I did want to chose another? Fuck! I hate having to even think about all of this stupid shit! Rubbing my hand down my face I glance over to Storm sleeping soundly beside me.

Do I want her for my Luna?

Would I actually fight with my brothers to have her as my Luna?

I don't think so. I may have an infatuation with her but I do not even come remotely close to even loving her. The only thing I love about her is how good she is in bed but that's definitely not enough for me to make her my Luna!

So why do I keep fighting this so damn hard?

Hell if I know. I throw the comforter off of me, sliding out of Storms bed, I walk into the en-suite bathroom.

Standing in front of the mirror I take a good long look at my reflection and what I see in front of me is not someone I can even recognize anymore.

The good fun spirited jolly guy that I use to be has vanished and in its is place grew a selfish bastard who seemingly only thinks of himself.

I need a damn drink!

I sigh, turning away from the mirror I jump into the shower with the hot water spraying all over my body I place my hand on the shower stall rolling my head under the hot steaming water trying to will myself to relax.

A picture of Thorn comes crashing through my mind like a damn speeding bullet suddenly. Fuck!

Slowly wrapping my hand around my stiff cock I start stroking it vigorously all the while I keep Thorns image in my fucking head.

I picture those soft supple plump lips I want so damn much to surround my dick in ongoing pleasure. I keep imaging them as I pick up my speed jacking off torturously to them.

Oh and those vibrant oversized breast I would just love to straddle her body placing my large cock right in between those beauties and fuck them so damn hard and rough.

Damn!

My spine starts to tingle thereafter my balls clench up tight as fuck, I groan and cry out Thorns name as I spray my juices all over Storms shower wall. Fuck! Fuck! Fuck!

Why the hell am I even thinking about her? I pant heavily as I release my half limp cock from my hand trying to get her damn image out of my fucking head! Dammit! Slamming my hand against the bathroom stall I bite down on my cheek in frustration. I shouldn't be thinking about her this way. Fucking lusting after her. The woman is already getting to me.

"Need some help with that big guy?" Storm ask suddenly, peering into the shower, she nods her head toward my half limp dick, she's completely naked as she steps into the shower with the water flowing down her body slowly dripping down her little breast I can't help but to think that she looks fucking immaculate.

Then fucking Thorns image pops into my head again. My fucking brain is apparently trying to compare the two of them. I push her image away focusing on the temptress standing in front of me.

Giving her my best shit eating grin I can muster up. I step closer to her wrapping my arm around her middle section I pull her closer to me roughly.

"You can." I manage to tell her and she proceeds to do just that.

Fuck!

Storming into my house after my illuminating shower with Storm a few minutes ago. I scowl when seeing that the living room and dining room is strangely vacant.

Stomping up the stairs I hear voices coming from one of our guest rooms.

I stop beyond the edge of the bedroom door listening in intently.

"The prophecy states that once the White Wolf Fire Fae reaches her full potential and finds her mates that she will rule once again over the Invivus Realm. A Realm that is has no ruler over it for many years because of the lost Princess. It's is rumored that she was kidnapped one night while she was attending a social event in King Zeniths Realm. There has been an interim ruler since she went missing a man named Samuel Drake, he is the Princesses long lost cousin so he claims and he is an evil and vile man. The Fae have been waiting patiently for their Princess to arrive and take back her Realm hoping that she will dispel them from Samuel and that appears to be you." What the actual fuck? Slay can't be for real can he?

She's the actual missing fucking Princess from the Invivus Realm?

I nearly shit my damn pants.

No fucking way! She can't be!

My ears pick up when I hear her emotional reply back to him.

"So you're telling me I'm this long lost Princess? That my mother was actually the Queen of this Realm? Then that would mean that my father...that my father either kidnapped my mother and held her against her will or.....but what about my brother? Wouldn't he be the rightful King? I mean, that would make more sense, wouldn't it?" She starting to panic I realize.

Stepping slowly away from the door I stomp back down heading to the dining room.

That's a lot to take in. I finally find my mate, well we do, and she's the fucking lost Princess?

I can't fucking believe it.

After hearing all of that I soon come to the realization that Thorn is going to be nothing but fucking trouble.

I have to find a way to get her out of our lives forever. I won't risk my brothers or my sister lives on her.

She isn't worth it.

I already lost my parents and I'll be damned if I lose anyone else because of her.

With that decision firmly set in my mind I turn on my heels and head straight to bed.

"Storm!" I yell for her as soon as I entered her house the following morning slamming the front door behind me I casually stroll into her bedroom assuming she's still asleep. Outside of her bedroom door I'm shocked when I hear faint moans coming from it.

When I reach her bedroom I open the door slowly and to my surprise Storm is in her bed with another man! Fuck!

And not just any man either, she is presently fucking my own damn Beta Pan Lawrence. I stand in the doorway folding my arms across my chest I stand back and watch as they both proceed to make out without even noticing my arrival. Typical!

Pan is in between Storms legs going at her pussy like a damned starved beast, Storm is enjoying every second of it moaning appreciatively as his tongue plunges furiously into her.

Not being able to withstand it any longer I clear my throat to grab their attention.

Storms eyes open suddenly seeing me standing here she starts to panic.

"Damn, Sin, Fuck!" She pushes Pan right off of her I watch as they both hurriedly stumble from the bed panicking.

"Damn Sin I'm so fucking sorry man." Pan grunts trying to apologize while he scrambles around the room trying desperately to find his clothing.

"Sin baby I'm so sorry. It's not....it's not what it looks like." She rushes to say. Yea right!

"It looked like you two were fucking to me." I say it so nonchalantly that it makes her hesitate when she reaches down to pick up her shirt that was cast about out on the bedroom floor.

"Yes but I can explain." She states as she pulls her shirt over her head causing her hair to be in even more disarrayed.

"Sin I'm sorry man. I came over here looking for you and one thing led to another and I..." I cut him off holding my hand up.

"Just happen to accidentally fall into her pussy? Happens to me all the time man." I grouse completely fed up with this bullshit I turn around headed for the door but before I exit her bedroom I turn back to them.

Looking Storm dead in her eye I give her my last parting shot, "I guess Slay was right all along about you. You are the pack slut." Before she can offer up a reply I storm out of the door and out of her house smiling.

By the time I make it back to my house my brothers, my sister, and Thorn are all sitting at the dining room table eating their breakfast.

Everyone stops talking as soon as I enter the room. I ignore their intense stares, grabbing a plate I fill it up with all my normal goodies.

Placing the plate on the dining table a little to roughly, I draw all of their attention to me. They all look at me confused but I just keep ignoring them.

I'm not in the damn mood to socialize so I just sit here eating my food and glancing up at them every now and again when someone begins to talk about something but I still remain silent.

"Did you hear her Sin?" My brother Sunny ask peering over the table at me curiously.

"What?" I ask between my bites of my food.

"Lila was talking to you. Are you okay?" Sun inquires with concern.

"Uhm. Yea I'm fine. What did you say Lila?" I ask her as they all stare over at me with a mask of confusion on their faces.

"I said I found my mate last night. Isn't it wonderful. His name is Marc Fuller. His a Beta at the Silver Moon Pack. He's going to pick me in about an hour to go live with him and I'm so nervous. I can't wait for all of you to meet him. He's absolutely stunning." She tells me with so much glee on her face and a new twinkle in her eyes that I can't help but to be happy for her.

She's wanted this so much, I'm so glad her dreams are finally coming true for her. She deserves it.

"That's great Lila. Wait did you say his name is Marc Fuller?" I ask.

"Yes why do know him?" Of course I know him.

"We went to high school together. Don't you remember Sunny? He was the captain of the football team. He use to date that girl....what was her name?" I snap my fingers. I can't believe I forgotten her name. She was a cheerleader at the time and a real hellcat. Blonde, big boobs, and an ass to die for. I groan just thinking about her.

"Oh you mean Chari. Yes I remember they had a really bad break up when she met her mate. It was all over high school about how badly she treated him when they broke up." Yea, now I remember. She did it right in front of everybody in chemistry class with her mate standing behind her. Marc was completely devastated.

"Well he doesn't have to worry about her now because he has me." Lila states with a touch of jealousy wrapped in her tone.

"Yes he does and he's the lucky one to find such a treasure like you." Thorn tells her placing her hand on her arm Lila beams over at her.

I growl.

Looks like Thorn has already got my family wrapped around her little finger.

"Thank you and you are a treasure also. All three of my brothers lucked out." She tells Thorn. Like hell I did.

I let out a deep growl.

Drawing everyone's attention again back to me. I jump up from my seat throwing down my fork on my plate with a huff I stomp off from all of them.

Heading straight for the living room I plop my ass down on the couch, reaching for the tv remote I start flipping through random channels aimlessly.

As soon as I hear the footsteps coming up from behind me I obnoxiously raise the volume on the tv wanting to block out whatever speech I'm about to get for my subsequently bad behavior.

Slay comes marching into the room with heavy footfalls indicating just how pissed off he actually is at me.

I rotate my head popping my neck ignoring him as he sits down on the couch next me.

He yanks the remote out of my hand turning down the volume on the tv. Then he throws the remote down on the homey design coffee table. The remote hits the glass with a chilling clink I actually thought he cracked it for second.

"What?" I whine out knowing that the inevitable is about to happen.

"Want to explain to me why you are being a damn jackass?" Slay cocks his eyebrow at me, I shake my head then lean my head back on the couch closing my eyes. Wishing that I didn't have to have this damn conversation.

"I heard you." I admit. I feel him shuffling on the couch then I hear him give a low sigh.

"And what is that you think you heard?" This time I'm the one who sighs.

"I heard you and Sunny talking to Thorn about the prophecy." I don't elaborate any further. I sit back patiently and wait to let what I just told him sink in.

"So you know she's the missing Princess then?" He ask. Well duh! I wonder how long they were actually planning to keep it from me?

"She needs our help Sin." He whines.

I bet she does.

"I'm not going to help her and I don't think you or Sunny should either. She's just not worth it Slay." Raising my head from off of the couch I glance over at him to read his expression and true to form Slay is obviously pissed at my suggestion.

"She's our mate Sin." His simple answer to the situation only riles me.

"And? That doesn't mean that we have to risk our lives to protect her Slay. Dammit man can't you understand if you decide to keep her around and protect her she's only going to cause yours or Sunny's demise! I won't have that. I can't." I slip the desperation into my tone along with my stern conviction.

He has to see this! He just has to.

"It's not your call. If you don't want her as your mate then that's fine, I'm tired of fighting you over it, make Storm your damn chosen mate. But rest assured that me and Sunny want Thorn as ours. We will stand and defend her. No matter what you may say or do it's our decision and I expect you to honor that." Now he decides to allow me to have Storm as my mate? Great fucking timing bro.

I can hear the determination in his voice and see it written all over face. I know that I won't win this argument not unless I can find away to show them just how bad Thorn is for them.

"Her birthday is tomorrow. She will be able to shift into her wolf and Fae then. Until then why don't you take the time to get to her know her better. You may change your mind about her." Slay suggest.

"How old will she be? Shouldn't she already been able to shift?" I ask him. Hell I shifted when I was just fourteen. She should already be able to do it.

"She's seventeen. She will be eighteen in two days like I said. I don't know why she isn't able to shift yet but she told Sunny that it had to do with her Fae side battling with her wolf side which has prevented it from happening. Hell I don't know all I know is that she hasn't done it yet." Curiosity instills within me. What an interesting development.

"I'm about to tell you something about her and I want you to remain calm when I do. I've debated with myself over this. At first I thought I might keep it from you but now I think you have a right to know but please try to control your temper. Thorn is innocent in all of this just remember that okay?" Now I'm more than curious. Leaning closer to him I just nod my head waving my hand for him to proceed.

"Her full name is Thorn Lee Rose." He tells me. I scowl trying to recall why that name sounds so familiar to me. When Slay sees the confusion on my face he goes on.

"Rose. As in Alpha Baker Rose." He elaborates.

I see fucking red!

You got to be fucking kidding me!

"Remain calm Sin. Remember she's innocent in all of this. She doesn't know about any of it." He says trying to calm me. Fuck that!

I spring up from the couch and start pacing back and forth in the living room desperately trying to calm my rising raging temper.

"I can't believe it and you still want to be with her. Fucking unbelievable!" I shout at him.

"What's going on in here? Why are you so damn upset Sin?" Sun ask as he walks into the living room with Thorn and Lila trailing closely behind him.

"You knew?" I shout at Sun, "you knew who she was and you still want to claim her as your mate? Are you fucking crazy?" I shout louder throwing insults at him.

"I know and I don't care." Sun calmly states glowering over at me. "She had nothing to do with it Sin. It was her father not her." He adds on.

"What? What did my father do?" Thorn interrupts us confused.

"Tell her Sun. You tell her or I will and she won't like it if I tell her." I insist angrily.

"Someone tell me." Thorn demands exasperated.

When no one goes to open open their damn mouths I stomp over to her. Coming right up to her face to face I glare down at her.

"Don't Sin." Slay warns me but I'm too far gone now to even care about what he thinks anymore.

"Your father is the one who called my parents wanting their help for the rogue attacks that was so called happening to his pack. He fucking lied about it. My parents got on that plane out of the goodness of their hearts to go and help a fellow pack in trouble, only to die for trying to help your deceiving father. There were no damn rogues attacking your pack. He bold faced lied and because of it they fucking died!" I scream all of it out right in front of her face and she has the nerve to blanch away from me.

She starts to fucking cry like a little child but I can't bring it in me to feel sorry for her ass at all.

"That's enough Sin! It's not her fault. You can't blame her for what her father did!" Lila reprimands me. I'm shocked that it's her that's actually taking up for Thorn.

Taking a step back away from Thorn I watch as my sister goes to comfort her. Placing her arm around Thorns shoulders she leads her out of the room cooing soft words to her.

I just realized in that very second as I observe them both walking away from me just how much I just fucked up!

Of course I did! Like I always manage to do apparently!

Chapter 6

My father, the ruthless bastard, is basically ruining my damn life.

I had no idea whatsoever about my father calling their parents for some made up bogus reason to help him out with some false scheme.

Why would he do that? Why would he lie to them? The only attack I can remember is when my mother died but that was two years ago and from what Sun had told me about his parents death that happened three years ago.

A year's difference between the two of them so it doesn't make any sense to me whatsoever as to why my father would even call their parents at all.

I've been sequestered in their guest room all day debating on what I should do. After Sins meltdown toward me Lila stayed with me for a while up until her mate Marc came and got her.

Now I'm desperately trying to decide if I should just take the chance and leave here on my own. Sin definitely doesn't want me here that much is definitely clear to me.

Slay and Sunny makes it seem like they don't mind me being here at all but after Sins declaration this morning I can't fathom the idea that they would actually want me around. Not after what my father did to their parents.

Although they did have a couple of she wolves go out and buy me some clothes and accessories that I needed, that did make me feel special but I can't stay where I'm definitely not wanted.

No. I have to get out of here. With my decision made, I look down at my hand viewing the ring that mother gave me for my birthday when I was just sixteen. Maybe I can pawn it for a bit of cash to survive on, for at least a little while.

Although it pains me to have to do it, I cant see no other options laid out before me. Sighing, I sit down on the edge of the bed twisting the ring on middle my finger.

Why does this all have to be so damn complicated?

I guess that's what I have to do then.

Hopping off of the bed I slowly creep my way over to the bedroom door. Opening it a small crack I peek through the opening eyeballing the hall. Letting out another sigh, I step out of the room looking both ways down the hall. With no one around to see me, I take off.

Sprinting down the stairs hurriedly. I jump from the bottom stair headed straight for the front door.

Blowing out a breath when I finally make it outside without no one being any the wiser I search the grounds for a means to escape. I'm fucking surrounded by a massive amount of trees. Fuck!

Traipsing over to the edge of the forest I thankfully noticed a dirt road that leads away from their house.

Choosing the dirt road instead of the foreboding forest I take off into another run. With my hair flowing wistfully behind me I leave the Vallors house with no fucking regrets at all.

How far back in the woods do these guys actually live?

I have been walking this damn dirt road path now for what seems like freaking hours.

There has not been one stupid car go by the entire time I've been walking. I'm exhausted and I want to kick myself for not thinking about bringing me any water or food along with me.

The sun is almost about to set and I haven't the foggiest idea where the hell I am. I hate being an unknown territory.

Trees is all see. Fucking trees! I grumble to myself kicking a rock in front of me down the dirt road.

I should at least be thankful that there's at least a small cool breeze to cool me down some.

Why did I think this was a good idea again?

"Because you wanted your freedom!" My wolf Maya invades my thoughts suddenly nearly making me piss my pants.

"No, I couldn't stay where I wasn't welcomed Maya. You saw how Sin reacted. He can't stand me!" He actually hates me.

"That's only because of his wolf, Malice is in control most of the time. Malice is a very cantankerous wolf. He's not like the other two." Figures.

"Regardless Maya, he doesn't like me. Besides, with this stupid prophecy hanging over my head I can't take the chance to be with them now. They might actually get hurt or worse." I couldn't live with myself if something happened to either of one them.

"You are going to need them Thorn. More than ever now. Can we please go back?" Man she's sounds whiny.

"No Maya I already told you. Please don't make this any harder." I plead.

"I'm not making this harder. You are. What do you think is going to happen when they find out you ran away from them?" I don't care.

"Hopefully they won't find me.Why are you on their side anyway? Aren't you suppose to be on mine?" Traitor.

"Because they are so yummy." Of course that's where her mind is at.

"Is that all you can think about?" Horny ass wolf.

"Don't blame me. I'm being deprived here!" Seriously! She's acting like a damn bitch in heat.

"Oh shut up its like your always in heat!" I complain.

"Can you blame me? They are hot! I wouldn't mind being tied up...." I cut her off.

"I said shut up!" I know just how damn hot they are. She isn't freaking helping any.

"Fine!" She grumbles slipping back into my mind.

Damn wolf!

"I can buy myself flowersWrite my name in the sandTalk to myself for hoursSay things you don't understand" I sing to myself completely bored as I keep travel down the dusty road.

The sun has set causing the darkness to blanket the land. Trees. Trees. And more trees.

Yes I think I'm losing my damn marbles, the boredom is starting to get to me. Maya stopped talking me now and all I hear is the wind rustling through the leaves, along with crickets, and hoots of some owls.

This is the longest damn road I have ever had to travel in my life and there still hasn't been one damn blasted car drive by. Nothing. Zip. Nada.

Just trees. Pretty little creepy ass trees. Trees. Trees. Oh and did I mention trees.

A wolf howls in the distance. I instantly stop in my tracks. Searching the area around me I feel a shiver creep up my spine. Chilling me to my bones. I may be half wolf but the sound of the wolf howling in the distance is ominous while I'm here alone the dark. By myself, with nobody freaking around for miles.

Why did I do this again?

Oh yea, because my life literally sucks at the moment. I'm not wanted anywhere. Well that's a lie. I'm wanted by my damn demented father. I get nauseous just from the thought.

Nervous and a little frightened I continue on my journey albeit a bit slower than when I first started. I'm wore out and hungry again.

Damn why didn't my stupid ass remember to bring some food along?

The ominous wolf howling kicks up again startling me as I come to a halt on the dirt road. I search the area around me yet again. Terrified.

Seeing a faint light in the distance, I smile, finally. Civilization! Yes! About time!

Taking off in a sprint I run toward the faint light as I draw closer to it I see that the light is coming from a small cabin that's a little bit off from the dirt road.

Should I? Or shouldn't I?

Is main question that keeps circling around in my brain but when my stomach lets out a grumbling roar the decision is made for me.

So I slowly make my way up to the cabin when a delicious fragrance suddenly hits me. I pick up my pace a little only thinking about the scrumptious food. As I come to the door I falter.

Standing in front of the cabins door, I hesitate, debating with myself now if I should knock or just keep on going. I mean, there could be a serial killer living in there after all.

But before I can make my mind up the door suddenly swings open making me squeak. Damn! I think I just tinkled on myself.

"Who the hell are you?" The guy standing at the cabin door stares at me with a deep scowl on his face.

I open my mouth then close it again not sure if I should to tell him who I actually am.

"I-I'm Thorn." I tell him, yea I can't lie worth a shit apparently.

"Okay Thorn why are you at my door in the middle of damn night?" He grumbles at me rudely.

Middle of the night? Really? I didn't even realize.

"I smelt food." I tell him dumbfounded I think my damn brain went on vacation.

He looks at me curiously probably trying to figure me out.

We both stand there glaring at each other for a few seconds I start to feel very uncomfortable under his grueling gaze.

"M-maybe I....maybe I should...just go. Sorry to disturb...you." I stammer out nervously backing away from the grouchy man at the door who won't stop glaring at me.

"Come in." He finally says with a huff opening his door a little wider as he takes a step back watching me avidly.

I hesitate again, not sure about what to actually do.

"Well are ya hungry or not? I don't have all damn night!" Rude, I think to myself but only hesitate a second longer the option of having some food in my empty belly finally wins out.

Painstakingly slow I walk through the doorway into his cabin never taking my eyes off of the grumpy beast standing slightly beside me.

Once I'm in the cabin I hear the door shut behind me when the lock clicks into place I shutter. Maybe I made a huge mistake after all?

"Over here." The grouch says waving his hand at his dining room table where there's a bowl of some type of soup sitting on it plus homemade bread.

I nearly swoon from the smell that hits me. Yes! I smell bacon. Nearly drooling I walk over to the table. Standing at the edge of the table I wait for Mr. Grumpy Pants to sit down.

He walks by me grabbing another bowl from his cabinet he takes it to the stove, spooning out some soup into it he then places it on the table opposite of him.

"Sit." He commands me. I don't waste a another second I sit down on the chair obediently just as he ordered me to do.

He grabs a spoon out from his kitchen drawer, turning he hands it to me I gratefully take it from him.

The grumpy man sits down in his chair opposite of me, without saying a word he begins to eat. I take the opportunity his given me to start eating myself. The delicious potato soup with chunks of bacon and cheese hit my tastebuds making me groan loudly from the delightful taste.

"So Thorn why are ya traipsing around in this woods after dark?" The grumpy guy ask although I shouldn't keep thinking of him as grumpy any longer at least he was polite enough to offer me some of his delicious food.

"I don't know." I tell him, what else can I say? The less people know about me the better.

"Ya don't know? What have ya got amnesia or something?" He ask.

"Something like that." I mumble taking another bite of the stew and bread.

"I think your lying. Don't ya think it's a lil bit rude to come to a man's house and eat his food that he so graciously offers ya for ya just to lie to him?" He ask cocking his eyebrow at me. Why is talking in a third person? Odd.

But he has a point I just don't know how much I should actually divulge to him. He is a stranger after all.

"I'm running from my mate." There that should do it. I feel no need to explain it any further.

"So I take it that ya are a mate to one of them Vallor boys then?" How does he know? What? Do I have it stamped on my damn forehead?

"Yes." I simply state.

"Well I be damned. Which one?" He ask me. All three?

Instead of telling him that I compromise with my fib. "Sunny." I lie.

"Got yourself a good one right there. So why are ya runnin from him?" This is getting to get a little bit to personal.

"What's your name?" I ask changing the subject. He looks a bit shocked from the sudden change of subject. I feel a bit guilty about it but I ignore my conscience and just take another bite of the soup and bread.

"My name is Barrik. Nice ta meet ya." He says with a little southern twang.

"Likewise and thank you so much for the soup. I was starving." I tell him as I finished up my bowl of soup. Slopping up the last drops of the soup with a piece of the bread. Feeling stuffed now I lean back in the chair sighing in contentment.

"Welcome it's the least I can do for ya. We are neighbors after all." I just love the southern hospitality. Why didn't Sin develop that habit?

"He's to classy for that." Yea right!

"Glad to see your back." I say sarcastically to her.

"I didn't leave I just took a nap." Really?

"Okay then."

"What? A wolf has to have her beauty sleep." Wow the ego my wolf has is astronomical.

"Sleep sounds good."

"At a complete strangers house? I don't think so!" She argues.

"Where else are we going to sleep?"

"The woods?" What the....?

"Hell no!"

"Fine!" She grumbles before going quiet on me. Ugh.

She's giving me the silent treatment again. Damn wolf!

"Talkin to ya wolf I see." Barrik states, while smiling over at me.

How did he know?

"You know I'm a wolf?" I ask him curiously.

"Of course. I smelt it on ya." Why does everyone keep talking about the way I smell! Do I offend?

"What are you?" If he knows about wolves then he has to know about other supernatural beings right?

"I am what ya call a bonafide vamp." He gives me an enormous smile clearly proud of being a vampire. His smile is so infectious I can't help but to smile at him in return.

"I've only met one other vampire before. He is so sweet. His name is Tristan, he's my brothers best friend." I tell him when I mentioned my brother I start to get a little sad.

I wish I knew exactly where he was or what my damn father did to him. I can only pray that he hasn't hurt him or done worse.

"There's plenty of us around. Im surprised ya only met one of us with ya being a wolf and all." He states with confusion on all over his face.

I was sheltered, that's why. My father always kept me away from others. He even had me home schooled. I couldn't understand at the time why my brother was allowed to go to a regular school and I wasn't. But now that I know about my father it makes the reasons for it all the more clearer to me.

"I didn't get around much." I lie again. The lie taste sour on my tongue. Barrik doesn't deserve my lies. He's been so nice to me. The guilt is starting to eat away at me.

"I understand that. Well if ya need a place to crash for the night ya more than welcome to crash here. I have an extra room in the back. It's not much but it will do ya in a pinch." He generously offers me now I'm really feeling really guilty. I feel a knot in my gut start to form from being so deceitful to him.

"Thank you. If it's no bother that is." I weakly smile at him. Why can't I just be honest?

"Tisnt a problem at all and ya are very welcome." He says rising from the table he grabs our dirty dishes from it taking them both to the sink.

"Let me wash those for you." I rush to say, springing up from my chair quickly.

"No. No what kinda person would I be if I made my guest do my work? I got it. Ya just take a seat and after I warsh these up I'll show ya to ya room." He says it so politely that I feel ten times worse now for being deceitful to him.

"I lied. I'm sorry. I am running from my mate that part is true but it's not just from one of them. I'm mated to all three of them. Sin...well Sin doesn't like me too much....at all actually. He doesn't like me at all and they all have issues with my family so I couldn't stay there any longer because I didn't feel welcomed. I'm so sorry I lied to you. I hope you can forgive me. It's just that...you've been so nice to me and I've been....well I've been misleading you. I'm sorry. Please forgive me." I confess to him in a rush my guilt overriding my own damn senses but I couldn't abide my own guilty conscious any longer. I'm a terrible person.

"Okay then. Well....thank ya for telling me the truth finally. Don't fret girlie it will all work out. I forgive ya. You just didn't know me is all." I sigh out in relief my guilt is starting subside a bit now, making me feel a little better.

"Thank you for understanding. But I don't mean to cause you any problems. If the offer is still on the table for the spare room I will gladly take but I will be out of your hair in the morning I promise." I tell him basically pleading.

"It's not a problem girlie. Here let me show ya to ya room for the night then." He says leading me to the spare room of his. I couldn't be more grateful for his help.

"Thank you so much Barrik. I will repay you somehow." I tell him as I walk behind me down the hall.

"No need for repayin nuthin girlie it's what neighbors do for each other." His generosity is completely immeasurable.

Barrik shows me to the spare room as I offer him my deepest gratitude. After he leaves me I hit the little twin size bed quickly thereafter falling to sleep instantly.

Waking up groggily to loud voices ringing throughout the cabin, I scrunch my face up in displeasure.

Sleepily, I grumble, raising up off of the bed listening to the screaming voices intently.

"They found us and they are mad!" Maya informs me a little scared.

"What? How? And how do you know?"

"I'm just good that way." Of course.

"Really?" I ask sarcastically.

"Well you asked." I guess I did.

"If you don't want them to find you here you need to run. Fast!" She shakily tells me.

Jumping up from the bed I search the little room but un-fortunately it only has a little window no bigger than a damn shoebox. Just my damn luck.

There's no way my fat ass can squeeze through that! Fuck!

The voices are starting to get closer now. I hear footsteps coming down the hall with no way to escape the room my stupid ass climbs under the damn bed.

Although it's dusty under here and I'm a complete moron for thinking I can hide under the bed, for some reason I feel like I accomplished something. I know stupid right?

Well I try to look for the good in everything.

Hearing the bedroom door open suddenly with a very loud bang. I jerk, closing my eyes shut tightly.

Okay, it's official. I have completely lost it. My dumb self is laying under the bed thinking that if I close my damn eyes they won't be able to find me? What kind of idiot am I?

"Come out Thorn. Don't make me get on my knees" Slay demands gruffly.

"Now there's an idea. I would love to see him on his knees." I bet.

"Oh, shut up!" I grumble.

"Rude!" I just roll my eyes at her.

"Thorn if you don't come out this second I'm going to tan your hide." Slay threatens.

"Oh, I would love...." I cut her off again.

"Shut up!"

"I'm coming!" I finally tell him. Sliding out from under the bed.

"He would like that." Maya purrs.

"For fuck sakes you horny ass wolf lay off it. Can't you see I'm in deep trouble?" I grouse.

"Maybe he will spank you." Now she has me thinking sinful thoughts. Damn!

Clamoring to my feet, I stand in front of Slay, Sin, and Sun as they are all glaring at me, I feel completely ashamed and embarrassed all rolled into one.

"You had us all worried sick Thorn. What we're you thinking?" Slay says definitely pissed.

"She obviously wasn't!" Sin adds with a lopsided smirk plastered on his face.

I don't know where it came from but I catch myself actually growling fiercely at Sin. He backs away from me when he hears my ferocious growl toward him. I mentally pat myself on the back.

"We're going home now!" Slay says grabbing me by my wrist roughly as he starts to drag me from the room.

I yank my hand away from his scowling up at him angrily. "Don't touch me like that!" I snarl at him. He shocks me by barking out with laughter.

"That done it. You are coming home with us and I'm going to spank that luscious plump ass of yours." I gulp loudly. Staring frightfully at him.

He can't really mean it? Can he?

"Oh yes he can and you better obey your master!" Maya pipes in happily.

"Oh shut up!"

Chapter 7

O f all the...

She ran away what fuck was even she thinking?

I can't believe this woman! I haven't slept all night and neither has my brothers nor has half of my damn pack for that matter. We have been out all damn night long searching for her ass everywhere.

We just happened to get lucky when we stopped in at Barriks cabin. Just taking a chance that she just may be there.

At first the bastard was denying that she was even fucking there. He held on strong to that damn lie for a while. He only gave her up when I told that damn country hick vampire that I could actually smell her fucking there and I had to go as far as having to threaten his ass multiple times before he hesitantly pointed to his spare bedroom. I commend the man for his loyalty to her but damn that pissed me the fuck off royally.

The entire time she was missing all I could even think about was that her father had somehow managed to get his hands on her. I was fucking prettified.

But when she climbed out from under that tiny bed, I sighed out in relief, thankful that my assumptions were completely wrong.

But then I got mad. Hell, I skipped mad and went straight to fucking furious. Seeing her safe and sound eased my worry but now that I know that she is safe she is going to have to pay for upsetting and worrying us all like she did. Damn this woman can be really pigheaded.

Pulling her into the house by her wrist roughly I yank her ass through the door. I only let go of her wrist when I finally have her standing right in front of me.

"Go get a fucking shower. I'll be up there in a minute to serve out your punishment. Do not leave the fucking room." I hiss rather aggressively to her. I need to calm myself down before I hand down her punishment to her or else I'm afraid that I just might lose control and fucking hurt her.

"But..." she starts to say but I cut her with a fierce glare.

"Go." I snarl. She squeaks, startled by my gruffness then takes off into a sprint headed up the stairs quickly without even taking the chance to look back at us.

I half chuckle watching her as she goes.

"Are you really going to punish her?" Sunny ask me as he's staring up at the empty staircase wistfully.

"Yes. She has to learn." I sigh when I see the doubtful look drawn up on his face suddenly.

"But it may make her runaway again Slay." Sunny's worried expression has me doubting the idea for a second. But then I recall how damn worried Sunny was when he couldn't find her.

He came rushing into the parlor with panic written all over his face screaming out to the top of his lungs that she was gone.

We all raced to her bedroom to find it completely empty.

She left everything behind though.

Even the clothes and items we just purchased for her were still left thrown about in her in room haphazardly. She didn't take a damn thing with her and that's exactly why I thought her father had actually found her. Fear suddenly imploded within in me when I seen her clothing laying about.

Both Sunny and I panicked, Sin on the other hand took it all in stride.

I actually hated him in that second. How could he act so damn nonchalantly about his mates disappearance? His attitude toward it all had me fucking fuming.

The entire time we were out searching for her all Sin managed to do the entire time was fucking complain and whine like a damn spoilt toddler.

I never wanted to punch him so badly as did in that moment last night.

"I highly doubt it. I promise I won't be rough on her Sunny but she needs to learn that she just can't do this to us." I finally give him my reply walking over for the couch I plop my ass down on it blowing out a huge ragged breath. Man I'm tired.

"Then I want to be there with you when you do it." Sunny states as he walks over to the couch crashing down on it beside me.

"I don't understand why you two are so worked up about it. You should have just let her go. It looks to me like she doesn't want to be here anyway." Sin replies shrugging his shoulder. He sits down in the chair opposite of us playing on his damn cellphone.

"Because of you," Sunny angrily states glowering over at Sin, "you have made her feel so unwelcome here that she probably thought she didn't have any other choice but to runaway." He adds heatedly. I hate it but I would have to agree with him.

I can refute than Sin has done nothing but make her feel unwelcome every since she got here. The dude is starting to get on my last damn nerve with his oblivious attitude toward her.

"It's because I don't want her here. She will eventually end up getting both of you killed just because of this stupid damn prophecy. I don't understand how both of you can so willingly just follow her around like two little lost fucking puppies. And I for one won't stand by and let her hurt either of you." Sin displays his anger well unfortunately. "Plus I hate her fucking father." He adds.

"The man doth protest too much, methinks" I quote to Sunny while eyeing Sin with a big fat smile on my face.

Springing up from the chair to argue with me further he starts to say something in return but he accidentally drops his cellphone on the floor in the process. The phone hits the floor with a clatter bouncing up on it then finally settling face down abandoned on the floor.

I haven't the faintest idea as to why but when I look down at the phone I burst out into laughter. Plus, with the added bonus of the astonishing look shrouded on Sins face it has me laughing at him uproariously. The idiot. That's what I call fucking karma.

"It's so not funny." Sin says as he's bending down to pick up his poor fallen phone up off the floor.

He studies his phone with a sadden expression, flipping it around in his hand he scowls down at it. I actually think I caught him pouting.

"Serves you right." Sun tells him holding in his own laughter he just offers him a little smirk instead.

"Look Sin. I know you have issues with Thorn but this is our choice. Either you stand behind it or you don't. I don't care anymore. Besides, I thought you were going to make Storm your Luna? Why should you worry about Thorn if you have Storm waiting in the wings for you?" I inquire confused as to why he hasn't actually done it yet especially after I gave him permission to do so.

"That's not going to happen." Sin admits, crashing back down onto the chair still staring down at his phone in his hand disappointed.

"Why not? You were so adamant about it. What changed your mind?" I question observing him closely. He holds up his hand toward me.

"Lila text me." He says suddenly changing the subject with a scowl marring his face. "Hey Sunny. Lila said that Nina is coming for a visit. She should be here in a day or two. She

said that she had something important to talk to us about."
Sin tells Sun with a devious smile erupting on his gleeful face.

Fuck!

Nina is coming? I always get a deep churning down in my
gut whenever I hear that woman's name.

"What? Why?.....why would she come here I haven't seen
her in close to a damn year?" Sunny questions Sin trying to
crane his neck to peer over at Sins phone. Sin pulls his phone
up to his chest giving Sun a disgruntled look.

"I don't know. Text Lila and ask. But things are about to
get a little more interesting around here." Sin chuckles darkly
staring back down at his phone.

"Fine." Sun says sliding off of the couch, giving Sin a glare
before he goes off to retrieve his own phone.

I shake my head at them both. They both are acting like
fucking children. Placing my fingers on the bridge of my
nose I lean my head back on the couch trying to steady my
breathing.

Nina. Damn!

She's Suns ex and that woman is more than a fucking hand
full. Their breakup as I recall was volatile to say the least.
They dated for almost six months give or take a week or so.

Her coming here for whatever reason now definitely could
only mean nothing but trouble for any of us. Especially Sunny.

Fuck!

I need a distraction.

"Tell Sun that I'm going to Thorns room he can meet me up there if he still wants to." I tell Sin scrambling off of the couch as I head off to her room.

"I'm coming to." Sin informs me as he raises up from his seat pocketing his cellphone in his jeans.

I look over at him confused.

"I thought you didn't want to have anything to do with her?" I ask.

"I don't but this could be fun." Sin affirms grinning mischievously. Why do I even fucking bother?

Rapping my knuckles on her bedroom door with Sin standing anxiously behind me I hear a faint 'come in' from beyond the door.

As I enter the room I notice Thorn nervously standing in the center of the room fiddling with her fingers anxiously.

And then my eyes latched on to her clothing. Seeing what she's dressed in my damn cock instantly hardens.

"Whoever went shopping for my clothes may have gotten me the wrong sizes." Thorn embarrassingly admits to me.

I roam my eyes down that delectable body of hers thanking whoever did go shopping for her profusely in my mind.

Fuuuck'

Those damn booty shorts she's wearing doesn't leave much to the imagination.

"Fuck." I hear Sin groan out huskily from behind me.

My thoughts exactly bro.

Closing my eyes tightly I try damn hard to fight down my own lust filled urges. Fuck I want her bad.

Inhaling in a ton of air deeply I shake my head vigorously to try and rid myself of my carnal thoughts but unfortunately it doesn't seem to be fucking working.

Opening up my eyes, I exhale out with a deep dark groan. Fuck!

Sin abruptly nudges me from behind with his hand pushing me further into the room suddenly. I glare at his ass over my shoulder. He clears his throat tilting his head in Thorns direction.

"Get on with it." He grunts, furrowing my brows at him I wonder why he's so determined to watch this shit now?

Sin steps over to the side of the room eyeing Thorn warily as goes. Interesting, I think to myself. I'm definitely going to have to delve into that later.

Suddenly remembering what I came here to do, I walk over to her bed, sitting down on the side of the bed I watch Thorn as she eyes me very suspiciously.

"Come here." I gruffly tell her. She hesitates shifting her beautiful dark blue eyes back and forth from me to Sin rapidly.

"Now Thorn." I add a little authority into my tone pointing my finger down toward my lap.

She jumps a little when I command her to come hither but eventually she starts taking light little steps toward me.

Sun chooses this moment to come prancing in through the door. When he closes the door behind him he turns and looks at each of us with a stricken look upon his face.

Cocking my eyebrow at him he just shakes he head at me granting me with a sour grim look. It must be about Nina, I think.

Sun steps up closer to Thorn he places his arms around her midsection gently urging her forward.

"It will be alright." He says trying to soothe her nerves as she comes a little closer to me.

Aggravated and losing my patience, as soon as she gets close enough to me I reach out grabbing ahold of her tiny wrist as I gently pull her to me.

"You know why I'm doing this right?" I ask her with a low soft tone she gingerly nods her head to me but remains quiet.

"How many do you think you should receive for running away and worrying us Thorn?" I question her, cocking my head to the side waiting patiently for her reply.

"I don't know. Maybe...two." She quietly tells me. I cock a lopsided grin at her and shake my head.

"You're not getting off that easy beautiful. I think maybe ten should do it? What do you guys think?" I ask my brothers but I never take my eyes off of her.

Her eyes suddenly widen in surprise from my direct question then she scowls down at me in confusion and ominously still remains quiet as a little mouse.

"Ten sounds good to me." Sin pipes up from the side of the room.

"Ten it is then." I agree nudging Thorn down to lay across my lap.

She fits there perfectly. I try to stifle a groan when I see her luscious ass popped up right in my face.

"You need a safe word beautiful. If it gets too much for you and you need me to stop you need to say the safe word for me. Do you understand?" I ask her as I flex my hand. She takes a minute concentrating turning her head so she can look up at me from her position then she embellishes a sweet smile toward me.

"Petals." She happily tells me. I quirk my eyebrow at her. Fitting I think to myself.

Placing my index finger down her shorts I pull them down to her knees and nearly choke on my fucking tongue. Daaamn!

Her plump round cheeks are fucking perfect. Not a damn blemish or mark lay upon them. I groan again with my dick getting harder, I know she can feel my harden cock laying up against the side of her stomach. She tilts her head back at me faintly smirking.

"Ready?" I ask her with my voice laced with guttural lust. She nods her head and lets out a deep breath.

"Words beautiful." I instruct.

"Y-yes." She timidly replies.

I nod my head about to smack her ass but I stop myself when I suddenly remembered something.

"Count them down for me." I demand huskily. Licking my bottom lip I rear my hand back then bring it down on that voluptuous ass of hers.

Smack!

"One, Papi." What the fuck!? Did she just....I still my hand instantly.

Now that was a major fucking turn on. I look up at Sun standing close beside us wondering what he might think about this new development, he just has an enormous smile placed on his face. The cheeky bastard. I guess we both just found a brand new kink.

Shaking my head again I proceed on with her punishment.

Smack!

"Two, Papi." She moans.

Again.

"Three, Papi." And I'll be damned if she didn't just purr. Looks like our mate has a brand new kink also.

I can live with that.

Smack!

I go all the way to ten and each time I spank that plump ass she just got more turned on by it. I can smell the intoxicating aroma of her arousal float wistfully up to me. Shit!

Massaging her ripe red cheeks after I'm finished she stiffens up under my touch suddenly. Pausing I look down at her then the smell of her arousal hits me even fucking more.

I decide to be a little risky. I drop my index finger down in between her little smooth folds, tracing my thumb along her clit I message her little nub as she lets out another trembling erotic moan.

"Fuck!" Sin grumbles.

I ignore him as I slide my finger into her wet walls. "You like that beautiful?" I ask leaning down closer to her.

"Y-yes." She purrs again. Adding another digit I crook my fingers inside of her then scissor them. Pumping in and out of her valley rapidly, I hear Sunny groaning beside me. Glancing up at him I see him rubbing his hand across his jeans right near his groin vigorously.

I smile up at him then pick up my speed plunging my fingers deep into her ripe little pussy she wiggles on my lap from the onslaught of my continuous ministrations.

My wolf, Demon, perks up inside of my head demanding that I fervently take her now.

"Fuck her!" Demon snarls.

I try to resist his demands but unfortunately I fucking can't.

Pulling Thorn off of my lap instantly I throw her sexy ass on the bed, yanking off her shorts quickly I jump in between her toned legs.

Raising both of her legs up in the air, I throw them both over my shoulders as I slide down on the bed. Lowering my head to that sweet enticing fragrance I don't hold back and dive right the fuck in.

Licking her tiny little clit in rotations I plunge my fingers back into her tight core.

"Damn!" Sin grunts from somewhere in the room but I still pay him no heed.

Thorn places her hands down on my shoulders urging me to go further. Sucking her clit into my mouth as I thrust my fingers into her drenched silken walls she starts to shiver as her walls start to heavily spasm around my fingers I bite down on her tiny pink sensitive bud.

"Fuck Papi!" She moans just as her juices explode out of her I suck up all of her sweet tangy cream with my tongue.

Fuck I could eat her delicious pussy out all day and night.

With her laying on the bed in complete bliss. I crawl up to her as I lick her juices off that's coating my drenched lips, I stare down at her post filled climactic face smirking down at her.

"You fucking taste divine beautiful. Here have a taste." I say lowering my head to hers I kiss her passionately. Swiping my tongue in between her lips I slip it in her mouth as our tongues embrace each other I groan out in her mouth. Fuck! She's so damn addicting.

Tearing my lips away from hers when I hear one of my brothers rudely clearing their throat from behind me obnoxiously.

"Well that was...inspiring." Sunny breaths.

I'd say.

After a cold shower I stopped back by Thorns room, wanting to ask her if she was hungry, walking into her room I see her sleeping peacefully on the bed with her hands tuck up underneath her face and her leg hanging off of the bed.

She looks just like a fucking angel.

Quietly stepping into her room I pick up her leg up to put it back on the bed then I pull the cover up on her tightly.

Peering down at her beautiful face I suddenly realize that she's definitely starting to get under my skin now.

What it means I don't know exactly but I'm bound and determined now to make her mine fully. Regardless of the obstacles that we have to face.

I can't allow anything to happen to her. I won't. I will kill her fucking father if he even thinks about coming near her and I'm pretty sure Sunny feels the same way as I do to.

And with this stupid prophecy hanging over our heads I need to start making plans sooner than later.

With that thought in my mind I slowly creep out of her room allowing her to sleep for now.

Closing the door softly behind me I mindlink my beta Flex. Flex has been my best friend for years now. He is dependable and I would trust him with my very own life. Actually I have on a few occasions. I don't honestly know how I would have made it this far without him.

"Flex I need to talk to you in my office." I inform him.

"Yes. Alpha."

"Oh and I hear congratulations are in order." He says with happiness laced throughout his tone.

"Thank you." I reply.

"When do I get to meet the woman who captured my Alphas heart." I laugh at his excitement.

"You mean Alphas." I correct him.

"No shit! Damn! Well congratulations to all three of then!" Well not exactly.

"Well two of us for now anyway." I say with regret.

"Sin right?" Of course.

"How did you guess?" I reply sarcastically.

"Simple, Storms been bragging about becoming our Luna with everybody." What the hell?

"I am going to kill that bitch!" I grumble.

"She's with Pan now. Does Sin know she's been hooking up with him?" Maybe that's why Sin has been acting so strangely.

"Not that I know of!" I quip.

"Well she's been all over him during our training today. You might want to inform him of it. Maybe he will change his mind about his mate then?" Yea right!

"I doubt it you know how Sin is man!" He doesn't know a good thing when he has it.

"That I do. Stubborn as hell!" Got that right.

"So true. Can you meet me in about an hour?" I ask.

"Sure I'm almost done here. See you then Alpha." Always dependable.

"Thanks!"

"No problem." I cut off our mindlink headed to my office to get some paperwork done before Flexs arrival.

Hopefully Flex will agree when I ask him to take over our pack and help Sin at least for a short time while Sunny, Thorn, and I travel to the Invivus Realm to get all of this shit settled.

I would ask Sin if he would like to travel with us to the Realm but I have a feeling that he would deny any of my request right now.

He needs to work through all of his shit anyway. Especially when it comes to Storm and her devious actions. If that bitch thinks she's pulling one over on my brother by sleeping around with Pan.

Then she has another think coming!

Chapter 8

"Happy birthday!" I yell out happily as soon as I entered Thorns bedroom carrying a pretty purple sparkling package in my hands that Slay and I got just for her.

But to my surprise and dismay her room is completely vacant.

The memories of her running away soon raced through my mind, in a virtual panic I ran from her room down the stairs and into the living room but all I can see when I get there is a empty damn room. Great!

Dashing to the dining room hurriedly, Thorn is still nowhere to be seen. Where the hell can she be?

I am just hoping she hasn't ran away from us yet again.

I search all of the bathrooms and even the damn closets. I even looked in Sins room but I should have known that she wouldn't have been in there. Fuck!

Where is she? She wouldn't leave again would she? What if her father found her? This woman is making me a damn nervous wreck.

Still not being able to locate her anywhere I eventually mindlinked Slay completely irritated.

"Where is she?" I ask him rather abruptly.

"Who?" Seriously?

"Don't be dumb! Thorn. Where is she?" I ask him aggressively.

"Relax Sunny she's here in my office with me." Slay replies with laughter expelling under his breath.

"I'm headed that way." I tell him overly relieved that she didn't disappear on us again.

"Fine." I cut off the mindlink with him headed for his office with her birthday present still firmly sitting in my hands.

Opening the office door I'm surprised to see Sin sitting next Thorn on the loveseat though neither of them is talking to the other it gives me a little hope, hopefully it can only mean that its a small step in the right direction for both of them.

"Happy birthday babydoll." I gleefully tell her as I stroll over to her I show her the present that I've been yearning to give her.

"For me?" Her beautiful face shows a wonderment of surprise. Her smile literally lights up the entire damn room.

"Yes. From me and Slay." I tell her as I side eye Sin briefly. We asked him earlier if he wanted to help with her birthday present but his dumb ass completely refused.

She grabs the present from my hands eyeing the gift in wonder. Gently, she unwraps her gift, tossing the paper to the side she pulls out the dress that we purchase her slowly, eyeing it in pure amazement.

"It's stunning. Thank you." She tells Slay and I. Her gratitude warms my heart. Glancing back at Slay I smile when I see his lopsided grin and a twinkle in his eyes.

"We also want to take you out to dinner tonight." Slay informs her, standing from his desk he casually makes his way over to her.

"But what about...?"

I cut her off, "We will have you back in plenty of time before you shift." I assure her. We've already planned everything out for the event ahead of time thankfully.

"Okay then. That sounds great and thank you both so much. You really didn't have to." She says with modesty riddled on her tone.

"You're more than welcomed to come along Sin." Slay tells Sin.

"Thanks." He mutters climbing up from his seat he exits Slays office in a huff.

Shaking my head at his stubbornness I decidedly just to let him go ahead and mope like he always does and return my attention back to Thorn instead.

"I hate monkey suits." Sin grumbles adjusting his black tie for the twentieth time tonight.

Damn dude is always complaining here lately. I ignore his complaints watching the staircase closely.

We're all waiting patiently for Thorns arrival standing at the bottom of the staircase constantly adjusting our suits.

I seriously can't believe I'm actually nervous about this date tonight.

I picked out one of my best tuxedos just for the occasion.

I want to make a good impression on her especially knowing that my damn ex Nina will be arriving here tomorrow. I'm nervously panicking on the inside.

Lila wouldn't tell me any information about Nina's unexpected visit. All she said was that Nina needed to talk to all of us urgently and that it was a matter of great importance.

Even though I haven't gotten along with Nina in the past I really hope it's nothing far too serious.

And I truly hope she isn't coming just to cause any trouble for us either but knowing Nina I'm sure she has something up her damn sleeve. She always does.

Thorns door finally opens, chasing away any thoughts of I have about Nina far away from mind when I see her anxiously descending the staircase in the dress we got her for her birthday.

She looks fucking ravishing.

The red formal dress shows off her dark sun kissed tanned complexion irresistibly.

She's a damn fucking Goddess.

"My Luna!" My wolf Stinger growls in my head in full appreciation.

"Yes she definitely is." I have to absolutely agree with him on that assumption.

I couldn't ask for a more beautiful Luna.

Thank you Moon Goddess!

The restaurant, Les plats désirés, is definitely crowded tonight. Streams of people are hanging around the building in a long awaited line.

We bypass the cumbersome line of people that's patiently waiting to enter, making our way up to the hostess without any disruptions whatsoever.

The hostess gives a sultry smile to us as we enter the building.

"Good evening Alphas, table for four?" She sweetly ask us with her eyes glued mainly on Sin standing roughly beside me in a very flirtatious and crude manner.

Sin just offers her a swaggered grin with a little flirtatious wink aimed right at her.

I nudge him with my elbow square in his ribs making him grimace up in pain as he lets out a disgruntled scoff.

"Yes please, Winona." Slays replies to her completely oblivious to Sins revolting transgressions from behind him.

"Right this way Alphas." Winona replies seductively as she sashays away, swinging her hips abhorrently, escorting us all to our designated table.

We reach our table finally, a giant round table with a cushioned bench surrounded it along with a white tablecloth and candles placed upon it. Thorn slides in the middle with Slay and I sitting on each side of her. Sin sets next to Slay on the far side of the bench scowling. I scowl right back at him.

If the asshole ruins this birthday dinner for her tonight I will be more than happy to kick his stupid ass right here in the middle of the damn restaurant.

"You're wine steward, Bernace, will be with you shortly." Winona informs us flashing her pearly whites at Sin before she saunters off swinging her hips again. Sin cranes his neck watching her as she walks away.

I kick him hard on his shin underneath the table.

Sins fucking pushing it tonight.

"Oh." Sin exclaims loudly. Drawing everyone's attention to him.

Smothering a smile I take a sip of my water, playing coy.

"What may I get you tonight to drink Alphas." The steward ask us with a genuine smile on his face.

"We'll have the Domaine de la Romanee-Conti Romanee-Conti Grand Cru, Cote de Nuits, thank you." Slay informs him, the steward nods his head at Slay with a slight bow of his head.

"Very nice choice sir." He replies as he walks off to get us our drinks.

Whatever the hell Slay ordered is a damn mystery to me but I'm damn sure glad he knows what the hell he's talking about. Because I'm completely fucking clueless.

A waitress brings us our menus. A tiny little brunette girl with a dimpled smile. She walks away briskly allowing us time to review our menus.

Looking over the menu I feel a bit lost this is definitely not my forte for sure.

Glancing over at Slay I feel a bit overwhelmed but he seems to have so much damn confidence flowing out of him that I decide to mindlink him.

"I have no idea what this shit is Slay. Just order something for me." I suggest.

"No problem." He agrees giving me a stiff nod.

The waitress comes back to take our orders but it is Slay who recites the order to her for all of us thankfully. When he starts rambling off the order in French I'm at a total fucking loss.

Shaking my head I glance over at Thorn to see her reaction, she seems to be just as confused as I am. Now I don't feel so bad for not knowing a damn thing about the French.

Forgive me Loup-Garou.

"What is this shit called?" Sin rudely sneers, peering down at the white bowl of food placed on the table before him.

"It's called Coq au vin Sin. Just try it I'm sure you will enjoy it." Slay quips.

Taking a tentative bite of the Coq au vin that Slay ordered for us. I revel in the unique taste of it. The chicken, bacon, spices and what I think is burgundy wine rest on my taste-buds delightfully.

"It's good." I reflect as I start gobbling down my robust meal.

"Well I'm out. This type of stuff just isn't for me. I need a damn burger and beer. It's a nice restaurant you have here Slay it's just not my style. Sorry." Sin sourly replies tossing his napkin on top of his bowl as he stands up abruptly.

"Pick me up down at my club when you're done here." He insist as he presumptively walks out of the restaurant hurriedly.

I'm definitely going to have a long conversation with him later and he isn't going to like what I have to say to him one damn bit either.

"You own this restaurant?" Thorn asks Slay with curiosity marring her face.

"Yes beautiful. I own this one and another restaurant called Slays Slaughter House plus a couple of other businesses around town." Slay is being overly modest.

He's a damn financial genius. He owns two restaurants and five small businesses plus two hotels all along our town.

Sin owns one bar and a strip club known as Sins Shop that he purchased from a long time friend of ours named Damon.

I personally own a mechanics shop called Suns Quality Auto Repair, that I purchased from a firemen that was wanting to retire. I've always had a fascination with cars.

"That's amazing Slay." She quaintly tells him.

By the time the dessert portion of our meal rolls around I'm completely stuffed but Thorn seems to want some type of chocolate. She ordered herself a chocolate soufflé when it finally arrived she seemed surprisingly happy but unfortunately she could only consume a small majority of it.

"I'm so full." She exclaims moaning softly, slightly leaning back on the bench with her face filled with contentment.

"I think Sun may want some dessert beautiful." Slay suddenly implies with a sly smirk. Thorn looks over at him inquisitively.

I cock my eyebrow at him curiously peering over at him.

"What are you up too?" I ask through our mindlink.

"Rest assured you are going to enjoy this as much as she is?" I'm at a complete loss at his suggestion.

"Enjoy what Slay?" I inquire.

"You will see!" He doesn't fill me in he only offers me another sly smirk. What is he up to?

"Well he can have the rest of mine." Thorn offers pushing her soufflé over to me across the table.

"No beautiful. I think he's hungry for something else." Slay gruffly hints to her. She looks up at him with furrowing brows.

"Slide under the table. She doesn't have on any underwear on under that sexy ass dress." He implies.

"How do you know?" I try to take a peek under the table but the table cloth is far too long for me to be able to see under it.

"I can tell. She has no panty lines Sun." Now this is interesting.

"With pleasure." Who am I to pass up such an enticing offer?

Slowly sliding the underneath the table I push the tablecloth off of me that latched unto my shoulder as I slid under it.

Crawling in between her toned legs I pry them apart with my hands gently, pushing her long flowing dress to the side of her leg I make my way in between her thighs.

Her intoxicating fragrance spirals over to me. The illicit smell of cinnamon and vanilla pierces me desirably.

Slay is absolutely fucking right she is definitely not wearing any panties whatsoever. Fuck!

Putting those slender legs along my shoulders, I slide two fingers into her delectably smooth folds separating them as I descend on her sweet pussy like a deranged mad man.

Licking, sucking, and flicking her tiny little button vigorously I can her moans cascading down to me.

"Shhh. You don't want the entire restaurant knowing what he's doing do you beautiful?" I hear Slay tell her huskily. She mumbles incoherently to him when her tiny hand suddenly comes down under the table she places it on top of my head grabbing a fistful of my hair she pulls me upward along her peaked bud. Damn!

Groaning, I slide my hand down my slacks pulling out my rigid hard ass cock I start stroking it as I continue to eat out her pussy happily.

As I bite down on her tiny swollen clit her legs begin to tremble uncontrollably. Her moans start to become louder as I thrust my fingers into her overworked pussy then I feel her scorching walls start to spasm.

She's getting close. Stroking my dick faster now I give her a few more licks before she comes undone around my tongue. Her juices flow out of her as her walls convulse around my fingers.

She lets out a quavering moan as soon as she hits her over induced climax. When her cream suddenly hits my tongue my balls tighten up then I spurt out my seed all over my hands and down my cock groaning out as I orgasm. Fuuuuck!

How I wish so badly that I can sink my long ass cock deep within her.

"Good girl." I hear Slay whisper to her. Good is right. Good and tight. Fuck she is so damn remarkable.

Stuffing my lax dick back into my slacks I gingerly make my way back up unto the bench panting ever so slightly.

Grabbing a napkin I feverishly wipe off my cum from my hand, staring at a blissfully happy Thorn beside me.

Peering over at Slay I quickly notice how is fidgeting in his seat trying to adjust himself without anyone being non the wiser.

Stifling a laugh at him I think to myself that this has turned out to be a very rememberable birthday dinner for all of us.

"Best damn dessert ever!" I quip.

Now we're all situated in the backyard close to the edge of the forest waiting for Thorn to shift.

All four of us are standing around with spare clothes that I brought along for all of us laying beside me in a little black backpack on the ground.

Thorn is currently in a little beige satin robe wearing nothing underneath it.

My thoughts have been going to naughty places every since she walked down those stairs with that damn robe on and nothing else.

Unfortunately, we have been back here for close to two hours now and nothing has happened yet.

We're all starting to get a little bit worried over it. She should have already shifted by now and I can see the worry etched all over her beautiful face and it's completely disparaging to see it.

Roaming my eyes over her I observe all of her closely. There has to be a reason why she isn't shifting like she should be but I have no idea why she isn't.

"What am I doing wrong?" Thorn ask us with a touch of anxiousness shrouding her face.

"I don't know beautiful." Slays tone holds a touch of anxiety also. If she can't shift then we won't be able to take her to the Invivus Realm for her to claim her rightful place as the Queen of the Realm and this is starting to turn out to be a major problem for all of us.

"Are you sure you're even a wolf?" Sin ask her snarky with doubt flowing off of him.

"Y-yes." Thorn stammers.

Then why isn't she shifting?

I know without a doubt that she is indeed a wolf. Hell, I can smell it on her!

But what can be causing this conflict?

"Is your Fae side stopping you from being able to shift?" I question her with my eyes still roaming all over her.

"No. Not that I'm aware of. What am I going to do if I can't shift?" She ask hurriedly, threading her fingers through her long silky hair.

"Then we will find another way beautiful." Slay insist but I don't know of another way that we will be able to accomplish this.

Grabbing her hands suddenly to comfort her my eyes quickly land on her ring that she has on her finger.

"Where did you get this?" I question looking down at her hand.

"My mom gave it to me on my sixteenth birthday. It was right before she was..." she trails off staring down at the ring on her finger sadly.

"Do me a favor babydoll can you take this off for me." I ask gently. I think I may know what's blocking her from being able to shift now.

"Why?"

"Please. Just this once. I will put in my pocket nothing will happen to it I promise. Just trust me." I tell her as I look deep within her eyes pleading with her to trust me.

"Okay." She lowly agrees, taking the ring off of her finer she slowly hands to me as I place in my front jean pocket I blow out a breath hoping I'm right.

It only takes a few seconds before she bends over crying out in pain agonizingly transforming.

Watching as she shifts into her wolf makes me cringe. The first time you shift is always the hardest. Remembering my first shift I recall just how painful it was for me.

I hate to see her in so much pain but I know she has to do it.

After what seems like fucking hours she has finally transformed into a magnificent White Winged Wolf.

Her beauty is beyond miraculous. I am in complete and utter awe of just how magnificent she truly is.

"Beautiful." Slay affirms my own thoughts.

"Stunning." Sin mumbles astonished at her ethereal beauty.

I have to agree with both of them.

Thorns wolf Maya is nothing but perfect.

"You are truly phenomenal Maya." I sincerely tell her.

She nuzzles her head against my arm her fur is amazingly the softest I have ever felt before. She tries to stand but she stumbles a few times before she finally gets the hang of it.

Bending down to her I comb my fingers through her wistful fur on her head she sways her head to the side and slightly up to me.

"May we run with you Maya?" I gently ask her still sifting though her soft fur.

She nods her head up and down.

I wish I would have marked her now. I would be able to talk to her freely with our mindlink if only I did have but unfortunately I haven't yet.

Taking a step back I remove my clothes swiftly then shift into my Red Wolf Stinger and my brothers do the same behind me.

My bothers wolves both look identical to mine.

Stinger walks over to Maya. He sniffs her then nuzzles her head gently placing his scent all over her.

Slay and Sin do the same to her.

Then we all rush off into the forest like a massive racing whirlwind.

This is what I so longed for. With my beautiful and loving mate running beside me I'm all of the sudden consumed with an over powering emotion.

One that I can only acquaint to it being an emotion of growing and aspiring love.

I just may be falling in love with her?

How can I not?

She is everything that I have ever wished for and more.

I just hope that someday she will be able to love me also!

Chapter 9

Last night while running through the forest with my brothers and Thorn at our side was truly inspiring.

I never felt so free and so damn exhilarated. It was like every pent up angry emotion that I have been holding on to for the last few years suddenly escaped me.

Laying in my bed remembering our joyful journey from last night brings me back to when I was younger. When Sun and I were finally able to shift and almost our entire family ran through the forest just as we did last night we were so damn carefree and didn't have one single worry in the world. A happy family.

Then later when Lila was able to join us it felt as we were absolutely complete.

How I wish I could enjoy those rememberable times again even if it was only for a second I would give anything for us to be together again just for that one more second.

But wish in one hand and well you know the fucking rest. Releasing a pent up breath I throw my covers off of me, sliding out of my bed I head straight for the shower.

All this reminiscing isn't doing me any good and fucking wishing sure isn't going to bring my parents back to us. To me.

Stepping into the warm shower I try to my best to relax. I need to find a way to relieve some of this damn tension that's barreling up inside of me.

Thinking of Storm for a fleeting second I push that thought aside immediately. She may be excellent in bed but after catching her with Pan I don't want anything else to do with her ever again.

Then my mind goes reflectively to Thorn.

If only.....

If only she wasn't such a damn burden I could honestly see myself with her but unfortunately with this ominous threat hanging over our heads with that damn prophecy. We all would be better off if she wasn't in our lives.

At least that way she wouldn't have a chance of getting my brothers killed.

And her father!?

Fuck! Her father I would gladly kill him in a damn second but not for her. No. It would be for my parents and my siblings. Never for her.

But damn every time I'm around her I feel like I just want to take her into my arms and never let her go.

It's the stupid mate bond doing this to me.

If only there was a way I could somehow retract the mate bond with her, I would do it in a damn heartbeat.

But I can't.

Because of my brothers.

Both of them seem to think they need her for some damn reason that I can't even fathom. They have been getting so damn close to her and they haven't even fucking known her that long!

Smashing my hand against the shower wall in frustration, I finish my shower aimlessly.

Maybe with Nina coming today she just might be able to help me drive Thorn away?

It could be possible.

Maybe just maybe if I could somehow manage to get Sunny and Nina back together then I could get Thorn out of the picture.

Slay would eventually lose interest in her, I'm sure, after he sees how much Sunny loves Nina and not Thorn. Right? It just may work.

With that affirmation of my thoughts circling confidently throughout my mind. I'm going to set out to do just that.

Watch out Thorn. Your time is coming to an end here!

"So when is she coming?" I ask my brother Sunny as soon as I entered the living room. Slamming down in the chair right next to him with Slay on his other side he gives me a look full of disdain.

"I have no idea and I really could care less." Sunny replies haughtily, I'm about to change his mind though.

"Alphas there is someone here to see you." One of our warriors Clyde tells us through the mindlink.

"Send them in." I rush to say knowing that it is Nina to finally come and help fulfill my plan.

Springing up from the chair I rush over to the front door ignoring my brothers confused looks tossed my way.

A steady knock raps on the door just as it starts I swing the door open but it's not Nina who stands before me.

"Who the hell are you?" I ask the stranger standing in the doorway.

I've never seen his ass before. Maybe I was a bit too hasty allowing whoever this is in? What if he's someone that's after Thorn after all?

"I'm Tristan is there by chance a Thorn Rose here?" His gravely deep baritone voice displeases me and why the hell is asking for our Thorn?

"Tristan?" Thorn yells just as she enters into the living room from just coming out of the dining room.

"Thorn?" Tristan says with surprise laced in his deep voice.

Thorn takes off into a run crashing into this Tristan, he nearly gets his ass knocked over from the sudden impact of catching her in midair.

He envelopes Thorn up in his arms with her legs wrapped around his torso and her arms tightly wrapped around his fucking neck.

What the hell is going on!?

Slay and Sunny make their way over to the happy twosome standing right behind them eyeing them both curiously.

I'm in a daze. I start to shut the door just watching this strange reunion when someone suddenly pries the door open with their hand making my own hand drop away from the doorknob.

"Fier?" Thorn says with astonishment flowing right through her voice. Jumping out of Tristan's arms she runs up to her brother jumping on him the same way she did with that Tristan guy.

Begrudgingly I shut the front door after Fier has made his way into our house still holding on to his sister tightly in his arms.

"So I take it your her brother?" Slay pipes in tilting his head to the side eyeing Fier curiously.

"Yes and I've been looking for this brat everywhere." Fier half laughs craning his neck to look down at his sisters face.

"H-how did y-you find me?" Thorn stammers with tiny tears escaping those dark penetrating eyes.

"Trackers and we need to talk." Fier grumbles turning serious instantly.

"Okay." Thorn replies climbing down off her brother with her feet finally planted firmly on the ground she takes his hand pulling him over to the couch with that Tristan guy following closely behind them.

I eye Tristan with suspicion as I make my way back to the chair I was previously in.

Fier sits down next to Thorn on the couch with Sunny and Slay standing off to their sides along with Tristan standing behind the couch it's a like a cute little family reunion I think to myself sarcastically.

"Dad has gone off of the deep end. I'm so sorry I wasn't there for you Thorn. He sent me on a little vacation to another pack land claiming that he was soon going to retire and that I should take this time to enjoy myself before I took over our pack. If I had known what he had planned I would have..." he trails off with his voice hitching.

"Stop. You didn't know what he had planned Fier. Nobody did. He...has some....deep rooted issues." Thorn tries to placate him rubbing her hand along his arm softly.

"I wanted to kill him. Nobody from the pack would tell me where you disappeared to. He just claimed you ran off but gave me no reason why. I was able to get a tiny bit of information out of that little she wolf Reny, you remember her?" Fier ask her slightly smiling.

"The girl with the little lisp?" Thorn quips.

"That's her she finally told me what happened or what she knew about your disappearance anyway. That's when I gathered a few trackers to find you. Tristan and I have been searching for you everywhere. I understand why you left but why couldn't you tell me Thorn? I was worried so much about you." Fier says looking at her lovingly.

"Dad told me he took care of you. He made it sound like you were dead. I'm sorry Fier but I had no choice but to run and get the hell out of there or else he would have...." Thorn trials off bowing her head and softly sighing.

"I understand Thorn. I'm just glad I found you and that your are safe but I still plan on killing that bastard for what he did to you. It's fucking disgusting, what he wants you to do and I still can't believe the entire pack is standing behind him wanting the same thing as he does. When Reny told me what happened I stormed off back to the pack house ready to kill his revolting ass but somehow he managed to escape. I have no idea where he is right now but I needed to find you to warn you that he also has trackers looking for you and he won't stop until he finds you. He's gone completely mad Thorn." Fier tells her with apprehension alighting his face.

"I know Fier why do you think I took off?" Thorn simply states. "He's fucking psychotic."

"How did you get this far anyway?" Tristan ask her.

"I sort of a hitched a ride on a train. I slept in one of the boxcars until it reached its destination then I took off walking through the forest and ended up here as they were having a party. They have been helping me every since." She says pointing at Slay and Sunny with a touch of pride showing on her beautiful face.

"Thank you for taking care of my sister and looking out for her." Fier says glancing up at Slay and Sunny with admiration written all over his face.

"I'd do anything for my mate." Sunny replies. Fier suddenly gets a look of surprise on his face.

"Mate?" Fier ask her dumbfounded.

"Yes both of them. Slay and Sunny are my mates surprisingly enough," she slightly giggles, "this is my brother Fier and my dear friend Tristan." She introduces them all.

Mates huh? Just Slay and Sunny? Well isn't that funny?

She just so conveniently left out one didn't she? I huff at her denial, rolling my eyes I lean back in the chair choosing to remain silent just observing all of them.

If she wants to deny me that's fine it's not like I accepted her anyway.

"And who is this?" Tristan ask nudging his head in my direction.

"That's our brother Sin." Slay states amicably.

"It's nice to meet all of you," Fier replies, he returns his attention back to Thorn, "so are you planning on staying here? The only reason I ask is because I have a safe house that you can go to where dad won't ever be able find you." Fier suggests.

What the fuck? I don't think so!

"She's staying here." I grouse bringing everyone's attention directed right toward me.

Fuck! Why did I say anything? I actually want her to go. It would be the most convenient way to get rid of her wouldn't it? So why the hell did I just open my big ass mouth?

"All I'm trying to say is that her dad doesn't know she's here plus they all have it planned to go to the Invivus Realm already." I backtrack quickly disappointed in myself for being so fucking stupid.

"Why the Invivus Realm?" Fier ask her curiously.

Thorn sighs out while eyeing me with displeasure. I just flash her my best shit eating grins.

Then hesitantly she fills her brother and Tristan in on the stupid damn prophecy of hers. Hearing the shit all before already I zoned them all out hating myself for destroying that brilliant idea of her brothers.

Guess I'm going to have to stick to my original plans with Nina then. How could I be so foolish? What the hell actually got into me?

I think it may have to do with that Tristan asshole that's now massaging Thorns shoulders tenderly behind her as she continues telling them her story.

Was I jealous? No, I couldn't be. I don't even like Thorn.

Watching her as she animatedly tells them about the damn prophecy I can't deny that I do find her attractive though. What guy wouldn't?

Tristan seems to find her attractive also I can tell by the way the asshole looks down at her with so much adoration closeted in his eyes toward her.

Then she's says something that instantly grabs my attention.

"All three of my mates are supposed to help me take back my rightful place on the throne. Without them it's said that I won't be able to accomplish it." What? I've never heard this side of the prophecy!

Glaring up at my brothers they both quickly shield their eyes away from me.

"Three? But you only have two right? Who is the other? Have you not found him yet?" Tristan ask with so much damn hope flowing through his tone.

"I'm her third mate!" I claim sneering at him with a touch of hostility escaping me.

"Really?" Tristan ask eyeing Thorn warily. "Is it true Thorn?" He adds looking down at Thorn with inquisitive eyes.

"Yes it's true. She's my damn mate. My other half. My destined one. My match whatever the hell you want or call it. She is mine!" I say unknowingly aggressively. Catching my brothers look of shock on their faces at my declaration has me faltering.

Man I'm stupid! Why would I claim her that way? Now their all going to think I really want to be with her.

"But..." I start to add but hesitantly stop before I finish my thought. What can I say now?

That I was just jealous and needed to claim what was rightfully mine? That would be so double standard and I would look like a damn asshole to all of them.

Instead I just sit there staring over at Thorn with a mystified look on my face.

"What he means to say is yes he is my mate but he doesn't really want to be. He already has another Luna chosen to be by his side. I think her name is Stella? Strain? Something like that either way Slay and Sunny are my mates. Not him!" She informs them with such maliciousness echoing throughout her voice that it actually has me baffled for a second.

"But if you don't have you third mate by your side then the prophecy won't come true, right?" Fier ask her worriedly.

"I'll go. I'll take his place. I may not be your true mate but I know someone who can fix that." Tristan insist.

Is he crazy?

"How the hell do you plan on doing that?" I ask him roughly.

"I know a witch who can switch her mate bond from you to me." Tristan says proudly. I note the hope he has captured on his self righteous face.

"I don't think that's such a good idea." Slay pipes in. Thank you brother I'm so glad that someone is actually on my damn side.

"You can come along with us that I don't mind at all but it has to be up to Thorn about the mate bond switching thing and since the Moon Goddess chose Sin as her mate don't you think that switching the bond might do some irrevocable damage?" Slay questions Tristan.

"No if we do it just right it shouldn't hurt anything. That is if you want this Thorn. You know how I feel about you. How I have always felt about you. If he has chosen another Luna then this may be your best option in the long run." Tristan states as he rounds the couch squatting down in front of Thorn with both of his hands holding hers.

"Why don't we put this decision on pause for now. Thorn, I have to go back to my pack and somehow find our father before he can get to you. Regardless if you decide to keep Tristan as your mate or not I will feel much better if you would allow him to stay with you while I'm gone. That is if your are not going to the safe house." Fier thankfully puts a stop to this moronic discussion of mate switching.

But when he ask if Tristan could stay with her something inside of me just snapped.

He already wants to take my place as her mate. How the hell am I going to be able to handle him staying with us? If he does he will always be around her claiming he's some type of bodyguard for her. Touching her and staring down at her with those damn love sick eyes of his! I so don't want to see that shit.

I don't know what's happening to me at this moment but I sure as hell don't like it.

"He can stay. The more protection for her the better." Sunny states completely oblivious to my feelings about this fucked up situation.

"Don't I get a say in this? What if I don't want to switch places with you Tristan? What if I want to be her mate? Did any of you think to ask me? Or even once think about how I might feel about any of this?" I growl out with my temper starting to flare up suddenly.

"Why would we? You made your mind up about Storm days ago. You have done nothing but push Thorn away ever since you met her. You claim you want nothing to do with her. That you don't want a mate. Or her for a mate so why are you arguing about this now? You should be happy little brother that things are finally going your way." Slay argues with me fiercely while glowering down at me.

I know deep down inside that I should be happy about it so why am I arguing so damn defensively about it now?

My emotions are in a damn upheaval.

"Stop. We don't have time for this. Sin you made your choice perfectly clear from the start are you saying now that you have changed your mind?" Thorn ask peering over at me with an inquisitive look on her striking face.

Have I?

I have no clue. All I know is that I am definitely jealous of this asshole before me still holding her damn hands tenderly in his.

Glancing at each person in the living room before me I suddenly start to feel agitation flow through my veins.

I honestly don't know what I want anymore.

"Never mind. Look Sin I'm not the type of person to play these little petty games with you. So how about I make this a little easier for you? I'll give you until the time we leave for the Invivus Realm to make up your damn mind. Only because the prophecy states that I need all three of my mates not because I want you either. If by then you decide that you don't want to be with me then I will gladly chose Tristan to take your place." Thorn lays down the final ultimatum with me with determination.

I sneak a peek at Tristan who is smiling over at me with pure delight erupting on his face. Then I look up at my brothers who both have disappointment planted on their faces at me.

Releasing a heavy breath I look back at Thorn eyeing me with those captivating eyes of hers like she's trying desperately to decipher me.

Even her brother Fier is looking at me curiously.

This is what I wanted isn't it? I wanted her out of our lives and she just so happened to give it to me on a golden platter.

I should just jump at this opportunity right?

"No!" My wolf Malice pipes in suddenly.

"Why the hell not?" I ask him confused.

"She is ours!" No she isn't.

"She will get my brothers killed Malice!" I state defensively.

"No she won't, you will!" Me?

"What? How?" I ask.

"By not going with them! You will leave them open and vulnerable! Maya is my mate and if you fuck this up for me I will never talk to you again Sin!" A bit over dramatic don't you think?

"Malice!" I scream in my head to my stubborn wolf.

"No! I agree with Thorn! Stop playing these petty little games or you will lose everything and everyone you care about! Stop being an arrogant asshole!" He quickly goes silent leaving me completely frustrated at him.

Fucking wolf!

Grimacing from his observant words he may have a small point though. I can't leave my brothers vulnerable. If something were to happen to them and I was the cause of it I would never be able to live with myself.

"Fine!" I grumble standing up from the chair abruptly. I start to leave the room wanting to get as far away from all of them as I possibly can.

I have a lot to think over and I need some privacy to do it. This has just turned into something that I never thought or even imagined it would be.

Then a sudden soft knock comes at the front door just as I was about to pass it. Sighing, I walk to the door yanking it open sharply.

I stand their immobilized at the beauty standing in the entranceway.

Fuck!

Now what? I so forgot about Nina's unexpected arrival today.

"Hey sugar are you going to let me in?" Nina states with a purr. I roll my eyes at her blatant flirtatious attitude.

"Come in Nina." I sprout in resignation, opening the door wider for Nina to walk through it.

Closing the door behind her I turn and notice that she is frozen in place.

Glancing around her I see my brother Sunny grimacing at Nina's arrival.

Fuck this is not what I had planned. Now what the hell am I going to do?

"Sunny baby come give your lover a hug." Nina purrs again holding her arms up in the air for Sunny to come to her.

"I don't fucking think so. What the hell do you want Nina?" I'm surprised at Sunny's outwardly opposition toward her.

He must really hate her? Now I'm glad I didn't go through with my stubborn ass plans.

"Don't be that way lover. I came all the way here just to see you. Play nice baby." Nina says seductively walking over to Sunny with a swag in her step.

I watch as Thorn slowly rises from her position on the couch pushing Tristan out of her way she steps around him heading straight for Nina.

"I don't think we have met yet. I'm Thorn, Sunny and Slays mate." She states with her arm extended out to offer Nina a handshake. There she goes leaving me out of it again.

Nina ignores her hand angling around Thorn she goes straight for Sunny instead. The defeated look on Thorns face is very noticeable as she watches Nina sashay her way over to her ex lover.

Nina leans up on her tiptoes planting a little kiss on Sunny's cheek. He wipes it off with the back of his hand looking down at her completely disgusted by her forward actions.

"Excuse me but if you touch my mate again I won't hesitate to kick your ass." Thorn says aggressively as she walks over to Nina glaring at her.

"Mate? She must be kidding? Tell me she's kidding Sunny?" Nina turns to Sunny furrowing her brows.

"She's not, this is my beautiful mate Thorn. Thorn this is. ..Nina." Sunny introduces them as they measure each other up everyone in the room stays silent just observing them.

"Well that's okay Sunny. You can just reject her now that I'm back baby. Go ahead and do it I'll be waiting for you up in your room when your finished" Nina bravely proclaims tracing her fingers along Sunny's jawline.

Before anyone knew what was happening Thorn suddenly raises her hand up slowly then without uttering a single word she rears back her hand creating a swirling tunnel of wind in her hand suddenly. She swings her arm directly at Nina the wind from her hand knocks Nina completely on her ass making her entire body slide along the floor rapidly. She crashes into a bookshelf that was in the corner of the room. Causing the items upon it to crash down on the floor with a resounding clatter all around her. "Mine!" Thorn roughly exclaims.

"Fuck!" Says Slay staring down at Nina's unconscious body lying on the floor in a heap.

"That's my girl." States Sunny as he is walking over to her.

Me? I'm fucking turned on so damn bad right now that I think my dick could actually explode from being so damn fucking hard.

What a fucking woman!

Chapter 10

"I don't care if your are having issues with the other Alphas I won't her found now!" I demand of my cowardly Beta Parker tossing papers from my temporary desk straight at him.

"Yes Alpha." Parker states nervously walking out of the office in a maniac rush.

Useless servants!

The entire lot of them are nothing but useless.

It's been days and they can still not even locate Thorns damn scent anywhere. What's the use of even having them around?

Sitting down in the office chair roughly I sigh out with frustration riddling all inside of me.

Why can't anything be easy?

My damn daughter must come to the realization that she will soon be mine. There is no other option. She can't keep hiding from me no matter how hard she tries I will eventually end up finding her. I have always gotten whatever I'm after.

She will have no choice but to return to me, regardless, if she likes it or not and soon.

"Is there anything I can get you Alpha?" Quinn a pretty little she wolf ask as she saunters into my borrowed office eyeing me seductively.

"Pick up those damn papers." I command as I watch her gracefully pick up the papers I tossed on the floor I admire her attributes closely.

She's not too bad looking for a little she wolf. I watch as she bends over right in front of me as her tiny little ass is so delicately showing through her little white shift making my cock unbearably hard instantly. She reminds of Thorn.

"Come here." I croak out decisively unbuttoning my pants as she slowly makes her way over to me.

Yanking out my stiff cock out of my pants, I present it to her knowingly. I register her sudden surprise with humor.

"Suck it!" I command gruffly. She hesitated for far to long for my liking though.

Grabbing ahold of her wrist I roughly yank her down to her knees.

"I said suck it cunt!" I tell her grabbing a fist full of her hair I pull her head down to my swollen cock with my other hand firmly holding my dick I push it up against her mouth nudging my cock into her resisting mouth forcefully.

Her little mouth springs open taking my cock into it slowly I can feel her teeth scrape along my tender flesh.

"No teeth!" I grunt pushing her head down on my cock more she eventually starts sucking on it without any further hesitations.

Leaning back in my chair I enjoy the feeling of her warm mouth gliding over dick slowly.

I close my eyes tightly as she bobs along my cock suddenly picturing my beautiful daughter Thorn.

I fantasize about her often, I'm picturing her just now imagining that its her mouth that is so delicately wrapped around my harden cock.

Yes! Thorn! That's my girl! Fuck you're a such good little girl!

Pushing her head with a touch a force harder along my long cock I envision my lovely daughter clearly enjoying sucking her father off.

"Thorn." I growl out as the lips wrapped around my cock suddenly start to pick up their speed rapidly.

Grabbing another fistful of Thorns hair, I slam her head faster up against my midsection. I hear her gagging from my forceful plunges around my dick making me sigh out in complete bliss.

"Oh Thorn baby. Just like that. You like your daddy's cock don't you baby?" I ask her mindlessly as I feel my spine tingle up suddenly. Forcing her head along my cock faster, my balls soon clench up as soon as I feel it I slam her head hard against the base of my cock. Forcing her to stay there until I can empty all of my cum down her throat.

"Thorn! Fuck baby!" I roar out. "Swallow it all for daddy!"

Ropes after ropes of my cum spew out into her mouth through my wonderful climax.

Panting heavily and fully sedated now I release the hair I'm holding. I finally open my eyes slowly only to see the damn she wolf Quinn staring at me with confusion as she wipes her chin with her hand.

"Who is Thorn?" She tentatively ask me.

"None of your damn business now get the hell out of here!" I scream making Quinn jump up to her feet quickly. She nervously runs for the office door slamming it behind her with a slight touch of force.

Placing my spent cock back into my pants sharply, I grab a tissue out of a box off of the desk wiping my hands thoroughly, feeling repulsed by my own activities.

That should have been Thorn not some nameless damn she wolf. I now feel bad for cheating on my love so easily.

What was I thinking?

Disgusted with myself I bound up from the chair swiftly knocking over a flower vase that was placed haphazardly on the desk.

One single red rose lays upon the floor with water cascading around it that poured out lying beside the golden vase.

Bending down I pick the single red rose up off of the floor as I hold it tenderly in my hands I think of my precious Thorn.

How I miss her.

Her genuine smile, those beautiful dark eyes and those succulent plump lips. I miss everything about her.

Every since she turned sixteen when I viscously had her mother killed I have always craved her far more than I should have.

My goal at the time was to take out her mother, the snobby bitch, and make Thorn mine.

Making her our packs Luna.

Then I would finally get what I so long desired for, to rule over the Invivus Realm with Thorn by my side.

Thorns mother would never allow me to rule beside her. When I kidnapped her from King Zeniths masquerade ball that evening the only thing in my mind was that I had to have her. Only because I wanted to rule over my own kingdom though.

I never wanted her sexually. Every time I had to force myself to fuck her. There was definitely no loved involved between the two of us at all.

I hated her as much as she hated me.

She was so damn presumptuous. Miss all high and mighty. At first I tried to use my charm to sway her but when that didn't work out so well I had to resort to using other methods.

Luckily I knew a witch that owed me a favor at the time. I made her use a spell on my dear wife blocking her magic from her so she couldn't ever escape me or use her abilities against me.

It was a wise choice one that I rejoice in even today.

Sitting back down in the chair with the rose still in my grasp I smile down at it deviously.

Thorns mother never stood a chance. I secretly got the Alpha who was a neighbor to our pack to find some risky rogues who loved money more than they did anything else.

I paid them all sufficiently to kill my wife in the most gruesome way fashionable along with a few other wolves from my pack but their lives were inconsequential to me. All that really matter to me was to get Silky, Thorns fucking mother, out of my life and for good.

I could no longer tolerate her insubordination toward me or my pack.

She was always fighting me. That's why her ass was mainly always locked up in my dungeon. I only allowed her to leave the dingy dungeon periodically for Thorns sake.

She was a very weak woman. Not like my Thorn though. Thorn is strong and a touch rebellious but I will soon have her seeing things my way. If only I could only find her.

Crumbling up the rose flatly in my hand, the torn petals of the rose drift down to the floor slowly. I watch them close as each one falls.

Now my son Fier, is off chasing his sister, trying his damn best to reach her before I do. I should have gotten rid of him when I had the chance.

But unfortunately I couldn't. Only because I was truly in love with his mother. She was my true mate after all.

Although I loved her immensely it didn't take long for her true colors to appear. Once she had Fier she changed dramatically.

All of her love that she once so happily gave to me she soon was giving to him and him only. She done everything for him.

Jealousy coursed through my veins every time I saw them together. She became spiteful toward me always throwing our son up in my face.

That's why I killed her.

I remember it fondly.

Wrapping my hands around her tiny delicate throat as I was fucking her mindlessly, I choked the life right out of her then I came so damn hard from it. It was actually the best sex that she and I ever had unfortunately.

Getting rid of Delia, Fiers mom, was exhilarating to say the least.

Feeling a stinging sensation on my hand I suddenly look down upon it. The thorns from the damn rose has cut into my palm from me holding it so fiercely.

I laugh diabolically at the tiny droplets of blood on my palm. It reminds me of Thorn. She is sharp just like the roses thorns. I can't wait to have her back into my arms.

Grabbing another tissue from the box I wipe my hand again removing all of the traces of the blood from my palm.

The door creaks open again slowly. Can't I get no peace at all? Turning in the chair I see the Alpha whose office I'm currently taking over standing in the doorway apprehensively.

"Alpha March what can I do for you today?" I ask abruptly with clear disapproval laced my tone.

"Well Alpha Baker it is not what you can do for me or rather what I can do for you." March says as he walks into his office halting only when he stands in front of his full length bookshelf, looking over at me with a hint of mischievousness arising in his precarious eyes.

"You found her?" I ask him astonished.

"Yes. We have." His defining tone sets my heart to racing.

"Where?" I question.

"She's in the south. There's only one small problem though." He informs as he walks over to his chair in front of the desk crashing down upon it.

"What's the problem?" I ask placing my elbows on the desk waiting for his reply patiently.

"She has found her mates." His declaration suddenly fills me with a questionable rage.

"Mates as in more than one?" I ask him quite dumbfounded at this new developing questionable information.

"Precisely. Three if I'm not mistaken." Three? How can that possibly be?

"How did you come across this information?" I ask him doubting it's notability.

"By a sentinel in the Blood Claw Pack. She gladly handed over the information willingly. Your daughter is mated to the three Alphas of the pack." Leaning back in the chair completely flabbergasted by this new information. I decidedly pick up a letter opener that was laying upon the desk.

Rotating the opener in my hand I sit back thinking about this new predicament I'm in now.

How can I get to Thorn now with Three damn Alphas standing in my way?

"Did you say the Blood Claw Pack?" I ask March curiously.

"Yes. Why? Do you know them?" He ask.

Oh what a delightful turn of events. Of course I know the Blood Claw Pack. I was the one who caused their parents demise after all.

"I know them well." I inform him absentmindedly still playing with the golden letter opener in my hand.

Reflecting back on my memories I recall asking the Alpha then of the Blood Claw Pack for his help with a bogus claim of a rogue attack all because I wanted his wives power.

She was a tri-promancy. A rare wolf that is seldom heard of. She had all the three affirm powers of the main elements along with her wolf she was a very powerful woman.

I had the same witch on call at the time that I used on Silky to claim all of her powers for my own but unfortunately the plane crashed before either of them could even arrive.

That was the reason I set my eyes on Silky. I lost that chance of power unfortunately but when I heard about Silky my plans changed dramatically at that point.

It was a damn shame though because I would have loved having all that damn power for myself. Mores the pity. I sigh out loudly when I recall it all.

"Do we have anybody watching over her there?" I ask March finally stepping away from my own sordid thoughts.

"Yes the same girl that told us about Thorn is watching over her for us." He tells me. Good. Then that means I still have time to formulate a new plan of action to retrieve her.

Eyeing March as he sits so casually in the chair before me playing with the hem of his shirt. I drop the letter opener on the desk with a click echoing in the room. Springing up from my chair I stroll over to him.

Stopping directly in front of him I tilt my head observing him lustfully.

"Strip!" I huskily demand. His head jerks up to me immediately with a flash of desire drifting through his dark brown eyes of his.

Quickly he jumps up from the chair stripping out of all of his clothes, haphazardly tossing them on the floor beside him.

"Go to the sofa." I insist pointing at the beige sofa in the corner of the room.

Swiftly he walks over to the sofa completely bare. I watch his ass jiggle as he goes.

Stripping out of my own clothes I walk back to the desk opening a drawer I grab out a tube of lube then walk back over to him with me being almost nude. I only have on my green boxers now.

"Bend over baby boy!" I croak gruffly squeezing out a glob of lube in my palm as he does so.

With his front facing the sofa and his pretty little ass up in the air I soak his rim up with the lube thoroughly.

Pulling down my boxers efficiently I stroke my throbbing cock a few times before I place it up against his tight little rim.

Pushing my dick in his ass fast and hard I start thrusting in and out of him like a rabid animal.

Grabbing ahold of his hair in my fist I push inside of him harder. Bringing my arm around his hips I start jacking him off with each powerful thrust I force into him.

"Fucking tight!" I grunt as I continue to plummet deep within him.

Bobbing my hand along his short but thick cock rapidly I lean over his back and bite down on his shoulder roughly.

Tasting that sweet tangy blood fuels my own desire more. Driving my cock into him rougher I start to imagine my sweet little Thorn again.

Her imagine comes to my mind swiftly. I picture her bent over the sofa just as March is now with my dick thrusting into her sweet little vagina over and over again, sucking her pert little nub of her voluptuous breast into my mouth. I ravage her ass completely.

Plunging into that tasty pussy of hers like I fucking own it.

Feeling Marchs cum suddenly dripping onto my fingers, I release his cock now grabbing ahold of both sides of hips diving deeper into that tight ass of his continuously and hard and fast I still picture my lovely Thorn in my mind.

With my spine tingling and my balls tightening up I imagine licking her sweet pussy now that's what drives me over the edge.

Spurting out my seed quickly I roar out loudly in the office, "Thorn Fuck me baby!" As my cum overflows Marchs ass delightfully.

March jumps up from the sofa sporadically making my flaccid cock fall out of ass limply.

He turns and stares at me with mortification plastered all over his face.

"You just imagined fucking your own daughter?" March states with revulsion all over his face.

I just shrug my shoulder at him dismissively.

"Yes I did. She will be my Luna March. Have I not made that clear?" I question as I go to grab my clothes off of the floor.

"That's sick Baker. You have to see how wrong that is?" His abhorrent attitude is staring to rile me up.

Dressing quickly I go back to sit down in the desk chair grabbing the golden letter opener again. I play with it as I think over his sudden declaration.

"I do but you will not change my mind on this. I want her. All of her. I have since she was sixteen. I almost walked in on her one time while she was in her bedroom. You see she has had this crush on Fiers friend Tristan for a while now. Anyway her door was cracked opened just a smidge. When I went to go get her for diner she was laying upon her bed completely bare playing her with little pussy and moaning out Tristan's name." I tell him recalling my own startling emotions then.

"I watched her closely. I just couldn't seem to take my eyes off of her. Her delicate round big breast with those dark husky nipples called to me. As I watched her fingers slip inside of her cunt I pictured myself doing it to her. I wanted so damn badly for that to be me. For me to be the one pleasuring her. I wanted to stick my hard dick into her pussy and fuck the shit out of her until it was my damn name she was screaming out in desire." My dick is getting hard just recalling it.

"I knew then I had to have her. No matter what and I still want her. You don't realize how many nights I have crept into her bedroom just staring down at her. One night I almost lost control with her. I climbed into her bed softly so as not to wake her. I slid in right in behind her and slowly moved my finger down into her cute pink little panties. When my finger finally came into contact with that sweet smooth pussy

I almost came in my pants. I quietly pushed it into her little canal ever so slowly pushing it in back and forth. I almost woke her up though. My heartbeat was beating so damn fast I thought it was going explode. Then she moaned. She moaned so irrevocably that in fact I released my semen right there and then in my own underwear. It was the most beautiful experience I have ever had in my life. I can only imagine how it would feel to have my cock sunk deep into her now." I confess to him with my breathing picking up very erratically now.

"Baker that is the most revolting thing I have ever heard in my entire life! How could you think that way about your own flesh and blood. Your own daughter for fuck sakes. If I knew that this is what you wanted her for I would have never bothered helping you find her!" March yells as he stumbles putting on his clothing.

"I'm going to tell everybody what a sick fuck you are! You will not be able to come near her when I'm done!" March keeps yelling out aggressively.

Tilting my head I watch as he stumbles a few more times trying to hurriedly put on his clothing. Sighing I stand up from the chair walking casually over or him.

As he is bent over trying to put on one of his socks I slam the letter opener into the middle of his larynx roughly.

The sudden surprise showing up on his face makes me laugh under my breath. Observing him I watch as he tries helplessly to remove the letter opener from his throat but unfortunately or in my case fortunately he isn't able to do it.

He falls upon the his office floor gasping for breath like a fish out of water. Sitting down in the chair I cross my leg over the other waiting patiently for him to die.

It doesn't take long before I hear his last breaths finally escape him.

Too bad. I think to myself as I stare down at his now lifeless body on the floor, he was actually a good fuck. Oh well.

"I need a body removed now!" I mindlink my Beta Parker.

"Yes Alpha." He replies diligently.

At least this way I now have another pack that I can rule over. The Crescent Moon Pack isn't quite up to my standards but they will do nicely for what is about to come.

Now I need to focus all of my energy on getting my daughter back to me and one way I can start doing that is by locating my son. I will use him to my advantage in some way. Maybe even offer him this pack as an incentive to help. One way or the other he is going to help me.

I need Thorn back with me now!

I've waited long enough already!

Chapter 11

That bitch!

How dare she come up into my house and put her filthy paws all over my damn mate!

I will fucking kill her!

"Woah there beautiful you need to calm down. She is not going anywhere!" Slay tells me while his arms are wrapped around my waist holding me back from that bitch Nina!

It felt so damn good when I crushed her ass with my spiral wind and now I so want to do it again!

But Slay won't fucking let me!

She woke up a few minutes ago in a damn daze. When her ass hit the floor nobody moved for a second. Then suddenly Sin took it upon himself to rush over and help her stupid ass.

He unfortunately helped her to get back on her feet and as soon as she was on her feet she started sprouting out her hateful vile words to me again.

I was ready to hit her with another one of my spiraling winds but unfortunately Slay stopped me before I could. Why won't he let me go? All I want to do is murder her. That seems somewhat reasonable to me.

"Sunny if you don't get this crazy ass woman away from me I will hurt her!" She whines like a damn bitch to my mate! How dare she?

"Hurt me? Bitch you couldn't hurt a damn fly!" I yell at her trying my hardest to get out of Slays hold on me.

"Sun baby are you going to let her talk to me like that?" Nina purrs staring wistfully over at Sunny.

If she takes one mother fucking step near him. I will definitely rip her damn head off of her scrawny little neck!

"Don't call me baby Nina. Lila said that you had to talk to us. She said it was important. State whatever it is you have to say then fucking leave!" Sunny states angrily toward her.

Nina eyes him curiously as she starts to make her way over to him Sin steps in front of her, instantly blocking her way to him.

I smile when I see him do it maybe Sin is good for something after all.

"Fine but I need to talk to all of you privately." Nina replies with satisfaction. I don't fucking think so!

"That's not going to happen!" I speak up aggressively.

"Nina just say what you have to say before I release Thorn on you." Slay suggest. What a wonderful idea. Release me I would love to get my hands on her. Preferably around her damn neck. I'm fixated on her damn neck!

Sighing in resignation, Nina finally decides to speak up, "I wanted to ask if I could stay here just for a little while." She rushes out quickly.

"Hell no!" I scream loudly making the bitch flinch away from me to my great satisfaction.

"Please. I have no where else to go the Alpha of my pack is trying his best to sleep with me and he already has a Luna. She's not his mate but he chose her nonetheless and if I stay she will end up killing me if she finds out." Nina pleads so sweetly it actually makes me nauseous.

"Then let her kill you. I don't see the problem here!" I state rather briskly.

"Thorn." Slay drawls out my name.

"What? This is not going to happen Slay. If she stays I go, simple as that." I promise with determination lacing my tone.

Then the entire room suddenly gets hauntingly quiet.

"Seriously? It's not like either of you wouldn't do the same?" I ask begrudgingly glancing over at everyone in the room one by one.

"He tried to rape me!" Nina announces abruptly with a very forlorn look suddenly appearing on her face.

"Riiight!" I don't fucking believe the bitch.

"He did!" She presses.

"I don't want her around. I think she's full of shit! If any of you believe this shit then you are not the people that I thought you were." I vaguely state searching the room.

"Thorn we don't know the complete story. Why don't we all take a minute and try to calm down. We can't throw her out on the street when she is so upset like this." Sun insists as Nina just smiles on.

"No it's either her or me?" I state to them all, frustrated beyond belief.

They all remain silent. It's like a damn deja vu all over again.

Hell no! They are not going to make me feel guilty for not wanting this bitch around.

"Fine. Then I'll go." I simply state glancing over to my brother, "is that safe house still an option?" I ask.

"You know it is Thorn. Always." Fier says to me lovingly.

"Let me go Slay. I need to pack." I forcefully tell him. He slowly lets his arms drop away from me as he hesitantly releases me from his hold. Turning back to Slay the shell shocked looked on his face almost has me faltering. But then I remembered how they all just disregarded my own wishes so easily.

Blowing out a breath I peer over to Nina still standing beside Sin.

"You can fucking have them!" I grit out pivoting on my heels, I walk away from them all headed up to my room to pack. I hear Sunny and Slay calling out for me as I go but I ignore them both of them they had their chance to speak up just now and instead they both chose not to do it. Fuck them both!

Slamming my bedroom door behind me with bang, I walk over to the bags of clothes that Sunny and Slay purchased for me eyeing them all wistfully.

Fuck it!

I don't need their shit anyway.

Leaving the new clothes behind I pick up my own clothes that I wore when I first met them all and walk out of my bedroom in a huff.

Walking down the stairs with determination in my steps I ignore the others around me heading straight for the door.

Opening the front door I hear foot steps coming up from behind me but I don't turn around I just keep walking out the fucking door without even looking back.

"Thorn are you okay?" Tristan ask me as he's running fast to catch up with me.

"I'm fine. Can we go?" I ask my brother that's walking up behind Tristan with worry written all over face.

"Are you sure Thorn? They all seem pretty upset that you're leaving!" Fier states.

"I'm sure. Let's just go." I tell him walking off to his truck I climb into the cab sitting my one set of clothes on my lap. Sighing.

I hear my brother start up the truck with Tristan climbing in the back of the cab as he puts the truck in gear.

As we back out of the driveway I give one final look back to the house of my mates that's when I notice Sunny and Slay running after the truck.

"Go hurry?" I demand of my brother. He swiftly drives away from my mates as I glance back I see both of them standing in the middle of damn road looking at the truck with longing as we drive away from them both.

They should of spoke up when they had the chance like I wish they did. I feel my unshed tears fill my eyes instantly but I dare not let them fall.

The safe house is different than I thought it would be, in my mind I envisioned a quaint little cottage but this, well this is like something out of a damn Steven King novel.

The three story mansion is completely faded. Here there once was what looked liked a grayish color is now covered with a dark mildew like exterior. It daunting as hell. No wonder my brother would think that my father would never find me here. It looks like no one has lived in this house for years.

"Are you sure the is the place?" I ask Fier with trepidation standing in front of the haunted looking house.

"Yes Thorn. It may not look like much from the outside but the inside is up to date. You have a kitchen full of food and supplies enough to do you and Tristan for at least a month or so and I have bought you new clothes for you to wear they are up in room along with a few accessories for you." Fier states as we all enter the estate.

He's absolutely right though. The inside of the house looks nothing like the exterior thank goodness. It's fitted with beautiful furnishings all around. I blow out a breath in relief.

"I'll be back in about a week or two to check on you until then here is a new cellphone for you to use. I already have mine and Tristan's numbers programmed into it for you. Just in case you need us. So do not answer any unknown numbers that call it. Okay?" Fier ask handing my new cellphone.

Astonishingly it has a pretty little phone case on it that has a beautiful picture of a rose with a girl and wolf and moon on the back of it. I love it.

"Thank you but do you really have to go?" I ask him a little apprehensively.

"I'm sorry Thorn but we need to stop dad before he has a chance to get to you. Tristan will not leave your sight and I have a couple of friends casing the place just case there's any trouble. Don't worry you will be fine. I'll make damn sure of it." Fier replies solemnly to me.

I just nod my head at him nimbly wishing that he could stay. With Slay and Sunny now out of my life he and Tristan are the only ones I can depend on now. Maybe they were the only ones I could ever depend on really.

"I'll miss you." I lowly tell him.

"I'll miss you to but I will do everything I can to get back to you quickly." Fier assures me.

"Don't worry little one I'll be here with you we can play games or watch a movie what ever your little heart desires, we can do." Tristan quips.

"Thank you."

"Anytime little one. Now come on let's find something to eat because I am freaking starving." He suggest dragging me away by my hand to wherever he's taking us.

"I'll see you later Thorn love you." Fier hollers at me as Tristan keeps dragging me along with him.

"Love you too." I barely get the words out before my brother leaves out of the front door.

Bye. I mentally tell him wistfully feeling his the loss of his presence already.

"So what do you want to watch?" Tristan ask me after we finished up our dinner of tacos and chips we grab a few snacks to take along to living area to watch a movie.

"I don't know what are you in the mood for?" I honestly could care less about the movie at the moment. I feel so down about everything that's happened that my heart just isn't in to it.

But seeing the pleading look in Tristan's eyes that flashed at me when he asked me to watch a movie with him, I caved instantly. I can't help it I'm a sucker for those puppy dog eyes.

"How about a horror movie?" He ask me knowing that they are my favorite. I can see right through his little schemes but it's really thoughtful of him to do it.

"How about It I heard it was good?" Tristan tilts his head faking concentrating mindlessly.

"Seriously? Stop that!" I laugh at his childish behavior.

"At least I got you to laugh." Awe I could actually swoon. Why is he being so damn sweet to me?

"Yes you did, thank you." I earnestly tell him. I'm truly grateful for him.

"You're welcome. Now let's watch this movie!" He says with excitement as he turns on the movie for us to both watch.

Three longs days and nights has passed by slowly since I left my mates behind.

Tristan has been a complete saving grace for me. During the entire time he has been there for me to wipe away my tears or just to listen to me babble on about them.

I don't know what I would do without him.

When he offered to switch places with Sin at first I thought it was bad idea. Now I'm not sure about that. If my mates apparently don't want me then I just may see a future with him. Maybe?

I have been so confused lately. Questioning my every thoughts and actions pertaining to the night I left them be-hind.

Did I do it too hastily? Should I have stayed and fought for them? Was I being to presumptuous? Was Nina really lying?

I don't know any more.

All I know is that in my mind they should of spoke up right then and there without a second thought on my behave. Right?

But they didn't and I can't change that now. Regret and remorse is all I have to hold on to now. It's pathetic!

This desperation that I feel now is nothing but pathetic in my eyes.

I should be stronger than this! Why am I letting them get to me so easily? If they truly wanted to be with me then they would of found me already right?

I'm tired of all of the questions that keep floating around in my restless mind endlessly.

As I'm preparing our dinner tonight these continuous thoughts are driving me crazy.

Chopping the onions for our hamburgers I start to cry but I don't actually know if it's from these dry onions or out my own self pity anymore.

This is ridiculous!

Finishing up the food I place the food on our plates aimlessly going through the motions like a robot.

"Uhm, Thorn we have company." Tristan states startling me as he comes walking in the kitchen.

I nearly drop the salad bowl on the floor, luckily I caught it quickly before it was able slip out of my hands.

"Who?" I ask him confused. Who can possibly know were here? Fier said no one knew but us.

"Uhm, one of your mates." What? They actually came for me well at least one of them has I think.

"Okay." I reply numbly placing the bowl of salad on the table.

"Are you sure you want to see him Thorn. I can tell him to go." Do I?

Without thinking about it too much I just start to walk around Tristan.

"No I got this but thank you." I tell him as I pass by him.

As soon a I entered the room I stop right in my tracks surprisingly astonished at who I'm seeing standing in the middle of the living area. The last one I thought that would ever come for me.

"Sin?" I ask breathlessly out of all of my mates I didn't expect him!

He turns to me when he hears my voice the look on his face shocks me. All I see is regret and a touch of shame captured on it.

"Thorn. I have been looking for you everywhere." Sin says as he walks a few steps toward me. I take a step back away from him making him halt his progress toward me.

That seems to be the running theme when it comes to me though. Everyone is always looking for me everywhere it seems.

"Why are you here?" I ask him harshly.

"To bring you back of course." He states it so simply.

"Why?" I question. He scowls at me pondering me in amazement.

"Because you are our mate Thorn. Why else?" It makes no sense.

"That's not a very good reason for me to go back Sin! Where's the others?" I ask him a bit defensively.

"They are outside. They were to scared to come in knowing how upset you were at them when you left." They came for me? Elation hits me suddenly at the very thought then it subsides quickly remembering what they exactly did.

"No. I don't think so. They had a chance to speak up then and choose me and they didn't. They chose her. I won't go back." I define my determination simply.

"Thorn they are sorry. They were just surprised by Nina's revaluation that's all." Bullshit.

"I don't think so. Surprised or not they had their chance and they blew it. So I think you should just leave now." I tell him waving my hand toward the front door.

"Not without you." He exclaims assuredly. Why is he acting so different? He never wanted anything to do with me before so why the drastic change all of the sudden? It's strange.

"Yes without me and why you? Why did they send you to come in here to talk to me? You never wanted me as a mate. So why?" I ask him suspiciously.

"Listen Thorn I know I have been a major jackass to you and I am sorry for all that I have done to you. Let's just say I had a change of heart and I see the error of my ways." I don't buy it! Not one damn bit.

"Too little, too late. Just leave Sin. This is not how mates are suppose to act or be around each other. I can't take all of this negativity any longer. Don't worry I won't reject any of you but I just can't see a future for us. Not anymore anyway." I whisper the last sentence to him lowly. Full of regret.

"Don't say that please Thorn what can I do to make up to you?" He ask me with a soft pleading voice. I don't think there's any way to salvage this relationship any longer though.

"Nothing. There's nothing you can do Sin. Is she...is she still living there?" I timidly ask him. Feeling self conscious suddenly.

"Yes. I'm sorry she has no where is to go Thorn." Yea right!

"Really? Why can't she live in your sisters pack then? They are friends right?" I ask laughing under my breath at this stupid conversation.

When I see the sudden realization hit him I can't help but to laugh loudly at his surprised face.

"Just leave. You knew you had the option to let her live with your sister and all of you still allowed her to live with you anyway. What kind of fool do you take me for Sin? Is Sunny still in love with her?" I get my answer when I see the guilt written look on his face.

Without saying another word I storm over to the front door opening it up for him.

"Leave. Now!" I say with force.

He hesitates for a second then slowly starts making his way over to the front door. Before he exits the door he looks down at me.

I refuse to meet his eyes with mine so I keep them focused on Tristan that's standing at the edge of the living area looking over at me with a sadden expression on his face.

"Thorn." Sin drawls out my name.

"She said leave. I suggest you do just that." Tristan gruffly exclaims walking over to me.

Sin glances back at him over his shoulder glowering at him.

"She's our mate Tristan not yours?" Sin speaks out roughly.

"Not for long." Tristan states. I don't dispute his words I just lower my head staring down at my shoes instead.

"What is that suppose to mean?" Sin ask turning to face Tristan. I look back up to judge his reaction.

"Take it however you want." Tristan says condescendingly to him folding his arms across his chest he boldly glares over at him.

Sin doesn't offer Tristan a reply when I glance over at him I note that he is mindlinking with his brothers presumably. Panic soon consumes me.

"Just leave Sin." I demand scared of what's to come.

"You heard her. Leave." Tristan rudely tells him.

Before another word can be spoken Sin punches Tristan right in his face suddenly forcing Tristan to fall back on his ass onto the floor roughly.

"Sin!" I scream bending down to Tristan, I cradle his upper body in my arms as he holds his hand against his damaged nose.

"She's mine! Ours! And I'll be damned if I allow you to have her!" Sin yells at Tristan who is trying to rise up from the floor.

"After the way you all have treated her I don't blame her if she never goes back to any of you!" Tristan yells.

Slay and Sunny soon make an appearance behind Sin eyeing Tristan who has finally made it to his feet with me standing right behind him.

"You all chose a damn whore over her! How do expect her to act? Did you honestly think she would come running back into your fucking arms so openly? No! And she never will either. So just leave us alone. You made your choice!" Tristan keeps screaming at them.

I make my way around him standing directly in front of all three of my mates. This needs to stop now before it gets anymore out of hand.

They all seem to have disparaging looks on their faces and regret coursing through all of them. I wish I could just let this go and get back to the way we were but I don't know if I can trust them any longer.

"Thorn please just listen to us. We have a reasonable explanation." Sunny finally speaks up. I hear the desperation in his voice.

"No explanation will ever be good enough as to why you chose another over me. You know what I changed my mind." I discreetly tell them as I take another step closer to them.

"I, Thorn Lee Rose, of the White Moon Pack, reject...." I didn't get a chance to go any further before Sin descended on my mouth kissing me feverishly to shut me the hell up!

The kiss is so enticing I can feel the sparks alight within me firing me up to my very core. Without even thinking I deepen the kiss even more wrapping my arms around his neck I actually fucking moan while doing it.

Slipping my tongue into his moist mouth I hear him groan out huskily. He pushes his body against me deepening the kiss I can feel his erection clearly pressed up against stomach my eyes widen when I feel how damn hard he is for me.

Suddenly breaking the kiss I pull myself away from him breathing heavily.

I'm in a blissful haze and I truly don't know what to make of it.

It's all too much!

Pushing Sin out of the door, while Slay and Sunny go stumbling back on the porch behind him. Hurriedly I shut and lock the door once I get them out of the doorway.

Leaning up against the door I place my hand against my chest with my other hand going straight to my mouth I run my fingers across my lips.

"I can't believe you let him kiss you! How damn stupid are you Thorn? They have acted reprehensibly toward you and you still allow them to grope you like you're a damn slut!"

What the fuck did he just say to me?

I'm shocked or hear Tristan talking to me in such a manner.

"What the fuck Tristan I'm no damn slut. If you didn't notice he was the one who kissed me while I was trying to reject him! How could you think of me that way?" I question him mortified by his hurtful words to me.

"You were the one who wrapped your damn arms around him Thorn. You liked it. Admit it. I thought better of you, I guess I was wrong." He tells me shaking his head as he walks away from me stomping his feet as he goes.

I stand there watching him storm away from me with a questioning look on my face.

I try to but I can't lie to myself. Tristan is right I did enjoy it. Far too much actually. But he is my mate after all why should I feel guilty about it just because Tristan thinks it's wrong?

Now I feel like I have nobody left.

The loneliness hits me like a punch in the gut and I start to cry unabashedly from it.

Dammit!

I can't take all of this shit any longer. I'm done! Completely done!

I'm just going to fucking leave them all! Fuck it!

Chapter 12

I 've been watching this morbid house for a few damn hours now.

Sitting on my Harley I stare at the front door of the creepy Addams Family house waiting patiently for Thorn to exit it.

After yesterday's debacle with Sin and with Thorn so easily trying to reject us, I made it my mission to put an end to this stupid fucking war between us. I won't let her go. I just fucking can't.

But since she won't see us personally I have to fucking sit and wait for her to come out of her own hiding place unfortunately.

I should have spoken up.

When Nina announced to all of us about her Alphas brazenly advances toward her I was in complete shock.

Her Alpha is a dear friend of mine, I've known him for years now and to hear that about him from Nina's lips just fucking surprised me. I actually can't believe that he tried to rape her though.

That's why I didn't speak up when I should have. I could kick myself for allowing her to leave us again. I'm a damn idiot.

It's all my damn fault.

If I would have just fucking spoken up or even kicked Nina's ass out of our house then we wouldn't be in this damn predicament that we are in now. Damn! I hate myself for it.

Nina is definitely a problem. Every since she has arrived in our home she has been flirting with Sunny nonstop. She's also been acting very suspicious. I just wish I knew what her damn end game was.

I begged Lila to let Nina stay with her instead of us but she adamantly denied me. She's Nina's friend but she doesn't trust her ass either.

So now we're stuck with Nina's trifling ass until we can find her other accommodations.

I tried to reach out to her Alpha, Alpha Curtis, but he has yet to answer any of my calls. I need to visit him if I want to get to the bottom of this shit but right now my main concern is Thorn, seeing Curtis will just have to come later.

Blowing out a long breath I stretch my tired body out, it's stiff from sitting here on my hog for so damn long. Fuck!

Either I'm getting old or I need to exercise more. At least it's somewhat cool today. Winter will be creeping up on us soon, it's my favorite season. Especially when it snows, to me it's like a rebirth, a fresh blanket across the land, revitalizing it.

I can just picture Thorn and I running across the fresh fallen snow getting our paws wet and rolling happily around in it. It's something that I just don't want to visualize though. I desperately want it to be a damn reality.

But unfortunately that won't happen until I can manage to get Thorn to see just how much I actually care for her.

This separation is hard man. What's that saying? You don't know what you got until it's gone? Yea that's me. I didn't realize how much I cared for her until she wasn't there any longer.

And I'm pretty sure Sunny feels the same way as I do. He's been moping around the house like a little damn lost puppy every since she left.

Now Sin on the other hand well let's just say he's had a drastic change of heart recently.

I laugh remembering what happened after Thorn left us.

It surprised me though, he's the one that got up in mine and Sunny's faces screaming at us both, telling us that we were complete morons for not speaking up earlier.

To say I was pissed at him for being so brazen is an understatement. I rarely fight with my brothers but that night Sin and I threw down, we even ended up shifting into our wolves.

It's a damn good thing we heal easily or else we would both be in the well care center right now. It was a bloody and harsh rumble but for some reason after that Sin has been all about getting Thorn back.

But I'm not the one to look a gift horse in the mouth I'm just happy that he's finally come to realize that Thorn is his mate and that should absolutely mean something to him.

He finally confessed to both Sunny and I about Storms affair with Pan. I can't say I'm not surprised about it either. He should've heeded my warning when I did warn him about her.

I'm just happy there was no love loss between them or it would of been far worse for all of us in the end.

Hearing a door open finally, I crane my neck to see Thorn leaving the old daunting house. Scrunching up my face I watch as she tries to be sneaky about leaving.

She turns her head in both directions eyeing the street before her nervously.

Squinting my eyes I notice that she has a cyan backpack thrown over her shoulder. What is she up to? She's acting very shifty.

Is she planning on running away again? The woman damn sure is a runner, I'll give her that.

Suddenly she takes off in a dash down the broken sidewalk running fast like her damn ass is on fire.

Hopping off of my bike quickly I take off after her in a run.

She slows her steps down finally when she reaches an abandoned building sliding in beside it down an alleyway.

Huffing, I sprint to the building. Looking down the alleyway for her, I notice her at the end of the alley, she has managed to reach the end of it but unfortunately her path is blocked by another building and some green over filled dumpsters on the side of the buildings.

Time to make my move. Strolling over to her casually she suddenly notices me coming to towards her. Her eyes suddenly flash with something akin to fear trying to search for a way out I presume.

"Really Slay?" She breaths out defeated with her shoulders suddenly slumping.

"Thorn I just want to talk to you, that's all nothing more. Give me five minutes of your time, please." I ask holding up my hands in surrender as I keep advancing toward her slowly.

"You had your chance to talk and you blew it. What more could you possibly have to say?" She questions me in silent desperation. I can see the weariness in her eyes and now I feel awful because I'm the one that put that weariness there.

"A lot more, beautiful. Just please five minutes, that's all I ask." I ask her in my own desperation.

"Alright. Speak!" She resolves herself to listen I feel a twinge of relief spring up in me. So I rush to tell her.

"Nina's Alpha is a friend of mine. He's been my friend for years now Thorn. When she told us what he was doing to her I was....well I was in a state of shock. I couldn't believe that the guy I knew for years would be so...cruel. I just froze. I'm so damn sorry. I should have spoken up right then and there but it's like my brain wasn't cooperating with my mouth for some fucked up reason," I stress taking a few slow steps closer to her.

"I'm a moron Thorn. I will forever be regretful for not speaking up sooner. For not showing you that you are the one who is important to me. To us. You mean the world to us Thorn and I will prove that to you everyday from here on out if you would just give me the chance to." I finally reached her. Standing close to her I can smell her sweet fragrance that I've been yearning to smell for awhile now. It overrides the foul smell that's floating off of the rancid trash in the dumpsters.

"Why didn't you just ask your sister for Nina to stay with her then?" She questions me like she's daring me to repute it.

"I did. But Lila doesn't want her there anymore than we want her with us. She is her friend but she just doesn't trust her." I reveal it all to her pleadingly.

"Sunny is still in love with her Slay. When I asked Sin if Sunny was still in love with Nina his face registered a sadness that was overwhelming. That was proof enough for me to not even think of coming back." She says as her voice trembling slightly.

I stare down at her confused, "Sunny doesn't love Nina, Thorn. He will tell you that himself. He has been avoiding her ass ever since you left. He is repulsed by her. I don't know why you think that he loves her but I can guarantee you that he indeed doesn't." Sunny actually hates Nina. They did break up for a reason but that reason unfortunately it's not for me to indulge.

"Fine he doesn't love her. But that doesn't change the fact that all of you chose her over me. Why didn't you stop me?" She ask me as she drops her backpack to the ground in a huff.

"We tried. We ran after you, after you got into your brothers truck. We tried to stop you as soon as we came to our damn senses and realized what you were actually doing. I promise you Thorn we did fucking try." I tell her even though I can sense her doubt about my truth.

"After you left we got into an argument but then we went searching for you immediately after that. None of us wanted you to go. We were just too shell shocked by what Nina told us." I add trying my best to remove any of her doubts about it.

"I still can't come back Slay. Not as long as Nina is there. I just can't do it. I will end up hurting her or worse if I ever caught her trying anything with either of you and....I just can't risk that. I'm sorry." Her tone leaves no room for arguments but I'll be damned if I let her go because of such a flimsy ass excuse.

"Then I will make her move out. It's that simple Thorn. You come first before anyone. Just let me prove it you." I will kick Nina's ass to the curb faster than a speeding a bullet if only Thorn will come back to us. To me.

"Then where would she go?" She ask me breathlessly.

"I don't know and I don't care Thorn as long as I have you the rest of the world can kiss my ass." I tell her, as I reach out to her, I just so badly need to touch her.

She flinches away from me when my hand comes near her, I drop my arm right away from her, sadden by her disregard.

"Please Thorn. Just let us prove it you." I desperately plead reaching my arm out again to her. This time thankfully she doesn't flinch away from it. I breath a sigh of relief.

Tracing her jawline with the pad of my index finger slowly, I feel the sparks with each slow movement. Closing my eyes I revel in the feeling of just being able to touch her.

When I open my eyes I see unshed tears welling up in those beautiful deep cove blue spheres of hers.

"I'm so sorry Thorn." I croak out miserably, knowing that I'm the cause for those unshed tears, it truly breaks me. "Please come home." I plead.

Lowering my head down to her I trace my lips along hers lightly. Closing my eyes again I move in closer kissing those petal soft plump lips of hers agonizingly slow. So tenderly.

I break away from her, placing my forehead on hers I peer down into those hypnotic eyes, I sigh searching her face as I watch one tear slip away from her eye, I lower my head again kissing away the tear gently.

"Please." I whisper urgently as I back away slightly from her face, her eyes search my face now wearily.

"Okay but I want her gone Slay. Otherwise I will leave again and this time I won't come back." She vows determinedly.

"Deal." I acquiesce, wrapping my arm around her shoulders.

"Then let's get the hell out of here this place fucking stinks." I laughingly tell her.

As soon as we walked through the front door the shit storm started!

With Thorn at my side and a pouty lipped fucking Tristan standing quietly behind us we all halted in our tracks observing the 'brawl for all' before us.

Sun and Sin were both arguing with two very pissed off women, known as Nina and Storm that are apparently hand-cuffed with their hands behind them.

They were shouting and cussing at my two brothers with all three of our betas: Pan, Flex, and Trace standing haphazardly off to the side of them looking deservedly uncomfortable.

Blowing out an aggravated breath, I steel myself for the inevitable that's about to come from all of this. Shit! I can't catch a damn break.

"ENOUGH!" I bark out with my Alpha tone aggressively at all of them.

Everyone in the room with the exception of my brothers and surprisingly Thorn tilt their heads to the side in submission toward me.

Then I hear a small squeak coming from beside me, I tilt my head in Thorns direction watching her as she squeezes her legs tightly together.

Then her sweet arousal hits me like a damn lust bomb going off. The enticing aroma of cinnamon and vanilla drift up to me. Suddenly realizing that she just got excited by hearing my damn Alpha tone makes my dick react instantly, making my jeans feel uncomfortably tighter than they were before.

Cocking my eyebrow at her, I try like hell to regain my control, that is definitely something we will have to explore later.

Turning my attention back to the riled bunch of miscreants I push my desires aside so I can address the situation at hand. But fuck it's hard with Thorn so damn turned on at the moment. Damn!

"What is going on?" I grit out stomping my feet over to them, trying my best to calm raging dick.

They all start to explain simultaneously, with each voice rising above the other.

"I SAID ENOUGH!" I bark out again fuming.

When everyone in the room finally quietens down I turn to my brother Sin for the explanation.

"What's going on?" I ask needing to get to the bottom of this childish shit now.

"Nina as been lying to us all along Slay. Just ask Trace he knows all of the details." Sin growls pointing at Trace, Suns Beta, who is silently standing behind Sun.

"Well?" I push for an answer as Trace makes his way over to me.

"We we're out in the training field when I overheard a conversation that Nina was having with her Alpha on her cellphone. Apparently, Alpha Curtis has sent Nina here to spy on our Luna." Trace admits stoically, I glance over at Nina that's now fidgeting on her feet with her head bowed down discreetly. The fucking traitorous bitch. I knew her damn ass was up to something.

"What did you intend on finding here Nina?" I ask growling at her but deep down I have a bad feeling that I already know the fucking answer.

"Her." Nina whispers lowly. So low in fact I had to strain my ears to hear it and that's a rare feat with me being supernatural.

"Why, Nina?" I sneer as I stomp over to her standing face to face I reach down and roughly grab her chin making her deceitful ass look me in the eyes.

"They want her." She mumbles with my fingers pressing her cheeks together tighter.

"Who? Who wants her Nina?" I bark ripping my hand away from her face, her head bounces back from the roughness of my grip when I release her.

"Her father! Curtis is a friend of his and he asked me to come and spy on her!" She yells snarling at me.

"Why? Why did you do it? Don't you know what her father wants of her?" I ask her bewildered. I knew Nina was a bad individual but I never thought she could be so vile.

"Because Sunny is mine and this bitch took him away from me!" She glowers over at Thorn who is casually observing the scene before her so damn nonchalantly that it somewhat confuses me. Why is she being so damn calm?

"How did Curtis know that she was even here?" I question Nina. It seems a bit strange to me that they all knew where she was.

"Alpha that would be because of Storm. Apparently she has been spying on our Luna for awhile now." My Beta Flex enlightens me.

Now my attention goes directly to Storm who is glaring me down with a visceral snarl on her face. I knew she wanted the role as Luna but I didn't think she would go this far with it just to get it.

My lack of judgment lately has been very off kilter unfortunately it seems.

I happen a glance at Sin who is rightly glaring down at Storm with murderous intentions flashing in his heated gaze.

"Is this true Storm?" I question her wanting to hear it from her own treacherous lips.

"Yes," she snarls, "and I'll do it again willingly," she turns her fire filled eyes to Thorn, "she doesn't deserve to be Sins Luna, I do! I worked my ass off for the position and she just came prancing into our lives destroying all the hard work I put into it. She deserves whatever she gets from her fucking father and I hope he fucking kills you!" She screams viscously at Thorn.

Hearing a cute little giggle cascade up from behind me I look back watching Thorn as she starts to burst out with unsolicited laughter.

While she's bending over in laughter I search each person in the room and observe that every single one of them are all staring at her like she's completely lost her damn mind. I can't blame them either.

"What the hell is so funny?" Storm snarls starting to walk over to a hysterical Thorn but thankfully Sin stops her before she can draw closer to her by roughly gripping her arm and yanking her back.

"You. You are what's so damn funny. Do you honestly think I came here wanting to be their mates? I came here to escape my father. Not to find a mate and I know it's rude to laugh right now but when you said you worked your ass for the Luna position, well I thought it was funny because you actually did, literally!" Thorn says between her laughter.

I roll my eyes at the absurdity of her words but damn she does have a point actually.

Shaking my head at Thorns disrupted laughter I return my attention back to the two conniving bitches.

"Who did you tell Storm? Who all knows that Thorn is here?" I ask reverting the attention away from a giggling Thorn.

When she becomes tight lipped suddenly I march over to her yanking her head back by her hair roughly.

"Who?" I snarl.

"Her father knows I guess. I talked to a guy who was working for this Alpha named March." I don't recognize the name unfortunately.

But I drop my hand away from Storms hair when I hear Thorn gasp suddenly.

"Do you know him?" I inquire worriedly, observing Thorns face when it goes from the cute glow of being humorous to panic in a hot damn second.

"He's my fathers....lover." She quietly says with confusion marring her beautiful face.

"Why is this so upsetting?" I ask her scowling at her discomfort.

"Because I thought he was my friend." She mumbles almost incoherently.

Tristan decidedly comes up behind her then, placing his hand on her shoulder he looks to me with resignation on his face.

"He's been a long time friend of the family. He is like a Uncle to her." Tristan informs me. I nod my head at him noting Thorns sudden sadness.

"What are going to do with us?" Nina ask abruptly with fear absconded on her face.

"I don't know Nina. What do you two think I should do with you?" I question her calmly with a smooth terrorizing tone laced in my voice.

Honestly, I just want to rip both of their heads off from their damn necks but unfortunately I can't. There are laws set in place for this type of shit and unfortunately I have to abide by them.

"You can let us go." Nina whispers suggestively. This time it's me who laughs although it's half hearted.

"I don't think so. Throw them in the dungeons but keep the handcuffs on them. We wouldn't want them to be able to shift on us. I'll contact Queen Miracle to see what she wants us to do about them." I instruct all our Betas knowing that the handcuffs they have placed on their wrist are magically designed to keep them from being able to shift into their wolves.

"Yes Alpha." They all say as they make their way over to them.

"You can't do this Slay! I'm a member of your pack dammit!" Storm squeals while trying to fight my Beta Flex who has her tightly within his grasp.

"Not anymore Storm. You are no longer a member of my pack." I enforce, growling.

"Then I'll be a rogue Slay. Please don't this to me. I have a family." Storm keeps bellowing trying to plead with me.

"Then you will be a rogue. You should have thought about your family before you did this Storm." Sin pipes in angrily glaring at her.

"You can't make me a rogue Slay I am not a member of your damn pack!" Nina grouses.

"No he can't but the Queen can." Sun tells her smiling deviously at her.

"Take them both away." I command.

"Yes Alpha." Flex says as he drags a kicking and screaming Storm away as does Trace with a very solemn Nina. Pan hangs back hesitating looking at Sin with regret marring his face.

"Sin I'm so...."

"It's fine Pan. I understand. I know how Storm is man. We're good." Sin tells him after he cuts him off giving him a small grin.

"Thanks man. It won't ever happen again." Pan promises.

"It better not because this one's my mate and I will definitely kill you over this one." Sin states half laughing giving Pan a manly hug and patting him on his back.

Friends at peace again at last.

With the mention of Thorn we all turn our attention to her after Pan leaves the room.

"You're back?" Sun comments breathlessly as he is strolling over to her, the sudden loving expression captured on his face when he looks lovingly down at her as he approaches her makes me smile deliriously.

"I'm back." She assures him as she smiles up at him.

A sense of pride engulfs me as I watch the two of them suddenly embrace.

Tristan takes a step back away from Thorn eyeing her somewhat disgustingly.

Furrowing my brow at him I try to decipher exactly what his look toward her may actually mean.

The idiotic love sick gaze he once had for her is now apparently dissolved. As Sin makes his way over to her to welcome her back home I observe Tristans actions closely.

He aggressively picks up his suitcase off of the floor huffing as he is observantly is glowering over at Sin and Thorn who are now hugging.

Something happened between them two and I plan to get to the bottom of it. With Thorns father already knowing where exactly she is at now we can't have any further problems to worry about.

But first we are going to have to get Thorn away from here and somewhere safe and far away from her father, after the Queens visit that is.

"I'm going to go give Queen Miracle a quick call." I tell them briskly interrupting their loving interlude. Placing a kiss on Thorns forehead.

They nod their heads at me as I turn on my heels headed straight for my office.

This is going to be an very awkward situation though. With the Queen being both Sins and Suns ex girlfriend, I think Thorn may find it be a little uncomfortable but unfortunately I can't see no other way around it.

Sitting at my desk I pick up the phone, hesitating before I dial, wondering if this is the right choice. I don't want to put Thorn in a position where she may feel a little less inferior than she actually is to us.

Sighing out deeply I resolve myself to dial the number apprehensively. Fuck!

All I can do is hope it all works out for the best though.

"Queen Miracle we have a situation!"

Chapter 13

We're out on the training field, watching each of our warriors practicing their battle moves, waiting patiently on Queen Miracles scheduled arrival.

The day is brightly sunny, one of the few here lately with the autumn days springing up upon us we are also preparing for our basic essentials for the upcoming winter months.

Trackers and hunters are blazing through the woods for their fresh hunts of meat substances, hopefully finding enough to carry us throughout the long cold winter nights and days.

The she wolves are happily tending to their overgrown gardens that supply most of our pack with our remaining food essentials.

And the little pups are running around playing vicariously with each other without a single worry in the world. Their little giggles and laughter can be heard escaping all around us.

This is pure heaven.

Slay, Sin, and I are watching our pack warriors, analyzing them all closely, as Thorn is sitting down on an upslope hill watching them also while playing with some cornflowers that surround her looking like a sweet angel while sitting amongst them.

"Hey girlie what's up?" I hear my sister Lila yell as she quickly approaches Thorn with her mate Marc straggling along not to far behind her.

She came to say goodbye to her back stabbing friend Nina.

"Lila! Come sit!" Thorn calls out waving her hand over for Lila.

Lila crashes down beside her on the ground while Marc gingerly makes his way over to us.

"What's up?" Marc ask with a broad smile when he reaches us.

"Gas prices!" I deadpan.

He just rolls his eyes at me. He has a habit of doing that a lot apparently.

Slay and Sin fill him up on what's been happening with all of us lately. I zone them out peering over at Lila and Thorn that are both laughing and what I can only assume is gossiping with each other.

Straining my ears, I try to zero in on their conversation, nosily wanting to know what has Thorn smiling broadly about with Lila.

"So I take you are not a virgin anymore?" Thorn ask Lila quietly. Lila blushes a pretty shade of red at her forward questioning.

Maybe I shouldn't listen any longer? Not really wanting to hear about my sisters ongoing love life, I return my attention back to the others intent on listening in on their conversation instead, that is until I hear Lila ask Thorn a very prominent question that has my ears perking up instantly.

"Aren't you a virgin?" Lila ask Thorn lowly. Thorn releases a light giggle at her.

"No. Actually, I've been with two people. A guy and a girl." Thorn tries to keep her voice low but with my super hearing I subsequently heard every word of her statement.

What the hell?

She can't be serious! Can she?

"Did she....?" Sin starts to ask but trails off staring over at Thorn and Lila curiously.

"I think she did." Slay says cutting off Sin and staring at the them with awe and curiosity.

I guess I'm not the only one listening in. But both Lila and Thorn are oblivious to us rudely listening in their private conversation or what they seem to think is a private conver-sation to them anyway.

"Both? Wow I honestly never pictured that about you." Lila states. Hell me neither sister.

"Why? I mean, it was like playful experimenting. It was just two girls who were wondering what it would be like." Thorn shrugs her shoulders. I wish I could see her face but unfortunately her back is facing me.

"Was she like your friend or something?" Lila questions her curiously. My ears perk up again as I lean in closer to them really wanting the know the entire story.

"Actually, she was older than me, but not by much. She use to my friend Tristan's girlfriend. But one night after they had a major fight and broke up she came crying to me in my room and well one thing led to another. We only did it once but I will tell you that being with a woman is a lot different then being with a man." Thorn replies chuckling softly. I think my damn dick just exploded. Man that's such a fucking turn on, my mind automatically goes to picturing Thorn with another woman. Fuck!

"How?" Man, my sister is curious! But at this moment I'm really damn glad that she actually is.

"Well a woman is soft, gentle, and knows exactly what another woman wants. A man....well, a man can sometimes miss certain things that a woman likes, if you know what I mean?" Thorn must of had a bad experience with the one guy that she was with but I will gladly show her what a real man can do. After that I know she will be singing a different tune.

"Marc knows what I like. He's gentle and loving and always gives me orgasm." Like says proudly. We all turn to Marc curiously, who is now looking slightly embarrassed at Lila's definition of him.

"What can I say I got the right moves." Marc whispers to us very quietly smiling ruefully at us.

Ewe, I really don't want to hear that shit.

"Man come on that's my sister. Damn!" I state dramatically.

Marc just laughs while rolling his damn eyes at me again.

"I can't tell you his name." Thorn insist to Lila with me missing half of the damn conversation apparently.

"Why not?" Lila ask.

"Because Lila, if your brothers knew his name they would probably kill him and he's way too sweet to be killed." Thorn laughs rambunctiously. I crease my brows glowering at her back.

"She's right I would probably kill him." Slay comments with a growl that's just barely above a whisper.

"She said the asshole was too sweet! Sweet my fucking ass!" Sin snarls. "I'll show her sweet!"

"I won't tell them. I promise." Lila presses Thorn further. A silence awaits us all.

Just say his fucking name! I growl in my head.

"Nope not gonna happen!" Thorn shakes her head vehemently. Fuck!

Come on Lila press her some more. I urge my sister on in my head. You can do it.

"Alpha the Queen and Kings are here." Flex interrupts my prodding announcing the Queen and Kings untimely arrival.

Fuck! Just when it was about to get to the good part. I guess I'll have to find out later.

"Alright thank you just send them around the back Flex." Slay gruffly informs him.

"Fuck! What bad timing!" Sin mumbles under his breath. I have to wholeheartedly agree with him.

"Thorn, Lila. The Queen and Kings are here." Slay informs them.

Lila and Thorn both jump up to their feet quickly while dusting off their clothes, looking a tad nervously at the back gate entranceway.

I stifle a laugh at them, even if they are royalty, I know the Queen very well. We dated for just a short two weeks before we broke up. Thankfully though the break up was amicable. She did break my heart slightly mainly from being pushed away from her then but that was a long time ago and now I'm actually happy for her.

Miracle and two of the Kings, if I can remember correctly, I think their names are Trigon and Baron entered the back-yard with poise and grace.

As they come through the gates back entranceway every-one bows down in respect to all of them.

Miracle gradually makes her way over to us with a genuine loving smile on her face but before she reaches us she spots Thorn and Lila standing directly behind us. Her eyes widen suddenly when she's sees them, Miracles smile grows even more broader as she swiftly rushes over to them. Ignoring us completely.

"Thorn Rose! Oh my, it's been such a long time, how have you been?" Miracle ask her as she reaches her, giving her giant hug. Everyone looks on at them curiously.

How the hell does she even know the Queen?

"I'm great Miracle. How is the family?" Thorn ask Miracle grinning at her.

Okay now I'm really confused.

"How do you two know each other?" I ask stepping up closer to them while her two mates step up behind Miracle.

"Uhm, well she's a friend of ours Sun." Miracles simply an-swers me briskly. Leaving me more curious than ever before.

"Hello Thorn. It's been a while. How is your brother?" King Baron ask.

Alright this is getting to be ridiculous!

"He's good Baron thanks for asking." Thorn states politely.

"Alright, I give, how do you really know each other?" I question glancing at each one of them suspiciously.

"Sun like I said she's a family friend. So where are the two prisoners?" Miracle ask quickly changing the subject unexpectedly.

While Slay sorts out all the details with them I grab ahold of Thorns wrist dragging her along with me. She lets out a tiny gasp as I lead her away from the others hurriedly.

When we finally reach the end of the fence line, I stop, looking around making sure nobody else is around to be able to hear us.

"Okay. How do you know the Queen?" I rush to ask her.

"How do you know the Queen?" She retaliates by throwing my question right back at me, smirking up at me.

The little minx.

"I use to date her." I simply state making Thorn frown up at me.

"What? But...really?" She ask me astonishingly.

Why is that so damn hard to believe?

"Yes. It only lasted a few weeks but we did date her for awhile, me and Sin both did." I affirm determinedly.

"Did...did you...?" She inquired nervously.

"No we didn't have sex if that's what you were going to ask." I grumble. "We didn't date her that long."

"Now how do you know her?" I ask suggestively folding my arms across my chest.

Thorn nervously looks away from me, hesitating with her answer. Her cove blue orbs begin to search all around the backyard, deflecting, trying to look at anything around her, while her eyes keep avoiding me.

"Thorn." I say drawling out her name.

"I know her son." She reluctantly tells me still not able to look at me directly in my eyes.

"How?....how do you know her son Thorn and which one?" I inquire cocking my head to the side.

"Look Sun can we please just go back? It's very rude with us being out here while the Queen and Kings visit?" She says abruptly, with a bit of edge to her tone.

I quickly noticed how she is determinedly trying to divert the subject but apparently I'm not going to get any answers out of her right now anyway. So with a slight resignation, I just give in.

"Fine let's go." I reply sighing. She walks ahead of me a few steps as we go back to the house with my mind whirling around with a ton a questions cycling rapidly through it.

Who is this mystery guy that was her first? Who was the girl? How does she know Miracle? What the hell is going on? Why's is she acting so nervous?

Watching her as she walks ahead of me I can't help but to watch her ass jiggle in those tight ass blue jeans she's wearing that fit her to a damn T.

Then my thoughts go on a very different naughty path suddenly remembering her conversation she had with Lila about her being with another woman.

Just placing that damn sultry picture in my mind makes me instantly fucking hard.

"Are you coming?" Thorn ask with her head turned back regarding me.

"I wish!" My wolf Stinger speaks up, growling in my head.

"You and me both buddy!"

Queen Miracle and the Kings were nice enough to join us for dinner tonight before escorting Nina and Storm away to their Realm.

We're all enjoying our meal of juicy spicy venison that our she wolves worked extra hard to prepare for the occasion.

The conversation around me is lively with Slay and Sin each sitting beside me and the others across from us, I couldn't remember exactly the last time that I have laughed so much than I have tonight.

Although I still find it a little suspicious how easily Thorn is getting along with Miracle. They both act like their old friends. Laughing and yucking up, it only makes me more bound and determined to get to the bottom of that.

Deep into a heavy conversation with Sin about our trainers I overhear Thorn mention something along the lines involving her father.

Instantly quietening, I horn in on their conversation noting Thorns distress.

"He's gone completely and utterly mad. The things that he said to me was revolting. Now he knows exactly where I'm at and I'm terrified that he will now come for me." Thorn tells Miracle with a slight tremble in her tone. Miracle reaches out for her hand placing her hand on top of Thorns hand lovingly.

"I will do all that I can to help you Thorn. We all will." Miracle assures her with resound determination laced throughout her features and tone.

"Thorn I had the same particular problem happen with my own father the only exception being that my father was not after me but one of my brothers. I unfortunately ended his life brutally in a fight we had over it. Spent years in the dungeon for it. But I couldn't tell anyone why I did it or who my father was trying to violate. I did, after all, kill him so in my misguided assumptions I thought that I actually deserved the punishment for it. But Miracle showed me how wrong I was on that assumption. So I sort of know what you're experiencing and like Miracle said we will do anything to help you, in anyway we can." King Trigons confession rattles me to the very depths of my core.

To know what he must of went through then and still come out aspiring to be better is a rare accomplishment indeed. I have nothing but respect for him.

"Thank you. All of you. Somehow I will stop my father no matter what it takes and thank you Trigon. I know that must of been hard for you to share with all of us." Thorns gratitude is infectious.

"Yes thank you Trigon and I'm also sorry that you had to go through such a unfortunate event but if you ever need anyone to talk to, I'm all ears." I smile over at him as I tell him and I devotedly mean every word I said.

"Thanks. I appreciate it. It was something that was definitely hard to overcome. That's why I think it's imperative for you Thorn to get far away from here as soon as possible. If your father knows where you are at then it won't be long before he comes to retrieve you. Maybe you might think about coming back with us? I know Cameron wouldn't mind seeing you again." Thorn looks directly at me and my brothers after Trigon mentioned Cameron.

Then it suddenly all fucking clicks. Cameron was the guy she was talking about earlier with Lila. Damn! This is so messed up.

My own damn mate had a love tryst with my former girlfriends son?

I know it may sound impossible but with supernaturals and are ability to withstand aging like others the improvable soon becomes the provable, in our world anyway.

"Thank you Trigon but we are probably going to escape to the Invivus Realm soon." Thorn informs him blushing slightly, looking a tad bit uncomfortable suddenly.

"The Invivus Realm?" Miracle ask.

It's Slay who fills them all in on the prophecy and all that it includes while I casually stare over at Thorn who still has a a shade of light pink caressing her cheeks from her apparent embarrassment.

Well I guess I don't have to prod her any further about her past lover then with the exception of the girl she was with of course but maybe I can ask Tristan about her or maybe not.

They way he has been acting today is fairly suspicious. Something must of happened between Thorn and him because he has been acting like an asshole today. He totally avoided coming to dinner with us tonight and has been treating Thorn like an enemy and not a friend all day.

He suppose to be the one protecting her but how can he if he constantly just walks away from her every time she even tries to talk to him?

"Maybe they had a lover's quarrel?" Stinger breaks through my thoughts.

"He is not her lover!" I disagree.

"But he wanted to be!" He can want all that he damn well wants, it's not going to happen!

"Well he's not. She's our mate not his!" I say very determinedly with a visceral growl toward Stinger.

"Mine!" Stinger growls.

"Yes ours!" I wholeheartedly agree with him.

"I love mate!" Stinger admits.

Peering over at Thorn who is observing Slay as he talks with Miracle and the others. I think about Stingers admission.

My heart begins to fluctuate rapidly. Do I love her? I love her smile, her tenderness, hell, I even love her spitfire attitude.

Whenever she talks to me she treats me like I'm the only person that matters at that very moment.

And every time she walks into a room I feel my heartbeat speed up a little bit faster.

Is that love? I don't know but I've never experienced this feeling before ever. Not even with my past lovers.

I long to be near here. I hate being away from her even for second.

Is that love?

I would do anything for her. Even lay down my very own life for her.

But is that love?

As I watch her beautiful blue eyes stare intently at every word Slay is speaking the overwhelming feeling hits me like a ton of bricks on top of my damn hard head.

"I think I may love her also!" I admit it to him and even more I finally admit to myself.

I love Thorn!

I love every damn thing about her. From the tip of her head down to her feet I love every damn inch of her.

It's a daunting prospect though. She has already left us twice. Although one was of our own damn doing, how can I make understand that she doesn't have to runaway from us any longer?

If I show or tell her how much I do in fact love her will she so easily just runaway from us again.? From me?

I can't risk that. So I decidedly will keep my love that I feel for her to myself for now. Just until I can make sure she will never leave us again.

I'm terrified if I tell her she may just do that though, runaway, and this time she may not ever come back.

"Wow. I never put two and two together. I should of known that you were the lost princess of the Invivus Realm. I knew your mother. Long before she ever had you that is. I met her a few times years ago and to say that you look just like her would be a vast understatement. I just knew, every time I looked at you there was always just something that was niggling at me at the back of my mind because you looked so damn familiar to me. I'm sorry Thorn I should have known." King Baron states with sincerity drawing me out of my love sick musings. "It was right in front of my face and I didn't even realize it" he adds

"You knew my mother?" Thorn ask King Baron wistfully.

But before King Baron could retaliate an answer the dining room door crashes open suddenly with a reverting bang against the dining room wall.

Standing in the doorway is a bloody and beat up Flex with his hand on his head where the blood is flowing freely down his face and breathing rather erratically.

"She's escaped!" He breathlessly announces.

Jumping to our feet quickly, me, Sin, and Slay run over to Flex immediately.

"Who escaped Flex?" Slay ask holding up Flex with his arm around his shoulders.

"Storm. She escaped. I...was guarding her like you asked and...out of nowhere....someone came and...bashed me on my...damn head...knocking me out, completely uncon-scious." Flex grumbles stumbling over slightly in Slays arms as Slay braces him tighter he lifts his body up to steady Flex better.

"Pan!" Sun snarls from behind me. Glancing back at him my brow creases in frustration.

"You think so?" I ask Sin. Pan has always been reliable and very loyal I can't picture him having to have anything to do with Storms escape.

"Yes. He's always had a thing for Storm I just didn't think he would ever take it this damn far." Sin barks combing his fingers through his hair clearly upset over this unfortunate event.

"Pan is loyal Sin. He even apologized profusely to you. I don't think it's him but if it is I will gladly let you deal with him. I'm going to take Flex to the pack doctor to make sure he's okay. Don't do anything stupid Sin before I get back. We will handle this but I need to know you won't go after him." Slay declares adjusting Flex to his side.

"What about Nina?" Thorn ask as she stands up from her chair walking slowly over to us.

"She still locked up. Only Storm...escaped." Flea confirms wincing.

"I'll be right back. Please excuse your majesties. I'm sorry for this disruption." Slay states nodding his head in Miracles and the Kings direction.

"Nonsense take care of your pack. We will escort Nina to our Realm right now and if you need any further assistance please don't hesitate to call." Miracles sweetly comments as her and the Kings make their exit.

But not before they tell Thorn and all the rest of us good-bye.

Left alone now with Sin and Thorn. I thread my fingers through my hair just as Sin did aggravated over all of this unexpected shit.

"We need to go look for Pan and have the others search the premises for Storm and him if he's involved." Sin instructs still looking overly upset.

"You need to calm down first Sin. You heard Slay. He doesn't think Pan had anything to with her escape." I don't either but I don't know Pan quite like Sin does know him.

"Slay might not think so but I damn well do. I knew Sun. I knew he was infatuated with Storm and I did nothing to dissuade of him from it. I got to find Storm." Sin stops his ranting glancing over at Thorn his face soon changes from being frantic to a steady eerily calm.

Then like a lightening bolt it's like something just clicked inside of him all of the sudden.

"I swear to you Sun I am done! I'm done with fucking women! They are always ruining my damn life. I just lost my best friend because of one!" Sin frantically starts pacing the room irritably again.

Something just doesn't seem right with him. He's acting very strangely.

"Not all women are like Storm Sin! I'm definitely not! And you don't know for sure if it even was Pan that helped her escape. You're just jumping to conclusions. Give him the benefit of the doubt and if your so done with women like you said then you might as well go ahead and reject me now! Because I will not wait around for you forever!" Thorn bellows loudly. I wince when I hear the hurt and disdain flowing out of her angry tone. "I'm tired of the way you're always treating me."

She stares at Sin for a moment but when Sin doesn't offer a rebuttal back to her and just looks at her scowling down at her instead, Thorn huffs out a deep breath before she stomps away from us dramatically. Slamming the dining room door behind her in her wake.

How can such a good day turn into a nightmare so damn quickly and why is Sin suddenly acting so damn fishy?

"I think she means it. You need to learn how to control your damn temper Sin or else we are all going to lose her and I promise you if we do I will blame you. Get your head out of your damn ass!" I snarl at him pointing my finger directly in his stubborn ass face. "What's gotten in to you? Why are you acting this way?"

"I'm going after Pan?" Is all he that he says before he dashes out of the door quickly, ignoring me, leaving me standing alone in the room looking at his back as he goes, sighing. What is going on with him?

Something seems different about him!

Chapter 14

I took off out of the dining room in search for my friend Pan or what I use to consider my friend anyway.

I'm fuming mad.

If Pan does have anything to do with Storms escape I will tear his ass to shreds with my own fucking claws and not even think twice about it. He doesn't even actually know what he has done. All of my strategic plans are just going to fucking waste.

Slamming the back door open I step out into the back yard sniffing the air for Pans own signature smell. A mix of pine cones and white ash that I can always detect no matter how far away he seems to be.

Walking through the backyard sniffing the air I think back to mine and Pans friendship.

While my parents were still alive I met Pan when I was around sixteen. He was a bit older than me by a few years but somehow we both managed to click. Especially after he saved me from some love sick girls who were chasing after me at the time.

Coming out of the high school doors after the last bell rang for the day, these damn girls would not leave me alone no matter what I did or said they were always constantly bugging me. Batting their damn false eyelashes up at me.

I was getting frustrated with all of them, trying my damnest to hurry up and escape them and when I wasn't paying attention to where I was going I accidentally bumped into what I now know was Pan, nearly knocking both of us flat on our asses.

He noticed the girls coming up from behind me fast and as I sighed out in frustration he laughed at me.

"Need some help?" He ask eyeing the girls as they drew closer to us.

"Yes. They are driving me nuts man. I just can't seem to shake them!" I huffed out frustratingly.

"Come here!" He insisted. I took a small step closer to him eyeing him suspiciously. When I finally got in front of him, he watched as the damn girls drew closer. As soon as they were close enough he hurriedly reached out for me grabbing me by my arms he pulled me closer to him.

As the girls got right up to us. He fucking surprised the shit out of me.

He lowered his head and kissed me full on, on my mouth grabbing the back of my head he pushed me closer to him. It was a mad lovers kiss.

I struggled to get away from him at first but then I started relax and enjoyed his kiss as his tongue slipped provocatively into my mouth. Making my dick harden instantly.

I got swept up in his kiss not really caring any longer about the random girls chasing me.

When he finally broke the kiss from me he stared at me with wanting desire caught up in his eyes and then just chuckled slightly.

I was completely taken aback. I have never kissed a dude before. It was something I never imagined myself ever doing.

"They left." He huskily tells me. I angle my head to look back and watched as all of the girls that were chasing after me were gingerly walking away from us both disappointed.

"T-thanks." I stammer as he lets me go.

"No problem stud. What's your name?" He ask folding his arms across his chest.

And from then on out we were the closest of friends.

It never progressed any further than that kiss between him and I. But sometimes late night I often wondered.

Now our relationship has turned into something that I can't even define any longer.

Hell I really didn't care that he was even with Storm but I did care about him. Mine and Storms relationship is something of a mystery. But he doesn't know that. Nobody does.

It will definitely hurt more than it should if he did help Storm escape. I honestly don't know if I could ever forgive him for such backstabbing behavior. I had a fucking plan and he just may have ruined it all.

I trusted him.

Maybe Thorn and Slay are right. Maybe I am jumping to conclusions?

I hope that's the case anyway because if it's not it's really going to tear me apart.

Walking against the fence line still sniffing at the air I catch a tiny whiff of Pans scent off in the distance.

Running fast in that direction, I follow his scent all the way to the backside of our property line.

Slowing my steps as I draw nearer, I keep following his scent until the scent becomes overwhelming stronger.

I stop when I see him at the edge of the forest standing alone but he seems to be talking with someone that I can't actually see. His lips are steadily moving as he animatedly talks to whomever is hidden.

Edging a little closer I creep to the other side of the yard to get a better view of whoever the hell he is talking to.

Pausing, I strain to listen.

"We can't tell them. I don't think they are ready to hear this Onyx. They have enough going on with their new mate Thorn." Pan speaks lowly to this guy named Onyx who is trying his best to hide amongst the tree line of the forest.

"I'm tired of waiting Pan. You need to tell them and soon or else I will." Onyx says sounding slightly irritated.

What the hell are they talking about?

Stepping closer I accidentally step on a fucking twig announcing my approach loudly. Damn!

They both snap their heads in my direction quickly. Fuck! Busted.

Coming out of the shadows I walk over to both of them. Pan looks at me like he's frightened of me which only manages to peek my curiosity even more.

"What's going on?" I ask as I approach them.

"Sin, what are doing out here?" Pan ask desperately. Looking very anxious.

"You first Pan. What's going on?" Waving my hand at this Onyx guy who is still hiding amongst the damn trees.

Pan sighs, "I found my mate Sin. This is Onyx. Onyx this my Alpha Sin." Pan introduces us reluctantly. Onyx steps out from between the trees slowly. Eyeing me with blatant curiosity as I eye him the same.

"Nice to meet you." Onyx says embarrassingly so.

"Same," I tell him then turn my attention back to Pan beside me, "so this is what you've been hiding? When did you two meet? What about Storm? Did you help her escape?" The questions start to flood out of me rapidly.

"Woah. Woah. Storm escaped?" Pan ask with confusion marring all over his face.

"Yes and I actually thought that you might have helped her." I admit to him though a tad to aggressively.

"I didn't help that bitch. I told you Sin that I was sorry and Onyx and I met just two days ago. He is Alpha Curtis's Beta, that's why we didn't tell you. You got to believe me. Storm was just a damn fling she didn't mean anything to me. I would never help her escape I value our friendship way too much to do that to you Sin." Now I feel like an utter ass. I should of had more faith in him but I hate hearing him call Storm such awful names. I just sigh.

"I believe you but why are you keeping your mate a secret? It's not like he's working with Curtis or is he?" I ask peering over at a very anxious Onyx that is now standing closely beside Pan.

"Never. I would never do something like that. I had no idea what Alpha Curtis was even planning!" Onyx says. I glare at him trying to find any deception clouding his face but thankfully I find none.

"I believe you. I'm sorry Pan. For thinking that you helped Storm. When I heard that she escaped I just saw red and I wasn't exactly thinking straight." I apologize to him determinedly. I don't want to lose his friendship not after all of these years. He means too much me.

"You're fine but we need to find her. She is probably meeting up with that guy that she's been passing information to about our Luna." Our Luna. The Luna I actually offended not even thirty minutes ago. What a laugh.

"Is Luna alright? Is somebody with her?" Pan asks me anxiously when he sees the stoic look on my face.

She's perfectly fine I left with her Sun. Who really cares anyway? I think to myself.

Then catching the confused look on Pans face I now grow anxious.

Fuck! I almost fucked up!

"I got to get back to the house." I rush to say as I turn toward the house in a quick and panicked run, headed back to make sure Thorn is safe: supposedly.

I found her in the living room with Sun, both of them were sitting on the couch watching the damn television.

I stared at them both curiously as I entered the room wondering how either of them could be so damn calm with them both thinking that Storm is now free and out there somewhere probably more than likely planning something evil in their eyes anyway.

But they both seemed relaxed and way too calm just watching the fucking tv like they don't have damn care in the world.

"Did I miss something?" I ask as I stroll into the room sitting down in my usual chair just eyeing them both precariously.

"Nope. Just watching the tv." Sun shrugs his shoulder dismissively. Looking, quite honestly, like he's actually very happy.

Do they suspect something?

Leaning back in my chair I still keep watching them both as they stare at the tv screen, placing my hand under my chin with my elbow on the arm of the chair. I scowl at them, trying to my best to decipher their nonchalant attitudes.

Something just doesn't seem right!

"Okay what gives? Why are you two acting so damn calm? You do realize that there's a loose maniac out there right?" I ask but they both just give my dismissive shrugs returning their attention back the damn tv.

Creasing my eyebrows at them I lean forward in the chair just to see what has both of them so damn captivated at the screen.

The picture is a bit fuzzy but I can make out some of the features of the person appearing on the screen.

Leaning in closer to get a better view of the screen, I nearly fall off of my fucking chair when I realize suddenly who is actually on the damn screen.

"Is that?" I start to ask but trail off as I fall to my knees on the floor to squat down in front of the tv to get an up close view. I didn't know we had fucking cameras in the dungeon.

I'm fucked!

"Why is Slay on the fucking tv?" I ask peering over my shoulder at Thorn and Sun sitting on the couch.

Both of whom are smiling at me widely. Sun just points to the tv not ushering a single syllable.

My gaze hesitantly goes back to viewing the tv.

I watch as Slay stands in front of very familiar cell bars that's located in our own dungeon. Fuck!

His lips are moving frantically but unfortunately there's no sound coming from the tv.

"Why can't we hear him?" I ask absentmindedly still staring at the screen.

"There's no sound. Just watch." Sun informs me.

The screen begins to flicker somewhat, glitching in and out suddenly, then moves to a different angle.

The picture on the screen now is inside of the dungeon cell room.

It starts off a bit blurry then comes into focus suddenly showcasing a very pissed off Storm apparently yelling at Slay with her body half bent over and her hands swinging around in the air.

"He fucking caught her?" I question Sun turning my gaze back to him. Fuck!

"Yep! I don't know how he did it but when he came in here he turned on the tv and asked for both of us to watch. Said he had a surprise for us both. Then just left, smiling." Sun states never taking his eyes off of the screen.

"I'm going down there." I stand up from the floor quickly. "She's mine to deal with." I add before I pivot around headed straight for fucking dungeon. I got to stop this.

Just as I entered the dungeon I can hear Storms loud screams echoing up to me.

Stomping down the primitive staircase I hear bits and pieces of her tantrum. When I hit the bottom stair I halted, just to listen in to her frantic ramblings.

"Storm. You did this to yourself. Stop blaming other people for your own actions. What I don't understand is why Storm? Why did you risk everything over something so damn trivial? You knew you would never be our Luna and yet you kept on with this farce trying your damnest in every way possible to become our Luna." Slay questions her with a sound of regret whispering out through his tone. "Why?"

"I don't have to tell you a damn thing. You're not my Alpha anymore remember?" Storms snarky attitude will definitely end up getting her killed.

Stop it Storm.

"No I'm not but that's not my fault now is it? No. It's absolutely all yours. So why? You have a family Storm. What will your mother and father or even your sisters think about what you have become?" Slay states.

"I don't give a damn what they think. I was doing it for them anyway but they all thought I was just absolutely crazy."

Storm says, she sounds so damn defeated. Just shut your fucking mouth Storm, I keep protesting loudly in my mind.

"Why then? I don't understand." Slay questions.

"You wouldn't. You couldn't possibly understand Slay. You and your brothers have always had it so damn easy. A loving caring family that has everyone's damn respect. Now you all even have a damn fucking mate to make all of your lives complete but what do I have Slay?" Storm pauses. I hear her footfalls making their way closer to the cell bars. I can't stand to hear this.

"I have nothing! No damn mate! No one to love me like I damn well deserve! I don't even have anyones damn respect!" Storm screams heatedly I can hear her breathing picking up erratically suddenly.

Please Storm I'm begging you just shut up now!

"What about your family Storm? They love you, I know they do, I've seen it. Your parents has always treated you kindly. They never neglected you nor your sisters. Are you trying to tell me that they did something to you or are you just lying again just to save face?" I notice that Slay is starting to get pretty defensive. As each world he tends to utter just starts to climb a decibel louder.

"No they never did anything like your thinking Slay. They are good people. They love me and my sisters. Please don't think badly of them. This is all on me. They had nothing to do with this." She starts rushing her words sounding more desperate as she goes.

Fuck! I hear her pain through her words.

"Did you ever love Sin, Storm? Or was he just another fucking conquest for you?" At Slays questions, I take a small step closer to the cell. Desperately wanting to hear her answer.

Come on Storm don't fuck this up!

"Yes. In a way I do. I always have." She whispers it but I can hear it all very vividly.

She confesses her love for me to Slay. I want to scream at her. But I just fucking can't. Damn!

"So you really love him? That's what I don't understand Storm. If you really loved him then why would you want to hurt his mate? The Moon Goddess chose her to be his mate and not you for a reason. Surely you have to understand that? If you hurt Thorn then you potentially would be hurting Sin also." Slay states it so matter of factly that it does make some sort of sense. But unfortunately Slay doesn't know that I was the one that inevitably pushed Storm into this. It was all me.

This is all my damn fault. She's getting blamed for everything.

I bite the side of my cheek to keep from blabbering something out loud that I know shouldn't.

I did this. Not her. I keep repeating the phrase in my head.

Stop blaming her Slay and I just wish that Storm would shut the hell up already.

She's going to ruin everything.

"He doesn't want her Slay. He said so himself plenty of times. He even told you. Don't you remember? That night on my porch? I was suppose to be his Luna not that fucking bitch Thorn. He told me so!" Storm yells out uncontrollably.

Reflecting back on my own damn thoughts. I'm the one to blame. I have to get her out of this.

"Don't call her a bitch Storm your already walking on thin ice as it. I will not have you slandering my mate! She has done nothing to you!" Slay yells back at Storm tempestuously.

"Nothing? Slay she has stolen my damn happiness away for me. How can you stand there and say that she has done nothing to me when she most definitely fucking has? Don't you see? She has stolen away the love of my life and took my damn position away from me! She's not as innocent as you may think she is. She took everything away from me!" Storm loudly refutes Slay with a tremendous amount of anger.

Why can't she just stop?

"It's not your damn position Storm it's hers! She didn't steal away anything from you! You did this. Not her! Do you actually know why her damn father is after her? I can tell by the look on your face that you don't so let me enlighten you shall I? He wants to fucking make her his Luna! He wants to sleep with his own damn daughter. His own fucking flesh and blood and you just gave him the opportunity to find her so he can accomplish it! I hope you're fucking proud of yourself Storm! No. She didn't do this. You fucking did!" Slay screams. His screams echo all throughout the dungeon loudly.

I flinch hearing him so damn upset.

Now guilt runs through my damn veins because its not only Storm at fault I am also. I fucking did this!

This has to absolutely stop now!

"I didn't know Slay. Honestly I didn't. I just thought he wanted her back. I knew he hated her but I didn't think he wanted....that." Storm says breathlessly.

That's my girl.

"Exactly right Storm. YOU DIDN'T FUCKING THINK!" Slay screams at her maddeningly loud. I rear my head back from the very onslaught of his anger. I can't take this anymore.

"Stop!" I scream back finally making my appearance known to them.

Slay looks at me while furrowing his brows down in confusion. I just keep my eyes on him not even taking a chance to look over in Storms direction as I make my way to him.

"Just stop Slay. It's not all her damn fault. It's mine also. I did this. Blame me." I desperately plead with him still not looking over at Storm. I just can't.

"What are you talking about Sin?" He asks. He just doesn't get it.

Inhaling deeply I open my mouth to tell him then stop myself before ushering a single word.

How do I tell him? How do I tell him that this is all my fault because I was basically stupid?

"I did this Slay. If it wasn't for me Storm wouldn't be in this position. I used her for my own selfish gains. I did pushed Thorn away and I did tell Storm that I would make her my Luna." Swallowing my pride as I tell him I go onward.

"Don't you see Slay? If I wasn't such a damn hardheaded jackass Storm would have never done any of this. I didn't want Thorn. Hell I don't even know what I want anymore. I just know that I can't let you punish Storm for something that

I did. I have been lying Slay. I've been fooling everyone." Here comes the hard part I'm afraid that Slay may never be able to forgive me once I confess this all to him but I fucking have to. I can't let it end this way for Storm, not when I know that I'm the guilty party.

"I'm sorry Slay. What I'm about to tell you may destroy your trust in me. Hell you probably will even hate me for it." I take a deep breath before I carry on. Building up my courage.

"Sin don't." Storm pleas urgently to me coming closer to the cell bars.

"I have to Storm. He has to know the truth." I reply staunchly to her.

"Just say it Sin. What did you do?" Fuck! Here goes everything.

"I was the one who called Alpha March, Slay. It was me. Not Storm. I only did it because I wanted Thorn out of the picture. She was going to end up getting both you and Sun killed over this stupid fucking ass prophecy and I couldn't allow her to do it. I did it for you and Sun, Slay. Storm is pretty much innocent in all of it. All that she did was pass a few messages to Alpha Bakers Beta. Please understand Slay I did it to save your lives." I plead with him desperately. Hoping that he can at least understand why I did exactly what I did. "Because I love you." I add.

He just stands there silently staring at me.

"Say something Slay." I whine.

Slay lowers his head blowing out a huge strangled breath. When he finally does raise his head back up again all I can see on his face is clear disappointment.

"Sin. Why? I had it covered baby." Storm says but I chose to ignore her focusing everything instead on my brother Slay before me.

This foreboding silence that's hanging in air between us is daunting.

"Please say something." I beg reaching out my hand toward his arm but unfortunately he jerks his arm away from my hand immediately.

"Do you realize what you have done Sin! Her father will come after her and he will basically rape her into fucking submission." His voice begins to croak when he finally speaks to me.

"I know Slay but it was the only way that I could see to get her out of our lives quickly. I don't want her father to rape her Slay. I'm not that fucking uncaring. I just wanted her out of here and away from you both but this was the only way that I could of to do it." I try eagerly to make him understand exactly just why actually I did it. "We already lost our parents. I wasn't going to take the chance and lose you and Sunny also." I add.

"You we're both in on this?" He questions sadly.

"Yes. I'm sorry Slay. I asked Storm for her help. Please don't blame her." I rush to say still pleading with him.

"So this entire time you have been acting? Pretending to finally accept Thorn as your mate, for what? To leave? I don't understand." He inquires as he starts pacing the dungeon floor frantically.

"I pretended with her so I could get her back here so that her father could come and get her to take her away from here. From us. I did this for you Slay!" At my last sentence he stops his pacing turning to face me he sends me a visceral glare. "For both of you!"

"Do you love her?" Slay ask nudging his head in Storms direction.

I glance over to Storm who is now crying with little tears running down her beautiful face. Do I?

I stare at her for what seems like minutes before I hesitantly turn my head back to look at Slay.

"Yes. I really do love her." I finally claim holding my breath.

"I can't believe this! You love her? Her? No, you know what Sin. You did this for you and for her!" He points his finger at Storm, "Don't you even think for one second that you did me or Sunny a favor. We care about her! We want her here Sin!" He throws his hand up in the air while threading his fingers through his hair with the other hand. "You both disgust me!" He snarls.

"You both just signed her fucking death certificate and you don't even fucking care, do you? I should throw your dumb ass in that cell with her! Because you two fucking deserve each other!" He bellows at me, I take a step back from his viscous attack of words towards me.

"You're not understanding Slay!" I scream out very urgently. "She would of gotten you both killed!"

"No Sin, you just did," I scowl at him, "you don't fucking realize it do you? By you getting in touch with her father you are bringing him directly to our doorsteps and what do you exactly think that he is going to do with me and Sunny once he comes to get Thorn?" He ask me condescendingly.

"He will fucking kill us both and it will be all thanks to you!" He scolds me while jabbing his finger in my chest at each word he dispels toward me. "Not her! I told you that you could be with Storm. Why Sin? Why did you have to take it this far?" He spits out angrily.

His words hit my like a fucking wrecking ball.

Fuck! I didn't even realize. What the hell have I done? I just put my own brothers in danger without even thinking twice about it.

I'm worse than Thorn is.

Suddenly I can't seem to catch my breath. My heart starts racing inside of my chest rapidly and all the while I start getting very dizzy from it all.

"Yea, you get it now don't you and I just hope you can live with yourself knowing that you are the one who put me and Sunny in danger not Thorn. YOU!" He bellows the last word bending over to get right in my face as he does it.

"Sin. I love you. I truly do but after this I don't even know if I can call you my brother any longer? You are not the brother I use to know. You have changed so much that I don't even recognize you. I'm done with you Sin. Completely fucking done and as for you Storm. Miracle will be here in the morning to take you to her Realm to delve out your punishment and I truly hope it's something terrible. Sin. You are fucking lucky that I won't have Miracle taking you along with her. The only reason I'm not is because you are in fact my brother," he takes a step away from me eyeing me with so much disdain.

"On paper anyway." Slay determinedly quotes before he turns in his boots and leaves us both in the dreadful dungeon.

"Sin baby are you okay?" Storm ask but her voice seems like it's miles away from me. I can't even focus on it.

Absolutely repulsed by my own actions I start to feel nauseous running to the corner of the dungeon I throw up all over the dungeon floor.

What have I fucking done?

Chapter 15

I watched the television screen with a strong sense of despair hitting me straight down deep into my knotted gut.

I keep watching as I see Slay and Sin start to argue, over what, I have no idea about. But something is definitely not right.

Slay had so much repulsive anger on his face toward Sin that it nearly took my breath away from just seeing it displayed on his tortured face.

When I seen Slay finally walk away from Sin I jumped up from the couch, ready to chase after Slay but Sun prevented me from doing so by grabbing ahold of my wrist and pulling me back down on the couch beside him.

"Let them handle it Thorn." Sun insists softly but I still yearned to go find Slay. Something just wasn't right and by the look on Slays face just now I knew it had it be heartbreakingly horrible and I know Sunny had to see the same thing that I did.

"But Sun you saw the look on his face there is something wrong and we need to find out what it is." I desperately plead with him.

"No Thorn. Sin has been acting strange all night. I don't know what's going on with him either but let's just give Slay few seconds to calm down before we go barreling off after him." I hate it but Sun does seem to have a very valid point.

They are brothers after all, he may not like it too much if I intrude on whatever is going on between them but that still doesn't lessen my worries any.

"Fine." I relent turning my gaze back to the tv screen.

On the screen I watch again as Sin stumbles over to the cell bars grabbing ahold of them with his hands. Storm wraps her hands around his on the bars so tenderly.

The emotion flowing off of Storms face is one that I recognize fully, it's one of pure unadulterated love.

The thought of her loving him so deeply kept my eyes glued to the screen, mesmerized, by what I'm actually seeing. I just couldn't pry my eyes away from the damn screen.

Sin then leans into the cell bars a little bit closer as their faces press up against each others in what generally looks like a very passionate kiss.

I gasp out loudly, feeling shell shocked, at watching my mate kiss another woman so damn brazenly.

To actually see Sin kissing Storm like he is so desperately in love with her gives me a new found feeling of discomfort that I just can't seem to explain or even understand.

It's honestly strange: this new feeling I'm having toward my mates now. Since I shifted I have felt drawn to all of them even more than I ever have before.

Sun springs up from the couch quickly, jostling me on the couch as he jumps up from it then rushes to the tv to turn it off completely.

The screen goes black immediately but I still can't seem to take my eyes away from the television. My eyes seem to be transfixed upon it.

"Thorn." Sun drawls out my name in a very sincere but worried tone. Basically feeling sorry for me but I don't want his damn pity. There's no love loss between me and Sin, thankfully and there probably never will be.

If that's the way that Sin wants it, then, by all means, so fucking be it.

"It's fine Sun. It's not like there's any love loss between us anyway. I knew he was with Storm I just didn't realize how close they actually were." I tell him inhaling deeply I finally tear my eyes away from the blackened screen sliding them up to look at him.

His face shows utter remorse and a touch of regret on it but I just numbly shake my head at him. It's really not that big of a deal to me.

"Don't feel sorry for me Sun. Sometimes it just doesn't work out between mates. It's probably happened more times than either of us even know about." I state with slight conviction, though I hate that I noticed that I had a tiny tremble coming out in my tone. Shit!

"I'm so sorry Thorn. He has changed so damn much that sometimes I don't even recognize him anymore. I'm not saying this as an excuse for his behavior but he did start to change after our parents died and somehow for some damn unknown reason it just seemed to escalate." Sun tries to reassure me, although he is absolutely right. Their parents dying is not an excuse for Sin to rip someone's heart completely out of their damn chest. Rip my heart out? What am I even thinking?

"It does hurt Sun but not as much as you might think. Sin and I have never really been close. He has pushed me away from the start. I'm just glad I learned about this now rather than sometime later." Now I'm the one trying to reassure Sun. I give him a faint smile rising up from the couch I gradually make my way over to him.

"Stop worrying Sun. I'm okay. I don't blame you or your brother for Sins actions. He has made his choice and I'm fine with it." I try to insert my new found convictions to him. I don't know if it's more for him or for myself but no matter what I will stand strong through all of this. I just have too. I always have too.

"Just promise me one thing Thorn." Sun asks me while forming tiny crease lines on his forehead. It looks so damn cute that I want to take my finger and run it along the crinkled lines to stop his worrying.

"Hmmm." I hum to him as I take a tentative step toward him, cocking my head to the side. He looks so damn adorable I would probably just about promise him anything at this very moment. I gasp at my own inner thoughts. Calm your hormones down Thorn this is a serious situation, I chide myself. Get with the fucking program!

"Don't runaway again. Stay. Slay and I want you here. We want you as our mate and we want to make a life with you. Please don't leave just because my damn brother thinks out of his ass and not with his damn head." He thinks I'll runaway again?

I really want to dispel him of his worries completely and promise him that I will never leave his side again. I just don't know if that's a promise that I can actually keep though. Sometimes I just do feel like running. It's been my only escape mechanism.

Sighing, I rip my gaze away from him debating on how to explain my own irrational fears.

"Oh he thinks with his head alright just with the wrong damn one." Slay replies grumpily as he suddenly enters into the living area.

I watch him as he stomps his way over to me and Sun. His gait his strong but he looks so damn weary with a deep tormenting scowl etched all over his handsome face.

I hate this for him.

"What happened down there?" Sun ask just as Slay finally reaches us.

"I really don't want to talk about it." Slay attest with a deep baritone worried grumble.

"Tough because I want to know. There's something going on Slay. I could tell by the look on your face. We saw what happened in the dungeon. You were so pissed off at Sin that I actually thought you were going to hit him." I demand of him. I'm damn tired of not knowing what is actually going on around here. They always leave me out of these types of discussions and I'm damn well sick of it.

"Thorn please it's just going to hurt you and I don't want to hurt you beautiful." Slay pleads with me. His dark chocolate eyes gaze down at me full of determination and with a tiny hint of sadness encased in them.

Nope. I'm not falling for those damn puppy dog eyes again.

"Just tell me Slay. I'm a big girl I think I can handle it." I insist, Standing my ground, I place my hands on my hips to try and show more courage than I really actually have at the moment.

False bravado some might say.

"Fine but please after I tell you promise me that you won't runaway from me and Sun again." Slay pleads. What is it with these men and these damn promises!?

I look directly at him with a hostile glare aim directed right at him.

Why do they always assume I'll runaway? The first time, yes, it was clearly my doing but the second time was definitely on them and not me. Don't they have any faith in me?

Fine if it's the only way I can get him to tell me anything I guess I'll just have to surrender to it.

"I promise." I mock promise them both as I sneakily cross my fingers that lay upon my hip.

Slay eyes me suspiciously for a second, fully showing me how much he actually doubts my own word.

Rolling my damn eyes I uncross my fingers and with a heavy say I make my vow to them both.

"I promise I won't runaway again." I honestly vow this time.

"That's good but just remember the punishment you received from the very first time that you did it?" Slay questions. I just nod my head swallowing down a deep gulp. I remember it fucking clearly.

"I won't hesitate to do it again." Slay threatens while giving me a sexy ass smirk. Damn him!

I think all of the blood that was rushing through my damn brain just swooped straight down directly to my treacherous overheated vagina.

Squeezing my thighs together, I try to suppress a moan. Closing my eyes I take a deep breath and count to ten quickly.

"1, 2, 3, 4, 5, 6, 7, 8, 9, 10." Fuck! Didn't work! Opening my eyes again my gaze snaps right back to a still smirking ass sexy Slay.

Beside me Sun tries to hold in a laugh but doesn't seem to succeed at doing it at all. His breathy laughter escapes him unexpectedly.

"What?" I ask defensively with my eyes bouncing back and forth between a smirking Slay and a laughing Sun.

"You counted out loud beautiful." Slay informs me while trying to contain his own laughter.

Well double fuck!

"Do you want me to kick both of you in the balls?" I ask while furrowing my damn brows at both of them. It's so not funny.

"Oh beautiful we can smell your arousal." Slay says chuckling at me lightly. I huff, I'm so glad these two morons find it so damn amusing. "Do you need for us to take care of it for you?" Slay ask me huskily. Fuck!

"Well if you both keep laughing at me then neither of you will ever get close enough to even touch it!" I tell with snarky ass tone.

They both stop laughing immediately.

Each now showing straight firm thinned lips and serious expressions on their faces with straight stiffened spines.

That's what I thought. I harumph.

"Now can we please get back to the main subject here? What's going on Slay?" I grow serious glancing up at him. Trying to ignore my wanting arousal.

Slay blows out a ragged breath, hesitating momentarily before he actually decides to spill the beans to me.

I stand there stoically as Slay describes every horrid damn detail to me and Sun. With every word spewing out of Slays mouth his actions grow even more fevered.

Side eyeing Sun beside me, I notice his resolve quickly dissipating to an onslaught of complete unbridled mortification.

Well I'm thankful that at least two of my mates care about me.

"And I told him on paper anyway and then just left." Slay finishes his description of Sins betrayal with a distorted mixture of absolute anger and sadness written all over this face.

They both stare at me patiently waiting for my reaction, I assume.

I don't know what to tell them? If they are expecting me to break down from Slays news then they will both will be waiting it for a damn long while.

Honestly, the news about Sin and Storm doesn't bother me quite as much as they both probably think that it does.

The only thing that truly bothers me about any of this is how it's damaging their relationship as brothers.

My father already knew that I was here, regardless if it was at Sins doing or another's doing it was bound to happen anyway. I'm mad about it but what's done is done. I can't simply change it.

"Say something Thorn." Sun pleads to me desperately.

I can only presume that he actually thinks that I am going to runaway from them again. Since they were both so adamant about me promising them both that I wouldn't. Men ugh! Why do they always assume that a woman is weak and needs to run? Even though that was my first unavoidable thought actually.

"Okay." I finally reply shrugging my shoulder dismissively as I drop my hands away from my hips beside me.

"Okay? That's all you have to say? Where's the screaming, the cussing, the fucking tantrum? You just can't say okay Thorn. Don't hold it in! Show us exactly what you are feeling. It's okay to let it all out!" Slay comments waving his hands in the air clearly not understanding my resigned emotions.

"Slay. I said it was okay what more can I say," I reply to him softly, "the only thing that bothers me is that this is going to put a a very hard strain between you two and Sins relationship as brothers. He is going to eventually end up blaming me for it like he has blamed me for everything else that's happened so far but I just may have a solution." One that I truly hope both of them will come to realize that it will be for the best in the long run. At least I hope it will anyway.

"What?" Sun presses looking curiously down at me. As I watch both of them I start to get a tiny bit apprehensive. I just know that they are not going to like what I am about to suggest to them.

Steeling my nerves I clear my throat before I explain it to them.

"Before I tell you, you both need to please promise me that you won't get mad." I bristle away from them when I see the sudden fierce looks that they both glower at me with.

"Hey you made me promise it's only fair that you return the favor." I argue. Bravely defending my stance.

"Fine what it is?" Sun solemnly agrees I nod my head at him then turn my attention to Slay waiting patiently for him to agree also.

"Fine." He drawls it out but eventually agrees though somewhat sparingly.

"Alright. I promised I wouldn't runaway but maybe we can runaway together?" I stiffen up when they both look down at me with disputing looks on their faces, "let me explain." I rush to tell them.

"Sin and Storm require some time alone right now so they can both work through whatever is going on between them and I desperately want to get away from them both. We also need sometime alone to work on our own relationships too. We were planning to go to the Invivus Realm anyway right?

So why don't we just go now?" I sincerely hope they both can understand exactly why I'm asking them to do this. "It can be like a mini vacation." I add slightly giggling.

"There's only one problem with that solution Thorn. Storm is going to be taken away in the morning for committing treason against her Alphas. She will be punished accordingly for all that she has done just like Nina has." Oh. I didn't realize that. Well fuck! Now what?

We all grow silent standing around in the living area trying to formulate another plan of action. Well at least I am. There has to be a way that we can all resolve this situation without Sin hating me even more. Not that I really care how Sin actually feels about me but I hate that there is so much turmoil between him and his brothers.

"Oh wait! I think I may have it!" I tell them excitedly as I start pacing the floor.

They are really not going to like this one though. It's way worse than my other idea but it may be our only way to resolve our issues. In my view anyway.

"We still go to the Realm like we already planned to do but we have to put a hold on our own relationships." I assert.

"What are you talking about Thorn? I don't want to put a hold on our relationship! That's absolutely absurd!" Sun exclaims quite loudly. "Are you like breaking up with us?" Sun ask me as he lowers his voice then peers at me with a forlorn look.

He gazes at me with such heartsick look that it almost makes me crumble.

"Hold on Sun. I didn't mean that we would have to stop being together and no we are definitely not breaking up. I just meant that we won't take this relationship of ours any further. Like, well, we won't mark each other. We won't complete our bonding right now. I know it might be hard but I think that we can do it at least for a little while, right?" I ask them a bit unsure of my own idea.

Bonding and mating between wolves is a pull that most wolves can't go without for long but we are all strong supernatural beings so I'm pretty sure that we can accomplish it, if only until we can work something out between them and Sin that is. I just want all of them to stay a loving family unit.

"No." Slay absolutely denies my request instantly. "I will not put off bonding with you just because Sin has a damn stick up his ass! Our relationship now has nothing to with Sin at all. Just because he's throwing a damn tempter tantrum doesn't mean he gets to rule over what we do! I won't allow it Thorn!" He won't allow it? Just who the hell does he think he is?

"Then I will have no other choice than to leave Slay. Sin will make it his duty to get rid of me. He has already proven to you that he will do anything in his power to accomplish just that. He thinks I'm going to get you killed because of this stupid damn prophecy and he just may be on to something." I argue back terrified that Sin may be actually right, for once.

"I won't stand in your way. Not anymore. Go. All of you. If this is what you so desperately want to do then I can't stop either of you and I promise I won't hold it against Thorn either. I just want one thing. Let Storm go. I would do anything if you just release her back to me and if you do then all of you can mate or bond or whatever and I won't say a damn thing about any of it." Sin states suddenly as he starts to approach us.

I step behind Sun, shielding myself away from him. Looking at him now I hate that all I can see from him is someone who truly despises me and wants me out of the picture no matter what it may take.

"I'm not going to hurt you Thorn. You don't have to cower behind my brother." Sin exclaims with a touch of mild aggression toward me. I don't fucking trust his ass any longer.

But knowing that I will have to put up with him if I want to be with his brothers. We have to reach a resolution to our problems somehow, someway.

So I determinedly step gingerly out from behind Sun I stand face to face with Sin. Glowering up at him with hatred casting out of my steaming eyes.

"You have already hurt me Sin. I don't think you can hurt me any more than you already have." I discreetly state folding my arms across my chest while cocking my hip slightly to the side.

I have to show him that I'm not afraid of him. Even though deep down I know that am.

I'm doing this for Slay and Sunny.

"Yea well, sorry about that." Sin fake apologizes without any fucking real emotion at all behind it. The cocky slimy arrogant bastard!

"So do we have a deal?" Sin asks Slay.

"No. No fucking deal Sin. I will not bargain with you over this. Storm is not to be ever trusted again and I can't allow her to be released from her confines just because you think that she deserves it. You may say that you love her, which I'm beginning to think is just a damn made up fucking lie anyway, but that isn't a good enough reason for me to set her sorry lying ass free." I almost choke at Slays reply. "I just won't do it"

Sin glares over at Slay, they both continue to stare at each other like it's a damn western showdown meeting at high noon for the shoot out.

Giddy up everybody!

"What do mean that you think it's a damn lie? Haven't I proven it to you already? I love Storm, Slay!" Sin accentuates the last sentence trying desperately to get his point across to either Slay or himself. I don't know which one he is actually trying to convince though.

"Why? Well let's see. You didn't seem to have a fucking issue with Storm sleeping around on you with Pan, now did you? And I also remember how you kissed Thorn so damn passionately at that creepy Addams Family mansion. So I think you are completely full of shit whenever you say that you love Storm, Sin. I think there's more to this than actually meets the eye. You are fighting way too hard to get Thorn out of the picture and don't tell me it's all for mine and Sunny's protection. That's a load of bullshit. We can both protect ourselves. We always fucking have. I actually think that you're hiding something else from us. Oh but please tell me if I'm wrong?" Slay challenges Sin standing up to him very defiantly.

Is he actually hiding something else as Slay thinks he is? What more can he be hiding? Does he have a secret love child that we don't know about? Is there another lover? Is he in cohorts with my father?

The last question has me starting to breath more erratically.

No please don't let it be that!

Sun draws closer to me as he places his hand on my back the sparks alight up in me instantly. Calming me down somewhat. My breathing starts to regulate just from his simple loving touch. Thank you Sun.

I watch extremely closely as Sin has a bout of confusion scrambling up on his faltering features. Is he having doubts? I ask myself. All of these questions keep tossing around in my mind fluently.

"You're trying to fucking confuse me!" Sin is undoubtedly having conflicting emotions about all of this.

What's going on with him?

"Fuck!" Sin screams, suddenly stomping his foot down unexpectedly.

I flinch away from him instantly.

Sun wraps his arm around my midsection bracing himself against me.

We all watch now as Sin emotions start fluctuating between being indecisive to a very surprising realization of acceptance. It's actually tantalizing to watch. Sin seems to have a lot of conflicting emotions.

Then he suddenly turns on his heel and storms away from us, clipping Suns shoulder as he goes by, headed straight up the stairs, stomping down his feet hard on each one of the stairs beneath him as he angrily walks away.

We all hear his bedroom door slam when he finally reaches it. I flinch away again.

"Well that went well." Sun dryly states still staring up at the stairway landing.

"We're all leaving out in the morning after I call Miracle to pick up Storms ass, for the Invivus Realm, so pack a bag and be ready." Slay states a bit edgy.

"I'll inform our Betas about our departure but what about Sin?" Sun questions Slay.

Slay peers sadly up at the top of the staircase landing looking directly at Sins closed bedroom door a bit wistfully.

"I don't want to talk to him any further. If you want to tell him about what we have planned then by all means be my fucking guest. Right now I think it's best if I just keep my distance from him. Demon is on edge and I may not be able to control him." Slays comment rattles me. If Demon, his wolf, is on edge then that can only mean that Sin has definitely pissed them both off to a high extent.

And all because of me.

"I'm sorry." I tell them as the guilt starts to engulf me, "this is all my fault. Sin is only doing this because of me. I don't want to be the person that comes in between all of you. Maybe I should just go to the Invivus Realm alone. That way you can all work out some of these issues on your own without me being around to cause any further problems." It's a good idea in my opinion.

They need to work on their relationships and I'm just standing in all of their way.

"Not going to happen and this is definitely not your fault Thorn. This is all on Sin. He has to work on his own damn issues. Don't blame yourself beautiful. Sin had problems before you even came into the picture." Slay tries to placate me.

But the guilt still resides within me.

"He's right Thorn. Like I said before Sin started having these problems right after our parents died. You are not to blame." Sun smiles down at me placing his head on the crook of my neck as he nuzzles within it.

His intoxicating aroma, of musk and fresh rain water, wafts up to me suddenly calming my inner worries instantly.

Slay comes to stand behind me as Sun edges his way to stand right before me. Slay wraps his arms around my mid-section, embracing me, while Sun plants both of his hands on my neck peering into my eyes lovingly.

I breathlessly moan out when Sun lowers his head to my neck leaving tiny little feathery like kisses on it as Slay does the same on the other side of my neck.

As they continue to ravish my neck an absurd thought flashes into my mind instantly.

I'm wrapped up in a beefcake sandwich.

And I love the damn bread!

Chapter 16

After Queen Miracle and King Lucias left with a crying and wailing Storm in tow, I sat down to enjoy a cup of hot mocha bean hot coffee before our subsequent planned departure.

I desperately needed some alone time to work out some of these complex feelings and issues I've been having over Sin.

But unfortunately I was interrupted by a very disheveled and quite disgruntled Tristan stomping into the dining room angrily.

He halted the second he saw me sitting at the table then he just lets out a frustrated grunt before he walked around me to fix himself a cup of joe.

Ignoring him I just kept drinking my own coffee still trying relentlessly to relax. Tristan decides to take the seat across from me. As he pulls the chair back to sit down upon it the scraping noise from the legs of the chair against the linoleum makes me cringe.

He unfortunately deposited himself in the chair across from me with a ragged huff.

Agitating me so much that I just roll my fucking eyes at him. Asshole.

I don't know exactly what his damn deal here is lately but I am definitely not in the mood to deal with his obnoxious shenanigans.

"So you're leaving for the Invivus Realm today?" Tristan finally speaks up though I note the edgy tone in his voice. It's starting to really grate on my damn nerves.

"Yea." Is all that I reply. I feel no need to elaborate with him any further on the subject.

I just don't like this asshole. At first I thought I would give him the benefit of my doubt. He seemed alright when Thorn first introduced us to each other but lately he has changed his entire damn attitude for some unknown reason and I just can't seem to figure out exactly why that is.

"Do you think thats wise?" Tristan questions taking a sip of his coffee. I scowl over at him confused by his unexpected question.

"What do you mean?" I ask a bit gruffly it's way to damn early to have to deal with this damn dudes uncalled for animosity.

"I mean with Sin not going with all of you and all. The prophecy did state that she would need all three of her mates, is that not correct?" He asks me but he does it with a very condescending attitude.

"We will manage." I tell him taking another drink of my coffee. I just wish his stupid ass would just leave me the hell alone already. So I can at least have just one damn minute of fucking peace. Is that too damn much to ask?

"Well if you want my opinion I don't blame Sin for not wanting to be with her. He saw the light early on about how she truly is and I just hope that you and Sunny don't end up regretting taking a chance on her either." Tristan states rather bluntly. "She's just not worth it."

"I didn't ask for your damn opinion asshole and why the sudden abrupt change? If I can remember correctly it wasn't too long ago that you were willing to happily exchange places with Sin." His face morphs suddenly from the condescending asshole that he has been presenting to me to now looking completely aghast. I stifle a laugh.

"Things change." Tristan states simply as he just shrugs his damn shoulder after regaining his obstinate composure.

"They do. So what changed them?" I persist tilting my head slightly to the side while observing him.

"That's none of your damn business!" He replies aggressively.

"Oh, but you made it my damn business when you brought your condescending ass in here and starting making inappropriate remarks about my damn mate!" I bellow out while slamming down my coffee mug on the table, spilling out my lovely mocha bean coffee all over the side of my mug and onto the damn dining room table making a complete mess. Shit!

"You know what I'm fucking out of here. Good luck on taming that out of control two faced bitch you call a mate!" Tristan growls standing up from his chair abruptly with his stormy eyes never leaving mine he ends up accidentally bumping into a very upset Sunny that's unfortunately blocking his only exit from the room.

Sunny has his arms folded across his chest as he's shooting fucking heated daggers through his eyes down at now very startled and flustered Tristan.

"What the hell did you just call my mate? Slay, please tell me that I'm hearing things because I think that I just heard this little ass prick call my sweet loving mate a two faced bitch?" Sunny ask with fierce intimidation. "I know this dumb fuck wouldn't be stupid enough to do something like that?" He adds growling down at him.

I let out a deep dark wicked chuckle, "You know Sunny I do think that this little bastard just called our mate a derogatory word! What do you think we should do with him?" I ask smugly while walking around the dining room table coming to stand right beside Sunny.

"I don't know. Maybe we should just cut off his little bitty tiny balls?" Sunny states disbelievingly in a very childish mocking tone.

"I don't know. If we do that then we would have to go through all of the damn trouble of finding the damn tweezers so we can move his little bitty pecker out of the way to even reach them!" I snarl my upper lip growling down at him.

Tristan frighteningly blanches away from us literally shaking in his fucking boots now.

"I-I didn't m-mean it." He anxiously stutters making me release another deep chuckle at him.

Seeing him so damn shaken enlightens me but knowing that Thorn would probably be upset if we did something to hurt him makes me regain my composure, I take a deep breath to try and tamper down my escalating temper.

I take pity on the little cowardly prick, "Get the fuck out of my house before I rip your cowardly spine right out of your tiny asshole!" I growl. Tristan doesn't waste a damn second, before he's pushing in between us he takes off out of the dining room running like his little ass was on fire.

Peering over at Sunny we both bust out in uproarious laughter, "I think he might have just pissed his damn pants!" Sunny says between his bouts of laughter. I'm about to reply back to him but the dining room door suddenly opens.

"What happened with Tristan? He just ran by me looking like he just seen a damn ghost." Thorn questions as soon she walks into the dining room.

Instead of answering her both Sunny and I continue to laugh as Thorn looks on at both of us with valid worry and uncertainty.

After Tristan's hasty departure we all gathered in to the living area with suitcases in each of our hands.

I open the portal to the Invivus Realm promptly once we were all finally situated.

"Ready?" I ask both Sunny and Thorn as they look on at the portal before them a bit apprehensively.

"I'll go first if you're scared. There's actually nothing to be afraid of, all you have to do is step right through it and it will lead you straight into the Invivus Realm." I try reassure both of them. They both just give me a slight hesitant nod still looking slightly apprehensively over at the portal.

Stepping forward until I'm standing right in front of the portal I take a glance back over my shoulder and give them both a tiny reassuring smile.

Putting one foot in front of the other I finally reach the portals entrance as I place my foot into it I unexpectedly get thrown back, by an intense electric shock, all the way across the living room area flat on my ass until my back finally collides into the wall forcefully. My suitcase ends up flying across the room with me but I have no idea where it may landed.

"Slay!" I hear Thorn scream and her own suitcase suddenly dropping to the floor immediately while she's anxiously runs over to me with Sunny heavily running right on her heels. She bends down to me placing her soft hands against my cheeks.

The sparks from her touch seem to bring me around quickly from my disoriented and squeamish state thankfully.

"Are you okay?" She ask me worriedly.

Grunting I stumble to stand pushing myself up off the floor with the palm of my hands albeit a tad ungracefully.

Leaning against the wall I shake my head vigorously trying my damnest to dispel the dizziness from me.

"I'm fine." I mummer being a little bit embarrassed from the incident and still a bit fuzzy headed.

"It won't let us enter into the Realm." Sunny exclaims. Well no shit Sunny. I fucking know that!

"Maybe because the prophecy said she needed all three of her mates and by my counting I'm only seeing two." Sin exclaims as he entered the room smiling with a bowl of fucking cereal that he's eating in his hands.

"You knew!" Sunny states staring over at Sin disbelievingly.

Craning my pounding head I glance over at Sin who is just smiling egotistically over at Sunny while the bastard keeps eating his damn bowl of cereal.

"Un-fucking-believable! You knew all of this time that we weren't going to be able to make it through the portal without your ass, didn't you?" I square off with him, while strolling over to him a bit unsteadily. Once I reach him I get right up into his fucking face.

"I knew." Sin affirms my own conclusions while giving me a snide smile. The damn jackass. I want to fucking crush him.

Before I could punch him in his smug ass face Thorn beats me to it. She literally slaps the living hell out of Sin across his damn face and I mean fucking hard. Daaaamn!

Sins head swings to the side from the rough slap the force of it makes him drop his damn bowl of cereal in the process. The bowl of cereal crashes down on the floor with a clang spilling the contents of it everywhere. Cocoa pebbles and milk mix in with the white fluffy carpeting, it suddenly starts soaking irrevocably into the carpet fibers. I scowl down at the enormous mess.

"You bastard! What the hell have I ever done to you to make you hate me so damn much? You're so fucking selfish. Those people over there," Thorn points to the opened portal while never taking her heated glare off of Sin, "are suffering under a tyrannical leader and all you can fucking do is think about your damn self! I've had it! You are a dishonest low down dirty deceiving heartless prick who doesn't deserve a mate or even the love of your brothers. Why do you have to be such a giant ass? What are you even good for Sin? All you do is cause mayhem and for what?" Thorn starts to run out of breath, she pauses then inhales deeply. Once she regains her breath she lays into him again while pounding her tiny fist into his chest with unbridled fury.

"So you can save your brothers? What a laugh. You can't even save your fucking self. Look at you! You are nothing but miserable and you are making everyone around you just as miserable as you are. I hate you Sin! I fucking hate you!" Thorn screams out terribly loudly still pounding away at Sins chest.

Sin peers down at her with retracted lips and genuine shock written all over his face. Thorn finally drops her hands away from Sins chest, breathing heavily.

"Thorn I..." Sin starts but Thorn holds up her tiny hand cutting him off instantly.

"Save it. I've heard it all before and I'm not in the mood for anymore of your damn lies." Thorn retorts sharply, dropping her hand down to her side, her shoulders then sloop down looking utterly defeated.

"Thorn?" I drawl out her name reaching my arm out to her slowly but when she sees it coming toward her she jerks her body away from my touch quickly.

"I'll be in my damn room if you or Sunny needs me." She informs us lowly as she turns away from Sin, she sighs, then walks straight away from us all. I watch her back as she climbs up the staircase, she looks so damn sorrowful as she walks away from us that it literally breaks my damn heart to see her in such distress.

"She hates me?" Sin ask very despondently.

"What the hell did you think she actually felt about you Sin? After the way that you have treated her I would actually hate your ass too." Sunny tells him imploding. I would have to actually agree with him.

"Do...do you....hate me too?" Sin ask Sunny stammering.

Sunny releases a tiny breath, rubbing his hands over his jawline he stares over at Sin with pity.

"Yes and no Sin. I love you but I hate you. The way you have been acting these last few years are making me hate you. Every since our parents died you have changed so damn much and I can't say that I like it. What is it Sin? What is causing you to act this way? Tell me why please because I truly don't understand." Sunny practically begs Sin.

I huff lowly knowing that Sin will never divulge a damn thing to either of us. No matter how much we may plead with him he has always kept his feelings locked up tight like a damn bank safe for years now I just can't see him changing.

"Never mind. You wouldn't understand anyway." Sin grouses just shaking his head.

I knew the bastard wouldn't open up but I'm about sick and damn tired of all of this tireless shit that he keeps dishing out.

"Of course. Why wouldn't we understand? We're only your fucking brothers who have lived with you our entire lives and whom, I may add, have also suffered through the same damn things that you have suffered through our entire lives together. But for some fucked up reason you seem to think that whatever has happened to you makes you somehow more tangential than either Sunny or I. But, by all means Sin, keep rolling around in your self pity cesspool that you seem to have created just for damn yourself." I fume exasperated by the mere idiocy of my damn brother.

"I didn't create anything! I deserve whatever I get! You. Wouldn't. Fucking. Understand." Sin accentuates every word while screaming at us loudly.

"Then tell me! Help me understand Sin!" I scream back pleading.

"I can't. I just fucking can't! I know I'm a fucking asshole Slay! I fuck everything up! I always do. It's like it's imprinted into my own damn D.N. Fucking A!" Sin bellows out even more loudly than before swinging his arms around frantically and pacing the floor.

"What is? What do you think you actually fucked up Sin?" I ask more determinedly. "Stop keeping it all in!"

"I killed our parents!" Sin yells.

Everyone then goes dauntingly silent. The air seems thick with questionable uncertainty. The only thing around us that can be heard is our own heavy breathing and the ticking of the old grandfather clock that's perched in the corner of the living room area.

The clocks ticking sounds that echo out of it is so damn fucking ominous.

Sin drops his hands to his side with his shoulders drooping he walks slowly over to the couch sitting down upon it as he sighs out with pure raw disparity.

My mind goes on a damn sabbatical, I can't seem to think of an original thought. Everything just goes fucking unrealistically blank.

"They died in a plane crash Sin. What do you mean you killed them?" Sunny ask quietly as he walks over to Sin sitting down on the couch right beside him, bringing me out of my own morbid darkness.

I still stand in the same spot frozen. Staring at my brothers. Unsure of what to do.

"The night before they left. I was in dads office talking to him about a party I wanted to go to, when mom came walking into the office looking really upset. Her and dad starting arguing over them going to help that asshole Alpha Baker. You know how dad was, he would always help anyone out that was in need but mom was scared. She didn't want to go, she said that something just felt off to her about it." Sin sighs leaning his head back on the couch folding his hands his lap as he then closes his eyes.

I break away from my immobilized state, edging my way over to him and Sunny, I sit down in the chair right beside them waiting for Sin to continue.

"Hindsight is twenty twenty, so they say." He huffs, "Mom and dad went back and forth about this for a while. I was starting to get aggravated at them. I just wanted to go to the damn party with Grayson and the guys because I was suppose to meet up Shari there. Remember her?" He ask raising his head from off of the back of couch to look at each of us questionably.

I just nod my head wanting desperately for him to continue on.

"Anyway, I was already late for the party so I ended up interrupting their bickering by screaming at them to get their attention and boy did I. Dad was absolutely pissed when I screamed. Mom was just surprised. I told them to just go. What would it hurt? Dad never backed down from a problem before so I thought why should he now if someone was desperate enough to call him for help then I thought they should go at least. So I ended up arguing with mom about them going." Sin pauses, wiping away a random tear that leaked out of the corner of his eye suddenly.

"It was bad," he takes a deep shuttering breath, "She kept telling me that I was just like dad and wouldn't listen to her. I guess I sort of was. I told her that she was just being selfish and a coward. Why the fuck would I say that? Mom was never a coward. I was just thinking of myself and how bad I wanted to go to that stupid ass party." Sin whines in anguish, placing his elbows on his knees he buries his face in between his hands, shaking his head vehemently.

His entire body begins to shudder uncontrollably, Sunny reaches over throwing his arm across Sins shoulder as I place my hand on top of Sins leg. He drops his hands away from his face then leans back on the couch once again dislodging Sunny's arm from him instantly.

I remove my hand away from his leg lowering my head. I hate to see my brother in so much agonizing suffering.

"I actually told her that she was not a good Luna if she couldn't even help those in need. Dad jumped my ass but all I could think about was myself apparently because I wouldn't back down even after I made mom cry. I'm a fucking bastard. I made our mom cry and at the time I didn't even give a damn. The last thing I ever told them was 'I'm ashamed that you are my parents and if you don't go to help someone out who needs you then you should be ashamed of yourselves also, so get on that damn plane and act like the Alpha and Luna that you should be!' I remember verbatim every damn word that I told them and I've been living with the nightmare of it every since then." I'm basically shocked at Sins confession.

How can he blame himself for this shit after all of this time and never even once tell us about it any of it? Not even a fucking hint!

It's been haunting him for three damn fucking years. I can't believe he is actually blaming himself for this.

"I went to the party even after dad told me that I couldn't. I hooked up with Shari and got drunk off of my ass. When I finally came home I went straight to bed and passed smooth the fuck out. I didn't even get to tell them goodbye. They left while I was still stone cold passed out. I didn't wake up until Lila came crashing into my room crying hysterically to tell me about the plane crash." Sin is crying now with tears cascading down his cheeks. I peer over at Sunny and find that he is also crying along with Sin.

Our brother has been holding this torment in for so damn long and I didn't even realize it. What kind of brother does that fucking make me?

"Sin." I drawl out his name not quite so sure as to what to say to him. What can I fucking say?

That I should have been a better brother and been there for him? We were all grieving but that doesn't excuse me from not realizing how bad off my brother was.

I fell so damn ashamed.

"I'm sorry. I should have been there for you. I didn't reali...." I couldn't even finish my own damn thought. I start getting choked up.

Fuck!

This is all just too damn much!

I spring up from my seat quickly and start pacing the living room.

I'm the fucking eldest I should have known. It was my damn responsibility. What a fuck up I ended up to be? Mom and dad would sure be so fucking proud of me. I failed all of them.

All of these random thoughts keep blowing through my mind like a damn fucking wild ass hurricane.

"Slay it is not your fault. It's mine. I am always fucking up. Every time I think I'm doing something right it always seems to go fucking wrong. Like with Thorn. I thought if I called her father he would just come and take her away so she wouldn't be such a threat to you or Sunny. I didn't even think about him wanting her for his Luna or what he was planning to with her. Or even what he would do to you two. I only thought of how I could get rid of her. That's my problem Slay. I do things before I even think and I rarely think of the repercussions that it may bring." Sin stands up from the couch walking over to me. When he reaches me he places his hand on my shoulder gently, stopping my frantic pacing.

"This is all on me. I have lived with what I've done and said to our parents for three years now. It has been eating me up alive. I've lashed out and did some really shitty things that I will have to pay for, for the rest of my life. This is not on you Slay. It's all me. You have always been the best big brother any brother could ever ask for and I'm so fucking sorry for everything that I've done but I'm going to have to live with this. Not you. Do you understand me?" I can't understand why Sin is so desperately trying to console me when it should be the other way around. I look down at him in utter confusion.

"I'm the eldest it is my job to make sure all of your traveled on the right path. To know when you needed me and be there for you. To look after you no matter what. Why the hell are you trying to console me when it is I who should be consoling you? I'm sorry Sin, I knew something was bothering you but I didn't realize it was something so damn crucial. I should have fucking known!" I grit out, jerking his hand away from my shoulder mad at myself for not being a better damn brother.

"How could you have known Slay? It's not like you were in the room with us when I acted like a complete ass. I did this. Not you. I'm also the one who so callously hurt Thorn and I don't think she will ever forgive me for doing it either. But there is one thing I can do." he says pointing over at the still opened portal.

"I can go with all of you. She may not want me there but it's the least I can do after putting her through all of this I need to make amends and help my brothers and my mate conquer her Realm." I'm actually surprised that Sin would even want to do something so drastic for us and especially for Thorn.

Maybe his confession to us finally will actually start to help him? One can only hope so anyway.

"It's fine by me but I want to make one thing perfectly clear before we go. I will not ever mate or bond with you and I'm only doing this to help those in the Invivus Realm. I could actually care less about the damn throne. And when we have finish our task I will come back here and be Slay and Sunny's Luna but I will never be yours. We will never be officially mated Sin." Thorn exclaims to Sin standing at the top of the landing of the stairs. Looking down at us with clear disdain playing on her face.

Surprising all of us, she states what she wanted to say very venomously then turns around heading back into her bedroom, leaving us alone yet again, as the door quietly closes behind her. We all stare up at the landing.

I look at Sin standing in front of me, he's staring at the landing with remorse shadowing his face.

It's not like he didn't ask for this. A little part of me thinks but then again I can somehow understand now why he is the way he is. But no excuse is going to be good enough for what he did to Thorn. Not to Thorn anyway.

I sigh, as pity engulfs me, but not for myself. All of my pity is aimed at my foolish brother Sin.

Shaking my head robotically the one thing that flows through my mind as I stand there watching Sin looking upon the landing so broken heartedly is,

Let the fucking adventure begin!

Chapter 17

We all decided to get a good nights sleep before leaving for the Invivus Realm the following morning.

After Sins heartfelt confession I hesitantly went up to Thorns bedroom to quietly check on her. Rapping my knuckles on her door softly, I stand and wait patiently for her to come to her door.

When I receive no answer I place my ear nearer to the door.

Hearing soft snores escape out from the doorway, I start to walk away but suddenly become indecisive, debating with myself if I should or shouldn't. What the hell, instead of going to my room I decide to peek in on Thorn instead. I need to make sure that shes is okay after Sins tirade, I try to convince myself.

The door silently opens as I enter.

Standing at the side of her bed I peer down at her. Thorn is laid out upon the bed with the glow of the moonlight cascading through her window. With the light of the moon shining down upon her it makes her look just like a beautiful angel. How the hell did I get so lucky?

Reaching down, I push a strand of her beautiful hair that's clung to the side of her face behind her ear gently.

She suddenly stirs in her sleep, rolling over unto her back, her head nuzzles down into her pillow a little deeper. I silently sigh inward, to see her so calm and relaxed is a rare occurrence, she's been under so much damn pressure lately, seemingly so down and depressed. To see her like this actually makes me heart swell.

I wish I could take all of her damn problems away from her.

Sighing, I cock my head to the side then my eyes suddenly go wide when I see that Thorn is actually completely naked under the white cotton sheet.

How did I not notice?

The top of her voluptuous breast are peeking out of the sheet. My dick instantly goes hard as fuck as I peer down at her luscious perk nipples that's clearly visible through the white sheet.

Fuck!

Absentmindedly I start to rub my hand across my jeans right at my hardened groin. My throbbing dick is painfully hard now. Damn!

I need to get the hell out of here.

Without even thinking I clear my throat nervously, Thorn then starts to stir awake suddenly. Startled, I quickly drop my hand away from my groin as Thorn starts to open her beautiful eyes slowly.

I'm to stunned to even fucking move!

When she finally notices me staring down at her like a damn pervert. She blesses me with a striking smile instantly. Calming my racing heart somewhat when I see her flash that alluring smile up at me.

"I'm sorry. I didn't mean to wake you. Go back to sleep." I suggest while whispering it to her lowly, slightly grinning down at her.

Before she can reply I hastily turn around headed for the bedroom door.

"Wait." Thorn groggily says halting me in my retrieving tracks immediately.

Turning back around I glance over at her, she raises up from her bed unconsciously dropping the sheet down to her stomach, revealing those succulent breast to me. My mouth suddenly goes fucking dry.

Diverting my eyes away from her bare form I try to focus them on something other than her. Spotting a blue tooth speaker sitting on the dresser I make my way over to it. Faking interest in it, I start playing with the buttons on it trying to get my mind off of what I just seen.

Damn she's so fucking desirable. Those big mounds keep flashing in my mind every time I finger a button on the damn speaker.

I jump back from the speaker when music suddenly starts streaming out of it. Laughing at myself, I angle my head looking back over at Thorn who is now partially covered up again with her cellphone laying her hands.

"Will you sleep with me?" Thorn ask me almost hesitantly.

With the music flowing out of the Bluetooth speaker softly throughout the bedroom, the whimsical melody of Adele's Easy on Me, echo in the room almost mythologically.

I walk over to the other side of the bed anxiously standing at the side of it wondering if I should take off all of my clothing? I'm a damn nervous wreck.

As I watch Thorn watching me with valid curiosity, I decide to just risk it. She is my mate after all so I decidedly strip all the way down to only my blue boxers.

After I finish disrobing, I slide into her bed under the sheet beside her. Leaning back on the pillows I place my hands behind my head actually extremely nervous being this close to Thorn while she is completely naked.

Thorn turns away from me placing her cellphone on the bedside table, the music that was playing earlier suddenly clicks off leaving the room in virtual silence, once she's done she then turns back to me.

Smiling again, she slides comfortably over to me, laying her head under the crook of my arm and on my chest.

Her incredulous scent floats up to me. Cinnamon and vanilla drift all over me, I shudder slightly when I smell her intoxicating aroma.

This is going to be much harder than I actually thought it would be especially when I can feel Thorns breast pushed up against the side of my chest just calling to me.

My damn cock still hasn't gone down yet making this situation even more complicated.

"What are you thinking about?" Thorn asks me softly bringing me out of my naughty musings.

I really don't think she wants to know exactly what's going through my mind at this particular moment though.

"Uhm, nothing!" I boldly lie. She tilts her head up to peer at me with an inquisitive look suddenly appearing on her face.

"That's not what your dick is saying!" Thorn exclaims bravely. I nearly choke on my fucking tongue. What?

"I didn't know my dick could actually talk?" I question moronically.

"Yep. It's saying Feed Me Seymour!" She tries to say it in a mock tone. I can't help but to laugh.

"Who the hell is Seymour?" I ask pretending to be dumbfounded.

"You know, Little Shop of Horrors? The movie? The musical?" She tries to explain easing her head up as she is peering up at me, I just give her a confused look.

I'm just shitting with her. I actually know what she's talking about but it's so damn funny to watch her get so flabbergasted that I just can't help myself.

"Come on. You have to tell me that you know what I'm talking about? Everyone has seen that movie!" She excitedly replies.

Grinning lopsidedly at her she catches on rather quickly.

"Really?" She huffs out, laying her head back down on my chest. I take my arm and circle it around it, pulling her flush up against me.

"I've seen it before but was actually pretty good but I'm not really into musicals." I reply with a touch of humor.

"I love them. I would actually love to see one live someday." Maybe I could make that happen for her.

"Really? Which one would you like to see?" I feel her shrug her shoulder.

"Any really, but if I had to chose one I would probably have to go with Dear Evan Hanson." I've actually never heard of it but if it's possible I would try my damnest to take her to see it.

"Maybe one day you just may be able to see it." I suggest now thinking of ways that I might be able to make this certain dream of hers come true.

"Maybe." She mumbles while her finger traces across my tattoo on the lower part of my abdomen.

It's a signature Red Wolf howling in front of a blood red moon. All three of us have it in different locations ok our body.

The tingles flow along her finger as she traces the pattern causing my throbbing dick to twitch. I hear a faint giggle and light gasp coming from Thorn as she peers her head back up at me with a tiny smirk shadowing on her beautiful face.

I watch her watch me for a second before she surprisingly scoots down lower on the bed, as she climbs under the sheet, she starts leaving a little trail of kisses from my chest all the way down to my groin until she finally positions herself right in between my thighs.

Fuuuck!

I feel her tiny fingers slide inside of my boxers, pulling them down till they reached just right above my kneecaps.

I let out a gasp when I feel those tiny fingers of hers suddenly wrap around my painfully hard ass dick. Fuck, Yesss!

"T-horn." I huskily stutter arching my back up off of the mattress as I feel her silken lips encase themselves around the tip of my cock and then go lower down my shaft agonizingly slower. Oh so fucking slow. It's beautiful torture.

Her soft supple lips reach the base of my stiff shaft with her warm mouth sliding along my swollen member I close my eyes enjoying this sweet torture. My hands grip the pillow hard right above my head.

Fuck, she's so damn good at this.

She wraps that divine tongue around my tip and up and down my shaft like a damn pro, the sparks run along my cock with each desirable swipe of her moist tongue.

Taking me again fully in her magical mouth.

Thorns mouth continues to bob up and down my dick when I suddenly feel her hand start to massage my balls gently I simply can't fucking hold out any longer.

"I'm about to..." I damn well can't finish my own train of thought from the intensity of my balls clenching up so damn tightly along with the tingling in my lower back I end up exploding all of my juices into her mouth unexpectedly. "Fuck!" I roar when my cum spurts out of my cock, oh so, sporadically.

Daaamn!

I hear her release my cock from her delectable mouth with a hearty plop. As I'm panting like crazy Thorn climbs out from under the sheet, when her head finally appears there's a twinkle in those dark cove blue eyes staring deeply at me and a tiny drop my spent seed dripping off of her chin. I wipe the excess cum off of her chin grinning at her like a damn maniac.

She hesitates for a second more before giving me a little smirk as she crawls back up over my body to lay down right beside me again, resting her head back down on my chest just like nothing just fucking happened.

Uhm, wait what?

Confused but still turned on I want to return the favor. I actually long to return the favor to her.

Deciding to take a risk I push her body back unto the mattress, she gasp then let's put a tiny giggle as I rest my own body on top of hers. I kick off my boxers under the sheet quickly then nestle down back on top of her, with the lower part of my body laying right between those taught firm toned legs.

I slip my tongue into her mouth devouring her from the inside out.

I want to mark her so damn badly, the yearning to do so stays in my mind as I continue to ravage her mouth.

Breaking away from her supple lips I start leaving little kisses along her soft neck, right where I want to place my permanent mark on her.

I resist the urge as I travel downwards slowly to the junction in between her ample breast places tiny kisses all along the way.

Not able to resist, I start kneading those beautiful mounds as I lick around her areola then suck her little perky nipple right into my awaiting mouth.

Thorns hands grasp handfuls of my hair in between her hands, tugging my hair as she purrs out little moans of desire. Sucking in her harden button into my mouth even deeper I start kneading her other breast giving them both all of my attention.

"Sunny." She moans my name out so softly, hearing her say my name so pleasurably suddenly sends shivers all the way through me.

Popping her ripened nipple out of my mouth I hesitantly glance up at her, the pure bliss flowing off of her face is so damn alluring, I fucking desperately crave this woman lying beneath me.

So much so that I would do absolutely anything for her even lay down my very own life for her.

The sudden dawning of how much I truly love her cements itself fully inside of me almost scaring the very hell out of me.

Her eyes meet mine as they do I see her sudden confusion laced into those damn blue cove eyes, she furrows her eyebrows at me as she studies me.

"What's wrong?" She breathlessly ask as she releases my hair from her hands. Propping herself on her elbows she raises herself up on the mattress eyeing me with uncertainty.

"I..." what can I say?

Do I divulge to her exactly what I'm feeling toward her? How can I when there's so many problems we're all having to deal with right now and Sin isn't exactly making this any easier for any of us.

"Sunny?" She questions as I just lay there on top of her staring into her eyes with my conflicting thoughts racing around in my head.

I guess I took to long to respond because before I know it Thorn is pushing me off of her with her hands firmly pressed up against my chest.

She wriggles her body out from underneath me all the while rolling me onto my back on the mattress beneath me forcefully.

Fuck! It wasn't my intention to upset her.

"Thorn wait." I tell her raising my hand in the air but apparently I'm too damn late.

She storms into the bathroom slamming the door behind her so hard that the doorframe even rattles.

Boy did I just fuck up!

Scrambling off of the bed I hurriedly walk over to the bathroom door, lightly knocking on it I press my forehead against the bathroom door, feeling ashamed.

"Thorn please." I plead with her through the door.

"Just go away Sunny!" She yells out from the bathroom, I can hear her light little sobs echo out through the bathroom causing my damn heart to break.

"No Thorn we need to talk about this." I raise my voice a pitch higher assertively adding a demanding tone to it.

"What's going on?" I jerk my forehead away from the bathroom door, startled to hear some one else in her bedroom.

Sin stands in the doorway with his hand still on the doorknob peering at me with a riddled look of confusion on his face.

"Nothing. Just go back to bed." I grunt. It's none of his damn business anyway.

"Well I would but I can't seem to sleep with all of the damn yelling going on around here. What's going on Sun?" He ask as he walks further into the room.

I'm sure as hell not going to tell him if I can't even express my own tormenting thoughts and feelings to my own mate.

"Nothing Sin. This is in between Thorn and I so would you just kindly leave us the hell alone?" I can't deal with Sin right now I'm far too worried over Thorn at the moment.

"Why is Thorn crying?" Slay ask as he's edging his way into the room with a furious look aimed right at me. He must of heard Thorns sobbing all the way into his room. Sometimes I actually hate how advanced our damn hearing is.

Fuck! Why can't they both just let me handle this situation all on my own? I don't need fucking babysitters.

"I got this. It was just a huge fucking misunderstanding between Thorn and I. Nothing for you two to worry about." I dismiss their valid feelings over my own and especially Thorns.

I need to talk to her privately to sort out all of our miscommunication. I don't need a damn audience.

"I have a right to worry about her Sunny. She is my fucking mate also." Sin surprisingly grumbles narrowing his eyes right at me.

"Since when?" I ask with fury lacing my voice. Placing my hand on my hip I then realize that I'm standing there in front of them both completely naked.

Fuck!

Rushing over to the bed I grab up my boxers from under the sheet and swiftly put them back on, huffing.

"Since I opened my damn eyes and realized what was actually important Sun. I know I fucked up with her and with both of you but please give me a chance to make amends." Sin instills his words with firmness and slight regret.

I glare at him dumbfounded by his sudden but questioning revelation.

Deep within me I so hope what he says is true but I hold on to some of my own doubts about it knowing how swiftly Sins mood seem to fluctuate here lately.

"That's not up to me. That's all up to Thorn. It's her that you have to beg for forgiveness from not me." I state walking back over to the bathroom door.

I can longer hear Throne soft whimpers coming from the bathroom thankfully. Leaning my forehead back on the bathroom door I blow out a huge strangled breath.

"Thorn please open the door and talk to me." I plead once again with her desperately.

"Thorn are you okay?" Slay asks her as he walks over to the door to stand beside me.

"I'm fine. Please just leave me alone. All of you." She softly demands.

Sighing, I raise my head from the door peering over at Slay.

Man I'm such a fuck up! Why couldn't I just express my reluctant feelings to her earlier?

I know exactly why I couldn't. Because I'm a fucking spineless coward!

"Yes you are!" Stinger gladly informs me.

"Please don't start I feel bad enough already." I feel like shit.

"Why didn't you just mark her!" Now I wished I actually did.

"I was afraid okay!" I admit gruffly.

"Of what?" Seriously?

"I was afraid that she might not reciprocate the feelings I have for her." Terrified actually.

"Idiot! She loves you anyone can see that!" Yea right! How would he know that anyway.

"And how exactly would you even know that?" I ask a bit snarky.

"Because I'm not blind you dimwit!" Why is he always calling me names? Like he would actually know anyway.

"Whatever!" I snort.

"Don't whatever me! All you had to do was say those three little words and none of this would be happening now. Sometimes I think you're a bigger idiot than Sin is." What the actual fuck?

"Hey I'm nothing like him." I grouse.

"Could of fooled me with the way you've been acting with her." I think he's full of shit. I haven't been acting any differently.

"Just shut up!" I snarl.

"Fine I was only try to help nimrod!" Still with the damn names.

"Whatever!" I snort again. Stinger gets upset and blocks me from him instantly.

Damn wolf!

"Thorn I'm so sorry. Please forgive me." I beg through the door. I'm such a fuck up!

"What exactly did you do to her?" Sin ask me from right behind me. I didn't even realized he even moved closer.

"Don't worry about it!" I'm not sharing how big of an actual fuck up I am with him or even with Slay.

One, it's just too damn embarrassing and two, it's really none of their damn business anyway!

The bathroom suddenly clicks open, the door opens slowly finally revealing a very flustered Thorn, who now has a short silky blue robe wrapped around her sexy body.

She slides right by all of us, ignoring each of us as she strolls over to the bed. She sits upon it with her legs crossed crossed and her head bowed down low.

"Are you okay?" Sin ask disrupting the awkward silence.

"I'm fine but I just really want to be left alone right now." She lowly whispers without even raising her head to loom at us.

The guilt quickly swims all through me when I hear her trembling voice quake. Fuck! I'm an idiot.

"Thorn I'm..." I trail off when I feel Slays hand rest upon my shoulder halting what I was about to say.

"Why don't we just leave her alone liked she asked." Slay suggests.

Glancing down at Thorn I see how much I have upset her. Maybe Slay is right she just may need some time alone to work out her feelings before I can talk to her about my major fuck up!

"Fine." I sadly agree still staring down at Thorn.

Slay and Sin soon exit the room with me slowly trailing behind them.

Stopping at the door I take one last glance over my shoulder at Thorn alone on the bed.

"Thorn I'm sorry. I'll give you some time alone right now but please let me explain everything fully to you whenever you're ready. What happened between us tonight has nothing to do with you. It's all on me." I softly retort before I turn away from her and walk out of the door quietly closing it behind me.

"What happened?" Slay ask as soon as I closed the door.

I'm not up for a damn interrogation right now but knowing that neither of them will just let this shit go, I let out a slight cough before I turn to them.

"Let's go into my office and I'll explain everything." I inform them turning on my heels I head off to my office located just off of the stairway.

With both of them trailing behind me anxiously I start become nervous once again knowing that I'm going to have to finally admit my feelings for Thorn to both of them before I can even admit them to her.

This is so damn messed up!

Thorn should be the one to hear this first but maybe my brothers might be able to help me if I do confess my love for Thorn to them. They may have the answers I'm seeking.

Either way I'm going to have to find a way to fight these inner demons that keep haunting my very own thoughts here of late.

Entering my office, I walk behind my desk propping my hands on top of it with my head hanging low in unquestionable despair.

I resign myself to the inevitable.

Slay and Sin finally enter into my office with curiosity etching on their bemused features.

They both take a seat in black patten chairs located in front of my desk.

"So what happened?" Slay ask impatiently.

Raising my head, I eye them both with fear rivaling through me.

Swallowing down a huge gulp, I brace my inner conflicts and just come out with it.

"I'm in love with Thorn and I think I just fucked up royally!" I state rather dramatically.

And that's a fucking understatement!

Chapter 18

After our unplanned meeting with Sunny announcing his undying love and devotion toward Thorn. Gag!

I waited until everybody was finally asleep to sneak out of the house hopefully unnoticed. Grabbing an extra set of clothing. I exited my room almost silently.

Quietly creeping through the house like a damn professional ninja, I made it out into the side yard without anyone being the non the wiser thankfully.

Making sure that my current surroundings are clear I hurriedly jolted over to the forest in a mad dash hoping that the shadows of the forest would hide me amongst them, stripping off all of my clothing I swiftly shifted into my wolf, Malice.

Picking up my extra set of clothing off of the forest floor I place them in between my jaws and started running haphazardly in between the trees, jumping over fallen branches and logs until I was able to reach my final destination in record time.

I drop my extra set of clothing on the ground then abruptly transformed back into my human form.

Throwing each article of my clothing on rapidly, I walk over to the cabin. Under my bare feet the dried autumn leaves crunch out loudly with each step that I manage to take onward.

Still panting heavily, I hesitantly knock on the cabin door. When the door finally squeaks open I flash Barrik a genuine huge smile.

"Just on time." He says opening the door wider allowing me to enter into his cabin.

Walking into the cabin I notice Singa sitting down on the couch immediately.

Rushing over to her she spreads her arms up open wide for me to enter them with a tremendous smile that's just for me appearing suddenly on her beautiful face.

"My love." Her husky voice vibrates gently on the side of my neck as I wrap her up into my wanting arms.

"I missed you." I tell her, nuzzling my head deeper into her supple neck. Her scent of nutmeg and spices envelope me as I rub my face deeper into her long neck.

"Ah, my love I missed you too." She claims as I sit down beside her grasping her tiny hand into my own.

Singa and I have been somewhat dating for close to two weeks now. Although I can't recall exactly how she and I met. My mind is kind of foggy on that. She has been a constant force in my life that I have come to truly rely on and respect immensely.

Barrik strolls over to us, sitting down in a small blue and yellow floral chair across from us, eyeing us both with genuine curiosity as he always seems to do whenever I secretly meet up with Singa here at his cabin.

"Now love, just as before, I need you to lean your head back on the couch and close your eyes." Singa sweetly suggests. "Can you do that for me?"

I nod my head gleefully at her. Leaning my head on the back of the couch I close my eyes just as she asked me to do.

Singa starts to speak with her voice being very confidant and thorough. Her words that she quietly speaks are some that I cannot seem to comprehend but I allow her to continue on with whatever she is doing anyway. I completely trust her and I'm basically putty in her pliable hands.

I just can't seem to fight it even if I wanted to, no matter how hard I try to withstand. She has this certain strangled hold on me.

"Amica mea non confidebat.Nec ego confido mea. Ego non videbo lucem. Nisi tenebras licet. Insidiae manserunt. Cum veros amores tenere." I scream out in pain as soon her last words are spilled from her lips.

Doubling over on the couch I begin to whimper, laying my head down on Singas lap. Sweat starts forming on my upper lip with my entire body beginning to tremble uncontrollably.

"Is he gonna be okay?" I hear Barrik ask but his voice seems like it's million damn miles away from me.

"He will be fine. Just give him a few minutes baby it will soon wear off. He will probably need some water but other than that he will be perfectly okay. But I'm really sorry baby I need to rush off, the Alpha is expecting me and you know he is whenever I'm late." I barely hear Singa tell Barrik. I feel her rise up from the couch, as she rises my head falls down onto the couch cushion with me still writhing out in unbearable pain as I ball myself into up on it.

"Ya know how I hate sharin ya with him." Barrik exclaims.

"I know baby but it's what must be done, for now anyway. Once he has his daughter back he will no longer need my help. You know this baby." Singa tries to placate him.

"I know I just hate it and I feel so guilty bout it. She's a real nice girl and all." Barrik informs her with bitterness laced in his voice.

I try my hardest to listen in closely to their conversation but I start to become very dizzy and nauseous, which makes it hard to continue to pay attention to them but I try my damnest anyway I keep fighting through whatever this is.

"Don't let her fool you baby the Alpha said that she was pure evil. We must rise above her innocent facade and lay our trust in the Alpha." Singa retorts. "I must go now baby. Just keep an eye on him. He is pivotal to our plans." I hear Singa adamantly command him.

"Just be careful ya hear!" Barrik tells her right before my world suddenly goes black as I fade into unconsciousness.

Waking up groggily, I blink a few times to get my eyes to come into focus.

Fuck! My damn head is pounding out mercifully and my mouth is so damn dry you could actually call it a fucking desert.

Unsteadily rising up from a hard surface with my hand laid palm down on said surface I push myself up from it albeit a bit shakily.

"Easy there. Ya were just on one hella fine bender." Barrik?

I swing my head over in Barriks direction instantly when I hear his voice throbbing throughout my head.

Wincing from the pain I let my head fall back on the hard surface shutting my eyes and breathing almost erratically.

"Here ya go." Barrik says. Opening my eyes I see him holding out a glass of water in his hand for me.

I scowl over at him, trying to remember exactly what happened to me as I take the glass of water from his awaiting hand.

The last thing that I can fully remember was going to bed after I left Sunny's office. No that's not right, I also remember running through the forest but for what I haven't the foggiest idea. Damn, why can't I remember?

"How did I get here?" I croak out with my dry ass throat parched as hell. I decidedly take a generous sip of the water. The cool sensation automatically starts to soothe my aching throat instantly.

"We had a lil bit of a bender, ya and I." That doesn't make any damn sense to me. Eyeing him suspiciously I sit the glass of water down on his plywood coffee table.

"I don't remember coming here." I tell him bluntly. He looks on at me curiously then starts to laugh very unceremoniously.

"Magin not. Ya wa sure wasted last night." Last night?

Looking across the room to the big front plated glass window I can see the sunlight creeping in through the off yellow tattered curtains beaming throughout the living room.

"But I remember going to bed." I absentmindedly say, musing mainly to myself.

"Ya might have but ya ended up here late last night wailing bout that spitfire girl ya have in ya home." I was crying to him about Thorn? That makes even less sense that me being at his damn cabin.

Propping my elbows on my legs I place my head in the palm of my hands trying to fucking remember anything. After a few wasteful minutes of trying I still come up with nothing. Not a damn thing.

"Are ya good ta make it on ya own back to ya place?" Barriks ask.

Dropping my hands away from my face I just stare at him for a second contemplating his question.

"How did I get here?" I ask him suspiciously. Something just doesn't seem right about any of this bullshit.

"I guess ya runned. It dudnt take that long fur ya to get here in ya wolf form." He informs me but he seems a little rattled.

"Look I got stuff I need ta tend ta today so if ya are okay to get back ta ya place on ya own I'll be gettin tat it." He states as he rises up from his chair completely dismissing me rudely.

"Alright." I mumble unsteadily stumbling up from his hard ass couch a tad ungracefully.

Making my way to his front door a bout of dizziness hits me suddenly. I steady myself before I open the door and walk out of it, slamming it roughly behind me.

Leaning on Barriks front door the bright sunlight beaming down on my face instantly makes me squint my damn eyes.

Man I feel like utter shit! Whatever I drank last night must of been really fucking hard core.

I don't think I've ever had this type of hangover before. Out of the damn blue I start to feel nasty ass tasting bile rise up in my throat.

Quickly racing to the edge of the porch I unload my diner from last night all over the ground.

Fuck! I don't remember eating that shit last night! Once I'm finished throwing up all over the ground, I dry heave a few times before I wipe my mouth with the back of my hand, spitting out the nasty tasting aftermath unto the ground on top of my gross pile of vomit.

Bracing myself on the porch railing, I try to calm my fucking racing heart when I catch a glimpse at Barrik peeking his head out around his tattered curtains.

Once he spies me on his porch he swiftly closes the curtains but not before I was able to catch his surprised expression.

I feel like there's something that I'm definitely missing but I can't quite put my damn finger on it. He's acting way too strange for this to be just a casual drinking visit from me.

Regardless of my conflicting thoughts on the matter I remembered suddenly that we are suppose to leave out for the Invivus Realm today.

Fuck!

Hurriedly I run to the edge of the forest, once I'm there I strip out of my clothing shifting into my wolf immediately. I grab my clothing in my jaws then head off zigzagging into the forest making my way as fast as I can back home.

I don't know exactly what happened at Barriks cabin last night but I do intend to find out.

One way or the fucking other.

Arriving back home, after I redressed myself, I edge my way into the house. Trying to be as quiet as I can.

But unfortunately I get busted as soon as I entered the living area.

Every fucking body was all ready there apparently waiting on my slow ass to appear.

Along with my brothers and Thorn there is also all three of our Betas and one of our she wolf cooks Betty Pollard for some fucking unknown reason.

Unless it's to see Slay off that is. She had always had a crush on Slay every since he became an Alpha, Betty has been drooling all over him ever since then.

A flash of a derisive evil plan suddenly crashes through my mind, I try to fight it off, knowing that the plan will hurt my brother if I even speak a word of it.

But something inside of me just pushes me onward, it feels like an itch on my skin that I just can't seem to be able scratch. It's damn unnerving.

As I walk further into the room everyone looks my way, all of their attention goes directly to me, when I finally make it over to them I stand right in between Slay and Betty eyeing them both with a devious grin playing on my face.

My inner subconscious is screaming out at me loudly not to fucking do this. Struggling with my inner demons I open my fucking mouth before I could even think about it and spew out all of my unplanned hatred.

"Well Betty did you and Slay have fun last night?" I ask her almost coyly.

She looks up at me completely flustered by my abrupt question.

"What are talking about Sin? I didn't see Betty last night!" Slay obviously protests.

I ignore him still struggling to hold my tongue but for some unexplainable reason I just can't.

"Of course not because the entire time you had your eyes closed while you were fucking her brains out!" I announce nonchalantly. Hearing virtually loud gasp from everyone in the room, I start laughing out ridiculously.

Why did I even fucking say that shit?

Before I know what was happening I feel Slay punch me fucking hard directly on my nose.

My body hits the floor instantly. Pain is now designated right at the center of my fucking face.

Slay suddenly jumps on me, straddling me as he lays into me with punch after heated punch right into my damn face. My head hits against the floor painfully nearly knocking my ass completely unconscious.

Then a rush of air hits me as I watch through scrunched up eyes as Sunny and Trace pull a fighting Slay off of me.

Grunting out in immense pain I drop my head to the floor again groaning out miserably, closing my ever growing swollen aching eyes. Fuck! That dude can pack a damn punch!

"Why the fuck would you even say something like that Sin?" I hear Slay yelling.

How the hell should I know?

Something in me wanted me to do it for some fucked reason that I not even I can explain.

"I need...help....Slay. Something...is going...on with me." I stammer out between grunts trying to raise myself up off of the floor unsuccessfully.

Falling back down on the floor I just lay there moaning awkwardly.

"You damn sure need help! What the fuck is wrong with you?" I hear Sunny ask me astonishingly.

"No...some...one did...something...to me." I plead harshly breathing. I realized suddenly that someone is actually fucking with me. It's the only way that I can explain it. I'm just not my fucking self any more.

Ending up at Barriks cabin on drinking binge is something that I never have done before. Hell, I don't even know Barrik well enough to even fucking drink with him.

Climbing up from the floor with Traces help, I finally get to my feet, leaning on Traces body for support.

Squinting through my eyes I try to focus them on my brothers who are both understandably glaring daggers over at me. I noticed that Betty is no longer in the living area with us. I must of ran her off.

"Someone," I clear my damn dry throat, "someone has done something to me." I finally admit through gritted teeth.

They still look at me with hate filled glares.

Fuck! How do I exactly explain this to all of them when I don't even know what the hell is actually happening to me?

I eye Thorn and the others that are standing behind my brothers peering over at me like I'm fucking crazy. Hell I just may be.

Taking a huge breath I start to explain to them as best that I can what happened to me this morning at Barriks cabin or at least what I think happened to me.

During my telling they all listen in intently to my description of my precarious morning.

I finish wrapping up my story, almost out of breath and wheezing I accidentally stumble. Almost nearly falling over even with Traces tight grasp on me. Trace luckily catches me before I do. Good man! I think to myself.

He then walks me over to the couch, sitting me down upon it while I try to regain my limitless breaths. My body definitely needs some time to heal from this morning's activities with Barrik to Slay kicking my ass I'm feeling tremendously soar and very haggard.

"So Barrik did something to you?" Thorn ask me unbelievably. I can hear the doubts cascading out of her sweet voice but hell I can't blame her. It is quite unbelievable even to my ass.

"I don't know....if he did but I do know....someone did. I didn't want to say that shit about you and Betty, Slay....know ing it was a....damn lie but for some reason....I said it anyway. It's like something....or some unknown force was driving me to do it. I can't explain....it any better than that but....you have to believe me Slay. Every time I open my....damn mouth it's like it has a....damn mind of its own." Please fucking believe me. I plead inside of my head. I need someone to believe me. Anybody?

"I'm going to talk to Barrik." Slay informs us.

"So am I." Sunny exclaims.

"Not without me." Thorn inserts determinedly.

I feel a sudden emotion inside of me swell up as I listen to them all.

"I'll hold down the fort until you get back Alpha." Flex tells Slay. With Pan and Trace both nodding their heads in agreement.

I think the feeling inside of me is what one would definitely define as relief. Complete and utter fucking relief and maybe just a touch of pride in the people that love me.

Thank fuck!

They actually believe me!

"I'm coming too." I tell them slowly sliding off of the couch grunting.

"You need to stay here and recuperate. It won't take us long, just relax." Slay demands. I huff but crash back down on the couch after he demands me.

Damn that Alpha commanding tone.

I nod my head numbly as I watch all three of them walk out of the front door with determination in each of their steps.

Thank fuck they believe me!

"Malice?" I call out his name a few minutes after my brothers and Thorn left. Apparently not receiving any answers.

"Malice?" I question again calling out his name much louder this time in my head.

Not being able to reach my wolf I start to panic. He was with me just a short while ago. Where the hell could he actually disappear too? Why isn't he answering my calls.

"Malice!" I try again but all I hear in my head is pure daunting silence.

What the fuck is going on?

"Are you alright Alpha?" Trace ask me breaking me away from my panicked thoughts.

"Malice isn't answering me." I mumble almost incoherently.

"That's...strange." Trace replies with uncertainty. Well no shit! No wonder I'm not healing as fast as I should.

Maybe he's just asleep?

"Just try to rest maybe he will talk to again once you're awake." Trace suggested. Nodding my aching head I lay down flat on the couch, nuzzling my head on the plump couch arm.

It doesn't take but mere seconds before I slip into oblivion.

I awaken crankily to horrid muffling noises and mild scuffling echoing out in the living area disrupting my momentary peaceful bliss.

Disgruntled, I rise up from my sleeping position on the couch only to notice that my brothers and Thorn have a very pissed off Barrik within their grasp with a cloth wrapped around his mouth to muffle his screams apparently.

Shuffling off of the couch I gingerly make my over to them. Slay and Sunny have Barrik bound by a pair handcuffs with each one holding a firm grasp on each one of his flailing arms.

Barrik is struggling to fight each of them off of him but it's of no use.

Thorn is standing behind the three of them smiling but there's a slight show of contempt floating in those beautiful blue eyes of hers.

"He told us everything. Well, as much as the asshole says he knows anyway." Slay informs me still maintaining his firm hold on Barrik.

"What did you find out?" I ask with a noticeable crack in my voice, my throat is still dry as fucking hell unfortunately.

"Well as far as we can decipher it looks like that you have unknowingly been put under a damn witches spell. One that is called 'blinding spite'. His so called mate has been blind-siding you with it almost every single night since Thorn has basically came into the picture. Apparently, it's to block out your own heartfelt feelings toward the people you love and like, but mostly love. That's why you have been acting like a fucking mad man here lately." I listen intently to every word that Slay tells me.

So I have been basically spellbound? That's why I have been acting so irrationally? That's why there was always the nagging feeling in the back of my mind whenever I did something that I just knew wasn't exactly right?

And this has been going since we meet Thorn? It doesn't make any damn sense.

I remember my stern convictions about not wanting to have a mate. I have had that certain view for years now. Not just when I meet Thorn.

Maybe that's where the spite part comes in?

I made my decision, about not wanting a fucking mate, when I was just sixteen years old.

The exact same day that Pan laid that memorable kiss on me is the day that will forever be cemented in my mind. The day that I vowed to myself that a mate just wasn't in the cards for me.

The day that I knew that I was not only attracted to females but to males also.

How can a damn mate of mine understand that? When even I don't understand it fully. How can I expect my mate to even comprehend it when I fully don't?

I couldn't do that to my mate so I decided that pushing away or even rejecting my mate would be the better option for everybody in the long run. I didn't want to subject my mate to that.

I didn't realize that I've been pacing the damn floor, I was to damn caught up in my own dysfunctional thoughts to even notice.

"What does that mean exactly? What exactly we're they trying to accomplish?" I question Slay once I stopped my frantic pacing.

"To dissuade you from being with Thorn of course and more than likely trying their best to cause a rift between us all." Sunny inserts scowling down at Barrik.

"If you don't mind would you take him to the dungeon Flex?" Slay ask.

"Of course Alpha." Flex comes over grabbing ahold of a still struggling Barrik. Trace advances to them both to help Flex with them each taking an arm of Barriks they roughly trudge off down into the forsaken dungeon cells.

Good fucking riddance!

"I'll call Queen Miracle before we leave for the Invivus Realm to inform her of the new circumstances with Barrik but we're wasting time here. If Barrik and his mate has gone as far as to this something like this, then Thorns father won't be far behind. Pan, you Flex, and Trace need to look after our pack while we are gone. If anything untoward happens while we are gone don't hesitate to call either of us and if you can't reach us I have left Queen Miracles number on my desk just in case." Slay insist. "Oh and if there are any emergencies take the entire pack to Alpha Gordon's pack. I'll call him and inform him of everything that has happened lately." Slay adds

"Yes Alpha." Pan willingly states, giving Slay, Sunny and I a respectful nod before he heads off.

"Is everyone ready?" Sunny pipes in sparing each of us a glance but I can't help but to notice that he looks on at Thorn with a touch of sadness etched in his eyes.

Another damn issue we will all have to sort out apparently. Just great.

"I need to grab my suitcase. I'll be back in a flash." I reply running off to my bedroom to get my damn suitcase.

I honestly would rather be eating fucking gravel than going to this damn Realm with them.

I stop in my tracks right before I reached my bedroom door, why do these damn awful thoughts keep traveling through my subconscious?

Is it the damn spell? I never use to be so cruel or so damn aggressive. Yea, I vowed I would never want a damn mate but I actually never thought that I would be so damn viscously angry about it either.

What has that damn witch done to me?

Picking my steps back up, I open my bedroom door grabbing my black lined suitcase off of my bed with a resounding scoff. Then I remembered Malice.

"Malice?" I call him out once again. Still no damn answer. Where are you?

"MALICE!" I yell! But all I get in return is pure silence.

What the hell is going on? Where can his stubborn ass be? Is this because of the damn spell?

Shaking my head at the million question roaming around in my mind but finding no damn answers I just resign myself and head off back down to the others I keep wondering how long this spell will actually last? When it wears off will I be able to see things differently or will my views stay the same? Will Malice return to me?

And exactly why me?

Why did her damn father chose me out of all three of us brothers? Was I the perfect victim for his damn scheme? How the hell did he know me so well anyway?

I halt in my tracks again with a new realization suddenly dawning on me that has me seeing red.

Fucking Storm!

She must of been the catalyst to all of this? That damn deceiving trifling....no! I won't stoop down to her fucking level. Now I truly hope that Miracle is giving Storm exactly what she fucking deserves.

Preferably Death!

My love will not be trusted. Nor do I trust my love. I will see no light. Only darkness is permitted. Trickery will abode. With my true loves hold.

Chapter 19

The Invivus Realm isn't exactly how I pictured it to be.

When one thinks of a Realm that inhabits Faes, Faeries, and Sprites plus other well known supernatural beings, one might imagine a beautiful or whimsical landscape.

Full of divine multicolors scattered all throughout the land with delicate flowing floral that one's eye would greatly appreciate but one would never picture this!

What happened here?

It's looks so foreign, so haunting, and mainly so obviously obstructed.

Like a overcapacity city with a dire ruler who equates hisself to a God. Living high above others amongst the clouds like he thinks he's above the lowly peasants living savagely beneath him.

It's just completely ridiculous!

Before I have a chance to voice these certain opinions of mine something or someone suddenly comes crashes through the blackberry bushes to the right side of us.

Startling me so much that I gasp out loud and actually drop my suitcase on the ground below me.

"Shhhh." A female voice creeps over to us demanding for us to remain quiet.

Swiftly grabbing up my suitcase in my hand I cock my head to the side observing the awkward talking bush.

"Come here." Are they crazy?

Shaking my head on protest, I back away from the ominous magical talking bush.

"If you want to live follow me." The bush says sternly as the leaves on the bush began to rustle frantically.

How is a bush going to walk with no damn legs?

I facepalm myself mentally! Why the hell am I thinking so damn foolishly?

A bush walking indeed!

I peer over to my mates who stand directly beside the bush peering down at it curiously, immobilized.

Okay? I guess I'm making all of the decisions then?

Hesitantly, I walk over to the blackberry bush, squeezing my way in between the bushes I make way into what seems like someone's backyard. Although the yard is very minuscule in size it seems well groomed with little garden gnomes placed haphazardly throughout the yard and small fairy lights hanging down from one tiny dwarf tree planted directly in the center of a tiny floral garden.

Hearing shuffling noises behind me I look back over my shoulder. I have to hold in a laugh when I see all three of my giant mates struggling to make their way in between the blackberry bushes.

For big men they sure do have some ingenuity in them.

Rolling my eyes at their antics I turn my attention back to the yard searching for whoever was calling out to us earlier.

I catch a glimpse of a figure standing in the doorway of a discreet but humble looking cottage staring intensely over at me.

Gingerly, I make my way over to the cottage and the mysterious person before me.

As I draw in nearer I can see it's a woman with very defined and striking features.

She's beautiful, too beautiful for such a desolate place such as this.

"Hello." I lowly acknowledged her. Halting almost close enough to her than I can now distinguish every fine line and soft curvature of her face.

"My name is..."

"Thorn." She cuts me off before I was even able to finish introducing myself to her releasing a beguiling smile over at me.

"Yes. How did you know?" I don't recall ever saying my name.

"I know more than you realize young Princess. Please follow me." I arch my brow up at her in surprise. This is indeed a very strange if not interesting woman.

My mates finally make their appearance behind me. I guess they made it through the bushes.

Instead of acknowledging them though I just hastily walk up into the strange woman's cottage slowly.

The inside is very small but quite quaint. There's a little navy blue couch with one simple navy blue chair and a small rounded table that sits in between the two. The room is basically surrounded in all types of books precariously placed upon all of the walls on shelves with some type of medicinal bottles and candles haphazardly a scattered throughout the entirety of the tiny room.

The strange but beautiful woman is seated in the small navy chair, patiently waiting for us to enter with a cup of what looks like a steaming hot tea in her hand.

"Please sit, Princess." I narrow my eyes at her before I resign myself to honor her request and sit dropping my suitcase beside me.

My mates come to sit down beside me on the couch eyeing the woman before us with blatant curiosity. It's a tight squeeze but we all somehow seem to manage it. With me sitting on the edge of the couch with Slay sitting right down beside me then sits Sin beside Slay with Sun sitting at the very end, they all place their suitcases in their laps, we all peer over at the stranger with a questioning gaze.

"I'm sure you are all very confused at the moment," well that's an understatement, "Let me introduce myself. My name is Freya Sinclair, I'm a Fae Seer and I'm here to guide you all on your long awaiting journey." Freya informs us with a slight smile.

I've never meet a Seer before. This is actually really exciting!

"How do you know about me?" I ask. Recalling that she called me Princess earlier.

"You look just like her. When she was kidnapped at King Zeniths ball I thought for sure she passed on, especially after all of this time that has passed with nobody ever seeing or hearing from her again but seeing you here now I reason that's not the case any longer." Freya knew my mother? But she doesn't know that she is longer with us though.

"I'm sorry, she is....no longer with us." Freyas sadden expression at my unsuspecting news seems to fluster her quite a bit.

Shouldn't she know this already? She did say that she is a seer? I was about to question her when she spoke up suddenly giving me the obvious answer.

"With the Realm now covered in an almost irreversible spell I can longer see beyond this Realm unfortunately. Thanks to Lord Samuel and his evil cohorts. I'm so sorry that Silky is no longer residing in the land of the living. She was and will always be a very becoming woman who will be remembered, revered, and respected above many." Her genuine sympathy toward my loss sets my mind at ease instantly. No wonder she didn't realize that my mother, the lost Queen, was no longer with us. At her mentioning of a certain spell, I scowl reflecting back, is that what caused the electric shock to Slay? Probably, I reason.

"Thank you." I appreciate her sympathies.

"Now on to far better and brighter things. This journey of yours will undoubtedly be very challenging. As you can see our dear Realm is not what it once used to be. Lord Samuel and his self appointed army have made sure of that. No one here believes that he is somehow related to you Thorn like he claims he is but those who has challenged him in the past to dispute his words have all fallen to a very gruesome and volatile ends I'm afraid." Freya suddenly becomes silent. Her face soon reveals a mediocre of unrelenting sadness upon it.

"My brother being one of them," Freya inhales deeply on a somberly breath. "There are people here who will help and stand by you to defeat this monstrous diabolical man but it will be a trying and difficult task." Now her face seems to reveal an abundance amount of hatred.

It makes me wonder just how this Lord Samuel has gone on to maintain his facade for so long just to sit upon the throne. What all he has done to others just in the name of power? It's down right revolting.

"First we must discover a reason for your sudden arrival here. If I may, I do have a ideal on how we may go about it. I know someone who runs the local magazine company who just may be able to help. That is, if you would allow me to announce your arrival to him?" She looks on me with hope filled eyes.

Glancing over at my three mates beside me, I search for their approval, but all I receive is scowling undetermined looks and dismissive shrugs of their shoulders.

Men!

"That would be wonderful." It's actually not a bad idea at all. "But what would I do at this company? I haven't the faintest idea about what it takes to work at a magazine business." I couldn't even tell you where to start.

"Let me handle that. Just give me a few minutes while I make some calls." Freya suggest, sitting down her little tea cup on the little round table in front of her she juts up running off into a different room in the cottage. Leaving me and my mates alone to digest all that has happened so far.

"Do you really think that you can trust her? I mean, you don't even know her Thorn and what about working at this certain company? It all seems like it's just a little bit too easy to me." Sunny exclaims with suspicion clouding all through his troubled mind.

"I feel like I can trust her Sun. I don't sense anything deceitful about her but I'm honestly not the best at judging someone's character am I? Look at my past indiscretions, at first I actually thought that Sin was a nice guy." I try to refrain my laughter, curling up my lip at Sunny as I watch Sins reaction.

His face is priceless. He's biting his bottom lip while side eyeing me with obvious disdain shadowing his face.

Sunny let's out a breathless laugh while Slay scrubs his hand down his face.

Score one for Thorn!

"Thorn can you please ask her about Malice. I'm worried about him. I just can't seem to reach him." Maya cuts in through my rivalry, sounding precarious.

"What? Is he asleep or just ignoring you?" I question.

"He would never ignore me. No, I think it has something to do with the witches spell that was cast on Sin." That would make sense.

"It's okay Maya. Don't worry I'll ask her." I assure her.

"Thanks Thorn." She breaths out heavily.

Freya soon returns with her cellphone placed in one of her hands and little white cards placed in the other. She sits back down on the navy blue chair granting us all a broad smile.

Yes. I truly do think I can trust her and I really do hope that I'm not wrong about her like I have been about so many other people in my past. Case in point; is sitting down right between Slay and Sunny.

"Alright I think I have about everything worked out for you. His name is Striker Hatch, he's actually my brothers son, well he's my nephew, he wants to meet you early in the morning. So that you two may discuss what your role will be under his employee. This is his card with the address of his company on it," she hands me one of the little white cards in her hands. I flip it around noticing the inscription written on it with silver encased slanted lettering.

Fata Glamour Magazine inc. Striker Hatch pres. ceo. #1-***-***-***North Faline drive 1970

"Thank you." I mumble lowly to her still looking down at the business card.

"Welcome dear heart, and this one is my sister, Hope Hatch, she owns an inn about a half of mile from here due east. It's called the Fata Family Inn, I've already called her and told her about all of you. She has already reserved two rooms for you all, free of charge for the duration of your stay here." She hands me another card with her sisters information on it. I'm assuming that this city must be called Fata then, with the magazine and the inn both being named after it.

It must of been at one time such a wondrous place that they assuredly must of been proud of it, now looking at the city and all that it has become it all seems like such a damn wasted shame.

And all Samuels doing!

"Now this one you should probably remember verbatim then shred it into pieces once you do. He's my nephew, his name is, Grayson Hatch, he's Hopes son, he works for Samuels Royal Guard but he is unofficially working for us. If you ever get into any type of trouble while you are here, he is the one that you need to call first. Then call me. We are all going to help you in any way that we can to finally overthrow that callous bastard." She hands me yet another little white card, this one has a golden royal crest laying upon it.

One that catches my eyes suddenly making me recall a long lost memory. I remember this certain emblem. My mother use to always wear it on her lapel as some sort of broach.

The memory is staggering. I still have her broach locked away in my jewelry box back at my old home, that is, if my father hasn't managed to find it yet.

"I must say a few things to your mates before you leave my company, if you don't mind Princess Sides?" Wait? What did she just call me?

"That's not my name. My name is Thorn Lee Rose. Why would you think it was Sides?" Her face shows extreme con-fusion.

"Oh I'm sorry. I just....assumed. Are not King Winslow Sides daughter?" Who? I have no idea who she is even referring to. I take a chance and glance over at my mates. All three of them have the same expression on their faces as I do. One of sudden surprise and complete peeked curiosity.

"No unfortunately my father is Alpha Baker Rose. Who is King Sides?" I ask her bewildered.

"Well he was the King that use to rule here until he was murdered. He was your mothers mate. They have a son so I just assumed that you was his also. I'm sorry." They had a son? My heart starts racing in my chest. My mother had a son?

"A son?" I ask flabbergasted.

"Yes. Your, well I guess he would be your half brother?" What the actual fuck!

I'm just...stunned.

"But..." I trail off with so many questions that are racing through my shattered mind.

"He has been imprisoned in the castles dungeon every since he was five years old. There have been numerous attempts to rescue the rightful King from Samuels grasp but all have failed. That's why my nephew Grayson is working at the castle. We're all trying to rescue our King out from underneath Samuels clutches so he can take his rightful place on the throne." Well fuck! I fall back on the little navy couch in complete and utter shock.

This started out as a journey for me and my mates to rescue all of the citizens from this corrupted leech now we're going to have rescue my brother from his vile clutches instead?

Damn! I have another brother? Why didn't my mother tell me? This is...hell I can't even think of a word to describe this.

"What's his name?" I mutter almost incoherently.

"King Austis Sides. He is the spitting image of his father. Well he was the last time anyone ever laid eyes upon him. The only people who get to see him now is that of Samuels choosing. That's what I thought you actually came here for. Was to rescue him, but now I can see that you had no idea that you even had a brother. I'm so sorry Princess." I'm actually sorry myself.

I should have known about him. My mother should have told me about him. How could she keep this is as a secret from me for sixteen damn long years?

I love my mother but at this very moment I truly resent her. She should have fucking told me!

"It's not your fault. My mother should have told me!" I reply with a touch of scorn developing in my tone.

"Are you okay beautiful?" Slay ask me worriedly. I just nod my head absentmindedly at him.

"What did you want to tell my mates?" I ask Freya desperately wanting to change the current subject.

Freya clears her throat apparently feeling uncomfortable from my disparaging discomfort.

"Yes. Well, uhm, first I would like to speak to you," she points her finger at Slay, "you were chosen to be her protector. You have an agile and swift determination about you but you are also very proud. So do not let your pride become your downfall. You are not in anyway responsible for others actions. You will also need to stay strong for the path ahead.

She will need your guidance and especially your strong protectiveness toward her. Guard her with every ounce of being in you." She instructs Slay.

Slay peers at her with an dour expression etched all over his face. My protector? It fits him I think to myself.

"I will always protect her!" He says with determination making my heart suddenly swell.

"And you," she now points to Sunny, "You are the very heart and soul of this group. Your compassion will reinforce everyone's willingness to go onward. To become one. Your encouragement can move mountains young heart, never lose that and always express your feelings from this moment forward. Stop hiding your secrets. For if you do not, you will lose the one new thing that you hold truly dear." Sunny eyes suddenly widen with his mouth going agape.

I'm more confused by her statement toward him, than I am of Slays. What is she actually talking about?

"And finally you," she quirks her eyebrow up at Sin, "you have chosen different paths than the Moon Goddess influenced for you. You are suppose to be her warrior but you have volleyed away from your chosen role. Mistakes tend to happen far too often where you are concerned. Listen well young warrior, your destiny has now changed thanks to your indecisive nature. There is another who has come to rival joyfully in your place. If you don't chose this route wisely then you will not only lose the one thing that will ever make you happy but you will also lose the few things you hold dear to your heart. Heed my warning! You are walking on thin ice and it's about to shatter all around you! Plus the one thing that haunts your mind is not by any means who you truly are. The way you feel for one does not mean you will feel that for others." Her voice grows a few octaves higher at her last few sentences directed at Sin.

"I don't understand. Feel for one? Feel for the others? What does that even mean?" Sin ask her obviously flustered.

"Just heed my warning young warrior. All will come to be realized in the future." Freya replies but it doesn't hold a lot of clarity for me and from what I'm witnessing on Sins face it doesn't for him either.

I am so damn confused about all of this with the exception of Slays reading. His is easy to decipher but Sunny and Sins bewilder the hell out of me.

"Last thing," Freya jumps up from the chair, walking over to a small cabinet located in the corner of the room.

She opens a small drawer with her back to us, when she turns she has a very large clear glass vial of some sort of dark brown liquid floating in it.

After she takes her seat again she hands the large vial over to Slay. He takes it as he peers down at it he creases his brow.

"This will mask your wolves. Here in Fata there are no wolves permitted. Even though your only half wolf, which I could sense right away, this will cover your wolf abilities but it won't cover your promancy abilities I'm afraid. Just the wolves. You must take a single drop of it every morning before you eat an ounce of anything." She instructs us once again.

"Will I have it take also?" Since I'm only half wolf I just may have to.

"Yes I'm afraid you will have to also. It's just a precaution. With the spell around the Realm, usually only Fae kind may be allow to enter. Since you are half Fae, it allowed you entrance." Freya explains. I've learned more from her tonight than I have learned from anybody else, even my own mother. I grimace mentally.

"Oh I meant to ask you. My wolf Maya would like to know if there's anything wrong with Malice, Sins wolf. She's been trying to reach him but so far she has received any answers from him." There you go Maya.

"It is the witches spell that's placed on Sin. It put his wolf into a sleep like trance for a few days. The spell should wear off completely within a day or two. By the way the witches name that placed that awful spell on you is Singa. She's been apparently working with your father for years. They seem to have an intimate relationship and Thorn, I really hate to be the one to give you this information but your father, Baker, he uhm, he had your mother murdered." I sit there stunned. How? What? Why? All keep rambling around in my brain.

The bastard! Why would would he do that to my mother? His own loving Luna! It's preposterous! What kind a man is he?

"Are...you...sure?" I inquire almost methodical.

"I'm positive. He is a very cruel and lascivious man Princess and what he's wants with you is absolutely disgusting, to say the least, but I do fear many will die in his imperious desire to have you." Oh what I wouldn't give to be able to rip my damn father to shreds.

I don't doubt a word she speaks. My father has killed many others in his lifetime and I guess now that includes my very own mother.

Now I feel just awful for resenting her earlier, from keeping my brothers existence a secret from me.

In all rationality I know somewhere deep inside of me that my mother didn't have a choice in the matter. Mainly because of my dickhead father but I wish she could of found someway to tell me.

I long for her so much to be here. This would all be so much easier if she was. I just hope that I can make her proud of me. Now that I know about my long lost brother I vow to do everything I can to help him escape. For him and my mother.

That's what my mother would have wanted. I'll do this for her and I'll do it for Austis. The brother I just learnt about tonight. It seems so surreal. It's absolutely amazing.

I need to get ahold of Fier and somehow tell him all about this new found discovery. I have been trying to reach his ass for the last three days but he hasn't answered any of my calls or text and with Tristan now gone I feel the need to speak to Fier even more.

I'll try again when we all get to this Inn Freya told us about. Hopefully this time I'll be able to reach him.

"Hope has a diner already prepared and waiting for all of you when you make it to her inn. Here is my number incase you need it but remember to call Grayson first if something untoward should spring up. He is a very strong powered Elemental Fae that some say out rivals even Samuel." She hands me a piece of torn paper that has a number on it. I guess this is our cue to leave then.

Rising up from the couch, I grab my suitcase form the floor then squeeze my way by the table to stand in front of her.

"Thank you for everything. I don't know how any of us will be able to repay you for all of this especially your kindness and trust." She gives me a genuine smile.

"No thanks necessary, I'm doing this for our kingdom and just maybe because I can't stand that asshole Samuel." I give her a slight little giggle over her openness.

"Goodbye." I tell her as I make my way to her front door. My mates come scrambling up behind me offering their gratitude to Freya before we leave her small homely cottage.

Once outside I breath in the cool night air trying to steady my fragile nerves.

I have learnt a lot tonight. Far too much that I would have ever predicted.

The main thing is that I have a brother that now I can't wait to meet.

"Are you alright?" My heart ask me. I turn to Sunny grinning at him.

Some of what Freya said tonight about him does make some sense now.

Sunny does without a doubt have an extremely big heart. I just can't understand why he froze last night when I yearned for him so badly.

He just stared at me like he didn't even recognize me.

His rejection was clear. He didn't want to make love to me last night that much I could tell.

But what I don't know is why?

He acts like he cares for me so why would he not want to be with me?

Do I repulse him? Am I not good enough? Thanks to Sin, although he may have done it unintentionally, my confidence has come down a notch or two.

Maybe Sunny doesn't want me to be his mate either, just like Sin?

Maybe I'm just not what he's looking for in a mate? He may be missing Nina also? I have no idea.

Whatever is bothering him, it hurt when he so carelessly left me hanging like that, he may just need some time to work through it all?

Regardless, I'm so tired of always being left out on the back burner with all of them.

Even with Slay now.

Does he and this Betty girl really have something going on, that I'm not aware about?

Sin said he was lying but at this point I don't know who to believe anymore.

Maybe after all of this over I will just have to move on from all of them.

They would probably be better off without me anyway, especially with my damn father after me.

Who knows?

I'm weary of all of this doubt flowing through me all of the time.

Sunny is staring at me waiting for an answer. Shit! What did he ask me? Oh, I remember.

"I'm fine." I finally answer though he looks down at me with doubt shadowing his face.

"Really. I am. Let's get going!" I lie boldly to him but thankfully he accepts it. I'm actually amazed that he did.

Apparently, I'm getting much better at this lying now.

Chapter 20

T he Fata Inn is a very cumbersome and adequately designed but small bed and breakfast type of establishment.

Not too shabby a place considering their allowing us to have free room and board for the duration of our stay here. Hopefully though that won't be for too long. We still do have a pack to lead and major defining responsibilities to get back to.

The sooner the better.

Entering the little establishment we were met by a very striking woman whose eyes was the brightest blue that I have ever laid my eyes upon.

"Hello, I'm..."

"I know who you are. Welcome to the Fata Inn Alpha Vallor. I have two rooms reserved just for you. Your diner is already prepared and waiting in you rooms for you. Please have a delightful stay." What I am assuming is Freyas sister, Hope, tells us in a very formal manner. She hands me over two sets of silver plated keys that has our room numbers engraved upon them.

"Uhm, thank you." I reply to her but by the time I look back up she has already mysteriously just disappeared.

Scrunching up my face in confusion I lean over the desk searching for her. With a rattled huff I shrug my shoulder dismissively when I can't find her then turn back to the others peering at them with startled confusion blanketing my face.

"Well then I'll guess we will just head on off to our rooms." I suggest to them thinking about Freyas sister Hope, she's totally different that I pictured, a very peculiar woman. She doesn't seem nothing at all like Freya.

Walking up the stairs to search out our rooms, 222 and 223, I notice she has generously put us in two rooms directly beside each other.

Opening the door with the silver key we all enter into the room 222. I have to say I'm pleasantly surprised by the rooms defining beauty.

It has a cabin vibe to it, a little on the sparse side but beautiful nonetheless.

Then my eyes cast theirselves directly on the bed placed in the middle of room. Wait! One damn bed!

Unfortunately then I guess we will all have to share them.

Thorn strolls into the room walking along side of me. Her striking blue cove eyes take in the room with a longing gaze in them. She's entranced by its beauty as I am entranced by hers.

I hear Sin let out a deliberate scoff as soon as he decidedly enters into the room.

"Okay then who is sleeping with who?" Sin ask. That's apparently the question of the night isn't it?

"Thorn can sleep with me." Sunny suggest. Sin and I look back over at Sunny giving him a deadpanned look.

"Why don't we let Thorn decide that, shall we?" I exclaim while grunting.

Thorn turns her full attention back to us three. Eyeing is all with clear uncertainty.

"Why don't we just draw straws?" Thorn mildly suggest.

I harumph.

I hate these type of dilemmas. Besides, I'm always the unluckiest fucker out of us three. I'm the damn eldest shouldn't it be I who decides on these damn things anyway?

Yea, you can qualify me as a sore loser. I fucking hate it.

"Good idea." Sunny amends. Of course he would think it's a damn good idea. He has always been the luckiest out of us all. Jerk!

Thorn walks over to the side table searching all around it for something. She then turns to us with three tiny plastic wrapped straws in her hand.

Just. Fucking. Great!

She unwraps the straws from their wrappers throwing the plastic in a small side trash dispenser located in the corner of the room.

"Got any scissors?" She inquires.

I reach into my jean pocket and pull out a small silver folding knife that I have on my keychain and hand it over to her.

She diligently takes the knife, turning away from us and then proceeds to cut along the straws.

Done, she turns back to us holding three pieces of the cut straws in her fisted hand.

"Choose." She demands.

Sun is the first to go, of course, he draws out the cut straw from Thorns hand but decidedly doesn't reveal it us. Holding it into his fist away from us.

Damn Jerk!

Sin then does the same as Sunny.

I take the last piece of cut straw from Thorns hand not even bothering to look at it.

"Okay on three." Sunny exclaims excitedly.

This is like some childish fucking kids game to him. He just seems way too excited for his damn own good. Grow up man!

We all reveal each of our straws at the count of three.

And to my utter surprise I'm the one who drew the shortest straw out of them all.

Yes! Take that you fuckers!

A giant egotistical smile suddenly appears on my face.

"Figures." Sunny mumbles.

Sin just shakes his head, smirking.

I couldn't resist I just wiggle my eyebrows up and down at them condescendingly. I fucking rule!

"Well that's settled. So now shall we eat?" Thorn ask waving her hand over to the side room that has a tiny rectangle folding table with four folding chairs to go along with it.

When we all sit down we discover a virtual feast laid out upon the table for us. Lamb Chops with tons of vegetables and even a mushroom soup to accompany it.

It doesn't take us long before we ended up devouring the well prepared feast before us. Light conversation transversed throughout the entirety of the delicious meal.

The one subject we all seem to keep coming back to all throughout the meal was one that I genuinely despised.

Thorn going to work for this Striker fellow at the magazine in the morning.

We all seemed to have a difference of opinions on the matter at hand.

Sin seems to think that is a good cover for her.

Sunny is floating somewhere in the middle. He likes the idea of her having cover but hates that it has to be her to do it.

Me: I fucking hate it!

I don't want her away from any of us for such a long period of time. With Samuel and his evil cohorts out in the city of Fata, who knows what could happen to her, if they just happened to discover her and who she truly is.

Thorn on the other hand absolutely thinks it's a brilliant ideal. Although she is worried that she doesn't have any experience concerning the magazine industry.

Which is one of the reasons that I don't want her to do this.

"I think it's a bad idea. What happens if your cover somehow gets blown? I think that it would be better if one of us would do it instead of you. Samuel wouldn't suspect us but he may just suspect you. Freya did say that you looked just like your mother. That alone would be a dead giveaway. Maybe I can talk to this Striker fellow and see if one of us can switch places with you?" I wholeheartedly suggest with a full stern conviction.

"No. It has to be me Slay. I can somehow disguise myself or even change my name. Maybe cut my hair or even dye it? But I can not and will not allow any of you to this for me!" Thorn exclaims while shaking her head vehemently.

I don't want her to change a damn thing about herself. She is absolutely perfect just the way that she is now. Not even a wig or a damn dye job could hide such remarkable beauty as hers.

"A disguise wouldn't work. If you do look anything like your mother did then nothing would prevent anyone from recognizing you. Besides, your perfect just the way you are." I throw on the last bit trying to reassure her although what I said is absolutely true.

"Thank you but sweet talking me isn't going to get me to change my mind about this. I'm going Slay and I just hope that you can understand why I have to do it." I do understand but it doesn't change the fact that I'm beyond terrified for her.

If the bastard Samuel or anyone else even tried to get their grubby hands on her I would burn down the world just to fucking kill them all.

That's when it suddenly hits me.

Fuck!

I fucking love her!

I am without a doubt absolutely over the top, deeply over my head, in love with this woman.

Damn!

How did I not realize this bit of information sooner?

"Because your a dumb ass that's why!" Demon speaks up inside of my head grumbling his dismay.

"Like you have room to talk. If I'm in love with Thorn then you my friend must be in love with Maya also." I can't believe I just realize this!

"Well, yea! I have been from the start. It just takes you dumb asses longer to realize it than us wolves." Seriously!?

"Im glad you love her Demon!" Who knew a strong ass wolf like Demon could ever find love?

"Same to you! Now go mark her already!" I fucking plan on it and the sooner the better.

"Will do!" I agree.

"About damn time!" He lets out a halfhearted scoff then laughs at me lightly.

"I think it's time for bed." I suggest a little huskily. Clearing my throat I stand up from the table dismissing any further conversation about Thorn and the disconcerting job.

She's lying on the bed reading a book while barely wearing anything at all, just a short little cut off white T-shirt thats cut off just right above her navel and a pair of white laced thongs.

Just as I exited the ensuite bathroom with only a white towel wrapped around my waist I faltered.

Staring over at her with pure lustful desire coursing right though me.

She drops her book away from her, laying it on top of her legs as she glances over at me.

When our eyes clash with each other's I note her own desire flaring up in those dark blue cove eyes of hers.

All of the sudden the room seems intensely hotter than my previous shower was.

Grabbing ahold of the towel around my waist I quickly remove it throwing it across the room as I stand in front of her in all my naked glory.

Her beautiful eyes roam all over my body. Halting only when she sees my full engorged erected dick standing at attention just for her.

When her eyes suddenly widen I give her a lopsided swaggering grin as I stroll over to the bed with my own eyes stalking her like she was my damn fucking prey.

I grab ahold the book from her hands and toss on the floor below me. Climbing up on the bed I push her down on the mattress and straddle her luscious body.

"I think it's time to play." I exclaim huskily as I lean down lower to her planting my lips on her plump supple mouth, I grab ahold of the bottom of her little white cut off shirt ready to pull it over her head.

But with the kiss being so damn alluring I rip her shirt in half straight down the middle instead.

With the sides of her ripped shirt now hanging open I get the perfect feel of her exquisite breast pressed up against my broad chest.

Diving my tongue into her warm welcoming mouth I start to knead those tempting breast pinching her little pebble in between my fingers she lets out a soft purring irresistible moan that vibrates into my mouth.

Pulling myself away from her enticing lips I start peppering little kisses all along the soft spot on her neck all the while I'm still getting to know her breast very intimately.

"Slay." She breathes out my name on a gusty note of raw desire while her tiny cold hand finds its way to the back of my head.

The sparks flash against my lips whenever I touch them softly against her little lithe neck eliciting a carnal eruption of fervor inside of me.

Scooting down slightly on the mattress I crawl right in between her thighs, her arousal floats right up to me the mixture of cinnamon and vanilla cascade around me alighting my senses into overdrive.

I grab ahold of her little white thong and rip them off of her animalistic like just as I did with her damn shirt.

Thorn let's out a tiny exciting gasp, "Slay!" She admonishes, just as I rip them away from her sexy body, her ripped shirt falls off of her shoulders as she rises up from the mattress to glare down at me. I curl up my lip as I toss her demolished thong somewhere on the bedroom floor below, not even giving a damn about where they may have fallen.

"Mine!" I growl out possessively as I descend my head right in between the junction of her juicy thighs.

Thorn falls back onto the mattress letting out a sexily purring groan as my tongue slides along her folds.

I place my hand a on her thighs spreading them out wider as I continue to devour her pussy by licking ferociously along her sensitive clit.

Her nectar hits my tastebuds with every stroke of my swirling tongue.

Sliding my hand down from the side of her thigh I reach her sweet tantalizing core, sliding two fingers into it I bend them hitting her G-spot at just the right angle she starts writhing out on the mattress below her uncontrollably. "Fuck yes Slay just like that." She moans delightfully.

Thrusting my digits faster into her wet channel I suck and lick on her little bud full of gluttony. Devouring it like it was my last damn meal not being able to assuage my heady appetite for her.

Thorn becomes a panting mess underneath my onslaught of her, she's taking sharp intakes of air trying desperately to catch her breath.

Just as I start to feel her walls begin to spasm I slide my fingers out of her saturated pussy leaving her desperately wanting for a damn release.

She huffs out dramatically as I slowly climb on top of that delectable body of hers grinding my harden cock along her folds agonizingly teasing her with it.

"I'm going to fuck you so hard that you won't even remember your own damn name." I hungrily exclaim as I give her a little fiendish smile.

"Bring it on big boy!" She impiously replies adding a fiendish grin of her own.

The little minx!

I growl out predatorily as I wrap my hand around my shaft sliding my cock along her divide, I spear my dick into her with a driving force.

Her head falls back unceremoniously on the pillow with her eyes closed firmly shut she lets out a very satisfying mewl. "Yesss, Slay." Hearing my name fall out from her lips just eggs me on to go faster.

With an impatient longing I begin to propel my cock with an accelerated brisk speed.

She wraps her toned legs around my hips pushing my body against hers demanding more of me.

Then her tiny hands press down hard on my shoulders as she keenly sighs out in provoking passion.

Groaning, I quicken my pace placing my hands palms down on the mattress I propel into her while gyrating my hips in a very licentious mating dance of full desire.

Feeling closer to my climax I descend my head down to her pliable neck, extending my fangs I push my canines down softly into her neck, her body tenses underneath me instantly as my fangs invade her neck, marking her by me for fucking eternity.

She does the same to me. As soon as I feel her fangs sink into my neck my balls suddenly clench up so fucking tight with my eyes rolling into the back of my head I groan out breathlessly.

Releasing my fangs from her tender neck I lick her pierced wounds sealing them back together gain instantaneously. She then repeats my actions.

Our bond clicks automatically into place sealing our fates as one forever.

Still ferociously pounding my cock into her I growl out as my seed sporadically spurts all into her, "Fuck Yes Thorn!" I empty everything I have into her as soon as I do my knot quickly seizes up inside of her womb.

Her silken walls suddenly convulse around my dick clamping down on it tightly she scratches her nails down my back aggressively as she screams out my mother fucking name! "Slay!" That's right baby scream it fucking loudly. I want the entire world to know you are fucking MINE!

While catching our breaths from our pure unadulterated bliss of ethereal sex. I fall on top of her panting, leaning slightly off of her body without crushing her. We both lay there on the bed just waiting for my knot to eventually recede.

"I'm sorry I lost control I didn't mean to knot with you beautiful." I grumble still trying to catch my damn breath.

"Don't apologize for that because it was fucking amazing Slay!" She replies with unbelievable satisfaction lacing throughout her breathless tone.

"It was magical and soon as my knot recedes we can do it all over again." I suggest bravely. She huffs lightly while giggling.

"That may take hours." Fuck! I didn't even think about that!

"I'm willing to wait....for you!" My tone grows serious as I gaze at her with an officious smile.

"That was...so sweet." She says with sincerity.

Sweet? Really? I prefer sexy!

"Anything for you." I want to say those three special words to her desperately but I hold them back unsure of myself.

Instead she literally shocks me!

"I love you Slay!" She confesses demurely leaving me basically thunderstruck and in complete awe.

"I love you Thorn. More than I would ever be able to tell you or show you." I say with upmost honesty as I lower my head to her lips and devour her mouth lavishly.

It's like my damn dreams are finally coming true. I can't believe it!

She fucking loves me!

The following morning while we're getting dressed for the day I observed Thorn while she was putting on her makeup that I honestly think she doesn't need at all.

Peering at her in the mirror above the bathroom sink I catch a glimpse of the marking that I left on her neck last night. Two little puncture wounds that are just now beginning to form into a very picturesque wolf howling at up at a full bright moon.

I feel immense pride overflowing throughout me whenever I graze my eyes upon it.

Viewing my own marking upon my neck that she blessed me with, the puncture wounds are beginning to form into a beautiful white wolf with wings mounted on its back.

It's fucking magnificent!

Enclosing her in my embrace with my arms gently entrapping her midsection I run my lips along my marking eliciting a gentle moan from her.

"Ready?" I ask her with my lips still pressed against her neck.

She nods her head silently leaning her body flat against mine tilting her head to the side slightly allowing more access for me to probe along her mark generously.

Groaning I hesitantly back away from her dropping my hands to my side trying to calm my raging inner beast. We better leave before I throw her ass back on the bed and have my fucking way with her again.

"Then we need to go." I growl out almost viscously popping my neck from side or side grunting out in marring discomfort.

I need to learn some damn patience when it comes to her but patience has never been one of my serious virtues unfortunately.

Sighing I walk out of the bathroom gritting my fucking teeth.

"I'll just meet you at the coffee shop when you're done then." I gruffly tell her as I turn on my heels and walk the hell away from her smoothly.

As soon as we made it to the Fata magazine incorporated building, Thorn refused my offer adamantly to go into the building with her to escort her to her damn meeting.

She wants to do this shit all on her own! I tried to make her understand that we are now officially a mated couple and should do these things together now but she continuously denied me profusely no matter how much I fucking tried to plead with her otherwise.

Stomping into the coffee shop, Fata Frappe and More, I sauntered up to the counter in a piss poor sour mood.

"Hey stud what can I get you?" The barista behind the counter ask flirtatiously giving me a cocky little wink. I study the girl with feigned indifference no doubt she is striking but a little to far on the gothic scale for me.

"I'll take a large mocha bean coffee." I order my regular laying the money on the counter as I do her hand reaches across the counter to take the money from me, she places her hand on top of my moving it down slowly across the top of my hand before she takes hold of the bills I laid down before her.

Jerking my hand away from here swiftly she shrugs her shoulder as she walks off of make my damn coffee.

I watch her tiny ass as she strolls away from me, admiring her soft swish and sway as she goes.

Shaking my head I turn away from the counter watching the traffic go by out of the big bay window for a few seconds before the barista makes her way back over to me to hand me my coffee as she does she slides a napkin along with the cup of coffee to me. I pick them both up from off of the counter as she turns and walks away busying herself with another customer.

Turning the napkin over I see her handwriting gracing across it where she left her number and name for me on it. Half laughing I stick the napkin in my front jean pocket and just walk over to a booth next to the giant bay window sitting down upon it as I watch the outside activities I sip on my coffee waiting patiently for Thorn to meet up with me.

Almost two hours have passed before Thorn finally arrives at the coffee shop. I've already had two damn coffees and a blueberry scone while waiting for her. Hearing the door chime I look up at the door watching her enter the shop giggling maddeningly at someone who is walking in behind her.

The unknown guy is smiling widely down at Thorn focused mainly on everything that Thorn is saying to him with valid peeked interest.

As they both draw closer I scowl watching this unfamiliar guy openly flirt with my mate.

"Hey Slay. I like you to meet Striker. Striker this is Slay." Thorn introduces us as they both take a seat in the booth with me, Thorn sits across from me with this guy Striker sitting directly down beside her.

"Nice to meet you." Striker says holding out his hand for me to shake.

I grunt nodding my head but don't reach out to shake his hand instead I put all of my attention on my mate before me instead.

"So how did it go?" I ask clearing my throat ignoring Striker hand. He retracts his hand away from me grimacing.

"It went well I'll tell you about all of the details when we get back at the inn." Duly cut off from any information, I lean back in my seat glaring at her new boss Striker across from me.

The barista makes an appearance suddenly, she stops right beside me rubbing her hip across my arm as she does.

Thorn eyes the barista with suspiciousness, I just smile. I guess two can play at this jealousy game.

"What can I get you two?" The barista ask them but her eyes never stray away from me as she does so.

"Hot chocolate." Thorn mumbles to her a bit too unhappily.

"I'll just have a black coffee." Striker tells her.

The barista writes down their order but pauses before she leaves us all. She leans down lower to me with her face nearly right up to my ear.

"Need a refill?" She whispers into my ear lowly but I notice the explicit sexual nature to her viral comment.

"No thanks." I mumble almost quietly cockily smiling at her, she then stands to her full height giving me another flirty wink before she eventually departs.

Thorn doesn't mutter a single word about the confrontation instead she turns her full attention back to Striker instead. Making me thoroughly jealous, I don't know if that is what she intended to do but regardless if it was or not it's fucking working!

Color my ass green but every time I see Striker intentionally touch her in someway I just want to jump across the damn table and clobber his stupid ass.

After a while of me putting up with this flirtatious torture from them we gingerly all say our goodbyes as we head for the coffee shop exit the barista just had to give one last parting shot to me before I exited.

"Catch you later stud!" I hear from behind me. Thorn halts in her tracks immediately turning back to me. She narrows her eyes up at me then without uttering a word she stomps away from me in a very heated manner.

Fuck!

Resisting the urge to turn around and look at the barista I walk out of the door behind my angry mate sighing.

How did this go so damn bad so damn quickly?

After we made it back to the inn I knew there was going to be hell to pay   I just didn't realize how bad it was going to be.

It didn't take two seconds before Thorn was on my ass!

"Tell me about it stud!" She snarls.

Fuck!

Chapter 21

"Tell me about it stud!" She snarls!

Fuck!

"What is that exactly suppose to mean?" I snarl right the hell back at her.

"You know exactly what it's suppose to mean Slay?" She huffs stomping her way over to the bed she takes a seat right on the edge of it glowering her beady little eyes over at me.

"Are you jealous? Come on Thorn, she was the one flirting. I didn't ask for any of it!" But I didn't turn her away either, my guilty subconscious speaks up loudly inside of my head.

"Jealous? Like you have any room to talk! You wouldn't even shake Strikers hand! He is just trying to help us Slay! Help me! Why were you being so damn rude to him?" Pure fucking raging jealousy is exactly why? But I dare not speak that aloud to her.

"Why? Because the stupid ass jerk couldn't keep his damn grubby hands off of you! That's fucking why Thorn!" I scream just a little bit too loudly at her. I grimace when I hear the pure spite casting out through my regrettably harsh tone to her.

Calm the fuck down Slay! I berate to myself as I trample across the room, disgusted by my own childish behavior, I sit down next to her on the edge of the bed, inhaling deeply, trying to calm myself down.

"I don't understand you Slay. Striker wasn't doing anything wrong. Why would you get so damn jealous over him?" She ask almost too quietly, Bowing her head, sighing softly.

Dammit! Why can't she see where I'm coming from?

"How can you just sit here and say that he didn't do any-thing wrong Thorn? The guy was intentionally all over you. I set there and watched all of it and you didn't do a damn thing to even stop him either. You didn't even sit down next to me. You chose to sit down next to him! How do you fucking think that made me feel!" I growl right at her, making her flinch back anxiously away from me. She springs up from the bed angrily, turning around to challenge me eye to eye.

"So what are trying to suggest Slay that I'm some damn flirt who gets her jolly's off by a damn guy flirting with me? That's so damn hypocritical! Pot meet fucking kettle!" She yells defensively.

What the hell does that suppose to mean?

"Are you trying to say that I was the one flirting? If I remem-ber it correctly she was definitely flirting with me not the other fucking way around!" I stand up from the bed suddenly pissed off beyond recognition as I stand up she takes a tiny hesitant step away from me like she's actually fucking afraid of me.

What the hell?

"You may have not of been flirting with her Slay but you didn't do a damn thing to dissuade her from her flirting with you either. Don't you try to pull this little innocent act on me! I saw the way that you were smiling at her. You are so fucking double standard!" Her voice grows a few octaves higher with every word she spews out at me. "At least I didn't reciprocate Strikers flirting! Like you did with her!" She adds heatedly.

I'm not a fucking hypocrite or even double standard! I refuse to accept either of those terms of me.

"I didn't fucking smile at her!" I lie like a damn rug but she doesn't buy it unfortunately. She scoffs heavily throwing her hands up in the air waving them around irrationally.

"Yes you did. Don't you damn well lie to me! I have two fucking eyes! I saw everything! You loved the attention that she was fucking giving to you!" Thorn bellows out so fucking loudly that Sin and Sunny hear it from all the way in the other room.

They both come crashing threw the adjoining door of the room with the door hitting the inns wall with a very re-sounding bang so hard that the door bounces back from the impact.

"What's going on?" Sunny questions eyeing us both with obvious concern.

"Nothing!" We both scream out at Sunny simultaneously making Sunny blanch away from us.

"Well it doesn't sound like nothing. The entire inn can hear you both screaming!" Sin admonishes, walking further into the room to eye us both with derive interest.

"Your brother has his eye on another woman. Isn't that right Slay? Oh, or should I say stud?" Thorn sarcastically snubs at me. I snarl my lip up at her.

"I don't have my eye on another fucking woman Thorn!" I roar out madly infuriated.

Thorn crosses her arms over her chest while her eyes roam all over me indigently.

Her eyebrows furrow down intently as her eyes catch on to something suddenly. She takes a tiny step closer to me as I eye her cautiously. She holds out her tiny hand aiming it toward my lower region, her nimble little fingers clasp on to something that was hanging out in my front jean pocket.

She pulls it out gingerly when I finally notice what's surprisingly sitting in her hand I nearly choked on my own damn saliva.

Fuck no!

She turns the napkin over in her hand searching it thoroughly, I try my best to grab it away from her hand but she dodges away from me to damn quickly for me to even snatch it away from her unfortunately.

Fuck! Now I'm definitely in for it.

After she proceeds to read what is written on the napkin from the flirtatious barista she looks up at me with pure mortification marring her beautiful face. Great! Just fucking great!

"Are you for fucking for real?" She questions as she gives me a very vindictive glare. "This is just too damn much, have you actually read this?" She ask me exasperated while she's shoving the napkin directly in my face.

I just stand there to speechless to even offer her back a reply. Sunny and Sin both study Thorn trying their best to get a glimpse of what's written on the napkin in Thorns hand.

"Honestly, okay, let me be the one to read it to you then. 'Why don't you try your luck? If you want a good time and a good fuck, don't be a dud, just call me up sometime stud! Jessica.' And look, it even has her damn number on it." Thorn half huffs breathlessly defining me with a very churlish smoldering look.

I'm fucked!

"Get out!" She shouts with an acrid tone leaving no further arguments but my dumb ass tries anyway.

"Look, Thorn..." I begin.

"GET. THE. FUCK. OUT!" She shouts slamming her hand with the napkin flatly against my chest roughly. I grab ahold of the napkin aimlessly.

I open my mouth to apologize to her but I close it back up immediately when she gives me the worst icy glare that I have the misfortune to ever see from her.

Stumbling over Sin, I make my way over to the other bedroom door, walking backwards, trying to desperately plead to her with my eyes for forgiveness but Thorn just sniffles and turns away from me without utter a single fucking word.

My shoulders drop instantly when I see how broken she actually is.

Blowing out a heavy ragged breath I turn on my heel and walk into the other bedroom highly disappointed in myself. Spotting a small trash can in the corner I ball up the napkin in my hand and toss it right into it. Why didn't I do that earlier?

Hearing footsteps behind me I eagerly turn my head, hoping against hope that it's Thorn walking up behind me so I can apologize to her profusely but unfortunately it just had to be Sin!

He closes the adjoining door behind him as I slowly walk over to the bed, sliding back onto the pillows I let out a very discouraging huff.

"Boy did you just fuck up!" Well no shit Sin. Thanks for the obvious announcement! I scoff at him. Captain obvious this one is.

Asshole!

Sin strides over to the other side of the bed, he flops down on it making the mattress bounce as he does. With his body half laying on the bed and his elbow holding his upper body up he in turn fucking laughs at me.

"It's not funny Sin!" I can't believe the asshole finds humor in all of this. Folding my arms across my chest I give him a stern look.

"Oh, yea it is, welcome to the doghouse buddy, you want a biscuit?" The fucking asshole laughs again.

Glowering at him he suddenly quietens down but he still has a little devious smirk alighting up on his damn face.

"Why did you keep it?" Sin questions. Hell I don't know. Maybe I liked the attention? It's not like I was ever going to call her anyway but unfortunately Thorn is not in the mood to even listen to reason.

"Who knows!" I simply state lying my ass off again. Shame suddenly hits me when I see the cocky grin on Sins face. Of course he's enjoying this.

"You liked her didn't you?" I shake my head vehemently.

"No!" I didn't, I just liked the attention she gave me. Is there really any harm in that?

"Well you must of liked something about her. You just could of tossed the napkin in the damn trash." No shit! I could have but why didn't I?

Sin eyes me with suspicious, dropping the damn smirk off of his face finally. Everything goes quite for a few seconds then out of the blue Sin jumps off of the bed pacing the floor excitedly, combing his fingers through this short hair.

"Oh man please tell me you weren't planning on calling her?" I squint my eyes at him. How could he think so lowly of me?

"No I wasn't going to call her. I stuck the napkin in my pocket without even thinking honestly. I just thought it was cute the way she kept flirting with me but then Striker showed up and continuously flirted with Thorn right there in front of me. It was like I was invisible to both of them. Thorn just let him touch her all over. Well on her arm and hand, but still, it wasn't right. She could have pushed his ass away. Hell she didn't even sit down next to me. She sat down next to that asshole." I take a deep breath trying to calm down my raging fury again.

"So you were jealous and you used this girl, Jessica, to try and make Thorn jealous, for what, out of pure spite?" Well when he puts it that way it makes me sound just like a jealous fucking lunatic.

When the realization hits me like a fucking Mack truck going at hundred miles per hour, I grimace.

Damn I'm so fucking stupid.

"Yea that worked out great for you didn't it? Look, Slay, take it from someone who knows that using someone else just out of spite will get you fucking nowhere. I used Storm just as she used me and I regret it so damn much that it's nearly killing me." He says it with so much sadness laced in his tone that I actually feel sorry for his ass.

"Sin you were under a witches spell. You didn't have much choice in the matter. I fucking did! So don't be too damn hard on yourself. I'm sure Thorn will be able to eventually forgive you." I know she will. Thorn has a big heart full of compassion and my stupid ass just fucking crushed it.

"She won't even talk to me Slay. Hell she can't even look me in my eyes. How do I expect her to forgive me if I can't even forgive my damn self? She hates me and what's even worse is that I hate myself also for doing all of the bad shit I did to her. I don't deserve her forgiveness. I deserve to be locked up in the dungeon with Storm and Nina." Sin admits with a gravely tone walking back over to the side of the bed he sets down on it gently with his body half turned to me.

"But I'm going to work my ass off to prove to her that I can be just as good of a mate as Sunny is to her and maybe you should do the same." He suggest with clear sensitivity.

I can't honestly believe I'm even thinking this but I'm actually proud of him. He has definitely come along away from being the condescending asshole he use to be to now opening up about his feelings and being a hell of lot kinder and wiser. But there seems to be an underlining concern with me about him and what Freya quoted to us earlier. It's been bothering me.

'The one thing that haunts your mind is not by any means who you truly are. The way you feel for one does not mean you will feel that for others.' That alone raises the upmost suspicions in me.

"What did Freya mean when she told you about the way you feel for one does not mean you will feel for the others?" I question him methodically.

Sins eyes open wide in surprise for just a second then he lets out a huge shaky exhale closing his eyes briefly when he opens them back up again I note the change of color in them instantly. Malice is at the forefront now. Sins eyes are now a bright red blood hue that are frighteningly staring over at me.

"Malice?" I stammer.

"Yes." I guess Malice has finally returned, thank fuck, I was beginning to get worried about him.

"Did you need to talk to me?" I question peering at his red shot eyes.

"Sin is too afraid to speak on this matter so I decided to take over the reigns from him because you should know what's going on with him. I'm doing this for him. He is leaving it in my hands willingly." Malice states almost robotically.

"Okay what is it?" I ask.

"Sin finds himself in a complicated query. When he was sixteen years old, him and Pan kissed. Every since that day Sin has always had his doubts about his own sexuality. He loves Pan but he doesn't understand his own feelings." I click my tongue at Malice.

I'm actually not surprised about Sins confusion. I've seen the way that Pan and him interact with each other. I always thought that Sin viewed Pan as more than just a usual friend or Beta. It seems my suspicions may have been correct all along.

"Can I talk to Sin now?" I ask needing to have this conversation with just Sin.

"Yes." Malice exclaims as Sins eyes go from a blood red to now a dark honey hazel. He blinks a few times rapidly then shakes his head vehemently. He turns his head slightly away from me, trying his best to avoid my gaze.

"Sin. Can I ask you serious question?" Sin turns back to me with, staring over at me apprehensively.

"When you look at other men does it do something for you? Like, when you look into their eyes or even their body does it turn you on?" I ask with soft sincerity.

"Actually no. It's only because of the kiss that I find myself worrying about this, because I liked it Slay. It did turn me on. I got hard instantly when he kissed me, but no, other men don't do anything for me." Sins openness and honesty about his long kept secret is inspiring.

"Then you are definitely not gay or even bisexual. If it only happened with Pan then it's just because Pan did turn you on but that doesn't mean that you like men Sin. It only means that you liked Pan." Sin peers over at me slightly confused.

"When you look at Thorn how does it make you feel?" I ask him cutting straight to the point.

"I do get turned on by her. She is beautiful and it doesn't hurt that she has a rocking body either but more than that she is compassionate, loving, and a hell of a spitfire. I want to be with her Slay. I want to be her mate. Her lover. Her everything. I just doubted my own sexual orientation because of what I felt for Pan. That's all. Thorn is like my dream woman. My dream Goddess actually. She's damn near perfect in my eyes and I didn't want to hurt her if later on I found out that I'm actually gay or even bisexual. That would not have of been fair to her or or even to me in anyway." Well fuck! I'm seeing another side of my brother that I didn't think that was actually possible.

"Well then I guess that solves that. You are definitely not gay Sin. You were just attracted to Pan and you were so young. Too young to even know what you wanted." He has to see that.

"I think you may be right." He states while giving me his famous lopsided grin.

"So now what are we going to do about winning Thorn over?" I screwed up just as much as Sin has. I hate myself of it.

"Do you...love her?" Sin ask almost embarrassingly so.

"Yes." I answer him quickly without a doubt in my mind I do indeed deeply love her.

"Then apologize to her Slay. I'm sure she will understand once you explain everything to her" Yea right.

I hate it but I don't think it's going to be that easy to win Thorn over. For one she is very stubborn headed to a fault but I still love her even if she is and for another, I fucked up royally by using someone else to make her jealous instead of just facing my own damn jealousy demons.

Thorn may not find that so easy to forgive. She hasn't even forgiven Sin yet over Storm. This is going to take more than just a simple apology. I may just have to beg or do something else. This is going to take some ingenuity on both of our parts.

Maybe I should buy her some flowers? No that seems way too damn cheesy. A gift? Some jewelry? Everyone woman loves something shiny and sparkly right? All of these ideas rushing through my head just seem way to damn lame and far too common.

"Any ideas on how we may get her to eventually forgive us?" I inquire of him modestly.

"I have no idea. I have been trying to come up with that answer for a while now." Well hell.

Looks like we are, like Sin referred to earlier, both in the damn doghouse.

Woof! Woof!

Later that night I get awoken, while sleeping next to Sin who is snoring rather loudly, the sounds escaping from the other room apparently from Thorn and Sunny are just too damn alluring to drag me back into my slumber.

The moans and groans casting out from the other room put me on full alert instantly. They sound so damn illicit and alluring.

It even manages to awaken Sin who was sleeping soundlessly beside me just a second ago.

"Is that what I think it is?" He ask me groggily. Easing his head up from the comfort of his pillows peering over at the door. Yea I actually think it is.

Sliding out from under the covers and off the bed, I slowly edge my way over to the adjoining door pressing my ear upon it half way leaning in.

Sin soon joins me as he presses his ear on the lower part of door leaning over to it on the opposite side of me.

I feel like a damn pervert listening in on them but for some reason I just can't drag myself away from the door.

After a few slurpy kissing noises we hear someone walking around the room with light steps and a smacking noise that I can't seem to identify yet.

"Bend over!" Thorn commands in a very rough and de-manding voice.

"Yes mistress!" Oh fuck! Did I just hear that right? Is Sunny playing submissive? Interesting.

Pressing my ear firmer onto to the door I eagerly await for whatever is going to happen next.

Smack!

What sounds like a whip echos up to us. I suddenly hear Sunny groan out in insurmountable pleasure.

Another smack then I hear a loud strained grunt.

"Have you been a bad boy slave?" Thorn ask Sunny sexily. Fuck! I don't know about Sunny but I indeed sure have. My dick expands quickly, from hearing such a dominating and sexy tone coming from Thorn. I didn't know she had it in her.

Hell I always thought that I was definitely a dominant lover but after hearing this I just may change my tune. Submission does have its redeeming qualities also.

"Yes mistress. I'm sorry mistress." Sunny pleads with Thorn. We hear yet another loud whipping smack coming from the room.

I wince, from the sound of the sudden erotic impact.

"On your damn knees slave!" Well fuck me! It almost makes me want to bend down and get on my own damn knees just for her.

"Yes mistress." We hear faint shuffling, presumably it's Sunny climbing to his damn knees as she so delicately commanded.

After another few seconds of heavy breathing and slight movements we then hear Thorns demanding tone slashing throughout the room again.

"Come and dine on me slave!" What the actual fuck? I catch of glimpse of Sin that's just a few centimeters off across from me. His face is showing avid and general interest also. At least I'm not only one getting off on this. Thank fuck!

Then we both hear Thorn purring with delicious moans while the sounds of Sunny eating her pussy out transverse over to us. I fucking groan.

How I wish that was me. I can actually smell Thorns apparent arousal from here. Cinnamon and vanilla is such a heady mixture that non other can even rival it. Remembering instantly mine and Thorns own love fest from last night of when I tasted that sweet ambrosia. I get extremely hard just from recalling it all.

"Now come here and fuck the hell out of me slave!" Thorn defiantly demands. Oh shit! Now that's a fucking turn on! Command me baby! I've been a very bad boy!

"Fuck yes mistress!" Sunny's excitement is erotically influential. I would bow down to her commands just as Sunny is now. I would feel no shame in it either. Whatever she wished for I would immediately and obediently comply with her in a damn heartbeat.

Grunting noises come from the room now along with the sound of skin meeting skin rapidly and very brutally.

Damn! Sunny is fucking her unmercifully.

"Fuck yes Sunny. Just like that!" Thorn moans. Daaaamn.

I don't know if I can listen to this much longer before I end up blowing my own damn load right here in my fucking boxers. How fucking embarrassing that would be?

Then to my surprise I hear skin being broken open and torn. Did Sunny just mark her? A sudden fragrance of iron hits my nostrils immediately. It is a definite sign that he most assuredly did indeed mark her. Then following right behind it I can smell Sunny's blood mixed with the aroma of Thorns own defining blood signature.

I'll be damn!

They marked each other.

Good for Sunny. I can't help but to crack a knowing smile at that. With Sunny loving her like he does this will only cement their relationship even further.

Now I'm disappointingly turning very fucking envious of him. How did I get in this fucking position? I sigh, knowing I only have myself to blame for it though.

The skin to skin pounding sounds starts to pick up again. Slowly at first then rocket into a mad and unrelenting frenzy.

Grunts and moans still cascade over to us.

I can hear Sins breathing start to pick up dramatically over from me.

With all three of them breathing rather heavily my own breathing starts to pick up rapidly. This is titillating as hell.

Closing my eyes I can just picture the four of us all together in one steamy make out session. Fuck how I wish that was true right now.

"Papi I'm about...." Thorn doesn't get to finish before I hear a wave of guttural moaning coming from her and Sunny both.

"Yesss!" Thorn bellows out very loudly in heated desire.

"Fuck Yes, Yes, Thorn!" Sunny roars at what I'm assuming is his climax hitting him at full throttle.

Fuck! This is just too damn much for me. Too hear Thorn moan in such unbridled passion for Sunny sends my stupid jealousy raging out again.

I can't believe I'm jealous of my own damn brother.

Now all we hear is heavy ass panting coming from both of them.

I take away my ear away from the door, grunting very uncomfortably. My damn cock is throbbing in my boxers almost painfully now.

"I'm going to go take a cold shower." Sin informs me standing up straight to his full height while adjusting his boxers in mild discomfort.

At least I'm not only one painfully uncomfortable right now.

"Hurry up! I'm going to need one also!" I grumble as Sin laughs while steadily walking away to the damn bathroom.

Asshole.

Wobbling over to the side of the bed to wait on my turn for the shower. I sit down on the edge of it staring over at the adjoining door that connects our two rooms together forlornly.

I got to fix this shit between Thorn and I and fast. If I have to continuously listen to Thorn and Sunny or even Sin, in the future, make love to Thorn like that. I think I might just lose my damn mind.

I love her deeply and somehow I desperately need to show her just that.

But I don't fucking know how?

Chapter 22

Last night was perfect.

After our love session I asked Thorn out on a date. She replied yes quickly which in turn made me one very happy wolf.

The only exception I made for the date was that Slay and Sin would have to come along also.

She argued with me over it for a time but ended up succumbing to it eventually.

I only did this so we can work out all of the problems between us finally. Wanting desperately to finally put an end to all of this back biting and fighting that's been driving me completely mad lately.

First, I made us reservations at a fine restaurant called, The Fata Cibus, then off to dancing but the only thing I could find even close to a club was a western motif bar called, The Wrangler Wild Post, strange name but it was either that or some dive called, The Stripper Tease, I seriously don't think Thorn would of been too fond of that one.

As of now we're all getting dressed up for our evening out. Hopefully this will help after Slays and Thorns argument yesterday.

I hate to see all of us on edge like this. Tiptoeing around each other, too afraid to say a word, just in case someone might take what someone else should say too offensively. It's all just ridiculous.

Deciding on wearing a long sleeved buttoned up white silk shirt with black denim jeans along with it, I spray on a touch of axe cologne after I'm dressed.

Sin is dressed in a blue long sleeved buttoned up shirt just like mine but with blue denim jeans to go along with his.

Slay on the other hand decided to go per his usual with a plain black T-shirt and faded black denim jeans.

I should have known he wouldn't go against his usual style though.

Almost ready I slip on my handy Timberland boots slightly adjusting my pant legs over them.

While I wait for Slay and Sin to finish getting ready I edge my way over to the adjoining door listening for any sounds of Thorn on the other side of it. As I'm listening the door suddenly swings open revealing a very striking Thorn appearing in the doorway in a dress that in my opinion is showing way too much skin for my own liking.

She looks damn good in it though. My throat instantly becomes dry just from looking at her in it.

My eyes are glued to her, even when I hear shuffling coming up from behind me I can't seem to draw my eyes away from that sexy as fuck body.

"Hell no! Go back in there and change right now Thorn!" Slay rudely demands of her as he is stomping his way over to us.

"What? Do you not like it?" Thorn ask innocently peering down at her dress.

"Oh I like it. Just a little too damn much though. Go change into something more discreet." He commands again but when Thorn looks up at him with storming emotions brewing behind those blue eyes of hers Slay adds on a quick, "Please!"

"Fine!" Thorn grumbles going back into the other room slamming the door behind her as she goes.

Just fucking great!

"What's your deal? Why couldn't you just let her wear it? So much for a peaceful evening!" I taunt Slay.

"It was too short and I could see almost everything." Although Slay seems to think that his reasonable explanation for his outburst is warranted, I think he's just full shit.

"You just didn't want other guys staring at her." I state the obvious, huffing.

"Well, yea. She's fucking beautiful Sunny. I don't want to have to fight off other men over her tonight." His cavemen brutality is going to end up getting him and Thorn into another damn argument again if he doesn't calm that shit down.

Thorn then reappears into the room in another dress. One that I think is almost as revealing as the first one was but I'm not saying a word about it.

"Will this work your majesty?" Thorn ask Slay extremely sarcastically.

"No but it will do I guess." Slay relinquished.

Thank fuck!

"Now can we get the hell out of here?" I ask them all hastily.

The Fata Cibus, is a quaint but stylish restaurant that serves an abundant amount of variety of foods.

Finally seated with our food already ordered we sit amongst others talking around us in the lightly packed restaurant but between the four of us there remains an awkward silence.

Even after our meals arrival we all sit here measly eating our fine food without either of us taking to one another.

I can't stand this!

After a few more minutes of torturous silence I open my mouth up to speak finally but I get interrupted quickly by a cellphones piercing ring.

Thorn retrieves her phone out of her handbag looking down at the screen very curiously while deeply scowling down at it.

"Excuse me." She replies softly rising up from her chair then slowly walking a distance away from us with her cellphone pressed up against her ear.

Then Slays cellphone rings interrupting us yet again.

Slay answers his phone with sour gruffness.

"Hello." He answers rudely.

"Oh hey hello. What's up?" His tone immediately changes with whomever is on the other end of the phone talking to him.

"Really? Okay then I'll inform them. Thanks for calling." He states in a rather dour manner.

"Who was it?" I question Slay but before he can answer me Thorn returns sitting back down in her chair, then placing her cellphone back into her handbag looking back up at us with a very dour look upon her face also.

"Sorry." She mumbles as she scoots up her chair closer to the table.

"Well? Who called?" Sin ask them both impatiently.

"That was Cameron." Why the hell is her ex calling her for? "Storm and Nina got handed down their punishments today." Oh now I completely understand both of their dour expressions.

"And?" Sin presses.

"It seems that Nina will serve ten years with the addition of having her wolf killed." Slay informs us timidly.

As he says it all of the attention is directed straight at me now. What do they expect me to do or say? Are they waiting for my reaction?

The news about Nina is not surprising to me at all though. I knew she would get some fierce punishment I just didn't know what kind.

But for what she had done it seems rather fitting to me. I don't exactly like it but what can I do about it? She did this to herself.

"Alright." I reply very nonchalantly.

They all eye me with trepidation.

"What? She got what she deserved okay?" I admonished and that's my honest opinion, what else can I actually say.

Slay clears his throat then looks over to Sin sitting beside him, "Storms punishment was a little worse." Here we go!

Slay begins to fidget in his seat. Clearly uncomfortable with what he's about to tell Sin.

Thorn apparently sees Slays discomfort and informs Sin instead of Slay giving him a reprieve.

"She will be imprisoned for ten years but uhm, she also lost her wolf and....well, she foolishly backed talked the Queen while she was in captivity. Unfortunately she did it while in front of King Talon. She called her some very foul names. He uhm, well, he...ended up cutting out her tongue for vagrant disobedience toward the Queen." Thorn stammers out while not quite being able to look Sin directly in his eyes.

All goes silent again. We all watch Sin as he absorbs the information in quiet disparity.

"Excuse me." Sin mumbles slowly standing up from his seat, he walks away toward the back of the restaurant probably heading to the restrooms located in the back.

Silence resumes once again. Maybe going out tonight wasn't such a great idea on my part after all? I felt at the time that it was actually a good idea but now all I feel is an insurmountable amount of remorse for Sin.

"I guess he did love her or loves her. I actually thought he didn't. I guess I was wrong. If it wasn't for me this wouldn't have happened to Storm, Nina, or Sin. Or even you Sunny. I hate myself. This just isn't working out like I thought it would. Thank you Sunny for trying, with this date night and all but I think I'll just go back to the inn." Thorn states verily melancholically as she quickly stands.

"What? No Thorn this isn't because of..." I start.

"Yes it is. Please don't try to sugarcoat it with simple platitudes. This is all my fault but thank you for trying." She replies with a touch of regret.

Before either of us can utter a word to her she walks away from us leaving Slay and I totally speechless.

"What just happened?" Slay ask. I wish the hell I knew. Dropping my fork on top of my steak, I turn half way in my seat to find wherever Thorn may have went to.

I catch a glimpse of her at the exit talking to a strange man. My eyes widen when I see how easily they seem to be getting along. Who is that?

"Slay, who is she talking to?" I ask maybe it's Striker? I haven't formally been introduced to him yet.

"Is that Striker?" I ask him absentmindedly staring at the two of them by the exit in heavy conversation.

"No it's definitely not." Slay says while he stands up gradually from his seat with his eyes stiffly glued on Thorn.

Sin then makes his reappearance. He stands next to Slay furrowing his brows at him. "What are you looking at?" Sin questions Slay while following Slays eyes to the exit door.

I stand along with them eyeing the couple with curiosity plaguing me.

As we stand there observing them both, Thorn turns in our direction pointing her finger toward us. They both eventually start making their way back over to us. "They're coming over here!" Sin states. We all hurriedly sit back down in our seats acting semi casually.

"Slay, Sunny, Sin, I would love for you all to meet Grayson Hatch. Freyas nephew." I recall Freya mentioning him. The one that works as one of Samuels guards if I recall it correctly.

"Nice to meet you." Sin replies holding out his hand. Grayson shakes his hand smiling over at Sin.

We all do the same in return.

"Would you care to join us?" Sin ask him politely. What the hell has gotten into Sin?

"Thanks but I can't but I would love to steal away this one from you three for just a bit." Grayson replies smiling widely at Thorn standing beside him. She gives him a wide smile of her own. Making me instantly jealous. Now I know how Slay felt with Thorn over Striker.

"They won't mind. Shall we?" Thorn replies before we can even supply our own answers.

She waves her hand toward the exit, "I'll see you three in a just a bit." She states rather abruptly. Leaving the three of us at the table silenced yet again.

They both walk off from us talking with each other like their long lost friends.

What the hell just happened?

"Did we just get dumped?" I ask disbelievingly. I had this entire night planned down to a T.

"I think we did. What the hell happened after I left?" Sin inquires almost disapprovingly.

I sigh out with regret then start describing the encounter after he left to him in full detail.

By the time I am finished with the retelling Sins reactions go from mild interest to being mostly somber in flat second.

"I don't love Storm. I just feel guilty. Don't get me wrong I do have feelings for Storm or had but it was definitely not love. If you would like me for me to define it in more simpler terms I think what I felt for Storm was just pure lust and nothing more. Yea, I feel bad for what's happened to her. I don't think the punishment fits the crime exactly. Her mouthing off to Miracle was uncalled for and I know how much King Talon loves Miracle so that to me is understandable in a sense. But killing her wolf was extreme. If that is the punishment that Storm had gotten then maybe it's what I should receive also. There's no excuse for what I did to Thorn or to you guys. I can't blame the witches spell on everything I did. Before, what was her name? Song? Sang? No, Singa. Before Singa came along I absolutely wanted Thorn out of our lives. But now that I know that I'm not who I actually thought I once was I want her in our lives beyond a shadow of a doubt. I just wish I knew how to fix this. I hate it knowing that Thorn blames herself for what me and Storm did to her. She deserves better me. But I just don't know how to fix this guys." Sins raw emotions startle me. I never knew he actually felt this way. "Plus, I truly think Storm was the one to send Singa my way. I'm just guessing but I'm pretty sure it was her. But how do I explain all of this to Thorn and make her understand?" He adds.

"You can start by apologizing to me. That seems to always work some. Then you can all three take me out to dance and drink the night away. I think we most definitely need it." Thorn says suddenly from behind me.

Startling all three of us. For werewolves we sure are lacking in the in the sensing department apparently.

"I'm so damn sorry Thorn. Please accept my apology. I hope that maybe we can try to start anew, you and I? I'll explain everything to you about why I done what I did. If you would just give me a chance to." Sin states as he stands up from his seat strolling over to her.

I turn again in my seat to watch them both. Sin grasp ahold of Thorns hands in his own, pleading with her with his eyes.

"Oh, Sin. I accept your apology and yes, I will hear you out but not tonight. Tonight I think we should just let lose and enjoy ourselves for awhile. We definitely need it." That we definitely do.

Springing up from my chair I quickly go to stand beside them both.

"Then what are we waiting for?" I ask excitedly.

Wrangler Wild Post, here we come. The Only problem now is that I don't know a damn thing about country music.

Oh well, who cares, Yeehaw!

It's not exactly what I envisioned, that's for damn sure.

I thought there would be a lot of country folks in cowboy boots and hats, boy was I wrong.

There's a live band with tons of people dancing and drinking. Overcrowded is definitely understatement here.

As we shuffle our way in between the mounds of people, trying to find a spot somewhere near the bar, I get tossed and pushed around by very inebriated people who are jovially having a very rowdy time tonight.

When we finally were able to reach the bar, the music was loud we could barely even hear to order own drinks.

Eventually, we all got our drinks from a very happy and over eagerly bartender.

We ended up drinking a few rounds happily.

Listening the country drawl of the band playing at the end of the building I start to sway back and forth to the beat unknowingly.

"Would you like to dance?" Thorn ask while screaming at me.

I laugh then nod my head vigorously to her.

Making our way through the rambunctious crowd we end up somewhere close to the middle of the dance floor.

I haven't the foggiest idea how to dance to this type of music.

But hell I'll give it a shot. After five drinks already I'm starting to feel a little looser.

So we dance.

Although I have two left feet I'm somewhat pulling it off. Thorn is laughing at me as she grinds her hips to the foreign music.

She looks so damn beautiful and the woman can actually dance. Her body shifts and fluctuates like a damn seductress.

Then unfortunately the music comes to halt suddenly.

"Okay friends. Tonight we're going to light it up with a song that you all know and love. So sing it loudly with me folks. Here is suck my dick one more time." The performer or singer on the stage suddenly announces.

"Really?" I yell at Thorn eyeing the band up on the stage. "That's the name of the song?" I add. Shaking my head.

The band begins to play a trumped up rendition of One More Time by Britany Spears, although by the name of the title of the song I'm pretty sure it's not exactly the same.

I thought this was a country bar anyway?

The band begins to play we start dancing again to the trumped up song that sounds just a bit off key to me.

When it gets to the chorus everyone in the bar stops dancing immediately. I look around amazed at them.

Then we hear everyone start yelling out at the band all at once.

"My horniness is killing me, and I, must confess, I'm still horny,still horny. When I'm with you,I just want to grind. All the time. So baby, suck my dick one more time!" Everyone yells out along with the band.

Wow! Ok then.

By the time the chorus comes around again me and Thorn are both singing along with them.

"So baby, Suck my dick one more time!" We all sing simultaneously.

Have to admit it's sort of fun.

Makes me wonder what other quirky song the band has.

After a few hours of dancing and drinking we're about to call it a night since it's getting close to two in the morning and Thorn has to be at the magazine office building early.

As we're exiting the building another song picks up by the band that I actually had to halt in my tracks to listen in to before we all left.

It's another trumped up rendition but of a very different type of song. One that I actually love.

But it's a female singer at the front the band this time.

As I wait Thorn comes to stand beside me. I just have to hear how they will portray this particular song before we all leave.

The music kicks up. It almost completely sounds just like Wanted Dead or Alive by Bon Jovi, almost.

Then the chorus comes up quickly. I wait on it on bated breaths.

"I'm a cowgirl,on a big dick I ride!I'm wanted, wanted,Best when I ride."

Alrighty then. Yep I'm so out of here.

Back at the inn finally I stumble into the room clumsily. Way too many drinks are starting to hit my blood stream quickly.

Thankfully, Thorn was smart enough to limit her drinks tonight.

She and Slay helps me into the room laughing uproariously at me between each of my stumbles. I don't mind it's good to hear her laughter after her sudden announcement tonight, I honestly thought she was going to leave us.

I crash onto the bed, nearly falling off of the edge of it as I go.

"I'll see you in the morning Sunny and don't forget to take the elixir." Thorn replies walking away from the bed and from me.

"Wait. I want a goodnight kiss!" I mumble puckering my lips up toward her. She lets out another hearty laugh as she walks back over to me.

Her lips graze mine softly. Nope, not going to work.

I place my hand on the back of her head deepening the kiss.

Sparks soar right through me.

When we break apart I cock my head peering into those damn beautiful cove blue eyes of hers.

"Sleep with me!" I plead with her sweetly but she just shakes here head at me making me dizzy instantly.

"I'm sleeping with Sin tonight. Get some rest Sun. I love you!" Thorn softly whispers next to my ear.

"I love you too. Wait! You love me?" I ask her bewildered.

"Of course I do Sun." She states slightly giggling.

I can't believe my ears.

She loves me!

She loves me!

"She fucking loves me!" I scream out loudly.

"Shhh. Sunny the entire inn can hear your ass. Besides, she's already left." Slay informs me.

I crane my head up from the bed searching for my beautiful Thorn. Uhm, Slays right she left.

Bouncing my head back down on the pillow below me I peer over at Slay.

"Hey Slay... can I tell...you a...secret?" I whisper, slurring at him.

"Sure. What is it?" Slay says while blowing out a dire breath.

"Before....before I marked our lovely Thorn I...made...a... mis....mistake." I hiccup between my words.

"What did you do?" Alright now I'm seeing two of Slay. They keep floating against each other. I reach out trying to grab one of them.

"When did you get a twin?" I ask him dumbfounded. He slaps my hand away. Ouch!

"What? Damn Sunny just go to sleep you are way too drunk!" Well duh? Of course I am.

"Any...way...don't tell...Thorn okay?" I mumble while burping. Man my breath stinks. Nasty!

"Damn Sunny excuse you and don't tell Thorn what?" Huh? What was I saying? Then I remembered. Oh yeah.

"Don't tell....her....okay. She...will..leave me." And she won't come back. Not this time.

"What did you do Sunny?" Why is he so mad?

"I...didn't...mean to Slay. After....she left the...second no th ird...no second...time. The second...time after she uhm...left. I did...something...stupid." And I will regret it to my dying day.

"Sunny just tell me. What did you do?" Well hell he's getting more upset with me. Maybe I shouldn't tell him.

"Never mind." I murmured.

"No Sunny. Tell me what the hell you did!" Damn! My head is starting to pound now. Why does he keep screaming at me?

"I...cheat...cheated..on her." Fuck!

"You did what? With who Sunny? Nina?" Nina? Fuck no I would never.

"With...Shari." I confess as my eyes start to get very droopy.

"Sins ex? Damn Sunny what did you do? Why? Why would you do that to her?" Why is Slay so sad now?

"I...thought we..lost her...for...forever." I cough in between every word. "I didn't think she...would...come back."

"Fuck Sunny! Man did you fuck up! Why didn't you tell me? What made you so desperate? You are an asshole. If Thorn finds out, you're right, she will leave all of us and all because of you!" He's screaming again. Damn my head.

"I know." I half mummer almost asleep. "I'm sorry." I add.

"Fuck sorry. Sunny you just messed up our entire lives. She will never forgive you! You have to tell her!" Slay nudges me awake.

"What!" I grumble.

"Don't what me asshole. You just destroyed my relationship with Thorn beyond repair just because you were a damn pussy and wanted to get your damn dick wet! Wake the fuck up Sunny!" Slay shakes my entire body. Instantly I get nauseous. I lean over the bedside and spew out all of the steak had for diner earlier.

"Fuck!" I hear Slay yell behind me.

After a few seconds of my upheaval I start to dry heave, gagging a couple of times before it all eventually stops. Thank fuck! Now my damn breath really stinks.

Falling back on the pillows I place my arm across my eyes that are now glossy and watering.

I hear Slay grumbling as he is cleaning up my gross mess beside me.

"Dammit Sunny this shit is fucking gross!" Slay complains at me loudly.

I'm not particularly in the mood to listen to his complaints. After throwing up I sobered up far too quickly.

Slay finishes cleaning up the vomit then he climbs back into the bed beside me. Huffing.

"I fucked up. I know that Slay but how am I suppose to tell her that?" Man this could destroy us all.

"Don't tell her. Please. She just said she loved me Slay. How can I tell her now?" I plead with him earnestly.

"There's also another problem." This is has been tormenting me for days now.

"What now. Like you cheating on Thorn isn't enough?" Slay replies sarcastically. Yea I deserve that and more unfortunately.

"Shari is coming to visit our pack in the next day or two. She called me asking if I could meet her there. She has something very important to tell me apparently." Fuck I hate this. "She asked if she could stay there until we got back."

"Well she can't pregnant. For one it's far too soon and for another unless it was done under a special moon she wouldn't be able to get pregnant. So what could she tell you that's so damn important Sunny? Besides, I won't allow it. Not after what you just told me. I just can't. She can't stay with us either Sun." I knew he would say something like that.

"No I don't think she's pregnant but..." Fuck how do I say this?

"After we had sex a few times that night I did, in the heat of the moment, kind of promise her that I would make her my Luna." I grimace away from him.

"YOU DID WHAT?" Damn! Doesn't he realize he's going to draw unwanted attention to us?

"Shut up Slay. Keep it down. What if Thorn heard you?" I grit through my teeth.

"Well maybe she should jackass. I thought better of you Sunny. Out of all three of us I actually thought that you would be the one who would make Thorn happy. Not cheat on her. I never thought in a million damn years that you would be capable of that and to promise Shari that she could be your Luna? What the hell were thinking?" I have no fucking clue!

"I wasn't. I was just missing Thorn and so upset that she left. I ran into Shari at Sins Shop, Sin wasn't there thankfully but I got drunk and just slept with her out of pure loneliness. I don't know how else to explain it Slay." I bellow not realizing how loud I actually gotten until unfortunately it was too damn late.

Hearing a tiny gasp from across the room I automatically jerk my head to the adjoining door and there stands my beautiful mate looking at me with a terror stricken face.

Fuck!

Chapter 23

And I thought I was a major fuck up!

After hearing Sunny's ill timed confession, Thorn went crying off into the bedroom slamming the door behind as she went.

I turned my full fury rage on to a drunken stupor ass Sunny that is still lying in the damn bed looking utterly distraught.

But I don't fucking care how bad he actually feels. He just crushed my mates heart in to pieces and now I'm about to fucking crush him!

Storming over to the bed I double up my fist and punch him right square in his damn nose. Sunny flinched his head back from the mighty impact groaning out like a damn fucking ass whiny little bitch.

"You fucking deserved it. Just when I was starting to get somewhere with Thorn you go and do some dumb ass shit like this and for what? Just to get your damn kicks off! Don't ever look at me again like I'm the damn devil that aimlessly hurt Thorn. You even fucking rival me jackass!" I state my case with him snarling down at him.

"Sin take it easy. Maybe you should go check on Thorn. I'll take care of Sunny." Slay insist formidably. Fine with me.

I give Sunny a deep forced growl before I leave Slay and him alone to go and check up on Thorn.

I stop in my tracks as soon as I get to the adjoining door. Turning back around I peer over at Sunny.

"Did you say Shari? My ex? Please tell me you didn't sleep with my damn ex!" I growl out at him ferociously.

"Yes it was Shari. Shari White. I'm sorry Sin. It just happened." Sunny replies while holding his hand up against his bleeding nose.

Fuck! No! No! No! He doesn't understand.

"Sunny," I drawl out his name, "Shari has a mate. That's why I split with her. Don't you remember? He's the Beta of the Howler Pack, Simon Slayer. From Alpha Tyler Darks pack? Oh damn Sunny he will kill you. He's a mean ass son-of-a-bitch and anyone that comes near his mate ends up as fish food." Simon is a devious prick who gets away with just about anything because he has the powerful Alpha Dark supporting his ass.

"I didn't know." Sunny mummers. Of course not.

"Why is she even back? Alpha Darks pack is in the west. Why would she even be here?" I mumble the thought mainly to myself.

"Sunny you need to stay in this Realm until we can figure out exactly what is going on. Do not go home! If Beta Slayer gets any hint about you being with his mate Shari. He will definitely kill your ass." What the fuck are we going to do now?

"Isn't he the Beta that killed Alpha Darks daughter though? Why hasn't he been captured?" Slay questions.

"Because Alpha Dark wanted his daughter dead. They covered up everything. I can't believe that you two can't remember this. Alpha Dark hated his daughter because she was mated to the Alpha of his rival pack, The Shadow Moon packs Alpha. Alpha Dryson Taylor. It happened right after mom and dads plane crash. They went to war with each other. Alpha Dark put an end to Alpha Taylor's pack and took it over. He's a very visceral man." After I broke up with Shari and she found her mate I heard all about this.

It terrified me at the time. Thinking that Beta Slayer was going to come and hunt my ass down and kill me for sleeping with his mate.

Thankfully, that never happened.

"What am I going to do?" Sunny ask dropping his hand away from his face immediately looking very despondent.

Oh yea Sunny just fucked up royally.

"We will figure something out. In the meantime Sin can you please go check on Thorn? I can't hear her crying any longer!" Slay ask worriedly.

"Sure. I'll be right back." I inform them. We need it work out some type of plan now to protect Sunny.

Opening the adjoining door I step into the room quietly. Easing my way in I search the room for Thorn. Not being able to see her I walk over to the ensuite bathroom to check on her in there.

I rap my knuckles on the door softly. "Thorn are you okay?" I ask her timidly.

But she doesn't answer. Trying again I still receive no reply from within.

So I try my luck at opening the bathroom door as it opens with a slight creak I find it empty also.

Scrunching up my brows I walk over to the side closet.

Please tell me she didn't leave?

Opening the closet I find it virtually empty with the exception of mine and some of my bothers clothes, there is nothing else left hanging in it.

Then I remembered her suitcase that she stuffed under the bed.

Stomping over to the bed I kneel down pulling back the duvet to search underneath the bed.

Empty again.

Fuck!

She left!

Again!

I spring up fast running into Slays and Sunny's room.

"She fucking left!" I scream.

We can't find her anywhere.

After searching for hours we have come up empty handed.

We searched the magazine company and even at Freyas. We also asked Hope if she just might happen to be staying another room. Hope looked at us like we were crazy. Maybe we are.

Because we can't fucking find her and it's driving us all nuts.

She left with all of the little white cards that Freya gave her, leaving us clueless on how to reach out to even that guy Grayson. We asked Freya for his number or his damn address but unfortunately she had to go and ask us why.

We ended up telling her the truth and because of that she wouldn't give us the damn information we wanted.

She told us and I quote 'I warned you!' Very snidely.

Now we are walking down basically every fucking street looking for her.

Even Slay and Sunny can't sense her through their damn bonds for some reason. I know that Thorn is half Fae so I reasoned she must have used some type of magic on the bond.

I also realize that her powers or abilities aren't mastered yet so I actually don't know how she would have been able to do it but stranger things have fucking happened.

Getting tired and restless I stop in at the coffee shop beside the magazine company that Thorn was suppose to work at today.

The door chimes a soon as I entered. The place is almost empty, only a few customers are seated in the booths. They all look at me strangely as I entered but I ignored them all. Too damn tired to even care at this point.

Stepping up to the counter the barista saunters over to a another customer. A goth looking type of girl, I wait as she tends to the other customer.

When she finally notices me behind the counter she gives me a broad smile as she strolls over.

"What can I get you stud?" Why does that sound so damn familiar?

I ignore it and place my order.

"Large hazelnut coffee." I grumble to her.

She walks off with a sway in her hips to make the coffee.

I turn around at the counter just watching the traffic stream by out of the big bay window.

"Here you go stud." Flirtatious this one. I hand over the money grabbing up my steaming cup of coffee.

She offers me the change back. "Keep it." I wave my hand to her.

"Hold on." I scowl when she tells me this. The other customer to the side me watches on with valid interest at us both.

Watching her closely she grabs up a napkin and starts writing on it.

Handing me the napkin I read what she wrote. I laugh. I actually laugh at this. Now I remember.

"You miss thang have caused a lot of trouble lately. I don't want your damn number and I suggest for you to keep the flirting down to a minimum because one day you're going to find yourself flirting with the wrong man." She just huffs at me, I wad up the napkin in my hand and threw it right at her.

I just keep laughing at her as I'm walking out of the coffee shop, somewhat feeling accomplished.

It's not like she didn't deserve it.

Now, I need to find Thorn.

Two damn days have passed since Thorn has up and left us and we still haven't heard a damn thing from her.

I'm actually starting to get very worried about her now.

This isn't like her. Yea, she has ran away from us before but only once was that on her.

Sunny has been going crazy. Blaming himself consistently for Thorns sudden disappearance.

When all actuality we have all fucked up in someway when it comes to Thorn.

Slay has been nothing but fucking miserable. He's actually driving me crazy from his persistent nagging and belly aching.

His temper is at an all time high now. Every time someone even tries to talk to him he blows up.

I need to get Thorn back before my brothers have to check themselves into a mental asylum.

Me; I'm trying my best to hold us all together but it's not me they are wanting.

It's Thorn.

And I actually want her too. I'm the only damn one out of her mates who hasn't bonded with her yet and now I'm feeling very remorseful about all of that.

This would all be resolved easily if I could just fucking find her.

I hate this place. I so want to go back to our pack.

But knowing now that Beta Sawyer will be after Sunny's ass has made that quite impossible for us to do just yet.

Damn Sunny!

He just gave up on Thorn way too soon that's all. Well that's the way I see it anyway.

I'm not sure Thorn will be able to see it the way I do.

Only if she would just sit down and talk to all of us that would make this shit so much easier.

Instead I'm running around this stupid Realm, like a fucking chicken with his head cut off, searching for Thorn.

Night and day. Day and night. Endlessly searching for her is driving me into an early grave.

I'm damn tired and very weary. Completely exhausted to the point to where I just want to find a bed and fall out in for a week or two.

This getting beyond ridiculous.

Leaning against a street lamp, I sigh out heavily, trying to calm my raging worries.

People are walking by staring strangely over at me with confused and somewhat frightened looks on their faces.

It is just past ten at night and this city seems more crowded than ever. For it to be a Monday people are coming out in drones it seems.

I watch as a cute couple stroll by me clasping each other hands. They look like they're in their teens. So sweet though.

I reminisce as I watch them walk by me.

I miss her. I miss her so damn badly.

A few more stragglers pass by me eyeing me with valid uncertainty.

I just shake my head at them. I'm too tired to even care what they may think about me right now.

Way too tired.

Then I catch a glimpse of a person I somewhat know sneak-ily making his way across the street. As he gets to an unmarked building he looks all around his surroundings before he enters the buildings door.

Taking a chance, and full of hope I make my way over to the building stealthily.

Coming to the door I try the doorknob luckily it opens up without a problem.

Stepping into the building the cold air hits me suddenly. The place looks completely abandoned.

There is a stairwell just as you step initially into the building.

I close the door softly behind me then strain my ears to try and hear footsteps or something to alert me to wherever Grayson might be.

Hearing a faint sound at the top of the stairwell I climb each stair carefully. Trying to be as stealthy as I can.

I suddenly hear voices coming from a room located at the top of the stairs.

Off to my right two voices are in a heavy conversation.

I can't make out what they are saying just yet so I step a little closer to the closed door.

"I need to go back Grayson." I hear Thorns voice coming from behind the door. My heart starts racing from excitement. I found her.

I fucking found her and Grayson, the asshole, has been hiding her all along.

"Why Thorn? After what you told me why would you ever go back to them?" What the hell Grayson? Whose side are you actually on?

"Because they are my mates and I need to talk to them about...all of this." Thorn pleads with Grayson. Why is she begging him? What is he to her?

I step closer to the closed door, leaning in, listening in on them intently.

"Just reject them Thorn. Haven't they put you through enough already? How much more are you going to take from them?" Grayson is now pleading with Thorn but it doesn't make sense.

How close are they?

"It's not what you're thinking Gray. They need to know what's going on and they are my mates. How many times must we go over this? I can't keep this bond separation up much longer from them. It's making me weak. Besides, I know that Sunny fucked up but I have to think he has a reasonable explanation for it. He told me that he loved me Gray." Thorn sounds so despondent it nearly crushes me to hear her this way.

"It's just words Thorn. If he really loved you he wouldn't have cheated on you." Graysons voices starts to rise a little higher. I ball my hands up into fist. He's beginning to really piss me off.

What happens between her and myself and my brothers is actually none of his damn fucking business.

"I know Gray. I do but..."

"There is not but here Thorn stop being a damn a sidewalk for them that they can easily step on." The nerve of this guy! What gives him the damn right to speak to her that way?

I start to open the door ready to face them both that is until I hear Thorn speak up again.

"I'm not a damn sidewalk Gray. Can't you understand that, they are my mates and I can't do this without them. Freya even said so and you trust Freya right? So why are you not trusting me? I can handle this." So what? She just wants to come back to us so she can rescue her brother?

Is she using us? That doesn't make any sense either. Thorn would never stoop so damn low just use us would she? No not Thorn.

"We can do this without them Thorn. Stay with me please." Wait a damn minute.

Why is he begging her like she is his damn lover? Thorn would never betray us that way! That I have no qualms about.

She is just too faithful. Too compassionate. Too reliable and way too kind hearted to ever do anything like that to us.

I don't believe it. Not Thorn.

I shake my head even though no one's around to see it.

"Gray, I can't. I have to tell them. It's best to just get it out in the open and let the cards fall where they may." What is she talking about? I'm so damn confused right now.

"Then I'm going with you. You are not going to tell them without me being there. I don't trust them not after what all three of them have done to you. I just don't get it Thorn. Why? Why would you even care about telling them? It's not like they care anyway. No don't cut me off Thorn listen to me. Me and Seraphina have hidden you away from them all in the hopes that you would soon come to realize that I care for you. I don't want to see you get your heart broken once again. I just can't do that Thorn. If you chose to go back to them then I will have no choice but to stop helping you. Don't you see that? We are so close Thorn. Don't throw it all away on some false hope that your mates love you because from what I have heard from you and what they have done to you I truly don't think that they actually do." Grayson stops his rivalry. Pissing me off even more after what I've just heard.

I listen closely wanting desperately to here Thorns rebuttal to him before I go crashing through the door to rip him to shreds. Tell him we do love you Thorn.

Woah, wait a minute. What was I just thinking? How can I actually love Thorn when I don't really even know her that well yet. No it's just a turn of phrase. That's all it is. I'm sure of it.

"Fine Gray then I will have to go at this on my own. You can't lay down a threat like that with me. If you think you can then you don't know me to well at all. I'm a fucking fighter and I fight for what I think is right and I'm right about this. They need to know that my brother is sick and I have to get him out of there now rather than later. So if you don't want to help me then that's on you. Not me! Yes I understand that they may not love me like they have said they do but I love them Gray. All three of them and if you can't deal with that then just leave. Go! Im better off on my own anyway." Thorn screams.

She loves me? She loves all of us? Wow. I am beyond shocked at her reveal. How can Thorn love me? I have done nothing but make her life miserable every since we met.

She can't be that forgiving can she? How can she forgive me so damn easily? I can't even forgive myself.

The realization of her love for me leaves me confused and overwhelmed. How can she love someone like me?

And her brothers sick? That was the big secret she had to tell us? I knew she would never cheat on us. It's just not in her. Relief flows through me instantly. I actually almost had my doubts because it did sound like a lovers quarrel to me but now that I know the truth I feel horrible for even doubting her.

"Fine. If that's the way you want it I'll leave but know this Thorn. I do not support you in the slightest. They aren't worth it. They have broken your heart far too many times and you are just way too forgiving but because I care for you Thorn I will help you with your brothers escape. But know it's just not for you. It's for my kingdom and for justice. If you ever change your mind about your mates remember that I will be here for you but I can't stand around and watch you go back to them not after the way they have all treated you. You deserve better." Grayson lays down his final words.

I hear footsteps coming my way. I hurriedly dodge behind a coatrack in the corner of the landing.

The door opens suddenly revealing a very dispassionate Grayson. He closes the door behind him but doesn't walk away. He stands there for a moment looking overly morose. He looks back over his shoulder shaking his head at the door before he leaves down the stairwell finally.

I hear the front door of the building closing as I step out behind the coatrack I walk over to the door debating with myself about entering.

Swallowing down some courage I open the door revealing myself to a frightened Thorn who is standing in the middle of an old dusty room with one small bed in the corner and a single lamp and table beside it.

This is where she's been hiding? It looks so damn drab. No fit for anyone to live in honestly.

"What are doing here Sin?" Thorn speaks up suddenly breaking me out of my trance.

"I've come for you. I've been looking for you everywhere Thorn." My simply reply leaves her confused.

"Why you?" She ask me.

Why me indeed?

"Because my brothers are going absolutely crazy without you. Neither of them can cope with you being gone. Sunny is beside himself and Slay hates everybody. Please come back to us Thorn. Let Sunny and Slay explain their actions to you personally. I know they both fucked up but if you can forgive a sad ass bastard like me then why can't you forgive them?" I plead with her with a very calm and rational voice. Stating all of my thoughts very thoroughly to her. Hoping that she will see some reason.

"I don't know Sin. I mean, I want to come back. I need to come back. I have things to tell all three of you but I don't know if I can forgive Sunny so easily. When did it happen Sin? I need to know all of the details." I know she needs to know but it's not place to tell her.

"Come back. Let Sunny explain it all to you. Let Slay apologize for being a jealous ass and let me have a chance with you please." I beg. I'm not ashamed of it. I ain't to proud to beg. Isn't that how the song goes? I silently laugh at my dumb self.

"Alright just let me pack up. But I'm not saying that I will stay. I'm just giving them both an opportunity to state their case. That's all. Nothing more. Understood?" She lays down her terms efficiently.

"Deal!" I smile at her. Just a little crooked little smile to let her know how much I appreciate this.

"Don't look so smug Sin. All of you have been trying my patients lately. It's not going to be so easy for me to forgive this one." Thorn states very calmly.

I can completely understand that.

"I know. I just appreciate you giving us all another chance. None of us deserve it really. We have all fucked up royally when it comes to how bad we have treated you but I for one am truly sorry for being such a damn stupid jackass and I hope you can eventually forgive me and one more thing. That night after you told me about Storm I was upset but it's not because of what you were thinking. I was upset because I acted the same way that she did and I didn't get punished for it like she did. It was all regret Thorn. Nothing more. It was not because I have feelings for her. I don't. None at all. The only feelings I have are for you and I hope that someday we can move beyond this. I truly hope we can. I want us to be together and be what I think mates should be. Which is loving and caring mates to each other." I confess with all that

I have to her. Then I remembered one more thing I need to tell her. Here it goes.

"And I was having some doubts about myself that's why I pushed you away. You see I kissed Pan when I was younger. When I first met him actually and from that kiss alone I was confused about my own sexuality. I thought that I might actually be gay or bisexual. I had no clue that I just liked his kiss more than I should have honestly but still I didn't want to hurt my future mate if that was the case. I mean if I was actually gay or bisexual. It wouldn't be fair to them so I decided to refuse to have a mate because of that alone. It had nothing to do with you. Not personally anyway. It was all me. But now that I know that I'm heterosexual it removed all of my doubts. So I'm sorry for that confusion. I hope understand." I end my speech with hope alighting up in me. Trying to catch my breath from being long winded. Who knew confessions could be so damn hard to explain?

"That explains a lot actually. I'm glad you told me every-thing. Sin I would have accepted you either way. You know what? I think that you and I should just start from the begin-ning." I furrow my brows at her in confusion.

She walks over to me extending her tiny out to me.

"Hello my name is Thorn Lee Rose and I think I may be your mate." I breathlessly laugh at her antics.

I extend my hand shaking hers softly. "I'm Sin. Yes I think you may be my mate also but I must warn you I can be a real jackass at times." I chuckle lightly as I tell her.

"Oh that's okay because I can be a real bitch at times. Fair warning." I have to laugh at that. Dropping my hand away from hers I take a leap of faith and wrap her into my embrace. She hugs me back willingly.

This could be a start to a beautiful friendship or even more. I dare hope.

Chapter 24

Staring at Sunny across the way I note the trepidation in him.

Back at the inn with all three of my mates standing around me as I sit on the edge of the bed wishing that we didn't have to deal with any of this. I tell myself firmly that I will not let them see me cry.

I own my own tears and I will not dispel them for anybody not matter how much it may hurt me.

So I sit here listening intently to Sunny trying to explain to me exactly what and why it happened.

With each word that comes from his mouth my own heart breaks a little further in two.

I can understand completely that he thought I was never going to return. Because in my mind at that time I was never planning on returning to either of them.

What I can't seem to wrap my head around is the thought of him keeping this a secret from me for so damn long.

It's not the idea of him sleeping with her that makes me so angry. It's just the general idea of all the secrecy wrapped around a big fat lie.

I would be calling myself double standard now if I held it against him for sleeping with Shari, because at that time, I was also thinking about sleeping with Tristan to be honest.

I was in all actuality going to reject them all then and just be with Tristan solely.

So unfortunately I can't hold any fault against Sunny for that. He thought we were over completely just as I did. People do tend to move on and like he said he was missing me and depressed about my absence just as I was about them.

I was planning on moving on also without them. We were one in the same.

I just can't understand why Sunny couldn't be more opened about it. Why would he hide it from me? I would have understood. I was doing the exact thing to them although I didn't go through with it. It was definitely on my mind, a lot.

I can understand the temptation. I was definitely tempted to do the same. Maybe I should have been open about how I was feeling then to all of them. Then we would probably not be in this horrible situation right now.

As I listen to him drone on and on about his adulterous affair I begin to become very unsettled.

"It was only one night Thorn and I am so damn sorry." Only one night huh? So I guess that makes everything better? Just one damn night. He....just....should..have..told....me.

"Please say something Thorn." Sunny pleads with me. What can I actually say? Should I admit to them that I felt the same exact way? I wonder how they would all take that?

Biting the inside of my cheek, I decided just to tell them. Regardless, of whatever may come of it. I'm tired of all of the damn secrets and lies.

Basically, I'm just damn tired.

So I do.

I tell them how I felt and what I planned to do with them and especially with Tristan.

I unload all of it calmly. Not once did I ever raise my voice or have it dripping out with sarcasm.

I just plainly told them all of it.

I don't spare a damn thing.

By the time I finished telling them they all looked a little differently down at me.

Sin was looking at me like he understood me completely. Which I'm sure he did.

Slay was looking at me with a touch of anger but I did note a slight touch of understanding in his eyes thankfully.

Now Sunny. Sunny was looking at me like I just vindicated him. Like he was now off of the hook for what he has done. A look of pure relief.

But if he happens to think that then he is just fooling himself because he isn't off of the damn hook not just yet.

"But I didn't do it although I desperately wanted to. But Sunny this doesn't mean that I'm not still angry with you. You lied to me. You kept it a secret and that's what hurts me the most. Why did you think that I would not find out about it?

I'm not clueless Sunny. I do have a brain and I use it from time to time. Secrets always get exposed regardless if you want them to or not." I exclaimed to him still never raising my voice once.

"Damn Thorn if I could take it back I would in a damn heartbeat. Shari meant nothing to me." I don't think he realizes that what he just told me makes it all actually worse.

I just shake my damn head at him. Sunny will never understand.

"Did it mean something to you when we made love?" I ask him lowly now completely doubting myself.

"Thorn it meant the world to me. I love you. I'm sorry I hurt you. I should have told you." He states as he walks over to me kneeling down in front of me right in between my legs.

"Yes you should have. It's going to take some time for me to forgive you Sunny. Not because you slept with her that would be wrong of me if I held that against you when I intended to do the same thing to you. But because you lied to me and it didn't even bother you that you kept it from me." I plead with him for his understanding.

His face shows so much remorse and sadness suddenly. I blow out a huge strangled breath. This is so much harder than I thought it would be.

Sunny is indeed the heart of our unit but after this I don't know if I can trust that sweet heart of his like I use to.

I know Sin did the exact same thing to me with Storm but he was under a witches spell for a time throughout it. Sunny definitely wasn't. That's why it's so damn hard for me.

He lied to me deliberately.

I honestly don't think he was ever going to admit this lie to me. It was just by an unfortunate happenstance that I even found out.

Don't cry Thorn! Don't let him see your tears. You are stronger than that. I keep repeating the mantra inside of my head.

"It did bother me Thorn. It was eating me alive. I just didn't know how to tell you and if I did I knew that you would leave me. Us. Forever this time. I didn't want to lose you." He croaked out the last sentence to me looking completely broken. "I can't."

I sigh, what am I going to do with him? His heart is just too damn big while my heart is shrinking just a little toward him.

"Like I said it will take time. Right now I don't think I can trust you. I don't think that you will cheat on me again Sunny. I just think you are way too good at keeping secrets from me and lying to me now." He takes a hefty intake of breath as I tell him.

I hate that I'm hurting him but what else can I do? He hurt me too!

"I understand Thorn and I don't actually blame you either. I should have told you. I will beg for your forgiveness until I cant breathe any longer if that is what it will take to earn back your trust again in me." This time it's me that's taking a huge intake of breath.

I don't know why but I actually believe him. It's hard. So damn hard. To look him in the eye and try my best to hate him for this.

I could never hate him though. I love him too damn much to ever hate him. But right now I do despise him a little for hurting me. Why is my damn heart fluctuating between love and light hate randomly?

Sunny grasp ahold of my hands into his suddenly. The sparks as usual shoot straight through me signifying to me that he is my soulmate.

Why would the Moon Goddess make this so if it wasn't meant to be?

Why does it hurt so bad?

I yank my hands away from his immediately. Placing them on my lap away from his touch.

I can't handle that right now and I don't know when I will ever be able too again.

He looks so forlornly up to me that it breaks my heart in two just a little more if that's even possible?

"I'm sorry Thorn. I love you." Those three damn words are tearing me in two. Can't he see this?

"There's more." Slay informs me with regret instantly shadowing his face.

What more can there be? I don't think I can take much more of this.

"What?" I questioned.

Slay then tells me about Sharis mate Beta Sawyer. How he would probably be after Sunny now for what he did and how bad this Beta really is. What the hell?

Sunny sure stepped in to it this time.

What else are we going to have to deal with?

I peer over at Sin that's standing right behind Sunny's kneeling form.

"Alright Sunny has explained everything to me. Slay has even apologized for being a jealous jackass and you have told me everything about you right?" I ask Sin.

Let's get it all out on the table.

"Yes. Nothing else left to tell." Sin says with a smile.

Thank fuck! I don't think I could handle anything else at this point.

"Alright then I have a lot to think about. So I'm going to go into the other room for a long hot bubble bath to think. Oh and before I forget I have to rescue my brother now rather than later. Striker has set up an interview for me to do with Lord Samuel. Alone. I'm two days time. That's when I'm going to take his ass down!" I explain to them and then walk off without another word into the other room to take my long awaited bath.

Let them stew on that shit for a while.

Soaking in a warm bubble bath with scented candles surrounding me I tried my damn best to relax my erratic racing thoughts but all I ended up accomplishing from all of this pampering was nearly falling asleep in the damn tub.

I was almost completely zonked out when the bathroom door suddenly springed open.

Startled, I jerk up awake quickly sloshing the water out of the tub and onto the floor.

"Sorry I was just checking on you to make sure if you were okay. You've been in here for almost an hour now." Sin replies sheepishly trying his best to avoid looking my way. "I was starting to get worried." He glances back at me bravely devouring me with his eyes.

Peering deep into those honey hazel eyes of his I can see the notable lust casting out from those hungry eyes. Just what I so needed.

"Care to join me?" I ask him desperately yearning for his touch and so needing a damn release. Sins eyes widen un-expectedly.

"Are you sure?" He ask me with some trepidation. It's so damn cute. Hell yes, I am definitely sure.

"Yes." Leaning up I turn the hot faucet side of the water back on warming the water back up. By the time the water is warm enough Sin has already stripped out of all of his clothing.

Standing at the edge of the tub, completely naked, he's staring down at me a bit nervously. I stifle a laugh over how nervous he seems to be. It's fucking adorable to me.

Roaming my eyes down his delectable body from his hazel eyes down to his beautiful ripped stomach, I aim my eyes down lower finally stopping at his very over sized and very apparent stiff cock. My eyes widen suddenly.

He's bigger than Slay or even Sunny. Although Slay has more girth to his, it's still a very impressive package and he is hard as fuck right now. His enormous cock is standing at full attention and it's all for me. Yesss.

"Are you coming?" I ask, pun definitely intended, quirking an eyebrow up at him when I finally look back up at his face it is uncanny how much pure unbridled lust he has for me.

He deeply chuckles as he climbs into the tub to sit right down in front of me. The water sloshes again when he lowers that sexy body down into tub.

I admire all of his attributes as he sits down. Yum-fuck-ing-me!

Licking my lips I lean into him making the first move. I've only ever kissed Sin once before, this is like doing it all over again for the first time to me.

Climbing up on top of him, I straddle him with my legs bent and off to the sides of him.

I feel his erection hit my sensitive pussy as soon as I squat down on him, I automatically release a guttural moan.

Fuck he feels so good and I need this so damn badly right now.

"Thorn." He drawls out my name groaning. Biting my lower lip I watch him as he closes his eyes while scrunching up his face like his in some sort of pain.

"Do you want me Sin?" I question him worried that he may of changed his mind.

He opens his eyes peering deeply into my own. "Of course I want you Thorn. I just want to make sure that you are truly ready for this." Am I?

Or am I just using him to escape from my own worries? As I observe him closely I realize how foolish that thought even was. I definitely do want him and now!

"I want you Sin, now." I declare as I lean into him leaving peppery like kisses along his neck.

"Thorn I don't want our first time together to be in a damn tub." I stop kissing him instantly. Feeling a tiny bit rejected.

"Fine." I push away from him jumping out of the tub quickly I grab a towel off of the towel rack, wrapping it around me as I leave the bathroom in a bratty huff.

"Thorn wait! That's not what I meant!" I hear him yell out in the bathroom with the water splashing from him hurriedly exiting the tub.

I park my ass right on the bed, dripping water on it but I can't to seem to care about it. What it is with these men?

Aren't I good enough for any of them? Why do I always keep putting my heart out there just for it to get trampled upon?

"Thorn baby please I didn't mean it the way you are taking it. I just meant that I wanted our first time together to be special. Not a just quick romp in the damn tub for fuck sakes." He is standing there completely naked with water droplets dripping off of him.

I furrow my brows at him, is that what he really meant?

This is my fault I've been doubting myself so much lately that it's actually making me insane.

"Sin do you find me desirable?" I ask him anxiously.

He looks at me with a very perplexed look masking his face. " Damn Thorn I think you are the most desirable woman I have ever met. Look at this." He points down to his harden cock, "This is all because of you baby. No one else just you and you didn't even have to touch me for me to get hard. You are so fucking sexy Thorn. I just wish you could see yourself like I do. Like we all do. You are so fucking beautiful. Why do you think Slay gets so jealous whenever another man touches you or even looks at you like he wants to eat you up? It's because you are ethereal Thorn and so damn enticing."

He explains as he comes to sit down beside me on the bed. The bed dips when he sits down upon it moving me closer to him.

I grab ahold of his shoulders to keep from falling over luckily he catches me swiftly before my face eats the floor. How embarrassing would that have been? He chuckles grabbing ahold of my arms to help balance me.

"Falling for me Thorn?" He inquires rubbing his hands slowly up and down my forearms. The sparks light up instantly making me moan out unintentionally.

"More like crashing for you." I giggle at him. My hands fall from his shoulders I glide them down his chest gently.

He sucks in a breath as I glide my hands down even lower finally coming to rest up against his stiff cock.

Gripping his shaft tightly into my hand I start stroking him very slowly. Torturously slow.

"Damn Thorn!" He hisses reaching out he grabs ahold of my towel ripping it off me in one full fledge swoop. Tossing it on the floor he wraps his hand around my wrist stopping my progress instantly.

Yanking my hand away from him he pushes me back on the bed crawling right in between my opened and very willing thighs.

"Are you really sure about this?" I wish he would quit asking me that.

"Yes I'm really really sure Sin now please just fuck me already!" I grit through my teeth with my head raised up from the pillow. He lets out a deep chuckle at me again.

"Anything you say boss!" Is he fucking kidding? I get fed up with his snide little antics, unable to resist any longer, I reach my hand down and grab ahold of his cock, guiding it straight into my already wet pussy.

I push my hips up as I continue to guide him right into me. He fills me up so damn nicely.

"Eager are we?" Jackass!

To shut his ass up I push his head down to my breast. He latches on to my nipple quickly, sucking it in his mouth ferociously. I let a low needy moan again.

Damn he's good. He starts thrusting into my like a deranged mad man. With his hand kneading my breast and his tongue swirling around my areola I lose my own train of thought.

I feel him driving into my cunt exceptionally faster. Harder and harder he plows derivatively into me. I wrap my legs around his hips pushing him along even further into me. Man he's tearing my pussy up.

And fuck it feels so damn good.

My damn pussy is acting like a greedy bitch.

"Fuck Thorn you're so damn fucking tight baby!" Why does his voice sound so damn fucking sexy? His deep lusty groans are driving me absolutely crazy.

Before I lose all of my self control I raise my head up to his neck releasing my canines I bite down on his neck fucking hard. He groans immediately pushing into me irrevocably harder and oh so much faster. Releasing my canines he proceeds to the same to me as soon as his canines sink into my neck, my pussy starts vibrating uncontrollably. I feel a knot instantly twist up in my lower abdomen.

My over sensitive clit starts to tingle, over wrought pressure begins to build up in me. Sin releases his canines licking my wounds just as I did his. The bond clicks into place instantly. Now I can feel almost every damn thing that he does.

His sexual over drive is fucking startling. With my body bouncing on the mattress from the force of him pivoting so damn roughly into me, I arch my back up off of the damn mattress edging his ass on.

The pressure starts to get even stronger, placing my hands on his shoulders trying to tame my inner screams I end up losing when a five star orgasm rocks me so hard I nearly fucking faint from the catalytic bliss of it. "Fuck yes. Damn Papi!" I purr breathlessly as soon as my climax hits me but Sin doesn't fucking relinquish.

He just keeps plunging into me at a very high uncontrollable rate. He's grinding into me so damn hard I just may be bruised and sore as hell by tomorrow.

Fuck he's insatiable. Not that I'm complaining. He just keeps going. Okay, if he wants to keep going then I will make it worth his wild. I drop my legs around his hips pushing him off of me with all of the strength that I have in me. I roll his ass flat onto his back then straddle him. His big dick stays inside of me the entire time miraculously.

I start gyrating my hips on top of him in a very leisurely erotic dance. Pulling up my wet hair off of my shoulders I drag my hands through my hair provocatively. With my eyes closed, I tilt my head to the side moaning out sexily. "Fuck!"

Hearing Sins strained growls fucking excite me, placing his hands on the side of my hips he starts bucking up his own hips to meet mine roughly.

Dropping my hands from my sodden hair I lower them to my breast slowly, still rocking my hips like a porn star on top of him, I start kneading my own breast hungrily right in front of him as I keep my hungry eyes now locked onto his.

I take one hand and slowly drop it even lower straight down to my over stimulated clit, playing with myself as he watches me with pure heat roaring out of his hazel eyes. I moan provocatively.

The lust appearing in those hazel eyes of his is my own just reward.

He jerks my hand away from my clit, very demandingly, taking over for me, he starts playing with it with the pad of his masterful thumb. I start to lose all of my control again under his very skilled ministrations.

Placing my hands, palms down, on his chest I fluctuate my hips seductively. Gliding my warm walls along his cock exponentially faster.

Quickening my pace I go full on over the damn top pushing my body down with force to capture his cock extremely tightly in between my stimulated slippery center.

"You..are so..damn fucking good at this." Sin grumbles between each shattered breath that he takes. Making me feel treasured just like a damn goddess.

The intensity of our union begins to cause more pressure on my sensitive bundle of nerves. Clenching up once again I unexpectedly moan out naughty little raunchy words to him.

"Hmmm you're cock is so damn fucking good!" I purr as soon as my walls start to spasm up hard once again.

"I'm going to cum baby!" Fuck yes. Cum for me Papi! Scraping my long nails down his chest savagely, my pussy suctions up around his dick so tautly I was actually afraid that I was going to sprain the damn thing.

"Sinnnn!" I yell out when my orgasm suddenly over takes me. "Yesss Fuck me Papi!"

He drives his hips up, bucking them straight up into me again, with his fingers pressing down harshly on my hips and his other hand still massaging my clit vigorously, he squeezes his eyes shut tightly with his head lolling back down on the pillows beneath him. He goes completely still while he spurts his juices out all into me just like a damn rocket as he screams out my name. "Thorn baby Fuuuck!" I can feel his warm seed enter deeply inside of me. Ropes after ropes of his cum flood in me, slowly dripping out of me making me a huge wet sloppy but glorious mess.

Breathing heavily I fall down on his chest exhausted beyond recognition. My pussy walls keep vibrating sending vibrations all around clit.

I feel his dick jerk inside of me with his excess cum shooting out into my over drenched walls. Damn that was some good ass fucking sex!

"Fuck that was so unbelievably hot!" I giggle at his admiration. Causing his cock to automatically jerk in me again. I absolutely love that feeling.

"You will do!" I laugh breathlessly up at him.

"Really? I'll do huh? Care to go another round just to prove you wrong?" Sin asks me as my eyes suddenly widen.

Yes. There's no doubt that he really does have a lot of fucking stamina. I honestly don't think I can keep up with him but I'm willing to give it one hell of a damn try.

"You're welcome to tear this pussy up again anytime!" I reply back to him squeezing my walls firmly around his cock again as soon as he feels it he lets out another strained guttural moan.

"Jump off of me then because right now I'm going to chow down on a delicious Thorn pie!" He states huskily. Oh hell that was so damn fucking cheesy. Men!

After going two more rounds with Sin, I'm totally exhausted, laying down with my head planted on his chest tracing my fingers along his sexy ass six pack my mind starts to wonder off all on it's own.

With Sins light snoring above me, that's remarkably unbelievably cute, my mind is riddled with the problems pertaining to me and Sunny.

I already decided to just take easy on him for the time being and at least to try and work on learning how to trust him again.

After all he was the first one of the three to actually accept me. He has done nothing but treat me sweetly, with the exception of lying to me, he has actually been the perfect mate.

I know he cheated but like I said before I was going to do the same damn thing to him. That isn't the problem.

Trust is.

It may take a while but eventually I will learn how to trust him again. I hope.

And with my brother being sick now I need to push these negative things far away from me just until I can rescue him from Samuel clutches.

Seraphina, the girl I meet after I ran away from Sunny, that helped me, when I was so desperately in need of a friend she came through for me.

I met her at the coffee shop where that other girl, Jessica worked, the one who left the note on the napkin for Slay.

I went into the coffee shop to find her. I was going to challenge her ass face to face and demand an apology from her. Like I would ever get one. I was just so damn mad at her at that point. Now that I realize that I have sexy ass mates that any girl in their right mind would absolutely drool over, I just have to accept the fact that other women find them just as attractive as I do.

That still doesn't mean that I have to like it though.

Seraphina owned the building that I was hiding in. She offered me a room in it free of charge just out of the kindness of her heart. I need to repay her for all that she did for me. Somehow. Someway.

Suddenly my eyes start to get really heavy. Yawning, I close my eyes snuggling up closer to Sins body.

Even in his sleep he pays rapt attention to me. He automatically wraps his arm across my waist tighter.

When I told Grayson that I loved all three of them. I meant it from the bottom of my heart. I do love them immensely.

With the thought of my love for them all and me accepting that I should try to forgive Sunny. I start to drift off into a peaceful slumber. Relaxing finally. My last thought before I entered dreamland was of Sunny.

In my mind I rehearsed how I was going to tell him that I have forgiven him.

But this will be the very last time I will forgive them all so damn easily!

Chapter 25

S he's dragging us along with her to meet some girl named Seraphina.

With me, Slay and Sin straggling along behind her and for some odd unknown reason she seems awfully chipper today, as we are all headed off to a local park that's located in the center of the city to meet this woman that Thorn has initiated as her friend.

I'm a little suspicious about it but seeing as how Thorn is so damn happy even after what I did to her, I accept this meeting with a placid smile on my face and trying my hardest to push my own suspicions aside. Just for her.

I seen the mark that Sin left on her neck from last night clearly. It's located just right under my own mark. All of our marks that's on her neck look exactly the same. As does hers on ours.

I trace the pad of my finger along my mark slowly, as I do Thorn instantly halts her progress forward as she turns around and looks directly over at me.

She must of felt it when I touched it. Interesting.

Thorn tilts her head a little to the side observing me with mild interest before she turns back around to start waking off again.

This morning she came to me and actually said that she forgave me, surprisingly, for my stupidity, not exactly in those terms but that was just about the gist of it basically.

It shocked me to no end. I wasn't exactly expecting that from her. I honestly thought that it would take a hell of a lot longer for me to earn back just a minuscule of her forgiveness and trust.

I count myself very lucky, most women would just pack up their things and leave after what I did. But not Thorn. Sometimes I think she is just way to forgiving but who am I to throw this unique opportunity away?

Regardless, of what she might say, I can still see a semblance of doubt shadowing her features. I will find someway to earn back her trust in me completely. Some fucking way.

She may say she's forgiven me but I know she has to have a small amount of trust issues with me now. I can just see it. It's as bright as a sunny day.

I will never in my life hurt her like that ever again though.

She means far too much to me and just to think I nearly lost her completely over this.

I feel a ache in my chest just thinking about it. Absentmindedly I start rub my hand across my chest exactly where my heart is located.

No, I will never ever hurt her again. In any shape, form, or fashion. That is my solemn vow to her and to myself.

As we continue to walk along the sidewalk the cool air washes over my skin sending a chill right straight through me.

The winter months are not too far away from us now. I bow my head watching my feet as we go onward.

I wonder if Thorn celebrates any holidays at this time of year?

For some supernaturals celebrating human holidays is very much frowned upon but for me and my family we have always celebrated Christmas with each other every year.

With it being only another month and half away I need to ask her and find out if she would enjoy It with us. I hope she does though. It's a magical time of year that I absolutely love.

I remind myself to ask her about it as soon I can, as we keep trudging along to the park.

I wasn't even paying attention to my surroundings. I was too caught in my own inner musings, by the time I looked back up we were already at the local park now.

Families are here running about, doing different variety of familial things.

When Thorn mentioned a park I didn't expect it to be this type of park. I actually thought it was like some kind of opened land structure that hosted a few benches and walkways, maybe even a small pond. But this is a virtual park made just for kids and their families to enjoy themselves in.

There's swing sets, slides, and even a merry go round with some kids playing happily on them.

Watching them play with each other makes me long for a child of my own.

I never asked Thorn if she wanted to ever have kids. Maybe that's something else I should ask her about. I hope she does though. Because I truly do want kids one day, plenty of them.

"Sunny come on!" Thorn yells at me waving her hand in a come her motion to me at the side of the park.

She is standing by a very pretty young girl smiling hugely over at her.

As I stroll casually over to them I can hear their conversation before I even reached them.

"Thank you for helping me. I don't know how I will ever to be able to repay you?" Thorn says to her. Repay her for what exactly?

"It was no problem. I was happy that I was able to help you." Well she seems nice enough to me.

As I approach my eyes bounce back and forth between the two of them rapidly.

The girl looks very young, I'm guessing her age is probably around sixteen or seventeen maybe?

"Sunny, Slay, Sin, I would like for all of you to meet Seraphina." Seraphina smiles broadly over at us.

"Nice to meet you Seraphina." I tilt my head down to her out of clear respect she giggles at my apparent geekiness.

"Just call me Sera." Her smile soon escalates as she takes in all of us.

"How old are you Seraphina?" Slay ask her abruptly. Amazing he was wondering the same exact thing as I was.

"Twenty." She replies shyly. Wow she looks so much younger than that. That definitely took me by surprise.

"Come let's sit and talk," Thorn grabs Seraphina by her arm guiding her away. We start to walk with them but we soon stop when Thorn turns her attention back to us, "You three can go off and explore. This is girl time." Thorn diligently informs us. We are well excused then, I guess.

I watch as they both walk away across the park giggling and talking amongst each other.

"She looks happier today." Slay suddenly states. That she does. Her radiant smile could actually light up the entire world.

And I hate it that I'm the one who made that beautiful smile disappear from her face, even for a second.

I want that smile.

I need that smile of hers directed right at me. Not just the intimidating fake one that she has been trying so hard to give me all day. A real heartfelt genuine smile filled with the love and devotion that she use to have for me.

I know that she said that she has forgiven me but I can still see the wariness floating around in her eyes whenever she looks at me and I was the stupid one who put that weariness there and I absolutely hate it.

"Are you alright?" Sin questions me. No I'm actually not. The guilt and regret are all but consuming me.

"Yes." I lie to him. No sense in making him worry also since he is just now finally on the right path with Thorn now. I just wished so damn desperately that I didn't stray away from my own path with her.

But I only have myself to blame for my stupidity.

"Why don't we go ask our girl if she wants to grab some dinner?" I suggest putting on a fake ass smile just for them.

"Sounds good." Slay happily agrees with me.

As we all make our way over to Thorn and Sera, I drift slowly behind my brothers, not feeling quite as eager as them.

One step in front of the other, is all I can manage to do right now.

Two paces languidly behind them I hear Slay casually ask them both out to dinner.

Thorn smiles up at Slay, that's the type of smile that I've been so yearning for. The one I so need to see.

"Sera would like you to join us?" Sin politely asks her. Seras eyes dash around nervously locking on to each of us.

"I would love to." She quietly agrees with a slight blush creeping up on her cheeks.

"Great, but we also need to make plans for what we need to do tomorrow for your interview with Samuel." Slay abruptly adds and we all freeze, not realizing that he just spoke out of turn unintentionally right there in front of Seraphina.

With shocked faces we all go perfectly quiet, when Slay suddenly realizes his mistake he silently cusses under his breath.

"Do you think we can trust her?" I question Thorn through our mindlink.

"I don't know. She has helped me before and she seems honest enough." Thorn states with a questioning gaze aimed toward Sera.

"Should we just tell her?" I ask.

"Honestly Sunny, I have not been the best judge of character here lately but to me she seems genuine enough. I like her if that counts for anything?" I just knew that statement was meant for me. The guilt inside of me suddenly starts to escalate.

"You know it does Thorn. We trust your judgement. We always have." And we always will.

"Thanks. Yes, I think we may be able to trust her." Thorn exclaims with assuredly.

"Good, then I think we should at least give her a chance." I agree with her. I will always trust Thorns judgement I just wish she had more faith in herself.

"Me too." She nods her head. Reaching out for Seras arm she places her hand on it gently.

"It's a long story and I know you must be confused but we will explain everything to you over dinner. That is if you're still wanting to go with us?" Thorn assures her.

"If it's what I'm thinking it is then I would gladly love to help all of you. I can't stand him either. He's the reason my sister is no longer with us. She was my twin and unfortunately she was cursed with being that bastards mate. He looked down on her like she was worse than a bug under his shoes. My sister, Batina, couldn't understand why he wouldn't have anything to do with her. She actually loved the asshole. Why I don't know but she did. He ended up killing her just because he thought that she was beneath his ass. Now it's just me and my mother and she rarely ever comes out of our house now anymore because of it. So if you are planning to get rid of that cumsucker then count my ass in." Sera snarls. Her sweet innocent face turns heated instantly.

Samuel apparently is worse than I actually ever imagined him to be.

"I...I'm so sorry Sera...I didn't know." Thorn shows her undying sympathy.

"How could you? Just please allow me to help you. I need some type of closure and I desperately need this, not just for Batina or my mother but for me also." I can see the pure raw anguish reflecting off of Sera.

"Well we may actually need more than just Seraphinas help here. I may have a plan but we need to get ahold of Freya and her sister, Hope and possibly even Striker if they would be willing to help us that is?" Slay has a plan?

I should of realized that Slay has been formulating a plan all along. He is the protector after all just as Freya once said he was.

"I'll call her and see." Thorn replies, grabbing her phone out of her front jeans pocket, she walks off with it pressed against her ear.

"How did you meet Thorn?" I ask Seraphina curiously.

"Oh it's a funny story actually. She came into the coffee shop where I work storming mad at my coworker, Jessica. You should of seen her. She marched right up to the counter demanding to see Jessica. She even pushed a customer aside to get to the counter. Unfortunately Jessica was off that day, so I calmed her down the best that I could and we just started talking. She told me about what Jessica did to one of you. Jessica has a bad habit of coming on to all of the good looking customers," she unintentionally blushes again, "anyway, our manager was there and heard everything. He gave Jessica a warning for her disobedience." She stops her explanation looking back over her shoulder toward Thorn who is still talking on her phone.

"Then the strangest thing happened. A guy came in after that and Jessica just couldn't resist and tried it again with him. He told her off though, she sort of met her match," she starts giggling, "another customer was there and heard everything that went on between them both. So he went to our manager and complained about her. She got fired that day." Sera states while casting a beaming smile up at us.

"I talked to that customer that reported her. He's a regular that comes in the shop all of the time. He didn't like Jessica either. He said that Jessica got really mad after this guy put her in her place. I asked him what he said to her and he told me that one day she would mess with the wrong man and threw a napkin right at her. Not like she didn't deserve it though." She says with a slight shrug of her shoulders.

After Seras story. I recall what happened between Slay and Thorn. Glancing over at him I notice that he is showing no emotion at all regarding Seras statement. I risk a glance toward Sin. The bastard is smiling deviously down at Sera. He told me what happened at the coffee shop between him and this Jessica girl.

Sin actually got her fired!

Well I can't say that I'm not actually happy over it.

"They will meet us tonight after dinner." Thorn states as she is walking back over to us.

"Good. Then let's go eat." I suggest to all of them eagerly.

Thorn smiles and does something that I wasn't expecting.

She runs and jumps right onto Slays back. Slay grunts from the sudden impact of her body hitting him. He looks over his shoulder up at her smiling.

"What are you doing?" He ask.

"My feet hurt and I'm hungry." She whines while pouting, "Onward horsy. Giddy up!" Her legs clasp around Slays sides as she points her finger forward.

"I'm not a damn horse Thorn." Slay grumbles.

"Okay so you can be my stallion then." She demurely tells him. Lowering her head to his ear she whispers something to him. Luckily I could hear just what she told him.

"If you let me ride you now you can ride me later tonight." She whispers to him provocatively.

Slay grins over at her then neighs to her like a damn horse and takes off galloping down the sidewalk with Thorn laughing uproariously on his back, while waving her hand up in the air.

The rest of us watch them go, laughing at their dramatic antics.

"She's got him wrapped around her little finger." Sin leans in to tell me this.

"She has us all wrapped around that little finger brother." Sin lets out a deep chuckle as we leisurely follow behind Slay and Thorn headed off to dinner.

We ended up at Freyas house a little after nine.

All of us was there crowded around in Freyas small cabin.

Us along with Sera, Freya, Hope, and Striker we're all working out a plan for Samuels subsequentialdemise.

Not long after we got most of the plan dissected did Grayson feign to make an unexpected visit.

The entirety of his time there he kept making overly eager eyes in Thorns direction.

While observing him I soon came to the realization that Grayson is indeed infatuated with our beautiful mate.

I never quite understood how Slay could be so damn jealous all of the time over Thorn, but now, I can definitely see exactly how could be.

I use to not have a jealous bone in my body but since Thorn has ventured into our lives I find myself being jealous often.

As I watch him, he keeps trying his hardest to get closer to Thorn. He drifts all through the living room, acting as if he's pacing the floor just to make his way over to her.

Eventually, he manages to sit down right beside her, on the far end arm of the couch that were all sitting upon.

I'm not the only one that catches this.

Slay and Sin are both eyeing Grayson with clouded suspicious eyes directed right over at him.

"Thorn can we talk in private?" Grayson ask ending all of the conversations that are going on around us. Everyone in the room looks up at Grayson with apprehension.

"Uhm, sure." She says with slight hesitation. Her beautiful cove blue eyes dart all across the room finally landing on me and my brothers.

There's a noticeable tremble in her hands as she stands.

"I don't think so. Whatever you have to say to her you can say right here in front of us." Sin states as he stands up from the couch folding his arms across chest.

Thorn starts to stand up but Slay places his hand on top of shoulders, pushing her back down onto the sofa gently, stopping her progression immediately.

"Figures that you three would decide to go all caveman. Look Thorn I just wanted to talk to you in private. What's the big damn deal?" This man must have a damn death wish.

"Not in my house! If you got a problem take it outside!" Freya growls furiously.

"Sounds good to me." Sin declares glaring daggers at Grayson.

"Oh, is that the way you want to play it little man? Then lets go!" Grayson daringly replies gracing Sin with a visceral smirk.

"Stop this nonsense this instant. We have more important things to worry about right now than all of you having some type of dick measuring contest!" Thorns words go unheeded as Sin and Grayson still continue to glower over at each other.

The tension in the little cabin grows as each one of us wait on bated breath to see which of them will break first.

Slay is the one who puts an unquestionable stop to the bullshit.

He slowly stands up from the couch, positioning himself right in between them both.

"Thorns right. We don't need this shit right now. So put your damn dicks away and let's just get on with this." I peer closely over at Grayson, as I watch the asshole he takes a few seconds before he inevitably decides to just give in first.

He eventually scoffs at Sin and Slay jumping up from the couch suddenly he gives us all one last glare before he then heatedly stomps away, as he leaves the cabin while slamming the door fiercely behind him.

Laying in bed, as Sin sleeps soundlessly next me, I can't get Thorn out of my thoughts.

Tomorrow she has to walk up into that castle by herself, pretending to be someone that she's not, defenseless and all alone.

Well I mean she has mastered some of her abilities lately but I'm absolutely terrified that with her lack of skills over her abilities that she will eventually end up getting herself hurt or even worse: killed.

No matter how many times we went back and forth over the plans tonight there will always still be a possibility of something going terribly awry.

And with Thorn and I still not truly being able to mend our relationship like we should have, I'm afraid that we will leave things unsaid that should be brought out in the open before it's too damn late.

That's just something that I can't live with or even allow.

As quietly as possible, I slide out of bed, trying my best not to wake Sin in the process.

Creeping over to the adjoining door, I slowly open it, peering my head around the side of the door I search the bedroom for Thorn.

Amazingly, I only see Slay laying down on the bed sleeping.

Closing the door silently behind me, I catch a sight of a light cascading out of the bathroom ensuite door.

Edging my way over to the bathroom, I rap my knuckles on the door softly.

Thorn opens the door suddenly with a hand towel placed in her hands eyeing me with curiosity.

"Sunny?" She questions, as I close the door behind me without taking my eyes off of her.

"Thorn I have something to say to you and I don't want you to say a single word until I'm done okay?" She looks on at me with her eyes filled with concern.

"Alright." She drops the hand towel that's in her hands on the bathroom sink finally giving me her full attention.

"I know I've already apologized over and over again to you for what I did but I can't seem apologize enough to you. Thorn you are my life. My world. The air that I fucking breathe. I hurt you and even though you said that you have forgiven me I can still see the doubts that you have about me in your beautiful eyes. I need to know what I can do to remove all of those doubts about me. I will do anything Thorn. Do you want me to get on my knees begging you for forgiveness? I will, without even complaining, I would get on my damn knees right here and now, and beg you with all that I have in me, just so you would forgive me for being such a dumb ass. I love you Thorn and I know I can say that until I'm blue in the face to you and you may still have your doubts about my love for you but I do Thorn. I love you more than I love myself. More than I love anything. I fucked up and I know it. I should I have told you and believe me I will never in my life keep anything from you again ever. I swear that on my life. So please forgive me. Not this fake forgiveness you have been supplying me with all day with but your genuine forgiveness. I want to see that loving smile aimed at me again and it truly mean something. I need you Thorn. More than I have ever needed anyone or anything else before." By the time I finished telling her what I wanted to desperately get off of my chest I didn't even notice that she has been crying.

I take a step closer to her, reaching out to her, I gingerly wiped her fallen tears away from her face softly with the pad of my thumbs.

"Oh, Thorn, I love you so damn much. Please, baby, forgive me?" My own voice betrays me and croaks up when I see her so damn broken.

"I...forgive....you Sunny." I blow out the breath that I was holding in. Relief washes through me instantly. Grabbing her up into my arms I embrace her tightly.

"Thank you." I manage to croak out barely, with her head laying upon my chest I start to stroke her long hair lovingly.

"Listen Thorn about tomorrow, please promise me that you will be safe. I need to know that you will do everything in your power to come back to me unharmed." It's a ridiculous notion, I know, but I so desperately need it her say this.

We will be there along with her but nowhere close enough to her to keep her safe and out of Samuel or even his evil cohorts hands.

"I promise Sunny." She agrees nodding her head against my chest.

"As long as you promise me the same thing." She mumbles.

"I promise." I vow solemnly to her but who actually knows what the hell will happen tomorrow to either of us. It's just a chance we are all willing to take for her.

And only her.

Chapter 26

Nervous as shit I dispassionately make my way up the castles steps.

Two burly guards are standing regally at the threshold, swallowing a loud anxious gulp, I hesitantly make my way up to them with shaky hands.

"I'm here to see Lord Samuel, we had a interview set up for today." I anxiously tell them. Trying to display my best professional tone.

They both eye me and my attire with disconcerting looks.

I know I look rather strange right now, my hair is mounted high on top of my head in top bun, with fake glasses perched upon my nose and I'm uniquely dressed in a white buttoned up shirt with a black thin pencil neck skirt on. I'm the epiphany of a damn school teacher.

"Name." One of the guard asks me gruffly.

"Mabel Quartz." I lie brilliantly giving them my fake name.

"Do you have any weapons on you?" The other guard asks me while his damn eyes roam all over my body. Men!

"I have a pen." I breathlessly laugh swinging my pen in the air back and forth in my hand to show them.

One guard smiles at me while the other scowls. Tough crowd.

"You may enter." The scowling guard replies.

"Thank you." I quietly reply back as I walk gingerly up the the castles door.

The guards politely open the double doors for me, I nod my head in their direction before I enter into the castle.

This is it.

I take two steps forward, all the while trying to contain my anxieties.

In the entranceway I observe the castles intricate details. The beauty of the castle is unbelievably remarkable.

The beauty of it is truly defining and generally classical.

Walking further into the room with hesitant steps, I slowly make my way over to the oversized window, pushing back the sheer curtain I look out onto the scenery below me.

High above the city you can actually see the people below us bustling about happily doing their everyday routines.

"There you are my dear. I'm sorry I'm late." I hear a high pitched voice coming up from behind me.

As I turn to the voice I finally get a glimpse of the cruel bastard who has been haunting this Realm viscously.

Lord Samuel prattles into the room with an enormous smile plastered on his face.

I'm surprised to see just how incredibly attractive he actually is.

"Thank you for allowing me this interview with you Lord Samuel. I'll try not to take up too much of your time. I know you must be quite a very busy man." I plaster on a fake smile holding out my hand to him.

He looks at me surprise at first but eventually he takes my hand.

"Nonsense anything for the general public, after all, I would be nothing without my loyal subjects, now would I?" He grins at me sadistically, Oh, how I so wish that I could just plow my fist right into that obnoxious face of his.

"True. Where would you like to conduct the interview?" I cut to the chase wanting to get this bullshit over with as fast as I am possibly able to.

"We can sit right here at this table if you don't mind? Would you like a drink before we begin?" He ask me politely pointing at a little round glass table.

"No thank you." I reply, while going over to the table that he so graciously pointed to.

But to my surprise he makes no move to come to the table with me. He just stares over at me with a suspiciously snide smirk.

"Is there something wrong?" I ask him nervously.

"I know who you really are Thorn." What did he just call me? Fuck! The jig is up apparently.

"W-what do you mean? My name is Mabel." I lie again nervously searching the room frantically for anything that I may able to defend myself with. Unfortunately, I can't spy not one damn thing.

I anxiously fumble with the pen in my hand trying my best to disguise my the tension rising up in me.

"Oh, dear, you can't fool me. You see I've known who you were all along. I've just been biding my time just to see how this little game of yours would be played out." Double fuck!

He lets out a deep dark chuckle all the while eyeing me with devious superiority.

"You must have me confused with someone else Lord Samuel. I'm here to do a interview and my name is definitely not Thorn!" I try to persuade him with another lie.

Sitting up stiffly in the chair I glare back at him with a superiority look of my own. Trying to show more courage to him than I actually have at the moment.

"I don't think so. You are, and correct me if I'm wrong, the daughter of one Alpha Baker and half sister to your brother Fier? Plus, you are also the lost Princess to this Realm. Have I missed anything?" He questions me coyly. "I know every-thing." He adds.

Fuck! Fuck! Fuck!

All of our well thought out plans just flew right out of the fucking window.

What am I going to do now?

"Oh don't worry I'm not allowed to kill you like I want to and believe me I truly want to but unfortunately I just can't." He sighs out dramatically. He's acting like this is some big fucking humorous game to him.

Asshole!

"How do you know all of this about me?" I inquire curiously as I drop my onto the table.

"Well, you see I am in my unique position here all thanks to your father. Years ago we planned this little faux pas him and I, along with Singa. We managed to overtake the Invivus Realm from your mother and her mate quite easily I may add. I was able to rule this kingdom in your fathers absence he didn't mind anything I did here as long as I never got in the way of any of his plans nor was I ever allowed to touch or harm you." He states briefly while pouring him a glass of liquor.

I listened to him intently with nervous apprehension flowing straight through me. Damn! Damn! Damn!

"Why? Why did you do all of this for my father?" I ask him suspiciously. What deep secret could my father possibly have over him?

"There in lies my own little secrets but I don't mind sharing them with you. Knowing that your father is on his way here to retrieve you, I might as well humor you and myself, to pass the time, of course." This guy is so crass. After he finishes pouring his damn drink he saunters over to the table sitting down right across from me.

"You see, my sister was your fathers true mate. For a while he did actually love her but that love grew distant after she had your brother Fier. She paid more attention to Fier than she did your father and you father was jealous over this so he had her killed." He says it so damn calmly that it's actually frightening.

"I don't understand. Shouldn't you hate him for killing your own sister?" It doesn't make sense.

"I hated my sister. The entire time we were growing up she got all of the attention. She was just a spoilt little brat who was completely undeserving of our parents love. So no I don't hate your father for killing her, I actually cheered him along while he did it." What am ass! The absolute gall of this man.

"After he did kill her, me and your father, well, we became lovers some might say. Him and I, along with Singa have this type of relationship with each other, you see. Anyway, we all came together and worked out this plan to take over this Realm. Your father killed the King here and I imprisoned his son." I gasp out rather loudly.

He is telling me all of this information while showing no outward emotions about it whatsoever.

I've never seen anyone so nonchalantly talking about murdering people.

"Why? You ruined so many lives and for what? The glory? Power? Fame? Why would you do it?" I ask him incredulously.

"Why? Because we could. That's it. I know you may be expecting more like some miraculous reveal announcing that we did this all just for revenge or something silly like that but we didn't. We did it just because we actually could!" He incredibly lets a deep diabolical laugh.

"Unbelievable. You are probably worse than my father. Do you actually know what he wants from me? Do you even care?" This shit is so damn startling my entire body is starting to shake in pure raw fury.

"Yes. I do. He wants you to be his Luna. He wants desperately to sleep with also although I can't seem to see why he actually does? Don't get me wrong, you are remarkably beautiful I just don't see the fascination he has in you. Oh well, to each his own I guess." He states as he studies me in my entirety with his eyes disgustingly roaming all over me.

I feel repulsive and dirty just from his vulgar eyes so blatantly roaming over me.

"Well let my father come then. I can't wait to destroy his ass." I exclaim bravely.

Samuel chuckles at my bravery. "Dear girl you are something else. It's sort of cute the way you think that you would actually be able to. He said you were challenging and I tend to believe him." The condescending ass!

"I'm a challenge alright. So now that you know who I really am why don't you be a gentleman and let my brother out of your dungeon?" His eyes suddenly widen. I bury my own laughter within watching him.

"What you didn't know that I knew he was still alive? I thought you knew everything?" Giving him cocky smile I place my hand on the table, palms down, lifting myself up from the chair while eyeing him with defiance.

"Let's not waste any more of my precious time. Won't you be a nice little fellow and go fetch my brother for me will you?" I'm tired of these stupid games. It's time to get this damn fucked up show on the road.

"You think you command me? Little girl I will crush you!" He snarls slamming his glass down hard on the table.

"I thought you couldn't harm me? Isn't that what you said? What would my father say if you laid one little finger on me?" Now I'm being the condescending ass and I love it.

"Look here...."

"No you look here! Go get me my damn brother before I kill you!" I cut him off demandingly.

"Kill me? I would love to see you try little girl!" I'm getting tired of him calling me a damn little girl.

"Then let me show you." I exclaim as I raise up my hand, with my palm up, calling forth on my powers as I produce a ball of whirling fire within it.

He backs away from me with pure terror now encompassing his face. It's a delightful sight to see.

"Stop!" Someone bellows out loudly from somewhere behind me suddenly.

Looking over my shoulder slowly, I see my father walking into the room with proud steps along with another woman trailing up behind him, I begin to shiver all over from his sudden appearance.

"Father?" I ask disbelievingly.

"Thorn my beautiful daughter. I've come to take you home. Now be a good girl and just come with me. This tedious search that you have had me on is far to tiring now. It's time for you to stop all of this childish nonsense and come home." Is he kidding?

"I will never come home with you. You sick fuck!" I scream at him while still holding the fireball within my hand.

"Thorn," he drawls my out name egotistically, "You can not win my love. You are outnumbered here. Why do you fight me so hard? Either you come with me or I will kill your brother, your choice!" What is he talking about?

"Where's Fier?" He scoffs at me pathetically.

"I have him locked up. Him and Tristan both. Didn't it ever cross your mind why you couldn't get ahold of him? I seen all of your text and calls on his phone and I must say you are very persistent. Now stop all of this and come home or I won't hesitate to kill him." I stand before him immobilized in shock.

He has Fier?

I distinguish the fireball immediately in my hand.

"That's my good girl. Now come over here and give your father a hug and a kiss like a good little girl." He states victoriously. Fucking Disgusting! "And I expect for it to include tongues." Ewe!

With a slump of my shoulders I diligently walk over to him, as soon I draw nearer to him he quickly grabs me by my upper arms, pulling me against him roughly.

I collide with his chest almost painfully, his grip around me is so damn unbearably tight.

I fake a heavy sigh, grinning mischievously against his chest.

Reaching slowly up to him, I maneuver my arm away from his hold, rearing my arm back suddenly I yank it forward with all of my might and plunge my hand deep into his chest. He gasps out with sudden surprise.

Crashing though his ribs I wrap my hand around his still beating heart and pull it out firmly from his chest.

He stands frozen just for a second gasping, his eyes open wide staring right at me before his entire body crashes to the ground unceremoniously. I stare down at him, peering at my fathers lifeless body on the floor with his wretched heart solidify in the palm of hand felling absolutely nothing.

I tear my gaze away from his lifeless form on the castle floor to look at my hand when I suddenly feel his warm blood starting to slowly cascade down my arm. My entire hand and forearm are covered entirely of my fathers blood and still all I can feel is absolutely..fucking...nothing.

I hear a female voice from what I assume is Singa, screaming out in horrific terror, jarring me away from my cold dead stance abruptly.

Then all hell breaks lose in the castle.

My mates coming running out of their hiding spots headed straight for me with panicked stricken faces.

Sera, Freya, and Hope all come running out behind them.

Screaming and scuffling are reverberating all throughout the room. I hear it all but can seem to bring myself to move.

Sin was the one who reaches me first, he jerks me against his body, wrapping his arms around me rather firmly.

"Damn Thorn you scared the living hell out of me." He breathes out with his chin planted on the top of my head.

A lot of questionable commotion is going on around us. I feel hands gently rubbing against my back in a lovingly matter but yet I am still unable to feel any type of emotions.

Then I hear Seras screams coming upfrom somewhere behind me, I pull away from Sin instantly that's when I notice that Slay and Sunny were standing right behind me.

Peeking in between the two of them I find Sera is facing off with an amused Samuel. Her little finger is pointed right at him while she keeps screaming mercilessly at him.

When Samuel seems to have quite enough of her ramblings he goes to strike her but before he is able to do so Slay and Sunny have already reached him, holding him back by both of them restraining him by his arms.

Samuel struggles within their tight grasp on him. Yelling out obscenities at all of them.

Sin comes up from behind me enclosing me into his arms with his arms easily circling around my mid section I watch the scene before me unfold with apt attention.

Sera bravely and shocking pulls out a giant hunters knife she had somehow managed to hide on her unsuspectingly.

I start to walk over to them but Sin stops my progression by pulling me back against his chest, holding on to me tightly.

"Let her handle it baby." He whispers into my ear. I can feel his warm breath virally fanning out against my neck. I shiver again.

Sera keeps continually screaming maddeningly over at Samuel.

Then in a flash she takes the hunting knife that's in her hand and plunges it deeply straight into the right side of Samuels stomach.

Sera drags the knife along the entire width of Samuels stomach. Samuel is screaming out in horrendous terror.

His eyes are fully widen nearly bulging out of his head with his mouth shockingly agape he starts to sputter, he tries to speak by moving his mouth half way opened and shut but he can't seem to form the words.

Standing their immobilized by what I'm seeing my eyes automatically drop to Samuels opened stomach, Sera pulls the knife out of it very swiftly all the while laughing mechanically at him.

I watch as half of his internal organs drop out of him spilling out onto the castles floor with a resounding grotesque plop, guts and galore are slowly sliding out of abdomen as Slay and Sunny both are struggling to hold on to his lifeless body.

Bile rises up quickly in my throat, leaning over with Sins arms still wrapped around my own stomach, I projectile vomit all over the pristine castle floor unintentionally.

"It's okay. You're okay." I can hear Sin try to comfort me as I keep gagging, dry heaving mostly, trying to get all of the disgusting aftertaste it all out of my mouth. My breaths come out unsteadily as I spit on the floor a few times. Gross.

Rising back up, a bit unsteadily, I look back over at the scene before me but thankfully they have managed to already cover up Samuels lifeless body with a burgundy curtain they must of stripped off of a curtain rod.

Another scream shatters throughout the room as I turn my head looking over my shoulder I watch as Freya and Hope both have Singa frozen in some sort of magical force field.

Singa is anxiously crying out and begging for her release. Her hands keep pounding roughly on the force field that's surrounding her.

"So you're the fucking witch who put a damn spell on me?" Sin snarls over at Singa suddenly dropping his arms away from me, he slowly takes steps toward her as I follow aimlessly behind him.

"Sin my love please help me." Singa pleads with Sin as he draws closer to her. I scoff out loudly. The absolutely derivative gall of this woman.

"Your love? The only love I have is for this woman right here." Sin tells her with a sneer while pointing directly at me.

"Don't be silly love. You told me she meant nothing to you." Well that fucking hurt. I want to slash out at her but I know that Sin is the one that has to deal with this certain nuisance of a problem. She has deliberately put him through hell, so I decidedly just allow him to have at her and sit back and watch the show play out before me.

"She means everything to me you cow! Why did you fucking do this to me?" Sins voice almost croaks on the last comment. I feel an usual twist in my gut to hear him talk like he is so damn broken.

"He made me do it!" Singa bellows while pointing her finger at my fathers corpse on the floor behind me.

"No he didn't. You were both his and Samuels lover, don't try and deny it Samuel already informed me of it. You're also the one that helped him kill my mother, you piece of low down dirty shit!" I bark out her with my anger steadily rising.

I feel hands pressed against my back again lovingly, I automatically jerk as soon as I feel them though.

"It's okay beautiful, it's just me." Hearing that it's Slays voice behind me I relax instantly.

"Thorn?" I scowl when I hear my name being called. As I turn around I see Striker striding in from a doorway that's coming up from the other side of the room.

"I have someone here who wants to meet with you?" Striker informs me with a smile. He half turns peering back when a man comes walking up from the doorway looking a bit haggard.

My eyes grow immensely wider when I see him. This has to be my brother.

I float slowly over to them. At least it feels like I'm floating because I can't seem to feel a thing but amazement at this particular moment.

He almost crumples through the door before I was able to reach him. Striker was able to catch him thankfully before he fell completely over.

Nervously, I proceeded over to him. As I drew closer I can actually see the resemblance between the two of us.

"Austis?" I seemingly ask in a quavering voice.

"You...look just....like my mother." Austis stammers out, I give him a breathless laugh.

"She was my mother too." I tell him as I start fidgeting with my hands. When I suddenly notice my fathers blood that's starting to crust up on it. I try to hide my hand behind my back quickly.

Glancing back up at Austis, he has a notable grin plastered on his face which in turn makes me relax somewhat.

"We have a lot to talk about." I nervously tell him.

"Yes we do apparently." He smiles at me instantly reminding of me of my mothers smile.

"Thorn." I hear someone else calling out my name as I turn I notice Sera making her way over to me anxiously.

"Mate!" What the fuck? I turn back around swiftly only to see my new found brother staring over at Sera unabashedly.

You're kidding me!

Peering back over at Sera, the poor girl is already in a very flustered state after hearing my brothers claim on her.

Her eyes are widen and she's trying her best to look anywhere else in the room but at Austis. I would laugh if it wasn't such a strange occurrence.

"Uhm, Austis, I would like you to meet my friend Seraphina." I humbly say while waving my clean hand at a very shy and timid Sera.

They both just stare at each other both of them are acting like they just don't know what to do with each other.

Okay then.

"I'll let you two talk." I mummer as I walk over to Sera. I give her a little nudge on her back making her slightly stumble. She huffs but eventually ends up strolling rather slowly over to my love struck brother.

Glad I could help.

Leaving them two alone I intentionally drag Striker along with me, by his arm.

"But I wanted to watch!" Striker pouts and whines like a baby. I just roll my eyes at him.

I let his arm go once I make it back over to my mates, Freya, Hope, and a still imprisoned Singa.

"What are we going to do with her?" I ask them all glaring over at Singa.

"I can tell you what to do." I'm taken by surprise by the new voice suddenly echoing in the room when suddenly I'm wrapped up against a foreign chest with a damn knife lodged up against my jugular.

"Thorn!" I hear someone scream out in a panic as soon as I collided up against a hard chest. The cold blade of the knife against my throat makes my entire body seize up instantly.

"Grayson son please don't do this." Hope is pleading with her son with both of her hands held up in right in front of her.

Grayson?

"Why not? I told her how much I cared about her and she just threw it right back into my face by going back to these three assholes!" He yanks my entire body back to him forcibly. The knife slithers across my neck as he yanks back causing it cut me slightly. I grimace from the stinging pain.

"Please don't do this Grayson, they will kill you." Hope tries to plead with him again. He just gives her a robotic chuckle.

"I'm far more powerful than any of them mother! They do not scare me!" He yells at her. I suddenly feel the rumbled vibrations of his deep voice casting out through his chest.

"You better be scared because once I get my damn hands you, I.....will.....kill...you!" Slay threatens him with a torrential snarl.

Grayson laughs at Slay then begins to gingerly take a step away from everyone while dragging me along with him. My high heel shoes scrape against the floor, dislodging them both from my feet as he willingly drags me along with him.

"She's mine! Back the fuck away!" He's lost his mind!

"Don't! If you hurt her in any way there will be not one damn person in this fucking Realm that will be able to keep me from getting to you!" Sunny growls at him.

I squeeze my eyes tightly together when I see the look of anguish torment captured on all of my mates faces.

I'm terrified that this unstable Grayson will inevitably lash out at them all.

"Let her go Grayson. You and I can work this out with each other by fighting this out one on one or man to man." Sin sneers at him with valid hatred. "Just let her go please." He adds pleading with Grayson with true raw emotions.

"D-don't...I'm fi..." I try to tell them I'm fine but I can't get the words to form because Grayson suddenly applies more pressure on the knife at my neck. I feel trickles of my blood dripping down my neck slowly. My entire body begins to uncontrollably shake in staggering fear.

This may just be the last time I ever get to see them again. Tears suddenly start to well up in my eyes. When I open them back up everything around me is out of focus and fuzzy.

Then I can feel the first teardrops randomly start falling down my face.

"Don't threaten me boy! Now back the fuck up or I will kill her!" Grayson starts taking larger strides, walking backwards, still dragging me with along him.

"Please son. You're better than this. I'm begging you don't do this." I can barely hear Hopes pleas now with her son because my ears are now starting to faintly ring out. I begin to panic.

"I am better mother. Better than them! Thorn is mine and I will treat her far better than those asshat clowns." Grayson deeply laughs diabolically.

I'm going to die by a mad man hands!

I bring my focus back to my three loving mates before me. Pleading with them with my eyes to not do anything remotely foolish that will inevitably cause them any harm.

"I...love...you!" I manage to say with my voice lowly cracking between my declarations to them.

I will always love you!

Chapter 27

My heart nearly fell out of my fucking chest when I saw that knife pressed up against Thorns precious throat.

Im going to kill this cocksucker very very fucking goddamn slowly and love every mother fucking second of doing it.

"I....love...you!" Thorn barely mutters out with tears steadily flowing down her beautiful face. She thinks she's going to fucking die. I sucked in huge desperate breath when she utter those three longing words to us like they were going to be her fucking last.

Not on my fucking watch baby!

Grayson seems to think that he's more powerful than any of us but I have some really bad news for this fuckwit.

He doesn't realize that every single person that's in this damn room would do anything for our sweet loving Thorn, especially me and my fucking brothers.

Nobody threatens the love of my life and gets the fuck away with it. No fucking body! Not even this dime store hood rat low life hungry power grubbing Son-of-a-bitch!

"Grayson let her go. This is your last damn fucking warning!" I snarl out at him while bearing my fangs, taking a few mild cautious steps toward him and Thorn.

She's still helplessly struggling within his grasp but every time she makes a move the damn knife at her throat within Graysons weaselly hands seems to cut into her neck a little deeper.

Her blood is slowly trickling down her neck making me see fucking boiling red! Demon growls out fiercely within me.

Out of the corner of my eye I happen to catch a slight glimpse of her brother Austis slowly edging his way over to an unsuspecting Grayson quietly.

"Keep him occupied!" Demon pipes up viscously snarling.

"Will do!" That's wont be a fucking problem.

"You fucking better. Then kill his two faced ass!" No damn doubt about that shit.

"Gladly." I snarl back viscerally.

"Grayson we need to talk about this. Why do you want our mate when you know that she loves only us? She will never be able to love you!" Keep him distracted. "Not like you want her to."

"I'll make her fucking love me!" This guy is completely off his damn rocker.

"You can't make someone love you Grayson. It only comes gradually. Thorn will never love you. She loves us. Can't you see how much you're hurting her." I try to plead with him for understanding. "Just look at her neck!" I growl.

Keep him distracted.

I watch anxiously as Austis has almost made his way up behind him now thankfully going unnoticed.

"If you love somebody you wouldn't hurt them Grayson. Look at her, you are definitely hurting her!" I point aggressively to Thorns wounded neck. "She's fucking bleeding!" I add on snarling.

Keep...him...fucking...distracted!

Grayson luckily lowers his head down slightly to see the damage that he has inflicted on Thorns neck and just as he does Austis finally reaches his ass. I was so preoccupied with Grayson and Thorn that I didn't even realize that Austis had Seras hunting knife within his grasp.

Austis rears back suddenly and with a forceful plunge stabs Grayson right into his damn back.

Grayson lets out a mighty deaf roaring scream before he crumbles down to the floor but just as he does he unintentionally cuts a long line across Thorns neck, she screams out in horror right before she starts falling down to the floor completely unconscious.

I rush quickly over to Thorn grabbing her up into my arms right before her body was able to collide with the damn floor.

People are all screaming and shuffling around us but I don't give a flying fuck about them at the moment.

"Thorn?" I call out her name with a shaky breath. "Beautiful?"

Pushing her long hair away from her face I watch as the cut on her throat thankfully starts to mend itself back together instantly.

I release a huge scared ragged breath that I was undoubtedly holding in then I swiftly notice her steady breathing by the little rise and fall of her chest. Thank Fuck!

Squeezing her tiny body tighter flush up against me for dear life I start to fucking cry like a little ass baby. I actually thought I fucking lost her.

Sin and Sunny are on the floor beside us touching Thorns body wherever they possibly can with very worried and concerned expressions on their faces.

I foolishly wipe away the tears on my face completely embarrassed by them. I'm a full grown ass man I shouldn't be fucking crying like this.

"She's okay. She's okay." I mutter with my voice fucking trembling as I keep rocking Thorns body back and forth in my arms. "She's okay."

Thorn starts to stir awake suddenly in my arms moaning out egregiously as she rocks her head from side to side trying diligently to wake herself up fully. Come on baby you can do it. Please.

"Thorn?" Sunny whispers to her barely able to contain his own feelings.

"W-what h-hap..happened?" Thorn stutters weakly as she tries to rise up from the floor unsteadily, I tighten my grasp around her, preventing her from being able to do so.

"I think you might have went into shock!" Sin explains to her while falling roughly back onto his legs letting out a full drawn tiresome breath.

"W-where's t-that asshole?" She mumbles slightly.

"He's dead. I think." Sunny relays the information to her unknowingly.

I crane my head looking over my shoulder at Graysons body that's laying out on the castles floor unmoving. Peering my eyes closer to him I search for any movements of breath dispelling out of him.

Unfortunately, I see slight movements as his chest rise and falls slowly, the bastard is still alive.

"No he's still alive but barely." Hope is kneeling down by Graysons fallen body hysterically crying over him.

"Striker I know he's your cousin and I hate to do this to you or to his mother but will you kindly escort Grayson to the care center and I will meet you both there shortly. But first I would like to ask if I have your permission," Austis looks down at Hopes crying figure, "to remove his powers from him. That way I can keep him alive for you but unfortunately I will have to keep him imprisoned." Austis deems regally.

I see a sudden flash of hope light up in Hopes eyes. "Yes, King Sides you have my full permission." Hope softly mumbles. She stands up slowly wiping her tears away from her face to allow Austis access to Grayson that's lying helplessly on the floor below him.

I observe closely as Austis places his hand right on top of Graysons head.

He mumbles a few incomprehensible words as a bright yellowish light starts to form on top of Graysons head. Graysons body begins to shake uncontrollably under Austis onslaught of powerful magic.

Then the yellowish light from Austis hand suddenly re-cedes back into the palm of his hand just as fast at it once appeared.

"It's done you may take him away now." Austis tells Striker. Striker walks over to Graysons listless body and picks him up off of the floor, bridal style, then obediently carries him away.

Good fucking riddance to the trash. If it was up to me the guy wouldn't be leaving this damn room breathing at all. He would be leaving in fucking pieces. Limb by limb, organ by fucking organ!

"What about me?" Singa screams out suddenly, alerting us all. I actually almost forgot about the witch bitch.

Thorn tries to stand up again but this time I don't hold her back, I stand up along with her, with my hands placed under her arms I keep her steady until she is able to stand back up on her own two feet again finally.

"What foul crimes had this woman committed?" Austis ask.

"She put a spell on me, she also put a spell on this entire Realm preventing anyone other than Fae to enter it, and she was in cohorts with Samuel and Alpha Baker." Sin informs him finally standing up to his full height.

"She also helped kill our mother and apparently she helped with killing your father to." Thorn adds on while she contin-uously rubs her hand across her throat.

Austis eyes widen and then in the next breath his face grows stern with fury you can actually see the anger rolling off of him in abundance.

"For that, you foul heathen, your penalty is death!" He vows with conviction and before anyone even realizes it, a flash of white light burst out of the palm of his right hand. The force field shield that was keeping Singa hostage dissipates right before are very own eyes when the white light hits it then without missing a damn beat the bright light crashes into Singas chest forcefully.

Her body absorbs the light within her as she yells out in horrific agony, her entire body starts convulsing, she lets out a strangled gasp as her eyes roll into the back her head.

Singas head lolls back and with one last beckoning cry her body goes completely limp then crashes to the floor as she lays there dying almost instantly.

When the last lone breath leaves her body the entire Realm begins to shake violently.

It only last for a split a second but it seemingly ends with a big roaring vibrating bang echoing throughout the entire Realm.

I squeeze my eyes tightly, flinching my head back when I hear the ear piercing bang.

By the time the piercing sound quietens I reopen my eyes only to view a heart stopping scene ahead of me. I watch horrified as Sins body collapses onto the damn floor falling completely unconscious.

Fuck! Fuck! Fuck!

"Sin!" Thorn screams.

I rush over to him quickly, along with Sunny and Thorn running up behind me. We all instantly fall down on to our knees beside Sins fallen body.

"Sin?" I ask with my voice cracking, reaching my hand out tentatively I check for a pulse on his neck.

Thump! Thump!

Thank Fuck, I was able to find one.

"Take him to the well care center!" Austis barks out the order loudly. The tone of his order breaks me from my traumatic trance immediately.

Picking Sins body up from the floor, I follow Austis out of the room with a crying Thorn and Sunny trailing along behind me.

I fucking can't stand this. Questions keep running around through my head. Why did he faint? Is he dying? What caused this? Why isn't he waking the fuck up? Why him?

After all that we have been through today I just can't lose my bother. I already thought that I lost Thorn today I don't think my heart can take anymore of this shit.

Please wake the fuck up brother! Please.

It's been two long days and nights since Sin fainted.

He hasn't woken up yet but the well care doctor assured us all that he will in time.

He said that the spell on Sin is what made him faint and put him in a slight sleeping paralysis.

Even though the spell on him somewhat dissipated over time he still had minuscule trace amounts of it in him.

When Austis killed Singa it caused a ripple effect on Sin unfortunately, causing his body to have a staggering reaction to it.

Anyone that was under Singas influence will be experiencing the same exact thing as Sin, according to Doctor Piedmont that is. Makes me wonder exactly how many people she ended up doing this to?

We have all been just lounging around here, hardly ever leaving the room, just waiting and hoping for Sin to finally wake up. Hopefully.

Thorn, predictably, hasn't left Sins side through the entirety of his stay here. The only time that she has been away from him is to use the damn restroom. Yesterday I did happen to finally coax her into a shower and to finally eat just a little bit of something.

Right at this moment she has her head laying on Sins bed asleep with her arm graciously laying upon his leg like it's a damn lifeline.

I tried to get her to sleep in a regular bed but she wouldn't dare leave Sins side no matter how many times I told her that he would understand, she just wouldn't have it.

Scrubbing my hand down my face I feel especially tired and weary. Sleep has been hard for me to come by these last two damn days and nights unfortunately it seems to be taking a heavy tow on my ass tonight.

Sunny is snoring mildly across the room, he's laying uncomfortably in a small leather green backed chair thats placed in the corner of the room while I'm sitting in another chair located right beside Sins bed.

With the room darkened and the only sounds that are echoing throughout the room is Sunny's snores and the sound of the heart monitor machine beeping ever so often, I start to drift off to sleep along with them.

That is until I hear a couple of soft grunts coming from straight Sins bed.

Cracking my eyes open a slit. I see Sins head starting to roll from side to side while he lets out a little soft whimper.

Jumping up from my chair quickly I stumble over to him, falling down to the side of his bed on my knees beside him.

"Sin?" I call his name out lowly.

He continues to grumble while trying to stir himself awake. His eyes creep open slowly into little slits, he then blinks once, twice, thrice then he finally rouses himself fully awake.

He suddenly whimpers out like he's in a lot of pain. Nervously, I reach my hand over to him, barely touching his arm softly.

"Sin?" I call his name out again. "Are you awake?" I add while whispering to him.

Sins eyes close suddenly then opens them wide again, I breath a hefty sigh of relief when I see those hazel eyes finally peering open widely at me.

"Thank fuck Sin. You had us all so damn worried." I state to him aguishly.

"W-what..." he croaks.

"You we're in a slight sleep paralysis." I cut him off, he tries to sit up but he struggles with it, hurriedly I jump back up assisting him to raise himself on his pillows to help make him feel slightly more comfortable.

"H-ho-how long?" He ask me with his voice croaking again.

"Two days." I state simply kneeling back down beside his bed.

He peers down to Thorns sleeping form cracking a tiny smile at her as he looks down on her lovingly.

"She hasn't left your side." I tell him quietly while smiling over at him.

"Water." He ask, I rush back up to grab him a styrofoam cup of water from the water jug left in his room. Handing it over to him, I see that his hands are starting to shake just a little.

I take the cup from him placing it against his lips, he drinks it all down thirstily to where it's almost completely empty.

"Thanks." He now sounds a bit better.

"No problem. How do you feel?" I question him curiously.

"Like a bulldozer fucking ran over me!" I cackle deeply at his remark kneeling back down once again at the side of his bed.

"Did everything goes as planned?" He ask referring to Samuels demise.

"Yep. All of the guards that Freya managed to put under were eventually arrested and placed in the dungeon cells. With Samuel now gone along with Alpha Baker and Singa, all is peaceful." I indulge him.

"What about Austis? Did he get to take his rightful place back on the throne without anyone disputing it?" Oh that he did.

"Yep. He is now fully the King of the Invivus Realm. With our very own Thorn being the Realms Princess." I explain peering back down at our beautiful mate still surprisingly sleeping with pride showing on my face.

"Good. I knew we could do it." He states proudly while smirking over at me.

I'm glad he did because sometimes I was having my own doubts about it.

"Is she okay?" He inquires glancing down at Thorn again.

"Yes. Although not entirely. She has been having nightmares when she does find to time to sleep that is and I still don't think she fully realizes the full extent of killing her own father just yet. Now she's worried about Fier and that asshole Tristan being locked up in her fathers dungeon. But I assured her as soon you we're capable enough to leave here that we would go rescue him." She has been so damn worried about her brother and with her worries compounding over Sins sleep paralysis she hasn't been taking care of herself properly.

She has had both Sunny and I extremely worried over her.

"You're awake!" Speaking of Sunny.

He spots Sin finally awake on the bed smiling enormously over at him. He stands up quickly from his makeshift bed strolling over to where I'm still kneeling.

"About damn time bro. I was starting to get worried about your stupid ass." Sunny happily exclaims while patting him on his shoulder. How damn sweet! I roll my eyes up at him.

"Why? You know I always need to take a good long nap after a battle." Sin brags sheepishly.

Here they are world my goofy ass fucking brothers and man do I love them.

"Sin?" A beautiful whimsical voice floats up to us suddenly.

Thorn finally awakens from her slumber staring over at Sin with shock cascading over her beautiful face.

"Baby?" Sin croaks out with a shaky breath.

Thorn springs up from her seat suddenly jumping straight into Sins awaiting arms.

He holds on to her so damn tightly that I'm afraid he may just actually break the poor woman in two.

I hear Thorn quietly sobbing against Sins chest. Sin rubs his chin all along the top of her head, kissing her head periodically as he does. I hate to hear fucking cry.

Damn I'm so done with this Realm.

I honestly think it's time for us to return back home now. Even with the problems we might have to face involving Sunny with Beta Slayer our time here has definitely come to end now that Sins finally awaken. We can all go home.

Thank Fuck! Because I really do miss home.

Three days later we are all gathered together near Freyas cabin once again to say our farewells to them all, for a time anyway.

Along with us, there is also a clutter of others waiting with us by the opened portal.

Freya, Striker, Austis and Seraphina have all come to wish us well and to say their parting goodbyes.

Hope, unfortunately couldn't make it, according to Freya she's been holed up at the inn, rarely leaving the place unable to face anybody.

I can understand that. Her son is now imprisoned in Austis dungeon cell for treason and attempted murder. He will more than likely be imprisoned there for years if not for life.

Grayson should consider himself very lucky that he didn't receive death for his outlandish crimes. The way I view it the bastard just got off with a little slap on the wrist when he should have been residing six feet under right now instead. But thanks to Austis compassionate nature Grayson will live.

Weary is the man that wears the crown.

Seraphina has moved into the castle finally accepting Austis has her mate. They actually make a pretty decent couple. I'm sure she will be an excellent Queen for the Invivus Realm.

There's a lot of work ahead of them both now but I'm sure they can both handle whatever is thrown their way. Especially with Freya by their side and Striker now being the head of Austis's Royal guard.

The bastard is even selling his own magazine company to honorably take up his position with Austis.

Freya is now assigned to be the Kings special Royal Seer. A position that I'm sure will fit her to a damn T.

With everything now being settled and the Realm finally being ruled by their rightful King, I have no qualms about leaving but unfortunately my beautiful mate is finding it hard to say goodbye to all of them, especially her new found brother.

She has been crying nonstop since we arrived at Freyas cabin. I realize that it's an emotional time for her but I have never quite seen her be this so damn emotional before.

Every since Sin has awaken from his forced nap I have noticed that she has been an emotional wreck.

Crying off and on at the drop of a fucking hat. She has also been a bit edgy lately.

She flew off on me just this morning just for me taking a tiny bite out of her raspberry scone and last night she actually threatened Sunny with a damn fork just because he had the nerve to ask her if she was finished with her food yet.

She has been acting rather strangely lately and I just can't seem to figure out exactly why?

Maybe it has something to do with us returning back home to our pack? There is a lot of bad memories for her back there after all.

It could also be from all the stress and pressure that she has been under lately or maybe even she's finally feeling the repercussions of killing her own damn father? But he damn well deserved it.

Regardless of what it may be, we need to get her back home and figure it the fuck out because it's driving me absolutely crazy.

"Slay don't just stand there like some damn statue come and say goodbye!" Thorn bellows out for me.

I reprimand myself immediately, don't say anything spiteful back to her Slay, you don't exactly know what's going on with her just yet.

So instead of saying something to her that I just might actually come to regret I obediently walk over to the rest of them to say my own goodbyes just like a good boy.

I feel like I'm fucking whipped suddenly.

I grumble as I go but eventually I plastered on a smile and said my damn goodbyes to them all.

Finally done and over with, thankfully, we all solemnly walk through the opened portal.

Once we're through it I sigh out heavily, happy just to be back home in my own damn territory.

Dropping my suitcase beside me as soon as I entered my lovely dwelling I soon closed my eyes and took a deep inhale of the magical scent known as home. Fucking Finally!

"Fier?" Hearing Thorn call out her brothers name I open my eyes back up instantly.

Searching around our living room area I spot a groggily Fier waking up from sleeping on our damn couch. He's rubbing the sleep out of his eyes roughly with the back of his hand.

When he spots Thorn he automatically springs up from my couch running over to her quickly, he wraps her up into his arms and swings her around, while laughing.

Sweet family reunion, I guess.

Fier drops her back down on the floor to her feet as he places both hands on the side of her face he looks at her with pure devotion sweeping his eyes.

"I was so worried about you. What happened?" Thorn ask him with her fingers clinging around Fiers wrist.

"It's a long story Thorn. I'm just so damn glad you're safe." Fier almost cries. Embracing Thorn gently he holds her in his arms tightly.

Well I guess we don't have to go out and rescue his ass any longer seeing as how he's already here.

"Sunny!" We hear someone excitedly yell out Sunny's name from the top of the staircase landing.

Craning my neck up I cringe when I see fucking Shari standing there in nothing but a damn white silk gown and robe on, that only goes down to her fucking thighs, she's peering down at Sunny with pure adoration lighting up on her face.

Fuck!

We just got home we really don't need this type shit right now.

Shari bounds down the staircase rapidly just as she reaches Sunny she throws herself into his arms enclosing her arms around his neck she then proceeds to kiss him all along his damn neck.

What the actual fuck?

I bet if I lifted up her damn silk nightgown right now I would find a set a balls on her that's bigger than my fucking own.

Sunny smartly pushes her away from him instantly.

"Get your fucking hands off of me!" Sunny growls out at her defensively. Shari nearly stumbles over from Sunny's push giving him a very snotty ass look.

I try my best to hold in my laughter at the absurd scene happening before me but I just simply can't.

I guess all of the tension from our past journey is staring to catch up to me? Plus with the added bonus of seeing such a fake ass woman trying her best to woo my brother sends me over the damn edge.

Bending over while holding on to my stomach I bark out in uproarious laughter, getting everyone's attention that's in the room quickly directed right at my ass.

Sin soon joins in on my ridiculous bout of laughter.

"What's so damn funny?" Shari huffs as she places her hands on her tiny hips while giving me an evil glare.

"You...are." I try to tell her between my bouts of laughter. "You...are so...damn...desperately naive." She fucking scoffs at me. The bitch.

"What is he talking about Sunny poo?" Shari ask Sunny with a fake pout. It's just too damn much!

I nearly piss my damn self from laughing so damn hard.

"Look Shari. I know I made you a promise but things have changed. I have my mate back and well, she is our Luna." You fucking bet she is!

Shari glances over at Thorn who is standing in front of a very confused Fier.

"Her? You must be joking?" Shari spitefully says with a fucking snarl on her face.

"No I'm not. This is Thorn my mate and she is our Luna!" Sunny states to Shari more intimidatingly.

"But Sunny poo you promised me." Shari whines pathetically.

"I know and I do apologize for that Shari but I love Thorn and I chose her. You were just as unfortunate mistake." I kind of feel sorry for Sunny now. My laughter dries up instantly when I see the anguish look that's aligning his face.

"Not according to this contract you signed Sunny." Shari states with a gleam in her eyes as she drags out a piece of tattered paper from her fucking bosom.

He fucking didn't? He wouldn't? How stupid could he actually be to sign a fucking contract? She has to be lying.

This has to be a fucking mistake! Right?

Chapter 28

He signed a damn contract?

The fucking fool! What is going to happen to all of us now? I'm so sick and damn tired of us never knowing any type of damn peace.

Can't there be just one damn day that we don't have to deal with some type of crazy ass bullshit in our lives?

Shari withdrew that damn contract from her bosom with a snarky stare planted right at Thorn.

Thorn, the incredible woman that she is, just took it with a grain of salt and shrug her shoulders dismissively at Shari.

I am absolutely bewildered by Thorns nonchalant reaction toward all of this shit.

Sunny tentatively grabs the contract from Sharis grasp like it was fucking diseased.

When he unfolded the paper in his hands he let out a very loud audible gasp after reading the fine print on the damn thing.

Impatient as hell I stormed over to Sunny ripping the damn contract from his hands.

As I viewed the almost ineligible script before me I couldn't help but grow madder with every damn word that I read.

There in fine bold fucking print states that Sunny officially makes Shari White his damn Luna it even has the fucking date issued on it.

What the hell was my moronic ass brother even thinking?

He clearly fucking wasn't thinking apparently. Unless he was thinking with his damn dick!

Dropping my hands to my side in complete and utterly disgust, I blow out a disparaging breath.

Slay soon comes over to me ripping the contract right out of my hand that still laid limply at my side.

As he reads it his face morphs from an earnest concern look to a full blown pissed off outright panic.

He did the same exact thing as I just did. He dropped his arms to his side in clear defeat sighing out dramatically.

Sunny not only fucked up this time his ass literally fucked up severely.

What the hell are we going to do now?

"See? Told you! It's right there in black and white and it's irrefutable proof that I am now Sunny's Luna." Shari states snidely. The damn bitch is nothing but a fucking con artist. I'm sure of it. There has to be something that we can do to refute this bogus ass claim of hers. "Oh Sunny poo don't look so upset. You know you actually had no control over it. That night I had a friend at Sins bar place a little spell on you. Her name was Esmeralda. Strange woman but very helpful. It only lasted for a few hours unfortunately. When you were so wonderfully making love to me you thought you were actually making love to her!" She snarls over at Thorn, "when in all actuality it was me you were with the entire time. You kept yelling out that bitches name over and over again. I almost got jealous over it." Sunny grimaces with every hateful word that spews out of this bitches mouth.

"Don't look so defeated Sunny poo. You got what you wanted which was an illusion of her but still in a way her and I got what I wanted. Which was this pack of course." Shari states cooing while fluttering her damn fake eyelashes up at Sunny.

Thorn then snaps out of whatever the hell that was keeping her from being so damn nonchalant before and walks over to Slay grabbing the contract from his hands roughly.

As she reads it I shove Sunny on his shoulder hard with the palm of my hand causing him stumble back from me immediately.

He huffs and then lower heads remorsefully.

He damn well fucking should!

I hear a cackle of laughter coming up from my left by Thorn. As I turn my head to view her I watch as she surprises me by suddenly conjuring up a small fireball in the palm of her hand lighting up the fucking contract between Sunny and Shari that's in her other hand on fire instantaneously.

"Stop!" Shari yells while hurriedly rushing over to Thorn trying to put the fire out in Thorns palm with her hands. She's flaying her arms around like a damn lunatic screaming and stomping her foot on the floor in clear outright desperation.

Little embers of residue fire are floating about all around Thorn as Thorn gives Shari a very triumphant smirk.

I guess the damn contract is pretty much null and void now.

"You can't do that!" Shari bellows.

"Well I did. I'm Sunny's fucking Luna. Bitch you ain't fucking shit! Now get your skinny little rag tagged ass out of my fucking house now before I set that little skanky ass of yours on fire next!" Daaaamn! Why was that such a fucking turn on? I love it when Thorn gets all aggressive and demanding. That's my fucking woman! A damn spitfire and sexy as fucking hell.

"I have a copy!" Shari rebuttals back at Thorn coyly.

"No you damn well don't. You wouldn't have been trying so desperately to put out the fire if you actually did?" Well she got her there.

Shari is pipping hot now. The daggers that she's shooting toward Thorn could actually pierce threw a damn stone cold heart.

"The jig is up honey. Time for act two." Shari loudly exclaims wickedly. Poking her tongue through the side of her mouth.

Our door crashes open wide suddenly with three very pissed off men standing at the threshold.

The man that's standing at the front and center must be Sharis mate Beta Slayer. You can obviously tell by the way he looks like he has actual steam coming out of ears.

The goons behind him must be twins just like me and Sunny except these two look exactly identical in every aspect.

"Who the hell are you and what exactly are doing in my damn house?" Slay questions them with his hands balled up into fist laying at his sides.

His knuckles have gone purely white from the firm tightness of them. Shit he's really fucking pissed.

"Beta Slayer at your service and this is now my pack." Slayer sneers. What the hell?

"You must be hallucinating because this is our damn pack!" Sunny instills with a deafening growl.

Slayer just hackles at both of them.

What an asshole.

"Not anymore dumbass you signed a contract stating that Shari was now your Luna and since I'm her mate that makes me the official Alpha of this pack now!" Slayer explains condescendingly as him and his goons make their way into our house unwelcome.

"There is no contract. Not any more. I burnt that shit right up!" Thorn tells him proudly.

Slayer curls up the side of his upper lip at Thorn with his beady eyes roaming all over her body. He licks his bottom lip suggestively then takes a few steps forward to her before he is even able to reach her I block off his path quickly by standing directly in front of her.

"I don't fucking think so." I snarl at him. Slayer let's out a humorless breathless laugh rolling his fucking eyes at me.

"Whatever that is here in this house is rightfully mine now. My possessions, every fucking thing here is mine and I have every right to fucking claim all of it and that includes her." He says while pointing his grubby finger over at Thorn.

"Slayer! That is not the deal we made. I'm your mate. What the hell do you want her for?" Shari interrupts, whining again.

"Relax baby cakes. I let you have your night of fun with Sunny boy over there. I think you owe me one for that and she will do very nicely." Slayer says huskily while eyeing Thorn with lust firing up in his eyes. "I mean check out that rocking body she has. Those big ass tits and that round firm ass. I love you Shari but I just have to have her." Not on fucking watch buddy.

Oh hell no!

"You fucking lay one finger on her and I will gladly cut the damn thing off." I growl.

"She is ours! Get your mind out of the damn gutter you fucking pervert. I won't allow you to touch her!" Slay pipes in angrily.

Slayer continues to hackle. It makes him sound just like a damn cracked out hyena.

"Like you can fucking stop me! Come her sweetheart. I want you to suck on my dick and then I'm going to make you feel really really special." Slayer says suggestively. Gag fucking me.

"No thanks if I wanted something small to suck on I'd just pop a lifesaver into my mouth." Thorn quips. Well fuck. Couldn't have said that shit better myself.

"You fucking bitch. I'm going to show you what small is!" Slayer barks angrily.

"That's my point exactly." Thorn states rather sarcastically. Damn my mate is definitely on point today.

I let out a deep chuckle only causing Slayers anger to fester even more.

He foolishly tries to dodge his way around me to get to Thorn.

Big fucking no no!

Balling up my fist I punch this asshole right in the middle of his fucking jacked up face.

The two goons that were standing at the door come rushing over to us hurriedly but they both get stopped quickly before they can even reach us by Slay and Sunny tackling them both down to the floor.

Slayer tries to throw a right upper cut at me in return. Dumb ass! I dodge it quickly.

Now all six of us are scrapping it out in our living room. Fier pulls Thorn back away from the battle but she keeps thrashing around in his arms trying her best to get away from his firm hold on her.

With me fighting Slayer and trying to keep a worried eye on Thorn at the same time makes it kind of difficult to get the upper hand on Slayer unfortunately.

He bashes my face in with a few good packed filled punches. For a little man he sure seems awfully fucking strong. I throw his dumb ass off of my body swiftly making him crash onto the floor.

Hearing Thorn scream out suddenly I turn my head in her direction instantly. Shari is pulling a shit load full of Thorns hair viscously in her both of her hands while Fier is desperate trying to pull Thorn out of Sharis grasp.

Slayer gets another damn punch in on me while I'm obviously distracted. Landing my ass right back on the floor. That was a low blow man.

Then a big popping ass sounds echos throughout the living room loudly.

Everyone that was fighting comes to screeching halt immediately.

Amazingly, when I rear my head up off of the floor I see Thorns entire body engulfed in ravenous flames. With beautiful fire wings protruding straight out of her back.

There's a small river of flames at her feet flaring up toward her.

She's nearly floating three inches off of the fucking floor from the flames that are softly whisking there way up up to her.

My eyes widen and my mouth hangs open widely as I view her ethereal beauty. She's fucking mesmerizing.

Stumbling to my feet ungracefully with my eyes still locked onto Thorns floating miraculous figure in the fucking air.

I try to gather my bearings taking two futile steps toward her, completely transfixed by her burning figure I try to draw myself a little bit closer to her, although hesitantly, amazingly I can't feel any warmth escaping out from her flaming form.

"Thorn?" I call out her name in a hushed whisper.

I can't actually believe what I'm fucking seeing. She's so damn enthralling.

Hearing footsteps coming up from behind me I unwillingly tear my gaze away from Thorns floating figure to see Slay and

Sunny, they're both transfixed on Thorns glorious transformation just as I am.

Catching a fleeting glimpse of Slayer and the two goons off to my right I watch as they all start trembling nervously over at Thorn.

Fier has dropped down to our coffee table sitting upon it while staring wide eyed and shocked up at his sister.

Shari, the bitch, is shaking like a damn leaf beside Thorn with her eyes nearly bulging right out of her eye sockets.

"I warned you. I told you to fucking leave. You didn't listen. How dare you hurt my mates! This is our pack it will never be yours. Now I will fucking finish you!" Thorn speaks but I don't recognize her voice.

It's a very deep scratchy baritone mixture of sounding somewhat like a damn evil demon and a full grown ass man. It sounds just like ten people are talking simultaneously through her at once. Fucking freaky as shit. I Involuntary shiver.

"Wha...." I don't get to finish my own damn questioning thought before Thorn quickly raises her hand up in the air and conjures up a streak of fire streaming right out of the center of her hand straight toward a frightened and immobilized trembling Shari.

It hits her full force, straight into her damn gut, as soon as the fire hits her, Sharis entire body goes flying right across the living room only stopping when she finally collides up against the far wall with a very harsh and brutal impact.

Sharis lifeless form leans up against the far wall with her legs laid out straight in front of her.

Slayer let's out a terrifying scream while running over to Sharis body he kneels down on the floor right beside her crying mercilessly.

Fuck!

"We're out of here!" One of the goons yells at Slayer. As they both take off out the door like two little frightened scaredy cats.

Hell I can't blame either of them. If I wasn't her mate I would be scared as shit of her right now also.

Slayer, bravely stands up from the floor, glaring over at Thorn with hate filled eyes and tears precariously rolling down his ugly ass face.

"You fucking cunt!" He bellows as he starts sprinting over to Thorn. "I'll fucking kill you!" He snarls.

I come out of my daze instantly, running over to try and catch him before he is able to make his way to my mate.

But I get cut off by a streaming mass of fire flying right by me headed straight for Slayer ass. The fire stream does the same exact thing to him as it did with his bitch of a mate Shari.

He goes flying against the far wall colliding with it harshly, Slayer slides down the wall limply landing right beside his mate dead.

Stone cold fucking dead.

Fucking wow is all that I could think as I stare at the two lifeless bodies sitting on the floor right beside each other.

I'm completely fucking shocked! I turn my head in a daze looking back over to my mate completely bewildered.

"Thorn!" I scream in a panic when I see Thorn laying helplessly on the floor completely unconscious.

Rushing over to her very quickly I slide across the floor on my knees giving my damn ass fucking knees carpet burn in the process.

Pulling her limp body into my arms as soon as I reached her.

"Is she breathing?" Sunny ask me anxiously.

Hell I don't know.

What the hell should I do?

Panicked I place my hand on top of her chest waiting for any signs that may show me that she's actually breathing.

I panic again when I can't feel any type of air escaping her. My entire body starts to shake uncontrollably.

No! No! No! Fucking no!

"Sin!" Slay bellows. "She's breathing relax!" She is? Peering down at Thorn anxiously and beyond fucking terrified I watch as her chest slightly rises up and down. I release a frazzled breath.

Fuck! Thank you Moon Goddess! Thank you! Thank You!

"We need to get her to the pack doctor." Sunny insist.

I stare over at him numbly.

What?

"Sin let her go. We need to get her to the doc!" Slay growls trying to pull Thorn away from me. I hold on to her tightly. No! No! I won't let her go!

"Sin please she needs help!" Fier pipes in with a desperate tone.

No! I won't let her go! I can't!

"Sin fucking give her to me!" Slay demands gruffly. Seeing the desperation caught up in his eyes I finally relent. Although hesitatingly.

Okay! Okay! She needs help.

Relaxing my hold on her finally I hand her over to Slay slowly. Very slowly. I don't want to let her go.

But unfortunately I know I have to.

Slay takes her from my grasp quickly, lifting her up off of the floor and out of my arms he takes off striding to the pack doctors office quickly.

I sit there on the damn floor trying to control my racing heart.

"Come on." Fier says urging me while grabbing ahold of my arm.

He pulls me up from the floor, I stumble over a little bit at first but once I'm able to stand up properly I take off to the pack docs office, running straight pass Fier in a blur.

Please. Please. Please. Be okay. I can't fucking lose her. Not when I just fucking found her. I just can't.

I can't take it.

She's hanging on by a damn thread. She expended almost all of her damn energy transforming into whatever she transformed into almost a week ago now.

Even her wolf Maya is locked up in a damn sleeping coma. We can't reach out to either of them.

And the worst part is we found out through our pack doctor that Thorn is surprisingly pregnant. What a wonderful surprise that was. I fucking love that she's pregnant with our pup but she needs to be here with us to enjoy it. It's so not fucking fair.

Now we are all not only begging and pleading for Thorns life but also for the life of our little pup.

It's been fucking torture.

Every single second that passes by that Thorn isn't awake I lose a tiny bit of myself. Eventually it will be mounting all up to losing myself entirely.

She has to wake up!

Slay has been getting stone cold faced ass drunk every night since this shit happened. He just can't deal with it and hell I can't blame him. It's starting to get very hard for me to deal with it also.

Sunny. Fuck Sunny has completely lost himself. He has locked himself up in his room. Never once venturing out of it. He has food brought up to him by our she wolves even though he's rarely eating anything now.

He has dived into a deep depression that neither Slay and I can seem to get him out of and we have tried a many of times but unfortunately nothing has fucking worked. He blames himself for this.

Fier will not leave.

He's been staying in our guest room this entire time, rarely leaving Thorns side at all.

Me: I'm a complete fucking disaster of a mess.

I'm not drinking like Slay is nor am I hiding up in my damn room. I'm just numb.

Completely numb.

I walk around this damn house like a damn ghost.

Lost and confused. I just don't know what the fuck to do.

"Thorn baby, please wake up!" I stress leaning over to her.

She's hooked up to a lot machines right now with an IV going right into her arm.

I can't stand it.

"Please. I miss you baby. Slay misses you and Sunny too. Hell Fier won't even go back to his pack until you wake up. So wake up baby please." I plead with her comatose body laying on the bed.

I do this everyday. Every since she's been in here. I come in at least five times a day to beg her to finally wake up.

But unfortunately she never does.

"I love you baby." I declare to her softly.

I tell her that every day to.

Just hoping against hope that one day she will hear me finally.

Exhaling a large breath I rise up from my chair as I do everyday and exit the room quietly.

I head out straight to Sunny's room to check up on him as I still do every damn day. I got this damn routine down pat now.

Rapping my knuckles on the door I wait as usual for Sunny to open it but as usual he never does.

"Sunny you have to go and see her." I beg through the damn door to him gently.

Again. No fucking answer. I just sigh.

I make my way down to the living room expecting to see a very drunk and sloshed out Slay sitting on the couch. As per fucking usual.

Day in and day out. It's the same damn thing.

And of course that's exactly where I find him. Half out of his mind in unnecessary grief, passed out drunk off his fucking ass. Knocked completely fucking out.

Shaking my head I walk over to him and remove the empty bottle from his hand. I lay him down flatly on the couch.

Throwing the afghan that was on the back of the couch loosely over him.

Again and again.

Fuck! We so need Thorn.

This is getting to be very redundant.

I crash down on the chair beside the couch leaning my head on the back of it.

I close my eyes and try my damn best to relax.

After a while I just reopen my eyes, giving the fuck up on even trying to relax. Relaxation doesn't ever come.

I haven't been able to sleep either.

Maybe a couple of hours here and there is all that I'm able to grab lately.

Too much shit keeps flashing through my mind to even allow my restless body to sleep.

Like, I should of handle the situation better. If only I would have just killed that asshole Slayer from the very start Thorn wouldn't be in the condition she's in right now. If only.

If only I would have kept us at the Invivus Realm a little longer maybe, just maybe, Shari would have gotten bored of waiting on Sunny to return and just fucking left.

If only I didn't deny Thorn at the very start none of this bullshit around us would have happened and Thorn would still be here awake with us and thriving.

If fucking only.

I stare at the far wall lost in my own damn thoughts.

Hearing footfalls coming up from behind me I don't even turn my head toward the person or even acknowledge them.

"Hey." Fier says as he's walking up to stand beside me but I keep ignoring him. I'm just not in the fucking mood to talk right now.

"Have you been to up check on her?" He ask me. I sigh, bending over I place my elbows on my legs craning my neck to look up at him.

He looks so damn depleted. Probably just as I am.

"Yes. Just a moment ago." I finally answer him half heart-edly.

"Still unconscious?" Please just fucking stop.

"Yes." I numbly answer him again.

"Maybe any day now." He says with a small amount of hope echoing throughout his voice.

Yea. Any day now.

"Right." I grumble perching my face in my hands wearily.

Please I like you Fier. But please just go the fuck away from me. I can't handle you right now.

Fier just keeps standing beside me.

Fuck this!

Jumping up from my seat quickly, I turn away from Fier.

"I'm going to bed." I murmur leaving Fier and Slay behind in the living room.

Not even worried about hurting Fiers feelings. I just don't fucking care anymore.

Another week and half passes and still no Thorn.

My routine is starting to get very fucking tedious.

Over and over and over again.

I do the same damn thing.

Here I am sitting in the same old fucking chair. Pleading with Thorn to wake the fuck up!

And she still doesn't do it.

I'm beginning to lose my faith in her.

And I fucking hate it.

She now has a tiny little baby bump. Not much of one but I can still see it. The doc said the pup is doing fine. Strong heartbeat and all.

I just wish that Thorn was awake to enjoy it. I know that she would absolutely love it.

Everything is still the same. Sunny stays in his room as always and of course Slay stays hammered all of the time.

No matter how many times I beg and plead with them they both still do the same old shit.

They don't know how to handle it.

I caught Slay in here by accident the other day finally. He was talking to her with so much pain reflecting off of him. It broke my heart just to see and to hear it.

He was rubbing his hand across her stomach tenderly. I actually cried then.

It was like a dam that suddenly broke lose in me. All of the anguish that I've been holding in came rushing out of me like a tidal wave.

It was the first time I cried over this.

But it wasn't the last. I have been crying off and on now for a week.

I'm losing my mind.

She just needs to wake the fuck up already!

"Do you hear me Thorn? Wake the fuck up!" I almost scream it out but refrain myself from doing so.

Maybe I should though. If I scream it loud enough maybe she would finally fucking hear me!

"THORN! WAKE THE FUCK UP!" I dared to do it.

But still nothing.

I sigh out in pure defeat.

"Please baby!" I plead with all of my fucking heart and soul. I grasp on to her hands that's laying promptly on her stomach beseeching her.

"Why the hell are you screaming at me?" My head jerks up so damn fast I probably sprained my damn neck.

"Thorn?" I choke out.

"Yes. Why are you screaming?" I can't fucking believe it.

Springing up from my chair that was beside her bed way too fucking fast I nearly stumble over but I catch myself on Thorns bed thankfully.

"Baby?" I croak out. "You're finally awake. Thank fuck. I have been so damn lost without you." I start to cry again.

"Sin? What happened? Why are crying?" She ask me innocently. Placing her hand gently on my cheek. The sparks light up within me instantly. Fuck I so missed that.

"Baby I have so much to tell you but let me go and get Sunny and Slay first okay?" She nods her head slightly smiling over at me. Fuck I miss that too! I plant a soft kiss on her check before I leave her.

I rush quickly out her room nearly falling over again.

I race off to Sunny's room first, banging on the door I scream out as loud as I fucking can.

"She's awake! She's awake! Thorns fucking awake!" I bellow out very ecstatically. "Get your damn ass out of there our mate is finally awake!"

My baby is finally awake. Thank fuck!

Chapter 29

It's been two weeks, six days, and eight hours since Thorn has returned to us and and yet, I still haven't worked up the courage to even touch or even face her.

I've been stonewalling.

Keeping her at a comfortable distant and all because I'm basically a fucking coward.

If is such a small word but it can make a hell of a difference in someone's life.

If I didn't go to Sins bar that night and meet up with that Bitch Shari, Thorn would have never been in a damn coma in the first damn place.

If I would have faced up to my own damn inner demons and challenged them all head on instead of letting my own stupidity get the best of me then Shari would have never even been in our damn lives.

And the biggest if of them all.

If I just kicked Nina out of our house in the first damn place when she came to us whining and not foolishly believe her lies, then none of this shit with Thorn and us would have ever happened.

If only.

If. If. If.

Lately, I have sequestered myself into my own damn bedroom again, like the fucking coward that I am, because I can't seem to look Thorn in the eyes any longer. My guilt is slowly eating away at me.

The day she woke back up I staggered out of my room happy as fuck and ran to her room.

As soon as I entered her room I stopped dead in my fucking tracks at the doorway just staring over at her.

I couldn't fucking breath.

It's like all of it hit me at once, just seeing her laying there peering over at me with so much regret captured on her face.

My body stood there frozen like an idiot.

I couldn't talk to her, I opened my mouth to try but unfortunately I just fucking couldn't.

What was I suppose to say?

Forgive me Thorn for being the guilty party who put you into a fucking coma? Who almost killed you and our pup?

I couldn't utter a single damn word to her.

Slay came running in behind me pushing me right out of his way just to get to her.

I watched them as they both embraced lovingly.

Sin came running in soon after Slay doing the exact same thing as him.

I just stood there immobilized by my own damn fear.

No longer being able to face her I just turned away from them all swiftly. Releasing a troubling breath I stomped my way back to my room slamming and locking my bedroom door behind me and that was fucking that.

I'm a damn coward, I walked away and haven't seen either of them since then.

Two weeks, six days, and eight fucking hours.

Throwing my plate of unfinished food across the room it clashes with the wall forcefully scattering bits and pieces of it all on the my bedroom wall and floor along with the leftovers remnants of my uneaten spaghetti and meatballs. What a damn mess.

Just like my life apparently.

Swinging myself back on the bed in a huff, I lie down on it placing my hands behind my head just staring up at my ceiling and contemplating my own damn failures.

How did my life end up like this? I put my one and only true love in danger and my unborn baby. I only have myself to blame for it. She could have died. They both could have.

Hell they almost did.

And all because of fucking me!

"Get off your damn ass and do something about it then!" Stinger growls out suddenly inside of my head, startling me.

"I can't." I whine. I just can't.

"Yes you can. She's already told you that she has forgiven you Sunny. Why are you torturing yourself like this?" As if it's that fucking simple. She had to tell me through our mindlink that she forgave my ass because I wouldn't even open my door to her. I just couldn't.

"Because I don't fucking deserve her forgiveness Stinger!" I growl at him. Stinger has been on my ass for the entirety of my little pity party that I have been throwing for myself unfortunately.

"Why are you doin this? It was that witch Esmeralda and Shari who did this, not you! You can't keep wallowing in your own self pity." Yes I damn well can. How could he possibly understand?

"I did it too Stinger. I was the one who brought Shari into our lives and put Thorns life and my pups in danger. Me! All fucking me!" Just me.

"You we're under a spell dumbass just like Sin was. If he can get past it why can't you?" Why can't I? Because I care too damn much. I'm obviously the weak link.

"I don't know!" I reply scrubbing my hand down my face completely exasperated.

"We'll gain some knowledge Sunny because Thorn is not going to wait around forever for you to come out of this stupid guilt trip that you have been indulging yourself in!" She won't leave again that much I know is true. She will always have Slay and Sin and now that she is pregnant with our pup I can't picture her ever trying to leave again.

"She won't leave my brothers. She loves them too much. She may just be happier without me. I have done nothing but cause trouble for her. She's way better off without me." I state simply. Everyone is.

"You clueless moron. She is carrying our pup and she needs all of you. Not just your brothers Sunny. She needs us too and for your information I need Maya. Have you even once thought about what you're doing between Maya and me. You are deliberately keeping us apart and it freaking hurts." He sounds so distraught. Fuck! I didn't realize how much I was hurting him, my very wolf. How could I be damn selfish?

"I'm sorry Stinger. I didn't realize how much this was affecting you and Maya." Now I feel twice as guilty. I'm messing everything up. As always.

"Well it is and I'm tired of being without her. So get your stupid head out of ass and go get our Luna back!" He growls out at me defensively.

"What if she doesn't want me back? What am I suppose to do then?" Damn I sound just like a pussy. When did I become so damn weak?

"Why do I have to continuously keep telling you this Sunny? Thorn loves you, she doesn't blame you for any of this shit and she is desperately missing you too." Does he happen to have a crystal ball somewhere that I don't know about? How can he tell if Thorn is actually missing me or not?

"And just how do you know that?" I ask him snidely.

"Because dumb ass I still talk to my mate unlike you do. Thorn loves you Sun. All you're accomplishing by all of this is hurting her by keeping her at a distance from you, can't you see that?" Great. Just fucking great. Now I'm hurting her even more. I just can't seem to win. I only stayed away from her because I truly think she deserves better than someone like me.

"Damn! I am so sorry. I just thought that if I kept my distance from her that she would be so much more happier and a hell of a lot safer from my own stupid fuck ups. It didn't even register with me that I could be hurting her in this way. I'm so damn stupid." So fucking stupid.

"You're not stupid Sunny just misguided. Go apologize to her. Beg her if you have to. Hell, maybe you should even get down on your damn knees. Just do it and quit pussyfooting around." Damn nagging ass wolf. But he does have a point though, I'll never get anything settled between Thorn and I if I don't swallow down my own damn pride and just face her.

One way or the other I'm an going to have to convince her that I am truly sorry. Even if I do have to get down on my damn knees and grovel like Stinger suggested.

"You're right. Sorry Stinger." I admit.

"It's fine Sunny. I'm not the one you need to apologize too. Just get off of your guilt ridden ass and go find our mate then apologize to her profusely for your own damn stupidity dumb ass!" Seriously, always with the name calling.

"Fine but knock it off with the name calling I already feel bad enough as it is." I plead with him.

"Sure thing nimrod." Ugh! Damn stubborn ass wolf.

Sliding out of my bed with a new found purpose I go in search of my clothes.

I may be feel guilty as hell about all of this shit but now with Stingers encouragement persuading me onward I need to find Thorn and apologize for being a dumb ass guilt ridden headstrong numbskull stupid ass shithead.

Like now.

"Thorn?" I call out her sweet name while walking into Slays office.

Slay is behind his desk, per usual, with Sin and Thorn sitting beside each other, holding hands, on the sofa.

I walked in on them all have a heavy discussion, about what, I don't precisely know yet.

Thorn looks up at me when I call out her name just staring over at me for a second or two before I notice that tears are beginning to well up into her beautiful cove blue eyes suddenly.

Without ushering a word I walk steadily into the room over to her, yanking her off of the sofa with my hands placed gently on her upper arms, I stare into those watery eyes that's filled with so much adoration and kiss her very passionately.

Dropping my hands away from her arms I pull her up against me by wrapping her up in my longing embrace.

The sparks ignite within me as soon as our lips pressed magically together.

I let out a low hard groan delving my tongue into that sensual mouth of hers.

Fuck I missed this. Way too damn much. Thorns arms both go around my neck locking me up tight to her.

How could I have been so damn stubborn to deny both of us this for so damn long.

She's my heart, my world, my fucking everything. I love her unconditionally.

I yearned for this.

Regretfully tearing my lips away from hers I press my forehead up against hers just drowning myself into those striking eyes that's full of love compassion just for me.

I've been a straight up damn ignorant fool.

"I'm sorry Thorn. I'm an idiot. Please forgive me." I lowly plead with her while trying to catch my shattered breath.

"I told you already that I have forgiven Sunny. Stop locking yourself away from me. It's not your fault." How could I have been so damn foolishly.

I should have known that Thorn would have easily forgiven me her heart is just way too damn big to do otherwise. I'm a very lucky man.

"I won't. Not anymore. I promise." I vow it all to her sincerely.

Light clapping interrupts our intimate moment. Slightly turning my head with my forehead still pressed against Thorns I watch as Slay repeatedly claps his hands together, generously smiling over at both of us.

"About damn time." Slay exclaims happily.

Yes it is.

Chuckling at Slays antics I wisely grab Thorn around her waist pulling her down to sofa as I sit down on it I bring her straight down to me to sit on my lap. Still holding on to her tightly.

"What we're you all talking about?" I ask them curiously.

"Well Thorn here has decided that it is time to announce her to our pack as their Luna at a upcoming ceremony." Sin informs me with smirk.

Well damn it's about time we actually got to it. It's been too damn long coming now.

"When's the next full moon?" It has to be done on a full moon with our pack. Thorn has to shift into her wolf in front of the entire pack to show them all her willingness and solidarity to all of them.

"Three nights from now. That should give us time to make all of the arrangements for it." Slay pipes in excitedly.

"What about her gown? Will they have enough time to make it?" I ask them. Thorns gown is a very crucial part of the ceremony and I want it to be perfect for her.

"That's already taken care of while you were a....on vacation." Sin replies unabashedly.

That's a nice way to put it. I scoff deliberately over at him. Jackass.

A soft knock interrupts our discussion suddenly.

"Come in." Slay grumbles.

The office door opens slowly announcing some she wolves arrivals. There's three of them that are timidly walking in with a silver rolling tray that apparently has our dinner for tonight upon it.

The alluring fragrance of roast and garlic hit me instantly.

"Alphas." Two of the she wolves bow their heads at us all respectively. "Luna." They add on next both smiling over at Thorn very politely.

I notice the third she wolf just stands at the back of the silver rolling tray ignoring all of us disrespectfully.

Betty is bravely standing there with an obnoxious look upon her face and her arms limply laying in front of her with her hands clasp together tightly.

I ignore her disrespectful attitude. That's definitely a problem that Slay needs to deal with and soon.

Maybe I should talk to him about it later seeing as of right now he is completely oblivious to Betty's disrespect, to caught up in arranging the food out for us with the help of the other two she wolves, Lisa and Courtney.

As the food and utensils are abundantly placed out for us the she wolves then generously lay our food out on the plates before us on a coffee table located in front of the sofa.

But I still keep my eyes on Betty that's still rudely not communicating with anyone in the room.

"Thank you Lisa, Courtney. It's very much appreciated." Slay shows his gratitude toward them giving them both a kind smile.

Betty unfortunately scoffs out with apparent deliberation as she rolls her eyes skyward.

"Is there a problem Betty?" Slay questions her softly with a worried expression plastered on his face.

"No Alpha." Betty grits out between her teeth. What the fuck is wrong with this woman?

"You may be excused." Sin tells them all. Lisa and Courtney bow their heads again as they swiftly start to exit the room.

Lisa goes to grab ahold of the silver cart but Betty rudely swipes Lisa's hand away from the cart with her own hand.

"I got it." She snarls over at Lisa with a very heated look.

"Fine." Lisa murmurs to Betty then exits the office quickly followed behind by Courtney.

"Betty is there something bothering you? You know you can always come to me talk about anything." Slay speaks with way too much kindness toward her. I glance up at Thorn who is eyeing Betty with a calculating look.

"I'm fine Alpha and thank you that's very much appreciated. Maybe I can...come and...talk to you later about it." Betty ask Slay nervously.

Something seems fishy to me about all of this but I just keep my opinions to myself. I've already caused enough damn problems already. No sense in adding more crap on to the shit pile.

"Sure my office is always open to all of my pack members." Slay tells her. Betty smiles brightly over at Slay.

"Thank you so much Alpha." She says then leaves the office humming softly to herself.

Strange ass woman!

"What was all of that about?" Sin ask Slay while eyeing the office door with suspension.

"I don't know but I'm sure she will fill me in later. Maybe one of the other she wolves are giving her hard time. You know how Betty is? She likes to keep to herself. She's just too shy and quite sometimes." Slay shakes his head then starts eating his roast before him.

Hmmmm, Maybe?

Lying in bed with my Thorn laying beside me fast asleep my mind wonders back to Betty and her rude attitude.

She's been acting awfully suspicious lately I know that she has always had a semi crush on Slay every since he became an Alpha.

I just looked at it at the time as a simple little crush but after all that we have been through with other women every since Thorn has come into our lives now I look at the opposite sex with a fair amount of suspension.

Betty seems like, to me, that she is definitely up to something but whatever it is I need to keep my eye out for her.

I will not let another woman come in between any of us. Not again. Not if I can help it that is.

Pulling Thorn a little bit closer to me I revel in her softness.

I will not let anyone ever hurt our Thorn again. I vow this to myself with wholehearted stern conviction.

After we ate our rather scrumptious dinner tonight. Thorn announce to all of us very sheepishly that she has been preparing herself for all of us.

At first I didn't catch on to what she was trying to say until Sin and Slay both started to get turned on by Thorns admission.

Our little Thorn has been using butt plugs for a few days now to stretch herself out pleasantly just for us.

I almost bit my check when she divulged this to us. Slay on the other hand got more excited about it than any of us.

He definitely is ass man. She even hinted around that she wants all three of us at the same damn time. Now that admission got me really excited.

Hearing a loud scream interrupting my wayward thoughts, I scrambled out of the bed hurriedly. Throwing my jeans on swiftly Thorn awakens just as I'm starting to head straight for the bedroom door.

"Who screamed?" She ask me tiredly.

"I think it was Slay." I rush to tell her while running out of my bedroom quickly with Thorn now hot on my heels behind me.

Sin is already at Slays bedroom doorway standing at the threshold of it blocking everyone's way.

Pushing him to the side I walk into Slays bedroom but find myself coming to quick halt when I see the awkward scene before me.

Thorn accidentally bumps into my shoulder as she comes running into Slays room only to come to a complete stand still beside me observing the scene before her just as I am.

Slay is on the bed half nude, with only his boxers on, fighting off a very disgruntled Betty.

Betty is on top of Slay, straddling him, without a stitch of clothing on, struggling to get out of Slays firm grasp with his hands wrapping around her wrist.

"Don't just...fucking stand...there! Get this...damn lunatic ...off of me!" Slay grumbles between each breath trying to fight off Betty.

His strict deep Alpha tone demand instantly robs me right out of my confused daze.

Jumping into action, I climb on the bed grabbing ahold of Betty's waist with both of my arms wrapped around her, I roughly pull her off of Slay.

Sin finally comes over grabbing Betty by both of her arms he holds them behind her while Betty continues to struggle to get out of his grasp, sputtering and spouting maddeningly.

"You wanted me. Don't deny it....Why? Slay?....Why would you push....me away. I love...you. I've always...loved you!" Betty bellows while still struggling fervently.

Slays jumps off of his bed breathing erratically eyeing Betty with valid repulsion.

"You are not my fucking mate Betty! You came in here to violate me! You're fucking sick!" Slay yells snarling ferociously at her.

"She did what?" Thorn ask astonished. I snap my head to Thorn when I hear the anguish in her questioning tone.

She has her hand planted firmly on her little stomach like she is trying to protect our pup from any unwarranted danger.

Even through the chaos I can't help but to smile over at her.

"You wanted it Slay! Tell her Slay. Tell her or I will!" Betty screams threateningly over at Slay.

"Tell me what?" Thorn ask taking a tiny futile step towards Slay.

"I have no idea what this damn psycho is even talking about Thorn." Slay replies to Thorn defensively.

"Really? You're going to deny it? Fine then I will tell her you coward!" Betty turns her attention to Thorn, "while you were in your coma Slay and I slept together, many times." Betty hackles crazily.

Thorn let's a very loud gasp slip from her lips.

"No Thorn. Don't believe her. She's fucking lying! I love you Thorn, you have to believe me. I didn't do anything like that to you and I will never do anything like that to you." Slay determinedly tells her.

He slowly makes his way over to a very confused and frightened Thorn.

Fuck! This is going to start a fucking war between them.

She has been through enough with me and Sin doing that same awful shit to her.

If what Betty is saying is true then we are all majorly fucked now and no doubt lose her permanently.

Please don't let this shit be true.

"Thorn, beautiful, I didn't do it. I will admit that I was drunk basically the entire time that you were in a coma but I would never hurt you like that. I love you too damn much to do that to you. Not after...." Slay trails off but I get the gist of what he was about to say.

Not after what Sin and Sunny did to you. I can fill in the fucking unreadable blanks.

"He did and I have proof." Betty snidely smiles over at Thorn.

She's lying. She has to be lying. What kind of proof could she possibly have?

"I recorded it." What the fuck? No way. She's lying. The bitch is desperately lying.

"Show me!" Thorn demands while sneering over at her.

Oh fuck!

"Let me go. My phones right over there." She nods her head over toward Slays dresser where there sits a cellphone upon it.

Slay huffs at her then walks over to retrieve the phone from the dresser cautiously.

He picks it up, after pressing a button a few times the room automatically fills up with the sound of people definitely making out.

I edge my way over to Slay just as Thorn does.

Peering over his shoulder I stare at the video with a keen eye.

There is definitely two people having sex in the video.

And it is without a doubt Slay grinding his ass into whoever is laying underneath him on his bed.

Then something catches my eye quickly.

The female suddenly appears under him but it's definitely not Betty I'm seeing. It's another woman. Not Thorn though.

I suddenly remember the woman who is now moaning under Slay lustfully.

"Slay that's not Betty. Betty has red hair this woman has brown hair and I know who she is." I proudly tell him.

He drops the phone to his side peering over at me with an inquisitive look on his face.

"That's Monica Steward your ex girlfriend." I exclaim with a broad smile. Who the hell needs Sherlock Holmes when you got me?

"I haven't seen Monica in almost three years now." Then it suddenly clicks.

"You recorded me and Monica together? Why?" Slay ask Betty. Now Betty looks utterly defeated.

"You're fucking sick! You recorded me with my ex? What else have you done Betty? Have you recorded all of us or just me?" He ask her bewildered.

"Check her phone." I suggest.

And he does. He goes through her phone like a fine tooth comb. Brushing it all out.

By the time we're done checking her phone we found ultimate proof that Betty is indeed full blown crazy.

She not only recorded Slay with Monica but she has been recording all of our sexual conquest.

She caught Sin with Storm and even me with that bitch Shari.

What a damn devious wicked cunt.

Hell the damn lunatic even caught Pan and Storm going at it.

Either she gets off on all of this or she is just plain whacked out.

I will go with the latter.

"Take her fucking ass to the dungeon I will deal with her crazy ass later." Slay tells Sin.

Betty still struggles within Sins hold thrashing all about.

"Slay please don't do this to me. I love you!" Fuck that woman is definitely bonkers.

Sin drags her away while she still keeps fighting and yelling out at Slay as she goes.

Slay throws Betty's phone across the room aggressively. The phone completely shatters against the wall, hitting the floor with loud clank.

"Well now that Betty is taken care of I'm going back to bed. Coming Thorn?" I ask holding out my hand to Thorn.

"If you don't mind Sunny I think me and Slay really need to talk." I assumed that was coming. Dropping my hand back down to my side I shrug my shoulder at her.

"Sure thing. I understand." Giving her a half hearted chuckle I start to t leave Slays bedroom but before I exit the room. I smile deviously and turn right back around.

"Hey Slay, uhm, do you think you might be able to repair Betty's phone for me?" I try my best to hold in my chuckle.

"Why?"

"Well that way you can forward me the videos that's on it." I state rather innocently.

"Why would you want them?" He ask me gruffly.

"Blackmail of course. I thought I might send the one of you and Monica out as a Christmas video card this year to all of our friends. Oh and Lila would love it." I try to irate him and damn if it didn't work.

He picks up the nearest thing next to him and unfortunately it's a damn thick ass book and throws it right at me.

I dodge the book successfully chuckling my ass off at him while running away from him like my ass was on fire.

Damn it's feels good to be back to my old self.

Chapter 30

I feel like my old self again with the exception of being pregnant I'm starting to feel more and more like my old self.

At first it was a dog and pony show. My energy level was at an all time low. I was basically tired, weary, and nauseous all of the time after I woke up from my coma.

Now the nausea has started to waver off some and my energy level seems to be back to a normal, thankfully.

But my emotions seems like they are all over the place. Fier went back home to his pack. I'm already missing him. He took over our fathers pack. After Singas death he told me that it seemed like a cloud had been lifted up over all his pack members suddenly.

They all apologized to him profusely. Claiming they didn't know what they were exactly doing at the time. I guess it was Singas magic that had them all acting the way that they were. I'm just glad that now Fier can run the pack without running across any unforeseen major problems like we use to have.

Speaking of problems there's two of them that we now have the unfortunate opportunity to have to deal with.

One being that Betty bitch.

It just seems like to me everywhere I turn there's always some woman who does literally will do anything just to get to my men.

I just don't get it.

There all plenty of other men in this world why do they always seem to go after mine?

The other major problem that we're having to deal with is Alpha Curtis. I honestly almost forgot all about him.

That is until he can storming into our house demanding to know where Nina was.

Getting right up in always face like a madman.

He can demand all that he wants but none of us here owes his ass a damn an explanation for anything.

He has some nerve coming into my house like he owns the damn place demanding some freaking answers.

He is the one that sent Nina over her in the first damn place to cause havoc and try to steal away my mate.

Why should we have to answer to him?

And all just so he could help my loathsome ass father. The prick!

Now thankfully he is in the dungeon along with Betty the bitch.

We are just waiting now for Queen Miracles arrival to deal with both of the psychotic morons that's locked up.

She should be here any moment now and I hate that we have to continuously keep bothering her over this trivial bull crap that keeps somehow happening to us.

But unfortunately we don't have a damn choice in the matter.

"Has she arrived yet?" Sunny asks me anxiously. It's kind of funny to me how every time that Miracle comes around him and Sin both start to get extremely anxious.

I wonder if they think that it upsets that she was with them once upon a time?

It all honesty, it doesn't bother me in the slightest but it is kind of nice to watch them both squirm just a little.

They are all three sitting on the couch in our living room watching the front door with some trepidation.

I'm sitting in the chair beside them enjoying the show going on in front of me immensely, trying my best to hide my smile behind my balled up hand with my arm planted firmly on the chairs arm.

Slay doesn't seem as anxious as the other two but he still has a cautionary view about our Queen. To me, she is almost perfect in all things.

So sweet and generous.

The entire time I was dating Cameron she has always treated me with kindness and respect, just like I was her own child.

I love Miracle.

One day I hope that I can be somewhat like her. I look up to her. She has struggled through a lot from what Cameron has told me about her and the Kings relationships.

"Does it look like she's here?" I finally answer him with a slight smirk.

He blows out a hard breath nervously. I just shake my head at him. Men!

"They're here!" Slay announces while springing up from the couch far too quickly.

With nervous anticipation he begins rub his hands along the sides of his jeaned legs.

I just stifle a laugh at them and shake my head again.

Sin hurries to the front door opening it for them before they could even knock on the damn door.

Queen Miracle walks into the house very regally with a broad genuine small planted on her beautiful face.

Following behind her is King Malik and King Baron. Both look handsome as ever in their kingly attire.

I get a surprised shock as I notice a familiar face strolling into the house behind the three of them.

"Cameron!" I boast excitedly running over to him, I throw myself into his arms, hugging him fiercely.

"Thorn wow you have matured!" I grimace when I hear the sexual innuendo in his voice. "And quite nicely I may add."

Cameron has always been a flirt not just with me but also with others. I don't mind his dirty playfulness but I'm pretty sure neither of mates will appreciate his flirtatious attitude.

Dropping me back on the floor he eyes me with mirth and I can spot quite easily the little gleam sprouting up in his soulful blue eyes.

I give him a little tap on his shoulder giggling up at him.

"Be nice." I hint eyeing my mates who are now eyeing Cameron with a touch of jealousy sparking up in their eyes.

"When am I not nice my little dove?" His sweet term of endearment toward me makes Slay instantly growl over at him.

I roll my eyes skyward at them all. Men!

"Thorn how lovely to see you again." Miracle pushes her son Cameron aside to get to me. She offers me a gentle hug as I hug her in return.

The Kings do the same a little bit after her then we all sit down and discuss Betty and Alpha Curtis and their crimes with them.

Describing in detail all of their criminally and insane actions.

When the sordid details are finished I'm surprised to hear King Baron ask me if I would like to be the one to accompany him down to the dungeon cells.

I obviously agreed to do so. Who would ever turn down a Kings offer especially one that is as fierce as King Baron is?

As we travel down into the dungeons cells I start to grow rather anxious.

I've never met Alpha Curtis officially all I have ever seen of him was when he came into our house running his damn mouth at my mates.

Disrespecting them without any regard whatsoever about whomever was in the room with them as he done it.

For those few short heated minutes I only caught little glimpses of him.

Now I'm anxious to officially meet someone who use to be friends with my father. None of my fathers former friends are even close to being nice. They are all despicably evil.

"Relax dear heart I won't allow anyone to hurt you." King Baron tries to assure me granting me a genuine smile.

My anxieties start to wither away a fraction thankfully from his sound encouragement.

Entering the cold dungeons walkthrough I immediately spot a hysterical Betty crying up against the far dungeon cell wall.

Then my eyes flash over to the other cell that holds the intimidating Alpha Curtis.

He doesn't resemble the type of man that would ever have anything to do with my father.

Most of the time you can actually see the evil floating around in my fathers friends eyes but not with him.

If I'm being honest with myself his eyes actually show a sense of kindness in them.

Which may frighten me even more, so they say, the devil was actually was a very well sought out and desirable angel after all.

Looks can be very deceiving.

"First we will deal with you." King Baron exclaims as he observes Betty still crying helplessly in her cell.

"Unfortunately we can't do anything about the recordings that you had on your phone since they were apparently destroyed." Damn Slay for his uncontrollable temperament.

"But you have committed a malicious crime Betty Pollard. You attacked your own Alpha with the intention of blackmailing and violating him. For that I will remove your wolf and banish you from this pack forever after you have served five long years in our dungeon." King Baron declares her punishment with a very regal tone. Betty begins to wail even louder.

Seems fitting enough to me. She undoubtedly asked for this.

"Any questions?" King Baron ask Betty while tilting his head for the side.

Betty just starts to hysterically cry even further, not even bothering to answer him. I hold no sympathy toward her but I hold no ill will toward her either. Killing one's wolf has got to be horrific. If I lost Maya I wouldn't know what I actually would do.

King Baron then walks a few steps over to stand in front of Alpha Curtis's cell.

He's sitting down on the dungeons floor with his back pressed up against the stone wall. His eyes are closed with his head leaning against the wall like he doesn't seem to have a care in the world about his current predicament.

"Alpha Curtis I hear you are the instigator for Nina's crimes? What do you have to say for yourself?" King Baron ask him while he folds his arms across his broad chest.

Curtis scoffs out at the King very disrespectfully. Not even deeming him worthy to even open his eyes for him.

After a few tense seconds Curtis begins to let out a deep darkening laugh.

I scowl over at him. The man is either very brave or just plain idiotic.

"I'll ask you only once more Alpha Curtis. What do you have to say for yourself?" King Barons patience seems to be running very thin.

Curtis finally opens up his eyes to view him with a very disdainful glare.

When he finally catches a swift glance of me standing directly beside the King he then seems more interested in us suddenly, he pushes himself off of the dungeon floor with his hands.

With his legs spread wide he folds his arms across his chest just as King Baron does then sends a heated glare directed right at me.

I timidly take a step away from the cell bars placing my hand on my stomach as I glare back at him. There is just something about those damn eyes of his. Looking in them sends a chill straight down my spine.

Alpha Curtis let's out another deep chuckle as he watches me. I feel a slight fluttering feeling within my gut. This man seems extremely intimidating or maybe that's just what he wants to appear to be?

"I didn't send Nina over here to do anything your majesty. She can squawk all that crap that she wants to but I have no cause to harm anybody. I just came over here to find out where she was. That's all. She's been missing from our pack for a long time now and her family was staring to get worried about her. Well I say her family but technically it's the people that she's been shacked up with at my pack." Curtis's deep voice resonates with a promising tone of the truth hidden somewhere within it.

Which is very surprising to me actually.

The way he came bounding into our home earlier made him look like a jealous raging lover of Ninas, like Nina mentioned he was before. When I look at him now I just can't picture him being a rapist liked Nina so vehemently claimed him to be.

But then again rapist comes in all varieties.

"How do I know you speak you truth?" King Baron asks him.

"You don't. You just have take my word for it I guess." Curtis insist giving a slight dismissive shrug of his shoulder.

"Did you know my father?" I bravely pipe up with curiosity lacing my tone.

"I did. He was a gruesome and fowl man. He did try to get me to help him in his search for you but I adamantly refused. There was just something telling me that he was being untruthful about the whole ordeal. He ridiculously tried to convince me that you were the one who was responsible for your killing your own mother. I saw right through him. So no I did not help Nina in whatever indenture she was on. I was searching her out for a pack member of mine who was honestly worried about her. Why, I don't know, she has always been a pain in my damn ass." He chuckles again lowering his head for a second before he looks back up at us again.

"I'm not guilty of any crime except for maybe being hot-headed but you can blame that on my wolf Titan. He has a mean and a short temper that is a mile high." I couldn't help it I had to chuckle with him. I know three other wolves just like that.

His eye clash with mine instantly as I let out my laughter. What is it about those eyes?

It's like they are drawing me to him.

"I'll return in just a few then. after I have talked to this pack member who asked you to come here. What is the pack members name?" King Baron ask, Curtis hesitates for a millisecond then lets out a hard breath.

"His name is Sylvester Walker. He's my gamma." Curtis answers with a tinge of regret foreshadowing him.

"Very well then just give me a little bit of time to see if his answer matches up to yours, if it's all true then I will set you free. But don't bother to try to mindlink him. These bars have magical crystal clusters that prevent you from doing so." King Baron instructs Curtis.

Curtis just simply nods his head over at King Baron.

The King then turns on his heel to exit the cold dungeon quickly but I find myself hesitating to leave.

Still far to absorb at watching Curtis from across the way.

"Are you coming Thorn?" King Baron ask from behind me.

I turn my head toward him and smile.

"Go on ahead there's a few things I like to discuss with Alpha Curtis." King Baron eyes me suspiciously but I can't blame him for that.

"I'll be fine. He's behind the bars and I do have my own abilities remember?" I insist.

"Alright I'll tell your mates that you will return in a moment. Be safe." He warns before he leaves me alone in the dungeon with Alpha Curtis and a still crying Betty in the cell beside him.

"Why did you stay?" Curtis shockingly ask me.

"I wanted to talk to you. There's just something that's been bothering me and maybe you can assist me with it?" At least I hope he can.

Curtis stares at me with a definitive look of uncertainty before he accepts my offer. Dropping his arms to his side he then lets out a long sigh.

He walks over to the bed that is situated at the far side of the wall sitting down upon it while still eyeing me with those damn eyes of his.

What is it about those damn eyes?

Curiosity gets the better of me as I step closer to the bars placing my hands upon the bars I stare down at Curtis with a touch of my own uncertainty now.

"What is it about you?" I just simply come right out and ask him.

"I think you already know the answer to that Thorn." Curtis replies to me with a lopsided smirk that starts to make me feel uneasy.

"I wouldn't be asking you if I had the answers Alpha Curtis. I can understand that you don't know me and I'm sure you don't feel compelled to tell me anything about you but...to be honest, whenever I look deep in your eyes....it's like I get spellbound. Why exactly is that?" I just bravely come right out and ask him again. Noticing his clear hesitation I start to get lightly aggravated, I take a marginal step away from the cell bars, huffing dramatically over at him.

"I don't like secrets Mr. Curtis I've suffered through enough of them to last me a lifetime and more, so please just tell me why I feel this way?" I desperately hate not knowing why every time I look into his eyes I start to get these damn deep rooted gut wrenching feelings inside of me.

"Look, Thorn I'm sure your a very nice....," those damn eyes then roam all over me straight from my head all the way down to my shoes, with a seductive undertone to them, "woman." He clears his throat then stands up slowly strolling over to the cell bars directly in front of me, "but if you want to know any secrets maybe you should ask your mate Slay." He states in a very authoritative manner. What does Slay have to do with any of this?

"Thorn!" Speaking of Slay, I hear him scream out my name loudly from the top of the dungeons stairs. Curtis cocks his eyebrow up at me when we both hear Slay suddenly descending the stairs heatedly.

By the time he reaches us Curtis has inexplicably taken a few steps away from me and the cell bars, looking sheepishly over at me.

"Thorn what the hell are you doing down here?" I ignore Slays gruff attitude locking my eyes back onto Curtis.

"Come on we're going?" Slay grabs ahold of my wrist pulling me forward.

"Don't be so rough on her you damn twit she's pregnant." Curtis demands Slay while glowering over at him.

Slay halts his movements quickly turning his attention to Curtis he gives him a piercing stare in return then snickers over at him.

"Mind your own damn business Cur she is my mate and I'll handle her however I damn well want." Slay sneers at him dropping his hand away from my wrist he walks over to the cell. "Get this through your thick damn head Cur. Whatever happens with my family and with whomever I am in love with has nothing to do with you. Ever. Are we clear?" He tells him while pointing his index finger straight at him through the cell bars.

I feel like I'm stuck in the middle of a damn war between them and I have no idea what the war is even about.

"Crystal clear Slay but maybe you should enlighten your beautiful mate here on exactly what your talking about? She just told me that she can't abide secrets and you my dear ex friend have been keeping the biggest secret of them all." Curtis's rebuttal sends my mind in whirlwind.

"What secret Slay?" I ask him anxiously. "What is he taking about?" I press him touching my hand softly against Slays upper arm.

He nudges my hand away from his arm swiftly, letting out a horrendous grumble toward Curtis and me.

I feel completely dejected from his spiteful rejection.

Dropping my hand back down to my side with my shoulders slightly drooping I let out a grumble of my own before I slid right by Slay to walk out of the dungeon away from the both of them with a lot of unanswered questions still haunting me.

More damn secrets!

I thought we were completely passed this but unfortunately not.

Not according to Curtis that is.

I'm so damn done! I'm fucking carrying their pup and they still don't have enough respect for me to even let me in.

Men!

Laying in bed later that night I kept tossing and turning with my mind filled with curious uncertainty.

Everything that Curtis said to Slay in the dungeon is coming back now to haunt to me.

I refused to sleep with any of them tonight, I chose to sleep in a guest room instead, which in turn upset both Sun and Sin, I'm just too pissed off at Slay right now to even care about the other twos feelings at this point.

Secrets upon secrets is all these damn men seem to know.

Miracle and the Kings left with a crying Betty in tow earlier today but they unfortunately couldn't get ahold of Curtis's Beta Sylvester just yet so Curtis is spending another night in our dungeon until they can at least get ahold of him.

Slay made me promise to stay away from Curtis tonight at dinner which resulted in another outstanding argument between the two of us. I refused to bow down to his damn commands.

I'm just fed up with all of this rhetoric.

If I want some damn answers I'm definitely not going to retrieve them from Slay. He's never going to tell me, a damn thing, no matter how many times I argued with him to do so he just shut his lips up tighter like a damn clam.

I need to talk to Curtis then.

With that thought in my mind I scramble out of my bed to head straight down to the dungeon, I don't give a damn what Slay instructed for me not to do I will do whatever I damn hell I want to do.

Creeping into the dark damp dungeon with slow measured steps I finally make my way over to the cell that Curtis locked is in.

I blow out a trembling breath when I see that he is thankfully still awake lying on his primitive bed just staring up the dungeons ceiling.

"Curtis." I murmur almost silently quickly grabbing his attention.

He springs up from the bed walking over to me with calculated steps.

"What are doing down here Thorn?" I keep asking myself the same damn question. Instead of answering him I tentatively walk over to the cell bars, desperately needing to see those hypnotizing eyes again.

The silence between us is all consuming. I can even hear his labored breathing flowing over to me between the disconcerting silence.

"Please tell me." I plead with him softly finally breaking the awkward silence between us.

"What did Slay tell you?" He ask as he comes closer to me.

"Exactly nothing. That's why I'm coming to you. Why do you hate each other? What happened between the two of you? Why do I feel this way? Please just tell me." I plead with him again desperately wanting some answers.

He lets out a very loud audible sigh while placing his hands on the solid cell bars.

"I can't tell you what happened between me and Slay. That's unfortunately his story to tell but what I can tell you is this; what happened between him and I is what one might call a family dispute. As for the feelings you have been having toward me, well, that one I'm pretty sure you already know Thorn. You just can't admit it to yourself yet. If you want any more answers they are going to have to come from Slay, not me. I'm sorry." He says with a troubling amount regret ingrate on his face.

I'm no closer to getting any answers now than when I first came in here with. I nibble on my lower lip while searching his face.

"Look, Slay will not tell me anything and I don't know why but I need some damn answers and if neither of you can give them to me then I'll just have to go to your pack and ask your so called chosen mate." I snarl toward him.

He looks down at me like I absolutely lost my damn mind.

"What chosen mate?" He ask and I scowl. I'm pretty damn sure Nina told us all that he had a chosen mate.

"Nina said you had a chosen mate." I mumble.

"Nina said. Oh come on! Are you truly going to believe a woman like Nina? Thorn I have no chosen mate. I've never had. I've been waiting for my mate for years now. I actually did find her recently but unfortunately I can't have anything to do with her over some stupid unfortunate circumstances regrettably." Curtis let's out a very resounding sound of laughter.

I search his eyes again for the truth and then it hits me, now I feel like a damn fool believing Nina's staunch lies. He must think I'm truly unbelievably gullible.

"I'm sorry I should have realized. I'm honestly not the best judge of character. I should have known Nina was lying." I apologize to him through my own embarrassing shame.

"Who is your mate? Maybe I can help you with that? That is if you would allow me too. I need to make up for having you locked up here in our dungeon anyway. It's the least I can do." Even though Slay hates him for some unknown fathomless reason that doesn't give us the right to keep him locked up in our dungeon over Nina's petty bullshit.

"Thank you for the offer but I'm good on that. You don't have to make up for having me locked up here Thorn. You did nothing wrong." Maybe but I still feel overly guilty over his unfortunate predicament.

"So you're not going to give me any answers are you? I should of known. Not one damn man can be opened or honest with me. Thank you for listening to me anyway Curtis and again I'm so sorry for you being here." I resign myself to never knowing the damn truth. With neither him nor Slay willing to offer me the answers I'm more than determined to find them all out on my own now regardless of them.

"Goodnight Curtis." I tell him with half hearted smile on my face.

"Wait. Don't go." He says abruptly as I start to leave.

"Look Thorn I am truly sorry I can't tell you anything. If I could tell you I definitely would believe me but unfortunately I just can't. If I let anything slip out it would be detrimental to others in the long run and I can't just can't do that because it would end up hurting someone that I'm finding myself starting to care about a lot. Please understand." He explains to me gently.

What else can I do but give be him the opportunity of my understanding when I unfortunately don't know all of the circumstances yet?

This time I give him a genuine smile, reaching out I place my hand softly on top of his that's around the cell bars.

As soon as our hands make contact with each other my eyes spring open wide in complete and utter unbelievable shock.

You got to be fucking kidding me?

Chapter 31

Un-fucking-believable!

The secret that I've been sheltering so closely in my heart for years is now coming home to roost and all because of my damn shithead ex best fucking friend.

Curtis has been a damn pain in my ass for years now. I fucking hate him.

I hardly ever talk to ass anymore only when a rash problem arises do I ever utter a single fucking word to him and you would have to force me at gunpoint to even do that.

This has been plaguing me for some time now. Sin and Sun definitely don't know what Cur is actually to them. Only Lila and I do. She only knows because she caught me one night at Sins bar crying tears in my beer over it all.

I hesitantly confessed it all to her that night. I have regretted it ever since. I made her vow to me that she would never tell our brothers then she unloaded her own dirty little secret to me that night also about Cur, making me vow to her not to kill him when she told me, now we both have secrets about his ass that we promised each other that we would never a speak a word about it to anyone.

But here I am about to unload my biggest secret to all of them

That's why I'm presently in the living room with my brothers and Thorn now having to explain to each of them my deepest and most daunting secret.

And all thanks to fucking Cur the prick!

"Just tell me Slay!" Thorn keeps repeatedly insisting with me.

Sun and Sin are sitting down on the couch staring up at me with hope filled and curious eyes while Thorn is sitting down in the chair with a very disconcerting look on her face aimed directly up at me.

I keep pacing the floor trying my best to come up with the exact words to explain this shit to all of them.

I hate to do it because I know that what is about to come vomiting out of my mouth will inevitably hurt my brothers to no end. Fuck! This is so messed up! I never wanted to hurt to them.

"Okay look, this is going to sound rather strange but I've been keeping a secret from both of you for a few years now. One that could possibly change your point of views about our own father." I remissly tell Sun and Sin.

"He and mom got into an argument a while back now. A huge one in fact. Dad moved out of the house for a few months over it. It was pretty damn bad. While he was out on his own he managed to hook up with a woman, who was as you might have all guessed by now was Curtis's mother." I stop speaking to let it all sink in.

Both of my brothers stare at me with different expressions written all over their faces. Sun is as usual looking deeply concerned over all of this while Sin is showing slight signs of prominent anger per his usual.

I carry on, "her name was Wilma Devine, she was at one time the Alpha's daughter of the Winter Moon Pack, which is now of course Curtis's pack. Dad reunited with mom a few weeks later but he didn't realize at the time that he got Wilma pregnant by some miracle while he was with her and apparently Wilma never bothered to tell him either." I blow out a pent up breath. Observing my brothers with blatant curiosity.

"I only know all of this myself because I was over at Curs pack one day and I happen to overhear his mom tell another woman about her relationship with our dad. At first I couldn't understand what she was even talking about. I was only eleven so hearing about our dad having another child with someone else kind of threw me for a loop. After I listened in on them for a while discussing dad I went outside to confront Cur over it. That asshole knew the entire time who his dad really was but he promised his mom he would never talk about it with anyone. He was even happy about it." Too damn happy if you fucking ask me.

"So are you trying to tell us that Curtis is our damn half brother?" Sunny ask me with astonishment.

Seriously? Didn't I just explain that?

"Yes that's exactly what I'm trying to tell you Sunny. Curtis is our brother." I tell him definitively.

"So why didn't you just tell us? Why keep it a secret? Mom and dad have been gone for three years now Slay. You didn't think you could of dropped that information on us at any given time?" Sin retorts rather sarcastically.

"Curtis and I had a falling out over this. He wanted to tell all of you but I would not allow him to do it. I was...ashamed of what our father did and I didn't want either you to have to go through that embarrassment or have either of you look at our father any differently than you did." I explain it to them with a touch of annoyance interlacing with my tone.

"Does Lila know?" Sunny ask.

"Yes. I admittedly told her while I was drunk a few years back." I admit.

"Did dad know?" Sin ask.

"No dad never knew because Wilma never told him and I chose not to ever bring it up with him. Mom and dad were finally in a good place and I didn't want to ruin it." I always thought that if I even spoke a word about it dad would probably leave us to be with Cur or Wilma and I couldn't do that to my mother. It would break her heart so I chose to be completely silent about it.

"So all of these years you have been keeping this secret from us for our own damn good? What? Did you honestly think they we couldn't handle it? And what about Curtis? How does he feel about all of this? Does he not want to be our brother?" Sunny rapidly runs through the questions faster than I can even answer them all.

"I don't know Sun. I don't exactly know how Curtis feels about any of this and I really don't care either. All I know is that I didn't want this to hurt either of you." I tell them scrubbing my hand down my face feeling utterly depleted.

"Why now? Why are you telling us all of this now?" Sin abruptly ask me. "What changed?"

Why now? Well because of the shocking information that Thorn informed me of just this morning.

I glance over at Thorn who is sitting in the chair with her tiny hands placed delicately into her lap trying her best to avoid my heat filled steaming eyes directed right on her.

"Because of me." She ultimately tells them both very softly.

They look over at her sharply with curiosity and concern streaming off of both of their faces.

"What do you mean Thorn? Why you? What do you have to do with any of this?" Sunny questions her ideally confused.

This is the part that I have been mulling over all damn morning.

I actually don't want to stand here and hear her speak those very heartbreaking words to them.

The same damn words that broke my heart earlier this morning, I'm damn sure they are about to break my brothers hearts also. Fuck I hate this!

But unfortunately I have to withstand hearing them all over again. For my brothers sake and mainly for hers regrettably.

"Curtis is..uhm, well he's..." she's understandably having trouble telling them.

Fuck!

This is so damn messed up!

"He's her mate too!" I grumble fiercely filling in the damn blanks for Thorn so I don't have to hear those heart wrenching words inevitably slip out from her lips yet again.

Hearing the gasp and distorted cussing from Sin and Sunny as I keep staring over at Thorn I can't suppress my own damn fucked up feelings over this situation either.

"Yea, I don't fucking like it either but unfortunately it's something that we're just going to have to deal with because Thorn here refuses to reject his damn ass." I growl.

We have already had this argument earlier this morning between Thorn and I.

I wanted her to reject him immediately but Thorn being Thorn shot that idea down very quickly.

"Why won't you? Reject him that is?" Sin quickly ask her.

Thorn scoffs out deliberately at Sin.

"I didn't reject your ass when you treated me like shit when we first met or even when you slept with Storm and I didn't reject your ass Sunny when you chose Nina over me or when you slept with Shari! I didn't even reject your ass Slay when you flirted with that girl Jessica or when you kept this big ass secret from me! So give me one good damn reason why I should reject Curtis. He is actually the only one that hasn't done anything wrong to me!" Thorn argues with very valid points for all of us.

But if she only knew the true Cur not this affront he's putting up just for her then she wouldn't be defending his ass so easily.

"Actually Curtis has been the most honest out of all you. So tell me why I should reject him? I may be carrying your pup but I will not put you three above him and that's final!" Thorn carries on getting even more fevered by the second.

"Thorn." I drawl out her name completely exasperated.

"No Slay! You three need to work through all of these damn issues and stop with all of these stupid ass secrets and lies. I'm calling Queen Miracle right now and explaining everything to her, then I'm going to remove Curtis from his cell and if any of you have a problem with it, well then you can just kiss my big fat ass!" Thorn heatedly tells us all quickly rising from her chair as she storms off from us angrily.

Well fuck me!

"Thorn." I call out for her but she just keeps walking away ignoring me completely.

"Well that went well. And I guess we have no other chose but to accept Curtis as our brother and her mate now." Sunny informs us.

Not if I have anything to say about it! Dammit all to hell!

She wants to go stay with him for a few days at his pack now to get to more acquainted with him.

What a crock of shit.

She can get to know his ass just fine while staying here at her own damn pack.

But she keeps on persisting that after the formal ceremony announcement of her being our Luna that she is going to his pack no matter if we agree or disagree with the shit.

And what's really getting my ass right now is that she is up there in our guest room with him completely alone. Behind a fucking closed door.

That has me scared out of my wits. I keep listening intently in case I hear anything out of the norm.

She called Miracle just like she said she was going to do and got his stupid ass released from our dungeon. Man I wish I could tell her just what a disastrous mistake that fucking is.

This is undoubtedly fucked up.

While us three are down here watching over our warriors train, she is up there doing things with his dumb ass that neither of us actually wanting or approve of.

Especially fucking me.

I don't know how to tell her that he's actually way too dangerous for her to be around him but I just fucking don't know how?

I keep grinding down on my damn teeth in pure aggravation while I'm standing here just imagining what them two may be doing up there with each other all alone or what he just might be attempting to do.

This so fucked up!

"Slay you need to relax. If you keep grinding your teeth like that you're just going to end up chipping a damn molar." Sin huffs at me while shaking his damn head.

How can he be taking this shit so damn casually?

"Why aren't you upset? There's no damn telling what them two may be doing up there." I question Sin completely perplexed by his calm emotions about all of this. I actually thought that he above anyone else would be more upset over this.

"Because he is her mate. What am I suppose to do Slay? The Moon Goddess chose him for her just like she chose us for her and since we are brothers it kind of makes absolutely perfect sense to me." He shrugs his shoulder continuing to watch our warriors as they practice on the field.

"It's not right. I refuse to accept this. She's ours Sin and nobody else's. Why should we have to share what's ours? Especially with him." I grumble.

I need to desperately get ahold of Lila and soon before something untoward happens with Thorn. She is the only one that can help me now. I tried to call her earlier but unfortunately I received no answer. It seems like that's always just my damn luck lately.

"Come on Slay. You're only saying all of this because you don't like Curtis for some odd reason. I don't know what you have against him besides him not telling you that he is our brother but you need to work whatever it is between you two out if you ever want Thorn to forgive you or if you ever want have her back in your bed again." Sin exclaims while letting out a deep annoying chuckle.

"I dislike his ass because I don't want to truly accept him as our brother. He just doesn't fit. He's really not a nice guy Sin. I wish I could tell you what I know about him and have you not once just stopped and thought about what we are all going to do now? If Thorn does decide to keep him as her mate, where exactly is she going live? He has his own damn pack just as we do. Do you even realize just how complicated this all is now? She can't divide her time between all of us. That wouldn't make any damn sense. So exactly what do you think she is going to ultimately do?" I ask him snidely. I'm just keep thinking up ridiculous excuses to try and get his ass away from Thorn as quickly as I possibly can. Hoping that my brothers will latch on to one of them and help me out without me having to tell them both the complete truth just yet.

Sins facial expression's fluctuates between morbid curiosity to outright baffled confusion. Come on Sin please realize what I'm so desperately trying to do!

"I don't exactly know how we would all actually manage it but unfortunately we are all going to have to find a way for us to all work it out, regardless of how you may feel about Curtis he is undoubtedly sticking around according to Thorn so I think it would be best for all of us if you and him would just sit down and try to talk this all out. Because I'm telling you right now Slay. I will not lose Thorn over both of your guys bullshit. So get your act together and work it the hell out." Sin inexplicably tells me before he turns on his heels and walks the hell away from me. I just wish that he could understand. Damn why couldn't he just catch on to what I was trying to do?

I fight down the urge to to tell him within myself. But fuck I have to do something.

"He has a point Slay. I don't want you to be upset with me either but I don't mind the fact that Curtis is our brother or that he's Thorns mate. I actually like him. He reminds me a lot of dad. He looks like him honestly. I think the reason that you dislike him so much is because with him being around you are no longer actually our eldest brother any more. He is about what? A year? Well a year and a half older than you are? I just think that you are uncomfortable with the thought that you will no longer have the highest rank above us all. Am I wrong?" Sunny challenges.

I would love to tell him that he couldn't be further from the actual truth of it all.

I don't offer him a reply back I just turn away from him and stare out over the field of warriors grumbling out my dismay.

Why is it that Sunny is always the one who can see right straight through any of our bullshit but he can't see through this? He has damn good insight that much I know for sure. It's rather uncanny at times but unfortunately this time he couldn't be further off from the mark.

"Thought so." Okay jackass! I'll just let him assume that he's right but it's eating me alive not being able to tell his damn ass the rightful truth.

"It's mainly because I know him better than either of you do Sunny. He's an asshole who only thinks of himself. He has Thorn fooled and now he is working his way up to fooling you two also. I don't trust him and you shouldn't either. There are things that's happened in our past with him and I and others that neither of you know about. I'm just saying Sunny that you should watch your back when it comes to him. He's the damn devil in disguise and now unfortunately he has our mate falling for his bullshit. Just help me keep an eye on Thorn. By the time this is all over I'm pretty sure that Cur is going to end up hurting her more than either of us will ever know." Sunny nor Sin could possibly understand how viscously evil Cur can actually be.

"Have you told Thorn any of this?" Sunny ask.

"I fucking tried to this morning but Thorn is just too damn headstrong and stubborn sometimes to even listen to reason. She's got it in her head that Curtis is more reliable than we are to her. Since you know you and Sin both have done the unimaginable to her to hurt her, she may just be thinking that he is the one that will be true to her and never hurt her like we did. Sort of like her savior in a way." I desperately try to reason for Sunny to understand.

"Can you please for once just stop bringing up me fucking Shari and how much I hurt Thorn? I already feel guilty enough over it. Okay? I can not change the past even if I fucking wanted to Slay. You know maybe you should just admit to her everything that Curtis has done in the past. I don't know what happened but maybe you should let us all know what did actually happened so we can keep Thorn out of any type of danger. That way we can all be prepared incase he does try to do something with Thorn." He makes it sounds so easy but unfortunately nothing is ever that easy.

"Maybe? But if I try to tell Thorn anything right now she probably wouldn't believe my ass anyway. Not after the way I acted this morning when she told me that he was her mate. I love her Sunny and I don't want her to get hurt but I also know how vindictive Cur is and trust me when I tell you that Cur is an egotistical asshole who is only out for himself. That's another reason I didn't want to tell you and Sin about him being our brother. I knew that once you two found about Cur that he would use you two to his advantage in someway. Cur always has a trick or two up his damn sleeve. He's just that malicious." If I could actually tell both of brothers and

Thorn everything that Cur has done in our past I would in a damn heartbeat but unfortunately I just fucking can't.

I'm locked down and kept a prisoner by own promises.

If I tell them then it will bring to light things from our past that I truly don't think they will be able to handle and Lila would never forgive me neither.

"Slay if he's this bad then we need to do everything in our power that we possibly can to remove him from not only Thorns life but our lives as well. Why can't you just tell me what he has actually done?" Fuck I so wish I actually could.

"I just can't. I made a promise to someone to never speak of it Sunny. If I break that promise then what kind of a man would that make me?" Or what kind of brother?

It is dangling right there on the tip of my damn tongue to tell them all another damn secret that I have been harboring from them. If not for my promise I would spill the beans right now just to get the asshole Cur out of our lives and for good this time but I just fucking can't. No mater how much I truly want too.

"Would he hurt her?" Sunny questions would uncertainty. I consciously suck in a deep a breath still listening intently to both Thorn and Cur upstairs. Thankfully all that I am able to hear is both of them still talking amongst themselves.

"I don't know but if he even comes close to trying I will end him. Look Sunny I wish that I could tell you all of it to you but if I do I will lose someone close to me that I dearly love and I just can't take that chance." I plead for his understanding yet again.

"Fine Slay but in my opinion you're putting a lot of things at risk here by keeping your damn secrets so close to your vest once again. One being our relationship with Thorn and the main one being her and our pups life. Is that really worth the risk of keeping your damn secret? You may love this person that you're keeping a secret with but as long as you keep to yourself you are going to hurt other people you love also. Is it really fucking worth it? I just hope that you will be able to live with yourself if it is. Because honestly Slay if I was you I just couldn't." Sunny deflated right there in front of me before my own very eyes. His face takes on a very sodden expression instantly and his shoulders droop down low in pure defeat.

Making me suddenly regret even saying a damn word about any of this to him.

"All I can do Sunny is call this person up and ask for their permission to tell you both or just kill him outright and if I do that Thorn would never forgive my ass. Until then both of my hands are fucking tied behind my back. There's nothing else I can do. I'm so damn sorry." I plan on calling Lila immediately. I can't stand the thought of keeping another gut wrenching secret from any of them and hopefully this time she will fucking answer me.

"Fine but do it quickly Slay, now that you told me all of this information about Cur. I'm more worried about Thorn than I have ever have been before. Especially now that she's carrying our pup. I will not let you or anyone else put either of them in danger over a stupid ass fucking secret that you are too damn cowardly to share. I'm also telling Sin everything that you have just told me so he and I can both be prepared for the shitstorm that you and Cur are so desperately willing to cause!" Sunny states rather aggressively before he turns away from me leaving me standing there all alone with my damn mouth fully agape.

If I don't do something about all of this now he and Sin would both end up blaming me over it and I couldn't blame either of them if they did and just like Sunny so ineptly reminded me I'm also jeopardizing Thorn and our unborn pups lives.

With that thought in mind I grab my cellphone out of my pocket and hurriedly call my sister up determined to put an end to all of this bullshit once and for fucking all.

"Hello," Lila answers my call on the third ring. Thank fuck!

"Lila we need to talk." I stress urgently.

"What's wrong Slay?" I swallow down a big ass gulp, I hate that I have to do this to her.

"I had to tell them that Curs our brother Lila. Cur...he is...he's..Thorns mate." I tell her. The line goes virtually quiet, my anxiety starts to peek.

"What? No Slay. I'm so sorry." She finally speaks with so much concern in her voice that it nearly breaks me. I fucking hate this.

"Lila, I have to tell them...what he did to you." I aguishly tell her while threading my fingers through my tangled hair.

"What? Why Slay? They don't have to know. Please don't tell them." She pleads desperately with me. I flinch when I hear the tormenting pain in her voice.

"Lila I have to. He's Thorns mate. She doesn't realize just how damn evil he truly is. If I don't tell her then I'm putting her and our pups life in danger. She actually likes the fucker." It's something that I just simply can't come to bring myself to understand.

"But Slay they will kill him if they find out, are you willing to take that chance?" Fuck I hate this, especially for her.

"And if I don't tell them he will do the exact same thing he did to you to Thorn. Are you willing to take that chance because I'm fucking not? This is my pregnant mate we are talking about here Lila and I love her immensely. I would die for her Lila. Either you tell them or I fucking will." I threaten her trying to temper down my own rage.

"Alright. I'm sorry Slay I should have realized that earlier. But I don't think I can face them and tell them both the horrid details about what happened. I just can't Slay." Lila is now crying through the phone. I can hear her softly whimpering along with her erratic breathing.

"Do you want me to tell them for you?" I suggest.

"Please. Honestly big brother I don't think I would be able to even face them or be able to get the words out to even tell them. I haven't even told Marc about it all yet. So yes if you don't mind can you please tell them and I will tell Marc." Her whimpers continue to echo through the phone. They remissly overshadow the sounds of the warriors still practicing ruthlessly in the background behind me.

"I'm sorry you have to do this Lila. I can only imagine how hard this must be for you. If you need me please don't hesitate to call or come over here. I will always be there for you baby sister, no matter what." And I always will be.

"Thank you Slay. I'll tell Marc tonight. I love you. Please take care of Thorn before it's too late. She doesn't deserve what I went through. No one does." Exactly. Fuck I'm so glad that she's finally seeing things my way. I release a calming breath finally.

"Love you too and I will. Be safe." I exclaim to her whole-heartedly.

"You too. Bye." She sadly sniffle.

"Bye."

I hang up the phone then my eyes automatically go searching the practice field for any sign of Sun and Sin.

My aggravation spikes when I see them across the field standing right beside Thorn and that asshole Cur happily laughing with each other.

Stomping across the backyard with determined steps I try to brace myself for what's about to come.

An all out fucking war!

Chapter 32

"We need to talk!" Slay says with a husky gruffness rudely interrupting are jovial conversation. I was about to jump on his ass until I looked over at him and saw the look on his face.

By the seriousness of the look plastered on his face I can tell that he means fucking business.

"Sure. Where?" I ask while glancing over at Sunny beside me.

"Inside. Now! You to Thorn. But not fucking you!" Slay exclaims rather aggressively while pointing his finger directly over at Curtis.

Curtis just huffs at Slay then shrugs his shoulders like he doesn't seem to give a damn. Strange, I think to myself.

We all immediately obey. Following after Slay with tentative steps toward our house.

By the way Slay is acting I'm starting to become overly worried. All day long he has been basically pleading with me and Sunny about Curtis, making me start to wonder if his attitude now has something to do with him.

Entering into the living room I take my usual seat in my favorite chair while Sunny and Thorn sit down on the couch across from me. Slay begins to pace back and forth looking very serious and way overly anxious.

"What is this about Slay?" I ask him very curious over why he's acting so damn odd and edgy.

"What I'm about to tell all of you will more than likely make you hate me and Lila from keeping this from you for so long but it needs to be said, especially now." Slay stresses.

"Alright. I don't think I could ever actually hate either of one you Slay but I'll keep an open mind." I try to assure him. He seems really panicked now. His entire body is tensed upped so damn tightly. I can literally see his muscles flexing against his black T-shirt.

"Same. I could never hate my siblings. Just spill it already Slay." Sunny pipes in.

"Slay are you okay? This can't be that serious, can it?" Thorn ask him worriedly. I guess I'm not the only one to sense Slays inner turmoil.

"Alright but before I tell either of you. I need both you Sin and Sun to promise me that you won't go all feral on me. It's a very sensitive topic and I know how hotheaded each of you can get. You're just like me in that area but this time I really need for both of you to try and stay perfectly calm." Slay asserts. Fuck now I know that this has to be bad, I scoot up further on my chair listening intently

"Promise." Sunny and I both say in unison.

"Alright. Years ago when Lila was just fifteen she went out looking for me because mom asked her too. She searched basically everywhere and couldn't find me. I had my mindlink blocked off from everyone because at that time I was with my girlfriend Monica at her cousins house while they were out of town and I didn't want to be distracted." Slay explains, I take notice of the touch of regret established all over his sudden crestfallen face.

"After a while she decided to go search for me at Curtis's house. She remembered that we use to hang out with each other sometimes not too long ago." I remember him being Curtis's friend for a while during our youth. He never would tell us exactly why they stopped hanging around each other. That is until today when he announced that Curtis was apparently our half brother.

"She went to his house searching for me but I wasn't there unfortunately. Wish I would of been now. Curtis invited her into his house on the guise of him wanting to help her find me. His mother nor his grandfather was home at the time. I don't know exactly where they were but that's what he apparently told her." Slay takes a deep shaky breath. He finally stops his frantic pacing deciding instead to sit down right on top of the coffee tables edge, facing both Thorn and Sunny now.

Not being able to see him too clearly I gradually stand up from my favorite chair to take a seat right in between Thorn and Sunny so I can peer straight into Slays face. .

I want to see his face while he finishes telling us yet another one of his secrets. I have a deep twisting knot in the pit of my stomach that's suddenly intensifying because I just may have a sense about what's coming but I hope like hell that I'm completely wrong.

"Unsuspectingly Lila walked into his house innocently thinking that Curtis was actually a good friend of mine and she fucking trusted him. He took advantage of the opportunity that was laid out before him. He tricked her then he forced himself upon her and continued to roughly violate her for hours." I hiss in a angry breath when Slay drops the fucking bombshell on us.

Curtis fucking raped my baby sister? For fucking hours? Fuck! He raped his own damn sister!

I hear Thorn let a horrid gasp beside me and I actually fucking hear Sunny grinding his own damn teeth together.

"He raped his own damn sister and he fucking knew that it was his sister the entire fucking time!" I go fucking livid!

Springing up from the couch quickly I start to make my way out the back door to fucking kill Curtis!

"Stop Sin! You fucking promised me you wouldn't do this!" Slay yells while jumping up from the coffee table to come charging over after me.

"You expect me to just sit on my ass and let this fucking slide? I'm going to fucking kill his ass! He raped our fucking sister Slay! His own damn sister! How fucked up is that? I won't let him get away with this Slay and you can't fucking stop me!" I bellow out far beyond furious now. I turn on my heels headed straight for the back door.

"Wait Sin I may have an idea." Thorn quickly says as she makes her way over to me.

"What Thorn? Because if this idea of yours doesn't involve me with my fingers wrapped around that assholes neck robbing him of his very life then I don't want to fucking hear it!" I sneer out at her unintentionally. She blanches away from the intensity of my anger.

"I know you're upset Sin. I am too but I may have a better way to go about all of this." She pleads with me. "A more vindictive way."

Sunny walks over to us slowly and by the look that's plastered upon his face right now I can obviously tell that it basically mirrors my own. Pure fucking hatred.

"What's your plan Thorn?" Sunny ask her gently somehow managing to contain his own anger amazingly. I give his ass props for that because right now I'm barely holding on by a single damn thread.

"I want you three to stay in here while I go outside and talk with Curtis....alone." Thorn explains. I scoff at her.

If she thinks that's a better idea than my own idea of ripping off his fucking neck from his disgusting body then she is unfortunately mis-fucking-guided!

"You are not facing that asshole alone Thorn. I won't permit it!" Slay intervenes with a threatening tone.

"Just listen to me please. Who is better equipped to deal with a damn family rapist than me? I have a plan that will end all of this bullshit without adding any violence into the mix." Thorn retorts with a desperate exasperated tone of her own.

"Fine. What's this damn plan of yours?" I hesitantly agree to at least listen to her plan. Although I hate it.

She dives right in into her well thought out plan with clear defined detailed determination.

We listen in intently to every single word she quietly speaks.

I have to admit it's not a bad one but I still adamantly refuse to let her do this shit all on her own.

"It's a good plan Thorn but you are not doing it by yourself." I lay down the law with complete conviction.

"I will be okay Sin." She tries her best to assure me.

Big fucking no no!

"You are carrying our pup Thorn. There's no way in hell you are going out there by yourself. I won't risk your life or the life of our baby. I'm with Slay on this one Thorn. You will do it with the three of us there or you won't fucking do it at all." I won't settle for any other damn option on this.

"I agree with him Thorn. It's just too damn risky. Who knows how he is going to react to any of this? You matter way too much to all of us to let you go at this all on your own." Sunny agrees with me and Slay, showing no signs of any doubt about our decision whatsoever.

"Fine. But just stand back and let me do my thing okay?" She finally gives in though halfheartedly. Regardless, I wouldn't let her do this all on her own even if my life fucking depended on it.

"Thorn are you really sure that this is what you truly want to do? I will completely understand if you can't handle this. Not a lot of people can." Slay questions her with full compassion and understanding. Which actually surprises me.

Honestly, I can't fully understand why Slay hasn't killed Curtis's ass already over all of this bullshit.

I don't know how he could of kept his temperament under control for so long now. If I had known exactly what had happened with Lila back then I would have already put Curtis in a deep underground grave.

"I'm positive Slay. I don't ever want to be associated with someone like Curtis ever. After everything that I went through with my revolting father wanting to do the same damn thing with me I find people like that to be just plain outright despicable." She's not the fucking only one.

How can anyone be so damn repulsive is beyond me.

"Then let's do this. Together." Sunny rightly exclaims.

Now that I can agree without a shadow of a fucking doubt.

He is standing at the edge of the training field as we all all saunter out of the house inconspicuously.

My eyes stayed continuously glued onto him as we drew nearer to the training field.

Slay, Sunny, and I break off away from Thorn, going to the outer edge of the fenced line where Trace, Flex, and Pan are waiting for us, while Thorn strolls on over to an unsuspecting Curtis.

We only get close enough to be able to hear them both just in case Curtis poses any type of threat or danger to her.

I place my arms on top of the fence post, folding them over, pretending to watch our warriors train right before us, all the while I am try to keep a precautionary side eye on Thorn at all times.

As she slowly walks up to him I can slightly see them from the angle that we're standing at while she sensually smiles over at him.

As I watch her with him my irritation begins to grow mildly.

"Relax will you. We don't need him to sense that anything's going awry with us. You will put Thorns life in danger if he happens notice." Sunny assertively whispers to me lowly.

I grumble softly over at him, but try to keep my general focus on the two of them mainly.

As she reaches him finally, she timidly leans her body in a tad bit closer to him while placing her tiny hands on his chest Thorn lets out a little light hearted giggle freely for him.

"Can I ask you something Curtis?" Thorn mumbles while tilting her head to the side as she peers up at him lovingly.

"Sure sweetheart. You can ask me anything?" Curtis responds with a very implied suggestive tone.

What a damn jerk face.

"Would you allow me to mark you?" Thorn just comes on out with it leaving Curtis clearly shaken with genuine surprise.

"Here? Now? I mean sweetheart I would love it if you would marked me but there are a lot of people around us." He retorts with snide smirk. "We would have a open audience."

"They don't bother me and I don't care who sees me do it. I just want to mark you so badly Curtis." She maintains her explanation with a provocative purr. "Please." She adds on for good measure.

I fucking can't stand this. This damn act she's having to put on with him. Giving him entertaining thoughts that will not be brought into fruition is only working to rile me up even more.

"Well if you are sure sweetheart then by all means I'm completely yours." Curtis replies with a veritable husky tone toward her.

I think I'm going to be fucking sick. I feel the bile rise up in my throat, burning away at me like acid.

Craning my head over to them slightly more I watch as Thorn grabs Curtis's chin firmly within her hand, strongly turning his head away from her face while she rises up on her tiptoes to lean further into him.

Her long beautiful hair drops off to her side as she tilts her head marginally toward his neck. Her plump lips separate as her canines elongate then sink right down into his damn pliable neck.

I cringe in disgust when I see her bite down harder on his neck. Curtis let's out a deep guttural lustful moan while he wraps his arms around her midsection pulling her body flush up to his.

I suck in a harsh hiss between my teeth, holding in my breath, just glowering over at them. I fucking can't stand any of this. My own jealousy eats away at me unhappily.

"Did she just mark him here?" Trace questions us ineptly. "In public?"

"She sure did." Flex affirms clearly astounded. "Damn!"

"But why?" Pan questions.

"Quiet!" Slay asserts as we all watch them both completely mesmerized and basically spellbound.

Thorn releases her teeth from his neck finally, I have to bite down on my lower lip firmly when I see her lick the puncture wounds she so generously left on him.

Thorn drops her hand away quickly from Curtiss face trying to step away from him but he ends up holding on to her a little tighter bringing her roughly against him again.

"My turn." He conveys smirking down at her.

I start to take a step forward toward them but Sunny wraps his hand around my lower arm preventing me from stepping any closer to them.

Jerking my head back over at Sunny I let out a low menacing growl at him, Sunny just sighs and shakes his head at me vehemently.

Blowing out a pent up breath, I yank my arm away from his grasp grumbling at him while returning my full attention back to Thorn and Curtis before me.

Thorn has her hands pressed up flat against his chest.

"Sure thing but first there's something I would like to say." She suddenly halts his advances by pretending to agree with him.

It's the first time that I actually smile during all of this charade because I know exactly what's forthcoming.

"Okay sweetheart I'm all ears." Curtis contends though hesitantly.

I can finally feel my spirits start to lift. Tensely waiting along with my brothers for her to utter those finalizing words from those sexy plump lips of hers.

Thorn then clears her throat a little dramatically, "I Thorn Lee Rose of the Blood Claw Pack, reject you Curtis Devine, of the Winter Moon Pack, from this day on and forward." Thorn clarifies loudly.

I hear all three of our Betas gasp out in shock behind me along with Slay and Sunny's joyful rising chuckles.

Curtis's arms fall away from Thorns waist dropping to his sides while his face instantly morphs into a wide state a shock as he grabs ahold of his chest with his right hand clutching it tightly and gasping out for random bouts of dry air.

"Why?" He croaks out in indistinguishable pain.

"Because of what you did to Lila." Thorn simply states while sneering over at him, she then takes a tiny step back away from him.

This is our cue. I take the first step quickly followed by Slay and Sunny toward her, only stopping when all three of us are directly behind her happily shooting deathly daggers at Curtis over her shoulder.

"You raped my sister you fucking asshole! This is just a small amount of what you truly fucking deserve!" I sneer my upper lip at him while growling.

Curtis bends his body half over while displaying an undetermined amount of pain. Groaning out breathlessly as he then collapses to the ground right underneath him on one bended knee with his other hand that's not clutching at his chest holding him up from the ground, palm down.

He lifts his head up at us as he lets out a groan with valid uncertainty crossing across his eyes, the asshole them smirks coyly in between his grunts.

"She...wanted....it. All...wom..en...do." He declares vigorously between each bouts of breaths.

"You sound just like my disgusting father, you swine! Not all women want it! Frankly, Curtis all women really want is someone to love them unconditionally. Not to be manhandled, abused, or violated from someone like the likes of you!" Thorn professes with inner rage boiling up inside of her.

"I should...have let..Nina...kill....you!" Curtis confesses during his wayward struggles.

"You lied! This entire time you have been lying to me? Did you try to rape Nina too?" Thorn ask him with an accusatory inquiry.

Cutis tries to laugh at her diabolically but ends up to only having a raging coughing fit instead.

"No..I didn't..Nina was more than....happy to sleep...with me." I can't fucking believe it.

"You were a couple, weren't you? She came to us all on her own free will. For you? Didn't she?" My eyes widen in complete surprise, I been so damn foolish. It was right there before us the entire fucking time. "There was no chosen Luna. You and her planned the entire coup! So you were, in all reality, helping Alpha Baker all along? How could have been so damn blind?" I deduced, with a fair amount of certainty.

My brothers turn to me with scowling faces in pure confusion. Thorn just keeps peering down at Curtis angrily.

"Can't you see? He has been in on this the entire fucking time. Him and Nina were working together. They were lovers!

He sent her here for whatever reason. Nina wasn't acting on her own!" I try to explain to both of them with some accuracy.

I can tell right when the realization dawns on them both. Slays temper starts to rise to a new degree and Sunny just looks reasonably stunned.

Curtis lets out a breathy chuckle still lowered on the ground below us.

"I sent her here...to break you apart...so Baker...could fuck...his..." He trails off as he begins to have another coughing fit. Curtis hacks up a good sized glob of dark red blood from his mouth, spitting it all out on the ground underneath him.

Fucking gross as fuck!

I spring back a hop away from him. Mortified by the congealing blood coming out from his mouth.

Rejection from your mate after bonding is a stone cold fucking bitch apparently.

Shuddering, I scrunch up my face in earnest disgust down at him.

"Then...he was going...share her...with his...friends. I was at the...top of the list." He reveals as his body falls back on the ground beneath him. Curtis balls himself up in a fetal position, moaning out in deserved agony.

"But you are her mate? Why would you do it just to be at the top of the list when you could of gone the easier route?" Slay questions Curtis, while he scratches the back of his neck.

"Was his mate." Thorn adds on with a visceral snarl aimed right at Curtis laying helplessly on the ground.

"I never wanted...a...mate. I just...wanted Nina." He pants while trying to stand back up onto his own two feet. Stumbling over a few times before he is able to finally stand upright again, still struggling to capture air into his lungs.

"I love Nina. I could...never love...someone as...hideous as you. You are...weak and...pathetic. Nina is...stronger and you took...away her wolf!" He imparts his misguided knowledge with a ineffective growl.

"I didn't take away anything from her the Queen and Kings did and you are a millions times more pathetic than any other person I have ever met!" Thorn loudly pronounces.

Then it all comes to a head quickly.

Curtis rages out at Thorn in just a matter of seconds. He throws himself at her clumsily will ill effect.

She takes ahold of his arms swiftly with both of her hands.

Before my reflexes were able to even kick in Thorn does something truly unimaginable once again.

She opens her beautiful mouth as Curtis is face to face and eye to eye with her while she holds him slightly away from her.

Trendils of smoke start to appear flowing up from out of her mouth.

Then a roar of a streaming flame exits her opened mouth going straight into Curtiss own opened mouth with only a half of an inch separating the two of them.

Curtis's mouth engulfs fully with her raging flame of fire as he swallows down the burning flames. He twists and tries to struggle away from Thorn unsuccessfully, but she nearly loses her grasp on him until Slay comes to stand right behind Curtis wrapping his two burly hands around Curtis's upper arms keeping him securely locked into place.

His eyes close up tightly as his face suddenly registers his own foreseen agonizing death.

Curtis's entire body quickly goes limp within Slays firm grasp on him.

Thorn relinquishes the flame with only small black and grey smoke trendils now exiting her mouth.

Surprisingly, she lets out a vibrating burp wile pounding her fisted hand up against her chest.

Slay unceremoniously drops Curtis's body. Letting his body fall listlessly to the ground beneath him, uncharacteristically dead.

My eyes travel back up to view Thorn standing before me looking down at Curtis's lifeless body, she seems devoid of any emotions whatsoever on her face as she studies him.

What the hell just happened? In a matter of only seconds Thorn has managed to completely strip Curtis of all life right before my very eyes.

Catching a glimpse of the others surrounding us, I notice that all of their faces are filled with recognizable mortification toward Thorn, their own Luna.

"She killed him! What did he do to deserve death?" One of our she wolves, named Harriet, ask out loud while aiming a heated glare in Thorns direction.

Oh Fuck!

Our entire pack starts to draw in closer to us with anger suddenly fusing all around us.

One brave and very ill reputable warrior steps out of the crowd shoving others aside to make his way over to us angrily.

"We should notify the Queen! She is a murderer!" Our warrior, Shengad, roars riling up the mob around him.

Shouts and jeers start rambling over to us, each one of them down casting and trying to shame Thorn for what she just done.

Thorn nervously backs away from the upcoming mob that's slowly trying to make their way over to her. I pull her over to stand right behind me, shielding her away from them all. Sunny comes over to us to shield her away from them also.

"Shut the hell up!" Slays Alpha command rightly diffuses all of their shouts and jeers instantly. Every single one of them tilts their heads to the side for him in full submission.

"This is your Luna and you will damn well respect her! She only did what she had to do to a professed rapist that raped my own sister! If any of you have one thing to say about any of this? Say it directly to me! Understand?" Slays Alpha tone leaves no room for any further arguments.

Each member of our pack bows their heads in submission to Slays Alpha commands.

"And you, Shengad. How fucking dare you threaten my mate! Your own damn Luna!" Slay is infuriated.

"I'm s-sorry. I didn't know Alpha. I apologize." Shengad stutters as his body begins to shake uncontrollably.

"It is not me who deserves your apology Shengad. For your unbecoming behavior toward your own Luna, you will patrol the outer property all night long for two straight fucking weeks! Are we clear?" Slay declares. "And I think you owe your Luna a formal apology."

Shengad obediently turns to Thorn wile still shaking some-what uncontrollably.

"I'm so sorry Luna. I didn't know the full circumstances involving the prior situation. Please forgive me." Shengad pleads with a notable tremble in his voice.

"It's fine, you didn't know. I can understand completely and please call me Thorn." She graciously tells him.

"Thank you...Thorn." Shengad comments while bowing his head down to her in respect.

I release a large exhale as I watch the crowd quickly dis-perse and a reprimanded Shengad walk humbly away.

What a damn day this has been!

"Are you okay?" I ask Thorn as I turn back to her searching her face any signs of discomfort.

"I'm fine. Let's just get rid of this damn body and call Lila." She suggest while waving her hand down at Curtis's lifeless corpses still laying down on the ground.

"Plus, I really need to remove this damn butt plug!" Thorn grumbles while scrunching up your her face catching us all by surprise, desperately trying to dig her jeans out of her ass crack.

Well fuck me!

Chapter 33

Tonight Thorn will be announced at her ceremony as our Luna finally.

I've been anxiously running around all damn day long trying my best to get all of the preparations done in order for this grand ceremony to be absolutely flawless, along with the she wolves that have so graciously volunteered their time to help me, I vow to make every thing to be just perfect for Thorn tonight.

It has to be.

After the fiasco with Curtis and our pack suddenly trying to solicit a damn riot over his well deserved death I want to insure that all of our pack members will soon see Thorn to be a reliable, respected, and secure Luna for our pack. One that will lead our pack to greatness just like I know that she can.

Poor Thorn has been a nervous wreck all damn day. Sin has been trying his best to occupy her time with various activities to keep her mind off of the upcoming ceremony, thankfully.

Slay has been busy with our pack warriors trying to secure everyone's protection for tonight's event.

Especially since there was a brutal rogue attack on the Saint Wolf Pack just last evening, located around thirty miles away just to the East of us.

Unfortunately, Alpha Wyatt lost eight good pack members including his loyal Beta Eaton.

Senseless mayhem.

Too many lives lost and for what?

Power? Corruption? Revenge? Greed?

Who knows?

It's all just too damn disturbing to even comprehend.

"Alpha Sunny, if it's okay with you, we would like your permission to leave so that we can all get prepared for tonight's events?" Cynthia ask me modestly.

"Is everything finished?" I search the entire room in amazement, the balloons, streamers, and even the moonflowers are all showcased properly around the room making it strikingly beautiful.

"Everything is as it should be Alpha." Cynthia establishes smiling anxiously over at me.

"Thank you ladies for all of your help. You may enjoy the rest of your night." I show them all of my deepest gratitude, for without them I would have been a damn nervous wreck myself tonight trying to get all of these damn preparations done in time.

"You're welcome Alpha." Cynthia replies softly before her and the others leave me to prepare themselves for tonight's occasion.

Taking a deep breath I head off for my room to follow in the she wolves footsteps to get my own self prepared for tonight's event.

My anxiousness starts rising within me as I go. Rubbing my hands together I can't help but to put on a grand smile.

This is going to be one hell of night I can just feel it.

"Tell me again why I have to wear a damn monkey suit?" Sin grumbles for the fifth damn time tonight, trying his best to adjust his tie again. He acts like the damn thing is choking him when in reality I know it's definitely not.

Rolling my eyes at him, I sigh out sympathetically, Strolling my way over to him I politely help his dumb ass with his tie. Sin has always had this compulsion with tuxedos. Slay isn't much better though.

Side eyeing him I try to stifle down my own aggravation as I watch him trade his white dress shirt for his usual black t-shirt and just forgoing the tie all together. He inevitably puts back on his vest and jacket. I should just glad the asshole has decidedly kept his dinner jacket and vest on tonight.

Realizing to myself that that no matter how much I would protest with him he would do whatever he wants to do anyway. I just shake my head and let him do it without any further arguments.

Finished with Sins tie I take a tiny step back to view all of him.

"How do I look?" He inquires with notable nervous antici-pation.

"Spiffy." I answer him truthfully.

He looks sharp as a damn tack. I proudly pat myself on my back mentally for picking just the right suit for the occasion. He turns around to look at himself in the long standing mirror behind him.

I join him by standing right behind him observing both of us with a genuine smile on my face.

Thorn asked us if we would all each wear some type of red tonight, I'm assuming it's because her dress will also be in red.

I can't wait to see her in it though, I bet she looks extremely lovely and with that thought racing through my mind I turn my attention back to Slay across the bedroom.

"Ready?" Slay grumbles a bit at me while scowling but then eventually sighs and nods his head.

"Come on Slay it's a special night what's with the grumpy face?" I question while walking over to him.

"The damn rogue attack on the Saint Wolf pack has me worried." Of course it does, who wouldn't be worried over it?

"We are heavily guarded tonight you made sure of that so let's just try to relax and enjoy the ceremony." I state as I place my hand on top of his shoulders, trying to reassure him. "For Thorn." I add on. He sighs again with resignation.

"For Thorn." He solemnly agrees with another nod of his head.

"Then let's go already." Sin pipes in rather excitedly.

Here we go then!

Standing at the end of the staircase waiting patiently for Thorn to finally make her grand appearance, each of us kept fiddling anxiously with our tuxedos.

I try to hold in my laughter as I watched my brothers painstakingly fidget continuously and how completely uncomfortable they are acting in their monkey suits.

Hearing Thorns bedroom door finally open all of my attention went from my brothers straight to her instead.

When I finally see her at the top of the landing I honesty started to fucking uncontrollably drool.

My goddess is nothing but an ethereal beauty in her new red flowing gown that matches up perfectly with her toned bronzed beautiful complexion.

"Wow." I so wholeheartedly agree with Slays sentiment toward her.

My eyes stayed perfectly glued to her as I watch her gracefully waltz down the staircase toward us like a damn rock star on parade taking my damn breath away from me.

Damn she's so fucking beautiful. I'm a very lucky ass fucking man.

"So how does it look?" Thorn ask while doing a little twirl for us, giggling.

"Beautiful." Slay asserts with a husky tone striding over it her.

"Stunning." Sin adds with his eyes roaming all over her delectable body.

"Fucking remarkable." I pipe in as I offer my elbow over to her for her to take. She flashes me that sexy smile of hers, placing her tiny hand in the crook of my arm as I escort her to the to the other side of the room to the opposite stairs that exits out to the opened balcony.

I can't believe this is finally happening.

"Dear fellow pack members and friends," Slay announces, "Oh, and family," he adds with a grin glancing down at Lila and Marc standing in the middle of the crowd, "we are all gather here this evening to induct Thorn Rose as our Luna of the Blood Claw Pack." Cheers and applause echo throughout the backyard from the audience below us.

"First we will do the ceremonies Luna ritual run then we shall all dine, mingle, and dance." Slay continues to announce after the applause soon dies down, "We will meet you all at the forests edge in just a few moments but in the meantime please help yourselves to a drink. Those that are of the legal age anyway." The audience then breaks out into laughter as we all step away from the balcony entering back into our home to change out of our clothes for the Luna run.

Standing now at the edge of the forest line with all of our pack members happily surrounding us in various robes and outer attire Thorn starts to get really nervous suddenly.

"Relax everything will be just fine." I console her, coming up from behind her I encircle her little baby bump waistline with my arms delicately.

She tilts her head to the side with her long hair wistfully falling away to her side I begin to leave little peppery like kisses along her neck trying to ease some of her tension.

"They will release the animals for the hunt but you don't actually have to catch one of them Thorn. This isn't a contest, it's just a way of welcoming you into our pack." I profess softly to her.

It has always been a family tradition in our pack to hunt down certain animals out of respect for our incoming Luna. To present them to her as a gift of honoring her and welcoming her into the pack.

Thorn thinks it's somewhat primitive but who are we to break years and years of family tradition?

"Alright everybody, at the sound of the whistle blowing everyone will shift into their wolves and begin the hunt. Remember this isn't a contest so let's just have some fun and enjoy ourselves. Good luck everyone." Sin announces to our pack. I take a step away from Thorn releasing her form my warm embrace. Then the whistle blows loudly.

Everyone in our pack, menand women alike, begins to strip out of their attire then automatically starts to shift into their wolves.

All around us you can hear bones begin to crack and morph along with some distinguishing grunting.

Howling starts echoing throughout the entirety of the backyard, I drop the black robe I was wearing onto the ground beneath me, then I start to shift into my wolf myself, along with my brothers and Thorn beside me.

"Yes let's go!" Stinger howls inside of my head excitedly.

"Hold on we need to wait for Thorn." I insist glancing over at our striking mate in her wolf form.

"Maya is beautiful." Stinger says wistfully.

"Yes she is." I agree. She is far beyond beautiful.

"I can't wait to meet our pup!" Stinger comments. I glance down at the little protruding belly Maya/Thorn has and smile internally.

"Me neither she's going to be the perfect mom." This time I'm the one with the wistful tone that's caught up on my own voice inside of my head.

"I so agree." Stinger replies then howls out happily.

We catch their attention with our howl, they all in return howl along with me.

Then we take off running and thrashing through the forest rapidly in search for our prey.

This is so much fun.

Best fucking time ever!

After the hunt we all got redressed in our formal attire to dance and drink the night away.

Slay and Sin ended up catching a boar and turkey tonight, lucky them. I only was able to snag up a small rabbit but surprisingly Thorn was able to get a capture a small doe. She of course decided to let it go on its little merry way but I couldn't have been more proud of her for doing it. It just goes to show how much compassion my mate truly has in her heart.

The party continued on to well past midnight, everyone actually really enjoyed themselves. I have to say it all turned out perfectly.

By the time we were all headed up to our bedrooms for the night I quickly remembered about Thorns wanting adventure that she so wanted to do with all of us.

Before we took the final step on the stairway I halted Thorns progress by grabbing ahold of her arm gently.

"Are you still wanting to do what you asked us about?" I ask her reminding her. Slay and Sin stop suddenly to turn their attention to us now extremely curious about her forthcoming answer.

"Of course just let me grab a shower first then I'm all yours." Well hot damn.

"Meet us in Slays room." I confer eagerly headed off to grab a shower of my own before our illicit journey begins.

I've been looking forward to this for days now. Every since she mentioned it I have been fantasizing about just this.

Slay and Sin both run by me eagerly probably having the same exact thoughts that I'm currently having.

Entering my bathroom I can't help but to rush through my shower while humming a sweet little old time tune in my head.

'Let's talk about sex baby' I start singing out loud in the hot refreshing shower. Very fucking eagerly and already hard as fucking hell.

Walking casually in to Slays room I nearly trip over my own damn two feet when I see that Slay is already laying halfway down on the bed against the headboard with Thorn leaning against him right in between his legs facing away from him, completely...fucking...naked!

Slay is carefully massaging her little perky nipples while Thorns head is thrown back up against his chest moaning out in pure erotic pleasure.

I don't see Sin anywhere in the room but I don't hesitate a damn second waiting around for his ass before I jump on the bed right in between Thorns opened and welcoming sexy as hell thighs.

Her legs are perched up with her feet firmly planted down on top of the mattress below her. I grab ahold of her tiny ankles then push her legs further up to her as I slide down on the mattress to ravish her delicious thriving core.

My tongue pierces her divide instantly, sliding greedily in and out of her. Her cinnamon and vanilla tangy taste hits my erogenous zone immediately causing my dick to jerk delightfully.

Fuck she taste so damn good.

I lap her up like I'm fucking ravenous, sliding my tongue upwards until I reach that little hot sensitive nub of hers, Thorn squeaks out a delightful purring mewl, arching her back up off of Slays chest lost up in her own carnal desires.

Slipping two fingers deep inside of her canal I lean back slightly away from her to watch as Slay pushes his own digits deep into her ass rim at the same exact time.

Thorn becomes an uncontrollable thrashing mess on bed under our continuous onslaught of her, "Oh, Yes Papi." She moans out desirably with her hips bucking up off of the mattress, placing my hand against her small belly I hold her in place as I continue to thrust my crooked digits inside of her rapidly. Then I hear the bedroom door open suddenly behind me. The bed soon dips down with Sin crawling up on it on his knees toward her.

He stops directly over her while slowly pumping his cock right in front of her face.

Slay scoots done on the bed from underneath her since I had no clue about what he was doing I removed my fingers from Thorns hot drenched core to sit back on my knees and observe him.

He eventually ended up trading places with me, after I stripped out of my boxers, now I'm underneath Thorn with her sweet body straddling me with her facing me, then Slay climbs right behind her, while he's doing whatever he's doing I start kneading on her breast firmly, leaning up I suck in one of her puckered nipples right into warm mouth.

Licking and sucking on her breast, Thorn keeps squirming on top of me rubbing her tantalizing wet pussy right up against my throbbing and aching swollen cock.

Fuck! Releasing her nipple I try to get a look over her shoulder at Slay wanting him to anxiously hurry the fucking hell up.

When I looked back over at Slay he was generously applying some lube thoroughly all over his harden dick and Thorns ass rim, I had to crack a smile at that. He's finally getting what he has always fantasized about with Thorn. That luscious plump ass of hers.

I suddenly feel the mattress moving, turning my head I see Sin wobbling on his knees back over to Thorn still pumping along his stiff cock vigorously.

As we all wait for Slay to get himself readjusted I reach down and start massaging Thorns little clit with the pad of my thumb to stimulate her along even further.

Her delectable moaning almost sends me over the edge far too fucking prematurely.

Damn! Hurry the fuck up Slay!

Slay finally gets his shit together thankfully, I don't think I could have waited much longer for his ass if he didn't.

He places his hand flat on Thorns back, pushing her down to me, leaning into her he whispers into her ear, "I'll go easy on you beautiful but just in case do you happen to remember your safe word?" He ask her huskily.

Thorn looks over her shoulder at him, causing her long hair to fall off to her side brushing along my chest lightly sending hasty chills straight through my entire body, "Petals Papi." She breathlessly replies to him seductively.

"Good girl." Slay says just as he starts pushing into her ass rim agonizingly slow, I grab ahold of my cock with my unused hand and slide into her pussy painstakingly slow also.

"Open up wide for me baby." Sin growls at her, his knees collide up against my side as he spreads his legs open wider still holding on tightly to his rigid cock, Thorn leans over to my side bending down to get even with him, she starts licking along Sins dick swirling her tongue along his tip making the fucker whine out very longingly.

Slay keeps grinding into her ass hungrily while I keep pounding ferociously up inside of her, meeting her hips with my mine brusquely.

I hear a loud slap suddenly peering over at Slay I watch as he slaps her rounded plump ass with the palm of his hand not once but twice, sending Thorn into alluring gyrating vixen. Rotating those magnificent hips on me.

"Fuck...your so...damn...tight beautiful!" Slay tells her with a breathy struggling long drawn out moan then slaps her ass again loudly.

I close my eyes and groan in pure ecstasy.

When I hear her fiendish purrs trying her damn best to answer him, I crack my eyes open a fraction to watch her, Sin keeps thrusting up his hips to meet her mouth with a fevered frenzy. His head his lolled back with his eyes closed up tightly in total fucking bliss.

Craning my head slightly I glance over at Slay behind her, his face is scrunched up so damn tightly while he pivots heavily into her, it's like he has an overwhelming voracious ache that's just for her.

"Damn Thorn...you have us...all gluttonous...over you." I grit out while gripping both of my hands now onto her exquisite hips while I start to savagely burrow up into her soaked contracting walls.

Her silken walls are squeezing my dick so damn tightly I think I might just abrupt inside far too quickly for my own damn liking. So I try my best to hold back with a thunderous pounding ache.

Releasing one of my hands from her enticing hip, I bring it up to her voluptuous breast pinching down hard on her little rigid nipple.

I watch as Slay begins to fondle her other breast also while still hammering into her with an unquenched insatiable need.

Throwing my head and closing my eyes up tight I grown out once again lustfully.

"Fuck I'm about to..." Sin trails off breathlessly, I peer open my eyes again to see Sin with a rapturous look planted right on his face as he begins to explode all inside of Thorns mouth. His body shakes uncontrollably, then goes perfectly still while he holds his breath in just for a few seconds. Finally when he undecidedly catches his breath again he falls back on his legs panting out very heavily.

I can see the secretion of Sins left over liquids flowing out of the corner of Thorns mouth. She licks it off of her mouth with her tongue, watching her tongue swirl along her lips so seductively makes my dick twitch automatically up inside of her.

Dammit!

Slay goes next surprisingly, catching a glance over at him he lets out an animalistic groan while throwing back his damn head. His face looks like he's in absolute rhapsody as he keeps feverishly plundering in her.

Slay lets out an arduous wail, "so fucking ass good!" He willingly unleashes his hungered beast directly into her.

While I continuously assail her pussy with my cock Thorns velvety walls suddenly tighten around my dick unrelentingly, her exotic moans echo throughout the bedroom when Sin suddenly reaches over and pinches her clit, she can't with-stand it any longer, her entire body goes completely rigid on top of me.

With her head tossed to the side she reaches her orgasm instantaneously.

"Fuck it all Papi!" Thorn wails out so fucking enticingly that I can't hold back my own climax any fucking longer.

With a few final drives up into her pussy I let lose a powerful surge into her releasing all of my pent up fluids sporadically all within her doused pussy like a damn shattering explosion.

Spent and irrevocably sated, Thorn falls down onto my chest breathing out erratically then Slay pulls out of her ass so very tenderly.

All throughout the bedroom all that you can hear now are the sounds of our own overheated panting and whimpering.

"Alphas we have a rogue attack on the southern border!" Flex announces hysterically through our mindlink suddenly.

"On our way!" Slay grouses.

Slay and Sin both jump out off of the bed amazingly fast. I slide Thorn gently off of me, springing up from the bed I run over to the side of the room quickly grabbing up my boxers from the back of the chair.

"I'm coming!" Thorn quips while sliding off of the bed.

"The hell you are! You stay your pretty ass right here until we get back. Sin stay with her. Sunny and I will go take care of this." Slay demands while slipping his shirt over his head speedily. Sin just nods his head at Slay.

"Why can't I come?" Thorn complains while standing right in front of Slay with her arms folded across her chest still completely naked.

"You are carrying our pup Thorn. I won't let anything happen to either of you." Slay asserts with a very final informative tone.

Thorn huffs but obeys him although a bit hesitantly, she returns back to the bed sitting down on the edge with a scowl permeated on her beautiful face. I want to kiss the damn scowl away until it completely disappears but unfortunately I fucking can't right now.

"Fine just please be careful." Thorn pleads with us so damn prettily. I just couldn't resist any longer. I stroll over to her to plant a kiss right on her wrinkled up with worry forehead.

"We will. Love you." I whisper to her right into her ear before planting another kiss right on her cheek. I crack a smile when I see her immediately blushing.

"Let's go!" Slay insist as he walks over to Thorn and plants a kiss on her pliable plump lips.

"Love you beautiful." He tells her before we both head out of the bedroom door swiftly.

I hear her soft I love you's in return as we exit the room.

Fucking rogues always showing up at the worst opportunity available for them and for mainly us.

Hitting the back door we both run our asses off to get to the southern border of our boundary line.

Shifting into my wolf Stinger I take off crashing through the trees. Jumping over fallen logs and branches, zigzagging between the trees Demon and Stinger finally reach the southern border.

There is all of our Betas plus our reliable warriors fighting off what seems like ten to fifteen wild rogue wolves.

Jumping into the battle sharply, I latch my canines fully around the neck of one the tan rogue wolves that was trying to attack my Beta Trace while Trace was trying to desperately to fend off another wild rogue wolf himself.

Thrashing my head about form side to side with my canines still sunk deeply within the wild rogues neck I hear a crack snap in his neck then he lets out a very painful whimper before he goes completely silent and utterly still.

Tossing his carcass aside I search the forest for any other unsuspecting rogue wolves roaming about.

Catching a glimpse of Demon fighting a rogue wolf off to the right side of me. I trot over to him to watch his back. Others around me are still fighting off the rogue wolves one by one.

When out of nowhere I feel a stinging pain suddenly penetrate my hind leg. Letting out a whimper I automatically turn around to find a brown rogue wolf clamping down on my hind leg while ferociously growing over at me.

Without wasting another second I call upon my pyromancy power and unleash a fire stream straight out of my fucking eyes right at the rogue wolf, the stream is so strong that when it hits him it sends him flying straight across the forest grounds, alighting his fur on fire instantaneously.

He starts thrashing about on the ground, rolling and whimpering around through the dead fallen leaves and branches, roaring out in decisive pain as the fire engulfs his entire wolf form completely.

I check my hind leg noting the blood that's casually leaking out of the side of my open wound. Licking at the wound, thankfully, it starts to close up immediately.

Then I get another shock when my body suddenly goes flying across the forest ground as some damn cowardly rogue wolf hit me from my side while I was distracted.

I hit my back up against a giant oak tree causing pain to shoot right through my spine.

Fuck!

Struggling I finally find my way back up onto all fours paws only stumbling over once before I was able to catch my balance.

I spot the cowardly wolf slowly creeping up to me with a menacing low growl escaping out of his mouth.

Alright asshole, let's get this shit show over with.

With a menacing growl of my own directed right at him, I pounce!

This is actually a lot of fucking fun!

Chapter 34

'm pacing Slays bedroom floor frantically worried out of mind for both of my mates.

Sin, after some begging and pleading went down to the kitchen to grab us a much needed snack and drinks.

Slay and Sunny still haven't returned from the damn rogue attack.

I tried midlinking multiple times to both of them but apparently their either far too distracted from fighting off the rogues or worse, something has happened to them.

Biting down on my thumbnail as I keep pacing back and forth I suddenly hear the squeak of a floorboard right outside of Slays room.

Expecting it to be Sin to come in. I just ignore the sound and continue on with my irrational worrying once again.

When the bedroom door finally squeaks opens I halt my steps instantly, strolling over to it but it's not Sin that's standing precariously in the threshold, it's some stranger whom I never met before.

His eyes clash with mine instantly sending a wave of striking terror right straight through me.

Taking tentative steps away from him I end up backed against the far wall with him standing right over me.

He leans his head down in closer to my neck, sniffing slightly at my neck rubbing his face across my jawline slowly. I can tell he's a damn rogue just by the offensive smell wafting off of him. A repulsive mixture of wet dog and old mud.

Holding in my breath I watch as he leans back away from me searching my face with his haunting eyes.

He harrumphs then takes a step away from me, I finally release the breath that I was holding in still just wearily watching him extremely closely.

The immeasurable silence in the room between us starts to become very daunting as we both just keep eyeing each other with some trepidation.

Finally after a few tense filled up moments I break the ever growing silence between us.

"W-who are you? What do you want?" I ask him nervously.

He lets out a deep forbearing chuckle while he continues to keep staring maliciously over at me.

"I am no one!" His dark overcasted voice sends frightening shivers right through me again.

"What. Do. You. Want?" I ask him again punctuating every word with a fierce snarl.

"I want nothing!" What is this man? A complete fucking moron?

"Fine, why the hell are you here?" I question him trying to take another route.

"I'm here to take you to your father." What? Yep he definitely is a complete fucking unadulterated moron.

"My damn father is dead. I'm afraid you're wasting your precious time here! Because I fucking killed him!" I almost laugh at the look that suddenly appears on his shocked face.

His cool relaxed demure suddenly goes from menacing to a mixture of bewildered and horrified combined together.

"So if you don't mind why don't you just get the hell out of my damn house!" I growl out at him intimidatingly.

"Fuck I'm sorry I was just trying to do a job." He rakes his fingers through his hair nervously, "I don't know what else to do? I only took this fucked up job because I desperately needed the money. Now what the hell am I going to do?" He gives me his sad sob story.

I say nothing.

I just lean against the wall and watch him start pacing the floor just as I was earlier.

"Now I have nowhere to live and fucking nowhere to go. Look, lady I know I fucked up but can you please just overlook this? I would do anything you would ask me to do. I'm literally begging you." He stops his pacing looking over at me with such desperation locked up in his eyes.

I don't say a word.

I just keep staring at him confused by his actions.

"Please. I'll even get on my knees if I have to, just please, please, let this go?" He begins to actually beg me.

I'm starting to feel really uncomfortable with all of this.

"Are the other rogues with you?" I inquire with uncertainty.

"Yes, they are. They are just like me with nowhere to go and with no hope left in them. We are starving, homeless, and helpless. We didn't want to do this lady. Usually we are just some easy going guys who are trying desperately to find our place in this world. Unfortunately we have ran into some really fucking bad luck lately." He grouses, I can relate with him though, he continues to peer at over at me with piercing but pleading eyes. Fuck! Why do I actually feel sorry for his ass?

"Call them off right now and I'll see if I can help you!" I give him a valid opportunity. Hoping that he's trustworthy enough to go through with it.

"Yes. I'll do it!" He closes his eyes tightly in deep concentration.

After a few seconds he reopens them then flashes me a genuine smile.

I still don't know if I should trust him so I mindlink my mates to make sure he actually did what I ask him to do.

"Slay, Sunny, are you two okay?" I ask them both anxiously.

"We're fine but for some reason all of the rogues are now bowing down their heads in submission to us!" Slay replies, I release a long pent up ragged breath of relief.

"Just come back home." I plead with them.

"On our way beautiful." Slays the one that answers me back.

"Thank you." I offer him my gratitude.

"I am so sorry. I knew this was an idiotic mission. I don't know why I was foolish enough to even take it? I'll just leave you alone and you will never have to hear from any of us ever again. Thank you so fucking much lady." He breaths a sigh of relief stretching out his hand toward me.

I take it hesitantly and firmly shake his hand. As I observe him I start to feel pity for him and his unfortunate predicament.

Dropping my hand away from his he starts to turn on his heels to exit the bedroom door but I stop him before he is able to reach it.

"Wait! If...if I was able to help you and your friends, would you allow me the opportunity to do so? It's not a hand out before you ask. I was just thinking that maybe we could all work something out for both of our benefits." He furrows his brows down at me utterly confused about my offer. I have to stifle my own laughter at the look on his face.

I actually can't believe it myself. I have to be out of my damn mind to trust him after he broke into my house for nefarious reasons but for some fucked up strange reason I actually find myself trusting him.

"Why would you want to help me after what we just did?" He ask me. Good question! I haven't really got a genuine answer for it either.

"Let's start this out on a different footing. What's your name?" I ask him while honoring him with slight grin.

"Jackson Pendergrass but my friends call me Slaughter." He replies with a smile.

"Well Slaughter, how about this? I'm in search of a Gamma for myself and I think you just may qualify for it." I surprise him with my question, hell, I even surprised my damn self.

"Why?" He ask me flabbergasted.

"My mother always taught me to never deny any stranger a helping hand. So that's what I'm offering, a helping hand. Not a hand out. You will work for me and in return I will pay you handsomely." Curse my mother for teaching me good etiquette.

"What about my friends?" He inquires. At least now I know he's loyal to a fault. Most people would only be worried about themselves in this type of situation.

"We can offer them housing and we can always use some good warriors. So...do we have deal?" I ask finally coming off of the wall as I slowly make my way over to him. He peers down at me disbelievingly.

I just shake my head and try to contain my giddiness.

"Look, I know this all seems a bit strange but I'm pregnant and I could use some help. Not that my mates don't help me but they do have a pack to run themselves. Some days I may need you for protection for me and my baby and others I just may need you to fetch my hungry ass some food. Regardless the job is here for you if want it." I try to reassure him.

I just may be going insane.

Who in their right mind would offer this to someone who broke into their damn home?

Me of course. Who else?

"I'll take it." He says hastily.

I tilt my head to the side observing him hoping against hope that I am making the right decision. I guess only time will tell though.

"Good. Do you have a place to stay tonight?"

"No I don't but I can work something out." He grimaces.

Damn!

"Okay then for tonight you can stay in one of our guest bedrooms." I suggest.

"There is one issue though." He comments while rubbing his hand along jawline worriedly.

"What?" I press.

"I have a mate and a child. He's three." Well damn! Okay then. Now I can understand why he was so desperate.

"Then they are more than welcome to stay here also. What's your mates name?" I curiously ask him.

"Kipper." I almost choked.

"Kipper Flax?" I ask him as he peers down at me questioningly.

"Yes. How?...Do you know her?" I almost bark out with laughter.

Oh boy do I know her.

"Yes I know her. We were friends when I was younger." That's all I give him. I'm not sure if his mate has told him anything about me. That would definitely be putting all of us in a very peculiar situation, though a very coincidental and humorous one.

"What's your name?" Slaughter curiously ask me.

"Thorn Vallor. Use to be Thorn Rose." His eyes widen. Oh fuck! Fuck! Fuck!

He knows.

"Sooo, you are the girl that my mate was....once with." I'm glad he put it so delicately.

She was the only woman that I have ever been with. Tristan's ex that came crying to me after they broke up.

Wait until my mates figure this one out. I'll never be able to live it down. I can only imagine what will be going through their perverse minds once they meet her. Damn Men!

"Yes. We were...friends." I actually do start laughing then along with him. "I hope that won't be a problem?" I add on between my bouts of laughter.

"Of course not. That was in her past plus I'm more secure with my manly hood than that to be worried over something as insignificant like that." He says when his laughter dies down. Thank the actual fuck!

But I'm not so sure my mates will be as easy to tolerate this as Slaughter is with it. I can actually hear the raunchy jokes in my head now.

Oh well they are just going to have to live with it I guess.

"Who the fuck are you and what are you doing with my mate?" Sin suddenly ask jolting me straight out of my musings.

He's standing in the doorway with a tray full of food and drinks with a very menacing look planted on his face. Oh boy!

I rush over to me and explain in discriminating detail everything that's happened. Well almost everything.

As I tell him he walks gradually into the bedroom eyeing Slaughter with a heated glare while he places the tray of food down carefully on the edge of the bed.

By the time I finished telling him everything with the exception of confessing about Kipper he has settled down somewhat. He lets out a hearty sigh then eventually makes his way over to Slaughter.

"My name is Sin. I don't know you and right now I can't say that I trust you completely either but if Thorn is willing to give you chance then I see no problem with it. Just don't fucking hurt her or I will definitely kill your ass!" Sin politely shakes Slaughter hand. I release another long drawn out breath of relief.

Slaughter and Sin start talking amongst themselves as I make my way over to the food tray laying on the bed. I'm freaking starving!

Snatching up a plump red cherry I quickly pop it into my mouth just as I do Slay and Sunny enter the bedroom, stomping their feet and scaring the ever living shit out of me.

The cherry that was so pleasantly encompassed in my mouth came flying out of it and across the room hitting Slay right squarely in his damn eye.

"Dammit Thorn I just got through battling with some damn rogues and now I get pelted by a," he searched the bedroom floor until he finds the culprit, "a damn fucking cherry! Are you kidding me?" Slay grunts breathlessly.

I hiccup very loudly covering my mouth with my hand swiftly completely embarrassed by my ill fated bullet of a cherry hitting Slay.

My cheeks are probably as red as the damn cherry now.

Sunny starts laughing first followed by Sin and then Slaughter.

Slay just keeps glowering over at me.

"Can I call you red eye Slay now?" I ask him innocently as I watch him trying to get the cherry juice off of his face while grunting.

Everyone then breaks out into even more laughter with the exception of Slay, of course.

"No the hell you may not!" He grumbles, I hiccup again.

"And who the hell is this?" He adds still grumbling.

"That's my Gamma Slaughter." I tell him proudly then fucking hiccup loudly again.

"What?" Slay and Sunny ask me simultaneously.

So Sin is the one to inform them now of what happened since I just can't freaking stop continuously hiccuping.

It's very irritating.

I observe Slay and Sunny's reaction to the surprising news. Slay is as per usual showing his temperament. Sunny just takes with a grain of salt.

"And she knows my mate!" I start swinging my arms frantically in a crisscross pattern behind my mates back over at Slaughter.

Willing his ass to just shut the hell up already. He finally catches me waving my arms around frantically like a damn lunatic behind them thankfully.

"Uhm, yea she uhm, she use to be her friend?" He states it like a question. The moron! I might just fire him earlier than I expected. Another fucking hiccup slides past my lips again.

"I see you waving your arms around behind me Thorn." Sin busts me. I drop my arms instantly feigning my innocence with a very innocent look plastered on my face.

"I don't know what you are even talking about?" I assert myself although he doesn't seem to buy my act.

Hiccup!

Damn!

"She was the one? Wasn't she?" Sin ask. Damn him for his unique ingenuity.

He has done it now.

Slay and Sunny both turn their attention back to me with little smirks appearing on their smug faces.

Fucking assholes and Sin is nothing but a damn snitch.

Hiccup!

"Yes. She's the one." I resign myself to tell them. They would figure it out eventually anyway. So why the hell not? Might as well get it over with sooner rather than later.

"Her name is Kipper. Now you all know. You actually win. Happy?" I ask them sarcastically.

Hiccup! Fuck these are very aggravating.

"Very." Slay growls at me seductively. Stalking his way over to me he wraps me up in his embrace pulling my body flush against his. I can feel his erection against my ever protruding stomach.

"Aren't you sedated yet?" I whisper lowly to him. The handsome bastard just smirks down at me.

"Never." Oh fuck!

Hiccup!

Long days and nights have passed since I initiated Slaughter in as my Gamma and just like I predicted my mates have been hounded me every since. My loving but irritating mates have accepted him completely into our pack now. Thankfully after finding out that him and his friends didn't have anything to do with the other viscous attack on the Saint Wolf Pack.

When they met Kipper they kept throwing out insinuating sexual comments toward us both just like I knew they would.

Thankfully, Kipper just laughed along with them.

Although having her around has been such a miracle.

She has helped me so much through this pregnancy that I actually wouldn't even know how to even start to repay her for everything she has so willingly done for me.

Her handsome little tike, Mason, has been a joy also. He runs around the pack house without a care in the world. Just playing and bugging the crap out of all three of my mates endlessly.

In all honesty though, it warms my heart every time I see them with him. They will make such great fathers.

Lila is pregnant now also. Although she's only a few weeks along, Marc will not let her out of his sight for a second.

Finally finishing wrapping up my last present for Christmas, I stretch out my body with my hand placed on the middle of my back.

This little pup of mine loves to pounce on his mommas kidneys.

Standing up from the dining room table I grab the present for Mason off of it to place it under the Christmas tree in the living room.

Opening the dining room door the door accidentally bumps into someone on the other side of it. I flinch back immediately.

I begin to hear awful grumbling coming from the other side of the damn door.

Oops!

I slowly open the door and peer around it. My eyes widen when I see that it's Slay that I hit, he's grumbling and rubbing his hand across his forehead.

"I'm so sorry Slay." I murmur, while flinching again when I see the angry look planted on my lovers face.

"Thorn every since you have been pregnant you have popped me in the eye with a fucking cherry, stepped on my foot not once but three times, spilt hot ass soup in my damn lap, dropped a heavy ass box on top of me that you shouldn't have been lifting in the first damn place, kneed me in the groin, and now nearly knocked me out with a fucking door. Are you trying to fucking kill me?" I form a firm line of my lips desperately trying to hold in my laughter.

He's not lying though I have been actually a lot clumsier lately especially when it comes to Slay for some odd reason.

Still trying my best to hold in my laughter, Slay grumbles again but snatches the present out of my hands rapidly as he storms over to the Christmas tree, he puts it under it then turns back to me.

"I think you owe me one!" Slay suggests. What? Now?

"Slay it's in the middle of the damn day. Anyone can walk in here." I try to dissuade him. But trying to dissuade Slay is totally useless.

He stalks toward me with a predatory gleam in his eyes.

I try to back away from him but unfortunately my back hits up against the damn dining room door.

By the time he reaches me I'm completely lost up in his gleaming eyes.

He places his hands right above my head blocking me in completely.

"Slay we can't." I try to plead with him but my traitorous voice comes out all breathy.

"Yes we fucking can beautiful." He seductively states while his hand reaches down to the bottom of my dress finding its way right up to my already heated core.

His eyes widen a fraction when he realizes I'm not wearing any undergarments.

"Already ready for me I see." He utters while leaning his down to leave little feathery like kisses all along my neck. Fuuuuck!

I moan out unintentionally, when he deliberately sucks the skin of my neck into his mouth. Leaving his brazen mark upon it.

His fingers slide into my pulsating pussy, pumping them in and out of me vigorously. When he crooks up his two fingers inside of me I lose all of my damn self control.

"Ah, Papi, right there." I purr when he hits just the right fucking spot.

"You like that beautiful? Tell Papi exactly what you want." He mummers right in my ear so damn sexily.

"You Papi I want you." I tell him while I arch my back up to him like a needy wanting bitch.

"What do you want beautiful? My tongue in that hot ass pussy or my big ass cock?" Oh fuck he's driving me crazy.

"Cock Papi. I want that big ass cock!" I finally tell him as I moan out desirably.

He raises my dress up over my hips while yanking out his formidable cock swiftly. I gulp loudly.

Not caring any longer if anyone does walk in on us, I grab ahold of his dick moving it over closer to my aching pussy.

"Patience beautiful." Yea right! Just fuck me already you damn tease.

As if he read my damn mind he plunges his big dick up into me making my entire body jerk up against the dining room door.

Slay has never been one to be known for his exuberant patience. Without missing a damn beat, he rips open the top of my dress exposing my uncovered breast to him fully. Since I've been pregnant they have grown in abundance and Slay has discovered a new found fascination with them.

As he thrust into me he lowers his head and takes my perky nipple right into his warm wet mouth.

My damn eyes nearly roll back inside of my head with the absolute thorough pleasure he's giving me.

I have to grab ahold of his shoulders tightly just to balance myself out from the onslaught of his sexual animalistic driving force while clumsily wrapping my legs up completely around his hips.

"Fuck Thorn you are so fucking tight baby." He grunts while he wraps his arm around my midsection still pivoting furiously inside of me. I lower my head to lay it down on his shoulder while purring into his neck.

"My little needy slut likes this doesn't she?" Oh fuck! Yes, talk dirty to me Papi.

"Yes Papi."

"Then tell me slut. Tell me me how much my little slut loves her Papis cock!" Dammit!

"I love your cock Papi, can I please have more?" I plead with him alluringly. Just give it to me already!

"Are you my little fucking slut? Tell me your my slut, whore." Well which one does he want slut or whore? I'm happy with either one of them.

"I'm your slut and whore Papi. Fuck me faster." He obeys diligently.

Slay invades my cunt faster with so much pivoting force that it nearly makes me see fucking stars.

"Fuck yes Papi." I moan. Slay surprises me when he bites down on my neck with his canines, sinking them into my pliable skin without any hesitation.

My walls start to spasm up instantly. I clench around his dick so fucking hard that he growls out loudly when he releases his canines from my neck.

"Fuck! Yes, damn you're so fucking good. Papis little cunt is working overtime." I honestly think he's trying to kill me. "You squeeze Papis dick so good my little needy whore!" Fuck me!

Slay doesn't slow down he keeps mercilessly jackhammering into me. Grunting and groaning.

He is definitely trying to kill me.

My desperate longing for him keeps me rooted up against the damn door while he continues to ram into my cunt without missing a damn beat. Fuck he's so good at this!

"Papis about to..." Slay trails off. As soon as he does I can feel his warm semen crash up into my cunt, overflowing it with his warm juices.

My walls constrict up again around me sending me over the edge again, "Fuck yes Papi!" I bellow out without any control over my raging senses whatsoever.

"Daddy are they wrestling?" Mason abruptly ask. Startling us both quickly.

Slay drops me to my feet as he slides right out of me, stuffing his still harden cock into his pants quickly. I can feel the fluids dripping haphazardly down my damn legs.

I swiftly try to cover myself from where Slay manhandled me and tore my damn dress wide open.

Thankfully, Slay turns around rapidly and blocks me from Slaughter and Masons view.

"No son they were, uhm, well. Yes. Yes thats exactly what they were doing, wrestling son....Let's go find your mother." Slaughter stutters out apprehensively.

I hear their footfalls exiting the room rather quickly.

I release a shattering breath as soon as I hear them exit the room.

Slay turns back to me with a shit eating grin plastered all over his damn face. Asshole.

"I told you someone would walk in." I grumble out embarrassingly smacking him right on his shoulder.

"Better get use to it because this one is about ready to meet us." He states firmly while running his burly hand across my oversized belly.

"Not yet and I think it will be a while before this one is actually walking around." I convey to him with a grimace.

"That was so damn embarrassing Slay." I confess.

"Oh come on beautiful. It was worth it. Want to do it again?" Is he kidding me?

"You are insatiable." I maintain with slight annoyance.

"Well I never hear you complain about it. My little needy slut. Now be good for Papi and meet me in the red room." He demands quite huskily.

The red room is a new added addition for their subtle addiction.

Tying me up and dragging out the bondage equipment has become the best highlight of my entire week.

I especially love the whips and handcuffs.

With a gleam in my own eye now I peer up at him.

"Will you role play with me?" I ask him pleadingly.

"Sure what do you want to be this time?" Slay agrees wholeheartedly.

"How about a dirty little schoolgirl and you can be my mean teacher." I suggest with hope filtering in my voice.

"Only if I get to spank you with the paddling board." Fuck yes!

"Yes, please Mr. Vallor I'll be good." I put on my best little schoolgirl accent while twirling my finger through my hair.

I can see the second that the lust fills up in Slays dark chocolate eyes.

"Get your slutty ass up there now!" I don't wait around another second before I take off running while holding my giant ass belly with my hand up the damn stairs.

Time to get in my kneeling position for my Papi!

Epilogue

"Look at that boys. Full fucking house, aces over jacks." The entire tables groans out with their dismay, I scrape in my winnings off of the table toward me with a big fat grin across my mother fucking face. "I win again!" I gloat.

Me, Sun, Sin, and all of our Betas along with Thorns Gamma Slaughter have been playing five card stud for close to three hours now and my luck has absolutely been outstanding tonight.

To be honest that's the way it has been for a while now. I've been one hell of a lucky bastard lately.

After Slaughters introduction into our pack things have changed around here for us for the better. There hasn't been a lot of drama like there use to be with us and I'm so damn thankful for that.

Which in all fairness does worry me somewhat slightly. I keep waiting for an unsuspecting bomb to drop down out of the clear blue sky to end up destroying everything that has been good for us but thankfully nothing untoward has even remotely happened yet.

What can I say I absolutely love the fact that my life has been pretty damn good for us all.

Thorn has blossomed into becoming a wonderful Luna for our pack, like I knew she always would.

Her self resistance and reliance has made our pack to become the number one pack ever known in these parts.

After Curtis's demise she made an actual miracle happen. She went to his pack and somehow ended up being able to combine our two packs both together.

Since we were his only living relatives, so to speak, it made the transition so much easier for us all and Thorn managed to make it all somehow miraculously happen.

She is indeed our little miracle.

"I call." Trace grumbles, I recognize all of his giving tells. He gives them away so damn easily. With just a twitch of his brow I know that he's definitely bluffing.

Looking down at the cards in my hand I remain emotionless on the outside but on the inside my adrenaline is pumping fast and hard. I'm luckily holding four beautiful tens and a Jack of hearts.

It was no surprise to everyone at the table that I won another hand. Hearing their groans and grumblings about my winnings, I just take it all in stride and rake in my winnings to my pot, smirking over at all of them.

"Guess I'm lucky tonight." I nonchalantly comment causing even more grumbling from all of them.

"I think he's cheating guys, what do you think?" Sunny accuses me while pouting down at his meager dwindling pot beside him on the table.

"Check his damn sleeves for extra cards because no one is this damn lucky." Sin grouses while throwing his cards down on the table.

"Hey I can't help it if you guys suck." I snidely remark as I start shuffling the deck of cards to deal them all out.

"I think the only one sucking around here is your mate." Pan haughtily indulges glowering right over at me while taking a swig of his beer. The entire table suddenly bursts out in light laughter.

"You're just fucking jealous Pan because she can suck better than a damn vacuum cleaner." Sin pipes in elbowing Pan right in his ribs. Pan fakes hurt by bending over while grabbing his side.

"Hey my mate can suck just as good as a vacuum cleaner too." Pan deflects while scowling heavily over at Sin. Making everyone of us groan at his subtle hint.

"Can we not bring our mates into this guys? Besides mine is way better than any of you guys mates are." Flex admonished with a sly smirk.

Flex met his mate a few years back now. She and him make the oddest couple to me. Where Flex is down to earth and humble his mate is the total opposite of him.

Raquel is two inches taller than him and she preferably thinks that her shit doesn't stink. She walks around the pack grounds acting like she's some damn movie star or something to that effect.

Don't get me wrong she is indeed beautiful but there in lies the problem. She's beautiful and she definitely knows that she is.

So far, lucky us, even though she thinks she is better than most of the people around her she hasn't caused any unforeseen problems.

Thorn somehow seems to tolerate her condescending ass but I truthfully can't stand her but Flex seems to love her ass so I'll give her the benefit of my doubt until proven otherwise.

"Stop bragging you guys. Not all of us are lucky to have their damn mate." Trace murmurs sadly while looking down at his cards.

Poor Trace use to have a mate not long ago but he lost him in a shocking home fire. Omke was a great man and is dearly missed by everyone till this day, especially by Trace. It took years of struggle, heartache, and pain but now Trace is finally starting to come out of his deep depression with the hopes of him maybe being able to find his second chance mate now and I truly hope that he does.

"You will find your mate soon just be patient man." Sunny tries to placate him. Trace just offers Sunny a half hearted smile but you can still see the sadness captured in his forlorn eyes.

"Look guys I don't know why all of you seem to think your mates are the best when you all know that I'm the one who has the best mate by far. My baby can top them all." Slaughter brags deviously leaning back in his chair with a broad smile on his face.

I shake my head vigorously at the numbskull but I'm very grateful that he quickly changed the subject again. Things were starting to get too damn depressing for a simple game of cards.

"Don't look at me like that Sin. You and I know for a fact that my mate is better. Hell, she is the only one of us that can brag about being with your mate also." And there we have it folks.

Every since Slaughter and Kipper have joined our pack Slaughter takes every opportunity in front him that he gets to always remind of us his mates and our mate's coupling.

"Shut the hell up Slaughter! One of these days I'm going to rip that damn vulgar ass tongue of yours right out of your fucking perverted mouth!" Sin professes with a stern glare directed right over at Slaughter.

Slaughter audibly gasp loudly watching Sin with a very honed in cautious look.

"Why are you being so viscous Sin? I'm sure Slaughter didn't mean anything by it." Thorn says suddenly as she waltzes gracefully into the dining room, casting one of her beautiful smiles down at Sin.

"Come here baby." Sin urges her while grabbing ahold of her delicate wrist to bring her down to him to sit upon his lap. Thorn giggles as she settles over on the top of him, then she reflectively wraps her sweet loving arms around his neck locking his ass in.

My eyes stayed glued on my striking Princess seated upon Sins lap. Her beautiful face has a mesmerizing glow to it. I can't believe how much I'm in love with this woman.

My eyes suddenly drop down to her swollen belly. Realizing that it won't be very longer until we all have another pup of ours running around here again causing a lot of trouble and mayhem very soon.

Dropping my cards on the table I reach across over to her while rubbing my hand across her protruding stomach I can't help but to broaden my smile.

"Where's Harley?" I question.

Harley is our oldest daughter. She is finally turning eighteen tonight, actually here in just a short while now.

We have been watching the clock steadily waiting patiently for the midnight hour to finally appear.

Then we will all go out into the backyard for our sweet daughters very first shift. She is so damn excited about it and apparently she's not the only one, we have all been anxiously staring at the clock with hidden anticipation for the upcoming event for hours now.

"She's upstairs getting ready. She's so nervous, poor child. She has been pacing the floor nonstop for close to an hour now. All she seems to be thinking about is finally meeting her mate. Can you believe it? Our daughter could actually meet her mate tonight." Thorn exclaims with her own excitement flourishing throughout her.

Me and my brothers just grunt out in disapproval.

Whoever her mate may end up being better make damn sure he treats my little princess right or else.

"I don't want to talk about it." I grumble leaning back in my chair as I fold my arms across my chest basically pouting now.

My little princess, to me, is far too young to even be thinking about men. The only men in her life she should be thinking about are her loving daddies.

"Oh, Slay she is a grown woman now. You are going to have to let her grow up. If you're this bad with her how are you going to act when Davina and Dalia shift?" She ask as she climbs up off of Sins lap to come over to mine.

She sits down on my lap sideways, I unfold my arms to wrap them around her while she tilts her head to the side just observing me with pure unconditional love settling in her beautiful cove blue eyes.

I nuzzle my head down on her shoulder inhaling her sweet intoxicating aroma trying to settle down my raging thoughts about our beautiful daughters.

"Davina and Dalia are unfortunately looking forward to it but at least we have another year before we have to deal with it." Sunny states while dealing out another round of cards.

"Well look at this way guys. You don't have to worry about any of this with Stax." Flex pipes in, I angle my head up at him thinking about our over hyper sexual son.

Stax is remarkably just like Sin use to be, a damn sex fiend with only one thing on his damn mind all of the damn time. He's a damn horny ass teenager. That just thinks about sex and nothing else, ever.

At fifteen he surely has already gone through a list of women like they were fucking sweet addicting candy.

That's exactly how he ended up with the nickname Stax. His real name is Harlen but he hates it. When he was only five the damn boy starting noticing the opposite sex right away.

He piles them up one after another without any regard for their feelings whatsoever, hence the nickname Stax.

But he's twin brother, Hank, better known to all of us as by his nickname Shark, simply because of his tenacity for anything related to blood, is totally different.

He's fascinated with it more than he is with girls. I only hope that in the future he may become a doctor or something like that because otherwise he may end up going the opposite route like his mom is so overly concerned about: a fucking serial killer or something in that area of unsociable expertise.

I grimace just thinking about it.

"Yes Stax doesn't give a damn about a mate he just wants them all." Pan laughs while I grunt.

"I don't know about Shark though I don't think his ever really mentioned anything about wanting a mate?" Trace adds on with a perplexed look plastered on his face.

I know exactly what the asshole is thinking about and I fucking hate it. Everyone seems to think that Shark is our strangest kid out of all of them.

I love my children all equally, I don't love one more than I do the other but I desperately fucking hate the way other thinks about my precarious son.

"Shark wants a mate but he has better things on his mind right now." I convey to him while a developing sour taste quickly starts to appear in my mouth.

Thorn peers up at me with a worried look on her face. Every time someone mentions something about Shark she always seems to get that same certain worried look.

She's afraid that he is going to end up being just like her fucking worthless piece of shit father but I always assure her that he is definitely not, even remotely, going to be like him at all.

I hug her a little tighter up against me wanting desperately to remove that worried look right off of her beautiful face.

"Well there is one kid you have that we don't have to worry about and that's Ridge. That boy is something else. I can't believe how damn smart he actually is." Trace affirms proudly.

Ridge is our other son, the youngest for right now until our next one is born.

He's only ten right now but Trace is absolutely right about him the boy is sharp as damn tack. His IQ is off of the fucking charts. Thorn says it's because he takes after Fier her brother. Fier has, as Thorn says, always has been remarkably brilliant.

He's fascinated with chemicals and substances, I haven't got a damn clue about what he's talking about half of the time but he definitely makes us all very proud.

Fier absolutely adores him. Since Fier found his mate, Parker, they have both adopted Ridge just like he was their very own son.

Glancing down at Thorns stomach, I'm overwhelmed with happiness, yes our family has our ups and downs but I think it's all absolutely perfect to me and I wouldn't trade any of it for the damn world.

She's having another girl this time. We have already picked out her name, soon I will be able to meet my other little princess, Arribella, making our family unit complete.

"Of course he's smart, he takes after his daddy." Sunny boast proudly.

We actually never wanted to know the paternity of any of our kids but you can honestly tell whose is whose just by their looks and their actions.

The pack doc told me each time though whose child was whose. Not that it ever really mattered to me but he only did it in case of any unforeseen emergencies.

Harley is mine, along with Davina and Dalia. Stax and Shark are Sins. Ridge is Sunny's just like he boasted about but he doesn't actually know that.

Arribella is Sunny's also but to all of us they are all of ours and that's the way it shall always remain.

"I think he looks more like me shithead!" Sin attests, I crack a smile at that.

They always argue about this stupid ass shit every time it's brought up. Sin seems to think that his sperm is somehow more magically powerful than mine or Suns. Claiming that every single one of our wonderful kids is definitely his.

"Now, now boys they are all of yours. But I promise you this after this one pops out of me we are completely done." Thorn proclaims as she leans her head back down on my chest. I rub my hand along her back lovingly.

Thorn refuses to have any more children. Establishing very loudly to all three of us that her baby factory machine is closing down permanently for business.

We all hate it though, we at least, want just one more and if any of us has our way with it we will definitely get it.

She said the same exact thing before she got pregnant with this one and look where that got her. Knocked up yet again.

No matter how much she complains about it we all always seem to come up winning in the end.

I think it's because we are just too damn irresistible for her to resist.

"Mooooom! It's almost time." Our daughter Harley comes crashing through the dining room door suddenly, whining out dramatically.

Thorn raises her head up from my chest to crane her neck to look over at her and with a heavy sigh she stands up from my lap regrettably. I already miss her loving warmth.

With a discerning pout I glance over to my whining daughter who is standing in the threshold fidgeting, amazingly she looks just like her mother.

Beautiful without a doubt. Sometimes I can even notice little parts of me within her. Mainly her hotheadedness and raging temperament.

"Okay Harley let's go outside and get ready." Thorn replies while waving her hands toward the door.

"Are you coming?" Thorn questions. I raise my eyebrows up at her giving her a little devilish grin.

"Well I would but there will be children around beautiful, what would they think?" I reply to her huskily.

"You know I honestly think Stax takes after you sometimes!" She rebuttals. Everyone in the room begins to laugh at that.

Standing up from our seats to follow them out I just shake my head again, smiling. I have been doing a lot of that lately: smiling.

It seems like that everyday that passes us by I have always found something to be able smile about.

I can't complain a bit about how our lives have turned out. I have a growing and happy and healthy family, one that I'm actually very proud about.

Who can ask for anything more?

Walking out the back door with my brothers behind me in tow we all travel to the edge of the forest to meet up with Thorn and the others.

As we approach I spot all of my rowdy kids there along with her. Our pack members are all surrounding them, everyone seems really ecstatic about my daughters first shift tonight.

Thorns standing right beside Harley holding a soft pink robe in her hands for our precious daughter.

Harley is still fidgeting nearly bouncing on her feet from the excitement. She is so strikingly beautiful.

"Daddies!" She exclaims excitingly running over to my brothers and me.

She barrels into Sins chest first giving him a rather large hug then she goes straight for Sunny doing the exact same thing to him. Each of my brothers seemed overwhelmed at the moment. Both have very solemn looks on their faces. They can't stand how vastly mature she has become lately, along with me.

Harley comes to me last wrapping me up into her tiny arms placing them around my waist, I return the hug to her, not wanting to ever let her go.

My little princess has grown up far too fast. Where does the fucking time go?

She releases her arms around me as she peers up into my eyes with the most beautiful smile I have ever seen.

"It's okay daddy even if I meet my mate tonight you three will always be my favorite guys." She tries to reassure us, seeing the innocent expression on her face nearly does me in.

I know she desperately wants to meet her mate tonight and with our pack being overgrown with extra members in it now she may just do that.

I really hate the very thought of my little princess finding her mate so damn soon. Shouldn't she wait until she's like close to thirty or at least somewhere around that prominent age?

I pull her back to me hugging her closely to me again.

"Even if he's not here princess. I'm sure you will find him but just remember that if he ever hurts you in anyway, shape, or form, I will kill him." She pushes me back away from her looking up at me disbelievingly.

"You won't harm a single hair on his head daddy. Promise me that you won't." She pleads with me so sweetly I can't help but to chuckle down at her.

"Okay I promise I won't kill him but I will definitely hurt him." I vow with all honesty.

"Same goes for me little one. He just better hope that he treats you right." Sunny exclaims thoroughly.

"I'll be the first on the list to kick his ass if he gives you any problems, sweetie." Sin pipes in aggressively.

Harley just shakes her pretty little head at us and giggles softly.

"I love you guys." She states making my heart swell immensely.

She gets I love you's all around from all of us in return.

"Better go get ready princess. It looks like your mom is about to blow a gasket over there." I state to her while laughing breathlessly.

Thorn is definitely showing signs of mild irritation now, she keeps glaring over at us with a stern look plastered on her face. More than likely probably thinking that we are all trying to talk our precious daughter out of having a damn mate and accepting him, she is not too far off from the truth about thinking just that.

I wouldn't be too damn disappointed if my princess rejected her mate tonight if she is able to find him but that would be selfish of me. Wouldn't it?

Strolling slowly over to Thorn I wrap her up in my embrace from behind her, placing both of my hands along her growing stomach.

"Relax beautiful, she will be okay." Thorn leans her head back on my chest sighing.

"I'm just worried about her." I'm sure she definitely is and she's not the only one. By the look on my brothers faces I could probably attest that we are all definitely worried about our sweet little innocent daughter.

"Daddy when is this going to be over with? I'm tired." Ridge protests sleepily. Glancing down at my sweet little son, I remove one of my hands from Thorns stomach to ruffle my fingers through his blonde hair.

"Not long now buddy." I assure him while peering down at him then I suddenly hear light gasps echoing all around me suddenly.

Jerking my head back up quickly I take notice that my daughter has now transformed into a otherworldly ethereal wolf.

My eyes widen with astonishment as I view her tantamount beauty.

She is almost the exact replica of her mother.

I take a tentative step forward toward her only halting when I feel someone grasp ahold of my wrist, I don't have to look back to know exactly who has ahold of me, I feel the sparks shoot straight up through my arm alerting me that Thorn is the one who has me within her gentle hold.

"Mate!" I hear my daughter shout excitedly through our shared mindlink.

Now I look back at Thorn we both have sudden surprise written all over our faces.

I take a chance and glance over at my brothers, they both have similar looks on their faces. All of us are rather surprised by this.

"Mate!" I hear a growl inside of my head that sounds vaguely familiar.

Searching the backyard for the attending culprit my eyes happen to land upon my daughters surprising mate located in the center of the crowd.

I stand there shocked and visibly shaken.

Harley comes to stand beside me, now back in her human form, dressed in her soft pink robe staring over at her mate with adoration on her face.

Sun, Sin, and Thorn are all on the other side of me observing Harley's mate along with me.

"Daddy he's my mate please be nice." Harley pleads with me while placing her tiny little hand on my arm.

I begrudgingly nod my head to her not being able to form a single fucking word. I'm literally in a state of complete and utter paralyzing shock.

"Go to him." Thorn insist trying to encourage her while waving her hand at Harley. I growl lowly but unfortunately I know that I'm going to have accept him if I want my daughter to be happy. So swallowing down my down pride I earnestly glance down at her.

"Go ahead." I encourage her although hesitantly, nudging my head in Traces direction.

"Thanks daddy." Harley mouths to me then plants a kiss on my cheek before she walks slowly over to her newly found mate: Trace.

I start to feel a little ashamed over my reluctance when I see the love captured on Traces face all of the sudden. He's been so desperately lonely for years and now he doesn't have to be any longer thanks to the Moon Goddess for matching him up with my loving daughter.

"Well I be damned at least we all know he will treat her good." Sunny exclaims and I have to agree Trace is definitely a good man. He will do right by daughter that I'm pretty damn sure of.

"Mate!" I hear another yell inside of my head through our mindlink.

Oh, you have got to be fucking kidding me!

I watch in horror as my daughters other mate makes his way over to her shyly.

"Damn she has two of them!" Sin exclaims. Fuck! Fuck! Fuck!

"Calm down Slay. Mason will be good to her also." Thorn tries to reassure me.

I watch as Mason, Slaughter and Kippers son, looks fondly down at my daughter along with Trace.

"They better be good to her." I growl out ferociously but I hate that I have to eventually accept this shit. That's my baby girl and it irks me to no end knowing that she now has two of them.

"Well at least she will be getting double the action." Sin chuckles making me growl even more ferociously over at him while punching the cocky bastard on his arm.

"Really Sin?" I grunt out in dismay.

"Well I mean, she is just like her mother. I'm pretty sure she will be able to handle the two of them." I can't believe he actually said that. I open my mouth to reprimand him.

"Fuck you Sin!" But it's not me that obnoxiously screams at him, I'm shocked to hear my beautiful precious mate express herself so violently toward him.

"Ah, it's like music to my fucking ears. I love it when a woman screams. Do it some more baby."
Fucking Sin!

www.ingramcontent.com/pod-product-compliance
Lightning Source LLC
Chambersburg PA
CBHW070335170726
48291CB00001B/49